CHRISTMAS AFFAIRS

A matchmaking aunt,
a sentimental journey
and children with dreams
of their parents' marriage on their minds.

Our gift to you at this holiday season—
three yuletide romances that warm the heart
and promise that wedding bells will be ringing in
the New Year!

Season's greetings from all of us at Harlequin,
and best wishes from

Helen Brooks

Sandra Marton

Sharon Kendrick

Helen Bianchin was born in New Zealand and traveled to Australia before marrying her Italian-born husband. After several moves, they settled with their daughters and sons in Australia where, encouraged by friends, Helen began to recount anecdotes of her years as a tobacco sharefarer's wife living in an Italian community. An animal lover, she claims her terrier and Persian cat regard her study as much theirs as hers. Helen's first novel was published in 1975 by Mills & Boon in London, and she has since written more than thirty romances.

Sandra Marton is also the author of more than thirty novels. Readers around the world love her strong, passionate heroes and determined, spirited heroines. When she's not writing, Sandra likes to hike, read, explore out-of-the-way restaurants and travel to faraway places. The mother of two grown sons, Sandra lives with her husband in a sun-filled house in a quiet corner of Connecticut where she alternates between extravagant bouts of gourmet cooking and eating take-out pizza.

Sharon Kendrick was born in west London, England, and has had occupations that include photography, nursing, driving an ambulance across the Australian desert and cooking her way around Europe in a converted double-decker bus! Without a doubt, writing is the best job she has ever had! When she's not dreaming up new heroes—some of which are based on her doctor husband—she likes cooking, reading, theater, listening to American West Coast music and talking to her two children, Celia and Patrick.

CHRISTMAS AFFAIRS

HELEN BIANCHIN
SANDRA MARTON
SHARON KENDRICK

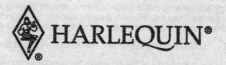

HARLEQUIN®

TORONTO • NEW YORK • LONDON
AMSTERDAM • PARIS • SYDNEY • HAMBURG
STOCKHOLM • ATHENS • TOKYO • MILAN • MADRID
PRAGUE • WARSAW • BUDAPEST • AUCKLAND

ISBN 0-373-83416-0

CHRISTMAS AFFAIRS

Copyright © 1999 by Harlequin Books S.A.

The publisher acknowledges the copyright holders
of the individual works as follows:

THE SEDUCTION SEASON
Copyright © 1998 by Helen Bianchin

MIRACLE ON CHRISTMAS EVE
Copyright © 1998 by Sandra Myles

YULETIDE REUNION
Copyright © 1998 by Sharon Kendrick

Visit us at www.romance.net

Printed in U.S.A.

CONTENTS

THE SEDUCTION SEASON

Helen Bianchin

Dear Reader,

Christmas is a wonderful time of year. I love the shops with their colorful decorations, the piped carols, the selecting of gifts, cards and wrapping paper. The sense of anticipation that goes with gifts and giving. I adore the mail—cards and letters from friends all over the world.

The feeling of joy, which is the true meaning of Christmas...children...kitchen smells...rich cake, plum pudding, turkey, ham, chicken, the sharp tang of wine.

Our Christmas is a pleasant cultural mix, leaning heavily toward Italian tradition. There is much food and wine, and always room at the table for any friend away from home. Christmas falls midsummer in the Southern Hemisphere, and with the sun high in the sky and soaring temperatures, the ambience reflects relaxation and informality. Icy cold drinks, a table beneath a large umbrella next to the swimming pool... Family, love and laughter, sharing and caring. Hopes, dreams and memories.

Wherever in the world you are spending Christmas, may it be happy and filled with joy.

CHAPTER ONE

It was neither wise nor sensible to drive for hours through the night without taking a break, but Anneke didn't feel inclined to covet wisdom.

And 'sensible' wasn't a suitable word to apply to someone who, only that morning, had told her boss precisely what she thought of him, then walked out of his office and out of his life.

Men. Anneke swore viciously beneath her breath. Words at which her sweet Aunt Vivienne would have blenched in dismay had she heard them uttered from her favourite niece's lips.

'Oh, darling, *no*,' Aunt Vivienne had responded in genuine empathy to Anneke's call. 'Come and stay with me for a while. The weather is beautiful, and you can relax.'

Family. How wonderfully they rose to the occasion in times of need, Anneke reflected fondly. Especially this particular member, who was surrogate mother, aunt, *friend*.

The small seaside cottage situated on a relatively isolated stretch of beach in northern New South Wales was idyllic, and it had taken Anneke only an hour to make a few essential phone calls before tossing some clothes into a bag. Then she locked her elegant small flat in Sydney's suburban Lane Cove, slid behind the wheel of her car, and headed for the main highway leading north.

'I won't arrive until late,' she'd warned her aunt, who had blithely responded it didn't matter in the least; the front door key would be left in the usual place.

Anneke glanced at the illuminated digital clock on the dashboard. Three minutes past midnight. It would take another hour to reach the outskirts of Byron Bay, a few more minutes to traverse the road leading down to her Aunt's beachside cottage.

It was a dark night, with no moon to cast an opalescent glow over the countryside, and she leaned forward to switch on the air-conditioning in an attempt to sharpen a brain dulled by more than nine hours of driving with only two minimum breaks along the way.

The car's headlights probed the ribbon of asphalt and its grassy fringes, and she held back from increasing speed. A semi-trailer barrelled past her, its rig brightly lit, followed a few minutes later by another. Drivers on a tight schedule hauling freight overnight.

Anneke stifled a yawn, rolled her shoulders, then turned on the radio, scrolling through the stations until she found one providing upbeat music.

It was one o'clock when she reached the familiar turn-off and only minutes before she drew the car to a halt on the grassy verge adjacent her aunt's garage.

The outside light was on in welcome, and Anneke switched off the engine, withdrew her bag from the boot, then trod the path quietly to the front porch, retrieved the key and let herself in.

It was an old brick cottage, renovated over the

years to incorporate modern conveniences, and immaculately maintained. Its design was basic, with rooms leading off a wide central hall that ran the length of the cottage. Lounge, dining room and kitchen on the right; three bedrooms, bathroom and laundry on the left.

Anneke shut the front door and locked it, then moved quietly to the rear of the house. She'd deposit her bag in the guest bedroom, then make a much needed cup of tea.

There would, she knew, be a cup and saucer set out on the buffet in readiness, and a small plate of sandwiches beneath film-wrap waiting for her in the refrigerator.

A thoughtful gesture by a very kind lady.

The guest bedroom looked endearingly familiar. A double brass bed occupied centre space, with its old-fashioned white lace bedspread heaped with lace-covered cushions. Above the headboard was a snowy white canopy holding a billowing mosquito net. Superfluous, considering the screened windows, but Aunt Vivienne had wanted to retain the old-fashioned ambience, so the canopy remained.

White lace frilled curtains at the window, old-fashioned wooden furniture, and highly polished wooden floors.

It would be so easy to slip off her shoes, shed her clothes, and sink into bed. For a moment she almost considered it. Her shoulders ached, her head ached, and she was so tired, not to mention emotionally exhausted.

She was inclined to add 'devastated'. Although that

wasn't quite the description she wanted. Angry, certainly. With Adam, her boss. And herself. Especially herself, for believing in him. She'd been a fool to think she was different from the steady stream of women who inhabited his life.

The type of man, she reflected viciously, who constantly sought challenges on a professional and personal level, Adam knew all the right moves, which buttons to press. He was very, very good at setting the seduction scene.

But not quite good enough. She retained a clear image of his surprise when she'd announced her intention of walking out. The practised hurt when she'd refused to accept his assurance *she* was very important to him. The slightly wry smile and the spread of his hands in silent acceptance of her vilification that he'd never change.

The only satisfaction she had...and it was very minor...was the knowledge she'd been the one to end the affair. Something she was sure had never happened to him before.

The bravery had lasted as she'd walked out of his office, and all through the long hours of driving.

Now that she was here, reaction began to set in, and she could feel the prick of angry tears.

A quick shower first, she determined wearily, then she would go into the kitchen.

Five minutes later she emerged from the bathroom wearing an oversize tee-shirt. Her face was scrubbed clean of make-up, and her hair hung loose halfway down her back.

In the bedroom she reached into her bag and extracted a few necessities, then she made her way towards the kitchen.

If she didn't know differently, she would almost swear she could sense the subtle aroma of freshly brewed tea.

A faint frown creased her forehead, and she suffered a pang of guilt. Surely she hadn't disturbed Aunt Vivienne, and the dear woman hadn't risen from her bed to offer tea and comfort at this late hour?

It was typical of her caring aunt, and she summoned a warm smile in welcome as she entered the kitchen.

Only to have the smile freeze on her face as a tall, dark-haired stranger shifted his lengthy frame from a leaning position against the servery.

A very tall man with broad, sculpted features, dark grey eyes, and black hair that fell thickly almost to his shoulders.

Anneke swept him from head to foot in a swift encompassing appraisal, and didn't like what she saw.

He was in need of a shave, and bore what looked like a full day's growth of beard that, combined with his dark eyes and long loose hair, gave him a decidedly devilish look. Add well-washed tight-fitting jeans, a black sweatshirt, and he resembled a man who was the antithesis of 'friend'.

'Who the hell are you?'

Uncertainty, defensiveness, fear. He glimpsed each of them in the fleeting emotions chasing across her expressive features.

He should, he reflected with mild exasperation, have taken the time to shave. And, if he'd had a mind to, he could have bound his hair into its customary ponytail at his nape. Could, perhaps should have changed into casual trousers and a polo shirt.

Except the story had been running hot, and he'd lost track of time as he transposed the images in his head into words on the computer screen.

And he'd promised Vivienne that he'd pop over the minute her niece arrived and explain in person why the cottage was empty.

'I've made some tea,' he indicated in a faintly accented drawl. 'Vivienne said you favour Earl Grey.'

Anneke's eyes narrowed. Vivienne. So he knew her aunt. That meant he wasn't an escapee, a felon, or someone of ill repute. Although, looking at him, she wasn't too sure about amending the last description.

'I locked the front door.' Eyes flashed a fiery emerald, then deepened in wariness. 'How did you get in?'

She was attractive, if you had a penchant for tall, slender, long-haired blondes, he mused. Natural, although these days it was hard to tell without getting intimate. Lovely green eyes, beautiful mouth. He felt something stir, then banked it down. Women could complicate a man's life, and he didn't need the aggravation.

Anneke. Pronounced Ann-eek. Scandinavian mother, English father, no siblings. Twenty-seven, para-legal secretary. Just walked out on a louse.

He took one long look at her, and just knew she'd hate it that Vivienne had confided in him.

'Sebastian.' He leant one hip against the servery, and attempted to keep the amusement out of his voice.

He partly lowered his eyelids to diminish the gleaming depths. 'And Vivienne gave me a key.'

For tonight? Or had he possessed a key for a while? Aunt Vivienne and a toyboy? The latter aroused an improbable scenario which she instantly dismissed.

Anneke drew herself up to her full height, unaware that the hem of her tee-shirt rose two inches up her thighs. Her voice rose a fraction. 'Sebastian *who*? And you'd better explain real quick why Aunt Vivienne asked you to come into her house at this ungodly hour.'

Dammit, was she wearing anything beneath that thing? Definitely not a bra. Briefs? If she lifted her shoulders much higher he was sure going to find out.

And precisely what, he mused tolerantly, did she think she could do to defend herself against him that he couldn't counteract and deal with before she'd even moved an inch? Kick-boxing, karate? He was trained and adept in each.

'Lanier,' he responded indolently.

So he was French. That explained the slight accent.

'Friend and neighbour.' One eyebrow slanted, and his mouth tilted fractionally. 'Requested by Vivienne to tell you in person news she felt would be too stark if penned in a written note left for you to read in the early-morning hours.'

Anneke was trying hard to retain a hold on her composure. 'So on the basis of good neighbourly relations you came over here at—' she paused to check her watch '—one-thirty in the morning, made me a cup of tea, and waited to tell me—*what*?'

'You're a mite ungrateful.'

His slow drawl held a degree of cynical humour, and it made her want to throw something at him. Surely would have if the sudden sharpness in those dark eyes and the subtle reassemblage of facial muscle hadn't warned her it would be infinitely wise not to follow thought with action.

'I've been on the road for eleven hours.' Her body stance changed, became more aggressive. 'I let myself in to my aunt's cottage and discover a strange, disreputable man calmly making himself at home in her kitchen, and I'm expected to smile and say, *Hi, my name is Anneke, what's yours? How nice, you've made some tea?*'

'And impolite,' he continued, as if she hadn't spoken at all.

'What do you object to? The "disreputable" tag?' Her eyes raked his lengthy frame, skimmed over broad shoulders, muscled chest, narrow hips, long, muscular legs, then slid back to his face. 'Sorry, Sebastian.' She gave his name faint emphasis. 'From where I'm standing, you hardly represent a trustworthy image.'

The eyes lost their tinge of amusement and acquired a perceptive hardness that changed his persona into something dangerous.

He watched those splendid emerald depths dilate, and felt a moment's satisfaction. 'Vivienne is in Cairns.' The unadulterated facts. He gave them to her without redress. 'She had a call an hour after yours to say her daughter had gone into labour six weeks early. She caught the late-afternoon flight out of Coolangatta.'

Colour drained from her face. Elise was expecting a second set of twins. Six weeks premature. 'How is she?' The words whispered from her lips.

His eyes narrowed faintly. So she cared. Deeply. That was something. 'Vivienne said she'll ring early morning with an update.'

The exhaustion seemed more marked, the faint smudges beneath her eyes a little darker. She looked, he decided, as if she should sit down. He crossed to the small kitchen table and pulled out a chair, then transferred the cup and saucer from the buffet.

'Tea. Hot, white, one sugar.'

Just the way she liked it. Anneke owed thanks to her aunt. And an apology to this large, faintly brooding stranger.

Neighbour? There was only one cottage in close proximity, and that was owned, according to Aunt Vivienne, by a lovely author who kept strange hours. He was also something of a handyman who had, Anneke recalled sketchily from her aunt's correspondence, fixed her roof, replaced a blown fuse, lopped two overgrown trees, and undertaken some heavy garden landscaping.

Anneke regarded the man standing at the table with a faint frown. Not by any stretch of the imagination could she call him 'lovely'.

Mid to late thirties. Ruggedly attractive in a dangerous sort of way, with the type of physical frame that seamlessly melded honed muscle and leashed power together to present a formidable whole.

Let loose, he'd present a ruthless force no man in his right mind would choose to oppose. The woman, she perceived, who willingly stepped into his space would never be sure whether she'd dice with the devil in hell, or soar to heaven with a tutelary saint.

'Are you done?'

Anneke's lashes swept high at his quizzical query, but there was no confusion apparent, no embarrassment. Just analytical regard.

OK, so men weren't her favourite flavour of the month. Justifiable, according to Vivienne, whom he'd driven at speed to the airport that afternoon. *'Such a dear girl.'*

Familial beneficence tended to be biased, he mused. 'Dear' she might be…as a niece, a cousin, a friend. But the woman who stood before him was cool, very cool. With fire beneath the icy façade. He had a very strong desire to stoke the fire and watch the ice melt.

'It was kind of you to carry out my aunt's wishes,' Anneke said formally. It was the closest she intended to get to an apology.

Sebastian inclined his head in mocking acknowledgment. Given the circumstances, and the late hour, he should simply wish her goodnight and leave.

'I'll make fresh tea.' Suiting words to action, he easily dispensed with the cup's contents, flicked the kettle to reboil, and took another teabag from a glass container.

Damn him, did she have to spell it out? 'I'm quite capable of making it myself.' She crossed to the refrigerator and extracted milk, then took it to the servery.

Big mistake. For it brought her within a hair's breadth of a hard male frame that seemed disinclined to move. Something that tripped the trigger on all her banked-up anger.

The silent rage she'd managed to contain all day burst free. 'You've more than done your good deed for the day.' Fine fury lent her eyes a fiery sparkle, and her knuckles shone white as she clenched her fists. 'I owe you one.'

He looked at her carefully, noted the thinly veiled anger, the exhaustion. 'So please leave?'

'Yes.' Succinct, with an edge of sarcasm.

'Gladly,' he intoned in a dangerously silky voice.

Something shifted in those dark eyes that she didn't want to define, and there was nothing she could do to avoid the firm hands which cupped her face, or prevent the descent of his head as he fastened his mouth over hers.

It was a hard kiss, invasive, with erotic power and a sweet sorcery that took what she refused to give.

No other part of his body touched hers, and he fought against leaning in and gathering her close.

A spark ignited deep inside and flared sharply to brilliant flame. For both of them. He could feel her initial spontaneous response before she refuted it. Sense her surprise, along with his own.

He softened his mouth, took one last tantalising sweep with his tongue, then slowly raised his head.

She looked—*shattered*. Although she recovered quickly.

He smiled, a slow, wide curving of his mouth as he regarded her stormy features, and he dropped his hands from her face. 'Now we're even.'

Then he turned and walked from the kitchen, trod

a path down the hall to the front door, then quietly closed it behind him.

It irked Anneke dreadfully that a few seconds of stunned surprise had rendered her immobile and robbed her of the opportunity to hurl something at him, preferably hard enough to do damage to any part of his anatomy.

Dulled reflex action, brought on by a degree of emotional, mental and physical exhaustion. Something that a good night's rest would do much to rectify, she perceived as she set the kettle to boil again and made fresh tea.

Men, she brooded as she sipped the delicious brew, were arrogant, heartless, self-oriented, entirely governed by their libido, and not worth a minute of her time.

A thought which persisted as she finished her tea, then she crossed to the bedroom and slid in between crisp, clean white sheets.

On the edge of sleep, one image invaded her mind, and it wasn't the sleekly groomed city lawyer in his three-piece business suit.

CHAPTER TWO

HAMMERING noises in close proximity were not conducive to restful slumber.

Anneke heard them in the depths of her subconscious mind and slowly drifted into wakefulness. Still the noise persisted.

What the hell...? She opened one eye and looked at the clock atop the bedside pedestal. Dammit, it was only *seven*. On Saturday.

Surely her aunt hadn't arranged for a contractor to do some work and forgotten to mention the fact?

Maybe if she buried her head beneath the pillow she could go back to sleep, she decided, suiting thought to action, only to groan out loud minutes later as the sound still penetrated with no seeming loss of intensity.

Annoyance had her sliding out of bed and pulling on a pair of shorts, and she paused briefly to drag a brush through the length of her hair before storming into the hall to assess where the hammering seemed loudest.

Rear, she decided, and made for the back door.

Quite what she'd expected to see when she opened it she wasn't sure. Certainly not Sebastian Lanier's tall, broad-shouldered, lean-hipped, jean-clad frame perched part-way up a ladder, wielding a hammer as he stroked in one nail after another.

'Just what the hell do you think you're doing?'

Well, now, there was a pretty sight to tempt a man's eye at this early hour. Nice legs. He followed the slender calves, the well-shaped thighs. Good muscle tone, he noted approvingly.

Narrow hips, neat waist, and the slight swing of her breasts made him itch to slide his hands beneath the oversize tee-shirt and see how well they fit his palms.

Slowly he lifted his eyes and took his time examining her mouth, and remembered the feel of it beneath his own.

He moved up a few inches and looked straight into a pair of bright, furious eyes whose emerald depths threatened nothing less than murder.

Sebastian smiled. A long, slow, curving movement that lifted the edges of his mouth and showed the gleam of white teeth. 'Good morning.' He positioned another nail and hammered it in.

Clean-shaven, his hair bound neatly at his nape, he looked almost respectable. It was the 'almost' part she had trouble coming to terms with. None of the men in the circles in which she moved resembled anything like *this* man.

Calm, she must remain calm. 'Do you know what time it is?'

Of course he knew what time it was. He'd been up since six, had orange juice, gone through his daily exercise routine, then assembled a high-protein drink in the blender and sipped it while he scrolled through his e-mail.

'Am I disturbing you?'

Oh, he was disturbing her, all right. Just how much,

he was about to discover. A last attempt at civility, then she'd let him have it with both barrels blazing. 'Perhaps you'd care to explain what exactly it is that you're doing?'

She possessed a fine temper. He could see it in her eyes, the tilt of her chin, the way she stood.

'Yesterday I removed a section of worn guttering. Today I'm putting up new.' He held another nail in position and nailed it in. Then he turned his head to look at her. 'I arranged it with Vivienne.'

There was that faint smile again. Anneke gritted her teeth.

He moved down the ladder and shifted it, checked its stability, then stepped up again. And hammered in another nail.

'I suppose you're one of those irritating people who manage to get by on an indecently few hours of sleep?'

'Five or six.' He lined up another nail and rammed it home.

Anger coursed through her body, heating her veins, and erupted in voluble speech. 'You're doing this deliberately, aren't you?'

He cast her a long, measured glance, noted the twin flags of colour high on each cheek, the firm set of her mouth. 'Is that an accusation?'

'Damned right it is,' she bit out furiously.

Sebastian hooked the hammer into his toolbelt and descended down to the ground. 'Let's get one thing clear. I boot up my computer at one in the afternoon. Vivienne needs something fixed; I fix it for her. In the morning.'

His voice was quiet, almost too quiet. And silky, she decided. 'You have to start at *seven*?'

'I'm due in town at ten,' he explained reasonably. 'I won't have time to do anything when I get back from town except grab some lunch, and—'

'Go boot up the computer,' Anneke finished for him. 'And you just had to finish this section before you left.'

'Yes.'

'Today.'

'It could rain,' he responded solemnly.

Most unlikely. Her voice rose a pitch. 'You waltz over here and begin hammering shortly after dawn?'

'Dawn was five-thirty, daylight saving time,' Sebastian informed her mildly.

'I don't give a tinker's cuss when dawn was.' She advanced a step, and crossed her arms across her chest. 'I want you to stop hammering so I can get some sleep.'

'Ask me nicely.'

Her jaw went slack. 'I beg your pardon?'

His lips twitched. 'Ask me nicely,' he reiterated.

So he was amused. Well, she'd wipe that smile right off his face! 'You can go—' she enunciated each word carefully '—jump in the ocean.'

The phone rang, its peal issuing an insistent summons she chose to ignore. Temporarily.

'That'll probably be Vivienne.'

It didn't help any that he was right. Elise was stable; the unborn twins were fine. However, Elise would stay in hospital, probably until the twins' birth, antici-

pated prematurely. Naturally Aunt Vivienne would remain in Cairns.

'I'm so sorry.' The older woman's voice was ach-
ingly sincere. 'I feel a little easier in my mind knowing Sebastian is close by.'

A sentiment Anneke didn't share.

'You've met him, of course,' Aunt Vivienne continued. 'Such a thoughtful, caring man. And so handy.
Oh, dear, I almost forgot—' She broke off, paused,
then launched into an explanation. 'I have an arrangement to prepare his evening meals. Anneke, could
you?' A hesitant apology swiftly followed. 'I hate to
ask, but would it be too much of an imposition?'

Yes, it would. If she never saw Sebastian Lanier
again, it would be too soon! The thought of preparing
a cooked meal for him every night was unbearable.

However, being Aunt Vivienne's guest, enjoying
her aunt's home, made it difficult to refuse. 'I'll organise it with him,' she agreed, hiding her reluctance.

'Thank you, darling.' Aunt Vivienne's relief was
palpable. 'You're such a good cook, far more adven-
turous than me. He's in for a gourmet feast.'

The word 'gourmet' struck a responsive chord, and
Anneke allowed herself a slight smile. If Aunt
Vivienne wanted her to prepare Sebastian's evening
meals during her sojourn here, then she would.
However, meat-and-potatoes-with-vegetables would
definitely be off the menu.

A contemplative gleam entered her eyes. Sautéed
brains, stuffed pigeon, pig's trotters. She gave a silent
laugh. Maybe this might be fun, after all.

'I'll take care of it, Aunt Vivienne.' Oh, she would, indeed! 'Is there anything else you'd like me to do?'

'No, sweetheart. Thank you. I'll ring again in a day or two, or before if there's any news.'

'Give Elise my love.' Anneke replaced the receiver, and noticed the absence of hammering.

Had Sebastian finished? Or was he merely being courteous? She moved towards the back door and saw his lengthy frame bending over a stack of neatly piled wood.

Nice butt, she acknowledged. Some men looked good in tight, worn denim, and he was one of them. As she watched, he straightened and turned to face her.

'Good news?'

She was on the verge of retorting that it was none of his business, but managed to catch the words in time. 'Elise is stable; the twins are expected to deliver prematurely.'

Succinct, with just a touch of resentment, he mused, wondering how she would react if he took all that fine anger and turned it into passion.

Probably try to hit him. He banked down a silent laugh and deliberately drooped his eyelids so the gleam of humour was successfully hidden. It might even be interesting to allow her to score the slap.

Anneke regarded him through narrowed eyes, unable to read him. And the inability didn't sit well. Usually she had no difficulty in pegging the male species. Smooth, charming, vain, arrogant, superficial, blatant. Whatever the veneer, the motive remained basic.

Yet instinct warned that *this* man didn't run with the pack, and that made him infinitely dangerous.

Damn his imperturbability. She wanted to shake that unruffled calm. 'Is six o'clock convenient for your evening meal?'

One eyebrow slanted, and she could have sworn she glimpsed a gleam of amusement in those dark eyes. 'Vivienne frequently shared dinner with me.'

She drew in a deep breath, then released it slowly. She even managed the semblance of a smile, albeit that it held a degree of cynicism. 'An example I have no intention of following.'

'You have an aversion to friendliness?'

Anneke could feel the anger rise, and didn't try to contain it. 'An aversion to *you*.'

His expression didn't change, although anyone who knew him well could have warned the stillness held ominous implications.

'You don't know me,' Sebastian intoned softly.

'*Believe* I don't want to.'

'Feel free to stow your bag in the boot of the car and drive back to Sydney.' His eyes were level, and resembled obsidian shards. 'The loss of a prepared evening meal won't negate my obligation to complete necessary chores for Vivienne.'

She drew in a deep breath, then released it slowly. She could, she knew, easily do what he suggested. Aunt Vivienne would accept she'd changed her mind, and be concerned about her ambivalence.

Except she didn't want to return to the city. Given a choice, she'd have preferred her aunt's company, her wisdom. And the solitude of a sandy stretch of beach in a gently curving bay where she could walk alone, meditate, and allow fresh emotional scars to heal.

A solitude she wouldn't gain if she went back to her small city apartment. Friends, concerned for her welfare, would ring and try to entice her to join them at any one of several parties, or attend the cinema, the theatre. Suggest lunch or dinner and attempt to play amateur psychologist.

Unburdening her soul and having her every word, every action dissected and analysed didn't form part of her agenda.

'I intend to stay,' Anneke responded with equal civility.

Sebastian hadn't been aware the small knot of tension existed until it suddenly dissolved in his gut. Nor could he explain the reason for its existence.

Sure, Vivienne's niece was a sassy, long-legged blonde whose captivating green eyes invited a second glance.

His mouth formed a slightly bitter twist. He'd known several sassy, long-legged women in his time, and bedded more than a few. Only to discover they'd coveted his wealth first and foremost. With the exception of Yvette, with whom he'd shared one precious year. In an unprecedented twist of fate, she'd been victim of a random road accident on the eve of their wedding.

For two years he'd buried himself in work, diced daringly in the world of high finance, only to wake one morning and opt for a complete change of lifestyle.

He owned apartments, houses, in several major capital cities around the world, and for a while he'd lived in every one of them.

It was in Paris, the country of his birth, where he'd first begun to pen a novel, the idea for which had niggled at his brain for months. The state-of-the-art computer which linked him to his various business interests had acquired a new file.

A file which had grown and totally absorbed him. His path to acceptance and publication had been a dream run. At a time when virtual reality teased the readers' senses, his futuristic upbeat plots had been a hit. International success soon followed, and in a bid for anonymity he'd returned to Australia, sought and found relative isolation in a picturesque bay in the Northern Rivers area, and snapped up a cottage he took pleasure in slowly renovating and refurbishing during the morning hours.

Once a year he flew to the States for the obligatory book launch. And each Christmas was spent in Paris. Occasionally he looked up old friends and joined the social set for a while, only to find the life palled, the new plot beckoned, whereupon he returned to the place he'd called home for the past five years.

Now he looked into the clear green gaze of the first sassy blonde who'd shown an active dislike of him, and relaxed his features as he proffered a faint smile. 'Six o'clock will be fine.'

Where had he been during that long minute of silence? Anneke told herself she wasn't interested. And knew she lied.

She inclined her head stiffly, and matched her voice

to the gesture. 'I intend going back to bed.' Her eyes held his, fascinated by dark slate-grey depths whose expression was difficult to discern. 'I'd be grateful if you'd stop hammering so that I can catch up on some sleep.'

'OK.'

She couldn't believe he intended to comply. 'You'll stop?'

Those sensuously moulded lips curved slightly. 'You asked me nicely.'

Anneke opened her mouth, then closed it again.

She watched in silence as he removed the ladder and stored it, gathered up the used section of roof guttering and collected his tools.

Without a further word he turned and covered the distance to his cottage with an easy, lithe stride.

Denim hugged every curve, hinted at superb thigh and calf muscle, and emphasised the length of his legs. Lean waist, fluid muscular grace evident in the breadth of his shoulders denoted more than average strength.

Dammit, why was she standing here *watching* him, for heaven's sake? Men weren't her favoured species at the moment, and *this* man irritated her beyond measure.

She retreated indoors, paused long enough in the kitchen to fill a glass with water and drink it, then she made for the bedroom and slid between the sheets.

The anger hadn't subsided; if anything it had intensified. Joined by the stinging realisation that she had no job, no salary, and running expenses to maintain on her apartment.

On the plus side, she had an annuity from inherited investments, sufficient to live quite comfortably until she found employment, and there was a reasonably healthy savings account from which she could draw funds to meet weekly expenses.

Anneke closed her eyes and deliberately summoned pleasant thoughts, employed meditation techniques, and resorted to counting sheep. Nothing worked.

With an angry jerk she tossed off the sheet, rose and pulled on a swimsuit. A swim, followed by a walk along the beach, then breakfast. After which she'd examine the contents of Aunt Vivienne's refrigerator and pantry, decide what to prepare for Sebastian's dinner, then drive into Byron Bay and collect everything she needed from the supermarket.

Anneke paused long enough to clean her teeth and run a brush through her hair, then she slid on a pair of sunglasses, caught up a towel, and made her way down onto the sandy foreshore.

The sun was warm, with the promise of increasing heat as the day progressed. A faint sea breeze teased the ends of her hair, and she inhaled the tangy salt air with pleasure.

There wasn't another person in sight, and she relished the solitude, choosing to explore the familiar shoreline for several minutes before opting to wade into the cool water.

Effecting a neat dive, she broke the surface and began a pattern of leisurely strokes parallel to the shore for a while, before emerging to towel the excess moisture from her skin and hair.

It didn't take long for the warm air to dry her swimsuit, and she wrapped the towel round her waist, then set out towards the outcrop of rocks at the furthest end of the bay.

Anneke could feel her body relax as the tension eased, and she increased her pace to a light jog, enjoying the exercise, the morning, the solitude.

It was almost an hour before she re-entered the cottage, and after a shower she dressed in casual shorts and a top, then caught up a pad and pen as she examined her aunt's pantry and refrigerator and noted what food supplies she'd need to collect from the supermarket.

CHAPTER THREE

BREAKFAST comprised cereal, toast and fruit, followed by ruinously strong black coffee.

Anneke tidied the few dishes, then she caught up her car keys, slid the strap of her bag over one shoulder, and made her way out to the carport.

Byron Bay was a pleasant seaside town, a popular holiday area, and the community centre for outlying banana, avocado and sugar cane farmers.

Parking the car wasn't a problem, and she took her time browsing through the supermarket as she selected her purchases and stacked them in the trolley.

It was almost midday when she returned to the cottage, and after unloading her various purchases she took time to have lunch before beginning preparations for Sebastian's evening meal.

At five she showered and changed into jeans and a singlet top, bound her hair into a single plait, then returned to the kitchen.

Artichokes stuffed and served with a rich cream sauce, marinated baby octopus, *risi e bisi*, two baby pigeons *confits aux raisins*, and, for dessert, her speciality—*bombe au chocolat*.

Anneke hoped he had a supply of antacid on hand, otherwise he was certain to be a victim of indigestion.

At precisely two minutes before six she trod the

short path linking both cottages and knocked on Sebastian's back door.

She heard a deep bark, followed by a curt command, then the door swung open.

Anneke saw the dog first. A huge Alsatian with liquid brown eyes, a dark velvet pelt, and possessing all the qualities of a trained guard dog.

'Shaef,' Sebastian qualified. 'Let him become acquainted, then you'll never need worry about him again.'

Her eyes travelled over snug black jeans, a black open-necked shirt, to features that bore a faintly mocking expression.

He was an arresting man, compelling, and possessed of a leashed quality that some would find vaguely frightening.

Anneke didn't question his authority with Shaef. She had a healthy respect for canines, and the Alsatian was an awesome breed.

'Will you come in?'

'No,' she responded quickly. Too quickly, for she saw the sudden gleam apparent in his eyes, and caught the slight quirk at the edge of his mouth. 'Enjoy your meal.'

'*Merci.*'

No man had the right to look so darned sexy, or possess a voice that sounded like melted chocolate being dribbled over ice cream. Smooth, very smooth, she perceived. Yet there was tensile steel beneath the smoothness. The hardness of a man well-versed in the frailties of his fellow men.

Without a further word she turned and retraced her

steps. In her aunt's kitchen she set about cleaning up, then when it was done she made herself a light, fluffy omelette, added a salad, and took the plate into the dining room.

Tomorrow night she'd serve him everything stuffed...carpet steak with an exotic sauce, stuffed mushrooms, zucchini, tomatoes and potatoes. She would even bake a vanilla sponge for dessert and stuff it with fresh strawberries and cream whipped with kirsch.

And Monday... She positively *glowed* at the thought of what she could do with seafood.

Anneke prayed fervently that if he didn't already have an ulcer, her epicurean offerings would soon provide him with one. Revenge, she determined, would be sweet.

Very sweet, she determined, upon waking next morning to the shrilling sound of an electric skill-saw cutting through wood.

Anneke spared a glance at her watch. Six-thirty. A half-hour earlier than yesterday. At least this morning she wasn't the victim of only a few hours' sleep.

If Sebastian Lanier was playing a game, then so, too, would she.

A slight smile played over her lips and she slid from the bed. A visit to the bathroom, then she pulled on briefs, shorts, and a singlet top. Her hair she deftly twisted into a single braid and let it fall between her shoulders. Then she slipped her feet into joggers and went to the back door with a ready smile in place.

He wore the same faded stonewashed jeans from the day before, and a different tee-shirt. Nice muscle structure, tight butt, firm waist, with no visible fat apparent on that mean frame.

'Good morning,' she greeted as she ran lightly down the few steps. 'I had no idea Aunt Vivienne needed more repairs. What is it today?'

He pulled the switch on the electric saw and straightened as he turned to face her. The dark hair was neatly bound, but he had forgone the morning shave. It gave him a distinctly piratical look, and heightened the planes of his face, sculpted hard cheekbones and emphasised the strength of his jaw.

If he'd suffered a restless night due to indigestion, it didn't show.

'A section of the picket fence needs replacing. New posts, new palings.'

She widened the smile, and her eyes took on a sparkling gleam. 'How kind. Aunt Vivienne will be pleased.' She turned towards the path leading down to the beach, then cast him a backward glance over one shoulder. 'Have a nice day.'

Anneke broke into a leisurely jog, and on reaching the sand she crossed down to the water's edge and ran parallel to the shoreline until she reached the outward curve of the bay, then she slowed to a halt and went through her usual morning exercise routine.

She deliberately took her time, and when she returned to the cottage Sebastian was nowhere in sight. The carpenter's horse, any wood cut-offs had been cleared away, and a brief glance along the length of picket fence displayed the new section in place.

A muted throaty purr from an engine sounded loud in the morning's silence, and she turned towards its source. Reversing from Sebastian's garage was a late model Range Rover, with, she soon saw, Sebastian at the wheel.

So he was going out. Good, she thought happily as she let herself into the cottage. She had a few household chores to perform, then she'd shower and put a call through to Aunt Vivienne. After lunch she intended to curl up in a comfortable chair and read until it was time to begin preparing Sebastian's dinner.

Anneke had just finished lunch when the phone rang, and she crossed the room and lifted the receiver from its handset.

Her usual cheery greeting brought no response, so she repeated it. Still nothing. She was about to hang up when she heard the soft sound of human breathing.

Even, steady, it became louder and faster, until there could be no mistaking the implied simulation.

She cut the connection in one quick movement, then stood transfixed for several seconds before shaking herself free from momentary shock.

It was simply a random call, she attempted to rationalise. Perhaps some kid with too much time on his hands was getting his kicks from indiscriminate dialling.

Yet it gave her an eerie feeling, one that was difficult to dispel as she tried valiantly to lose herself in the plot of the current mystery she was reading.

Preparations for Sebastian's dinner didn't take overlong, and at a few minutes to six she took the loaded tray and carried it across to his cottage.

Sebastian appeared at the door seconds after she

knocked. A white tee-shirt was teamed with black jeans, and both fitted snug on his frame.

He surveyed her with interest, caught the seemingly pleasant smile, and wasn't deceived.

His gaze flicked to the tray in her hand, and he didn't know whether to castigate or commend her.

Much depended on whether last night's meal had been a one-off, or if she'd duplicated dishes of which, while each separate one was a gourmet delight, the combination left something to be desired.

He thought of the rich *bombe au chocolat* reposing on a shelf in his refrigerator. Death by chocolate? Somehow he had the feeling the dessert was meant to be his *bête noir*.

'Enjoy.'

'Thank you,' Sebastian acknowledged as he took the tray, watching as she took a few seconds to fondle Shaef's ears. Then she turned towards Vivienne's cottage, and he viewed the elegant sway of her hips with male appreciation before taking the tray to the dining room table.

Shaef cast him an enquiring look and pricked his ears.

'That makes two of us,' Sebastian murmured as he placed dishes onto the table, caught up cutlery, and removed covers.

It only took a glance to interpret Anneke's meaning. Get stuffed. A slow, musing smile widened his mouth.

Vivienne's niece had gone to considerable trouble to exact revenge.

With deft movements he consigned the sponge, strawberries and cream concoction to the refrigerator.

Pride had prevented her from serving up burnt offerings, or the blandest of fare. Pride, and loyalty to her aunt.

Well, he wouldn't spoil Anneke's game.

He, too, could employ a little subterfuge. If most all of the minor repairs around Vivienne's property were completed within a week instead of the months she'd originally suggested, then so be it.

A slow smile curved his mouth, and the edges lifted in humour. And if he ran out of things to do, then he would invent some.

Sebastian sat down at the table and carefully removed a portion of stuffing from each vegetable, then sliced into the delectable-looking steak.

A man would need to be wary around a woman like Anneke. His lips twitched and his eyes gleamed with cynical amusement. If each prepared meal provided an indication of her mood, then the next week or two could prove interesting.

Afterwards he scraped discarded stuffing into the refuse bin, made recklessly strong coffee, then carried it through to the office, turned on the computer screen and began to work.

Intrigued to discover within a short space of time that a minor female character of his creation had developed a few traits that changed stoic to sassy.

Anneke surveyed the number of pots and kitchen utensils atop the kitchen benchtop and wrinkled her nose at the folly of creating culinary mayhem.

Rinse and soak, she decided, then she'd attack the dishes when she'd eaten her own modest meal of salad greens with nuts, fresh cantaloupe, mango and feta cheese.

Afterwards, she'd thumb through Aunt Vivienne's numerous cookbooks and plot a menu for tomorrow evening's meal, then list the ingredients she needed to buy.

At nine Aunt Vivienne rang, with an update on Elise's health and the latest monitor results on the unborn twins. It was a case of 'no change' being good news.

Almost as soon as Anneke replaced the receiver, her mobile phone rang, and she indulged in a lengthy chat with a friend in Sydney before ending the call and retiring to bed with a book.

The morning brought a light rain, and after a leisurely breakfast Anneke showered and changed, then drove to Byron Bay to collect fresh seafood.

On impulse she opted to spend the day baking, and purchased ingredients to make a Christmas cake. Several small ones, she decided, would make excellent gifts for friends, wrapped in red and green Cellophane and tied with decorative ribbons. She could take them back with her, or, if she chose to lengthen her stay, then she could consign them via the postal service.

It rained on and off all day. Alternate heavy and light showers with very little time in between.

The kitchen was soon redolent with various aromas, as Anneke washed and soaked a variety of dried fruit in sherry and brandy.

By mid-afternoon shortbread, cut in fingers, lay cooling on baking racks. There was one tin filled with rumballs, another with fudge brownies. Tomorrow she'd bake Christmas cakes.

A quick glance at her watch determined it was time to begin preparing Sebastian's evening meal.

A secretive smile teased the edges of her mouth. She almost wished she could see his expression when he uncovered a platter containing miso soup thick with seaweed and tofu, grilled eel in a rich oyster sauce, sushi with slices of raw fish and seaweed delicacies, and *faux* caviare. Flavoured tofu with fruit comprised dessert.

Sebastian heeded her knock, caught her carefully composed expression, and was immediately on guard.

He mentally conjured the thick T-bone steak he'd removed from the freezer earlier in the day, the makings for a salad he could put together in minutes, and sought to protect his palate.

'Why not join me tomorrow night?'

'I wouldn't dream of interrupting your work,' she responded with extreme politeness.

'An hour or two won't cause much damage.'

'Damage' was the operative word, and she didn't covet an hour in his company, much less two. Besides, if she shared a meal with him she'd have to resort to conventional cooking, and that would definitely spoil the fun.

'Maybe another time.' Without a further word she turned and retraced her steps.

It was as well he liked Japanese food, although he conceded her choice of dishes was probably as deliberate as it was unusual. The dessert joined the chocolate *bombe* and the strawberry sponge sitting in his refrigerator.

Anneke checked the dried fruit, stacked shortbread into one of her aunt's cake tins, then cleaned up the kitchen.

After a day of preparing food, she opted for something simple for her own meal, and followed it with a bowl of fresh fruit. She added ice to a glass, filled it with water, then carried it through to the lounge and switched on the television.

The phone rang at nine. She remembered the time, as she glanced at her watch. Even as she picked up the receiver she had the instinctive feeling this was going to be a repeat of yesterday's nuisance call.

Bingo, Anneke registered as no one answered her greeting, and within seconds she could hear audible breathing on the line.

Who would do something like this? It couldn't be aimed at Aunt Vivienne, surely? Yet who knew Anneke was here?

She cut the connection and replaced the handset, then stood staring at the telephone as if willing it to divulge relevant information.

For five minutes she hovered in the kitchen, wiping down bench surfaces that had already been wiped, checking cupboards, the refrigerator, the pantry. Just in case the call was repeated.

The thought crossed her mind that perhaps she should report it. But what could the police do, except relay advice she was already aware of?

THE SEDUCTION SEASON

talked aloud, but covering the... ha more quickly due to a longer stride.

Therefore, on the... Calf muscles be the saddles... less... Walker... ve steady going... her...

CHAPTER FOUR

SEVERAL friends were aware of Anneke's mobile listing, but she hadn't told anyone of her whereabouts or given out Aunt Vivienne's number. And no one she knew would make a nuisance, heavy breathing, non-speaking call then hang up.

She had no enemies, and no one she knew would wish her harm. So *who*? A frown creased her forehead. A misdialled number? Once, maybe. But *twice* indicated it to be premeditated.

The microwave digital display indicated a few minutes before six. Damn. There was no reason to front the day at such an early hour, and yet she felt too unsettled to simply sit around and do nothing.

A jog along the length of the beach followed by a swim in the cool, clear ocean would clear her mind, then she'd drive into Byron Bay and explore the shops for an hour or two. After lunch she'd mix the Christmas cakes and consign them into the oven.

This early there was a fresh newness to the day, apparent in the warmth of the sun's rays, the golden sand crisp from its tidal cleanse.

Anneke set a leisurely pace along the Bay's gentle curve to the outcrop of rocks before turning to retrace her steps.

It was then she saw a lone male figure closing the distance between them, his pace measuring hers in relaxed style but covering the sand more quickly due to a longer stride.

There was no disguising the tall, muscular frame, and if there was any doubt the dark hair sleekly bound at his nape provided recognition.

Sebastian.

Clad in dark sweat-shorts and singlet, he looked like something out of a health and fitness magazine. The sweatband round his head lent a credible likeness to an Apache brave.

The mental switch in image brought a smile to her lips and lit her eyes with a mischievous sparkle.

She watched with detached admiration as he drew close: the fluid flex of well-honed muscle and sinew, the lithe, animalistic grace of perfectly co-ordinated body movement.

At this stage most men would have bunched up their pectoral muscles, flung back their shoulders in an effort to impress a female of the species.

Sebastian merely slowed his stride and came to an easy halt. Lacking was the expected sheen of sweat; nor was there any evidence of shortness of breath.

'*Bonjour.*'

'Hi.'

The easy smile deepened the vertical crease in each cheek, and there was an appreciative gleam in those dark eyes.

'I didn't expect to see you out this early.'

Dammit, why did it take one glance at his mouth to bring vividly to mind how it felt to have it cover her own? And *why*, a silent voice taunted, should some internal flame ignite and flare into deep, pulsing life with anticipation that it might?

'I rarely sleep in.' She hadn't meant to sound defensive.

Touchy. Definitely touchy. And he wondered why. 'I wasn't aware I'd implied that you do,' he said quietly.

Oh, hell. She had the distinct feeling he could see inside her mind, and meaningful conversation at this hour of the morning wasn't her intention.

'Must keep the heart-rate up,' she indicated, preparing to sprint away from him.

'We could run together.'

'Sorry,' Anneke declared without compunction. 'I run for fun. You,' she said with certainty, 'adhere to a more professional pace.' She even summoned a slight smile. 'And I wouldn't suggest you alter it solely for my benefit.' She broke into a light sprint, then slowed her pace when she had put some distance between them.

It wasn't easy to ignore the faint prickle of awareness teasing the hairs on her nape.

His very presence irked her. He made her feel vulnerable, and she didn't like it any more than she liked him.

There were no messages on the answering machine, but her mobile showed one missed call, and when she checked voice mail all she heard was an indistinct whisper followed by the silent click of a replaced receiver.

Her stomach gave a small lurch, then settled.

Adam? Even as the thought intruded, she dismissed

it. Adam Lloyd Chambers was a legal eagle of impeccable lineage, admired by his associates and a pillar within his social community.

The fact he had a penchant for sexual dalliances didn't alter the fact he was an unlikely candidate to make nuisance calls. Besides, she couldn't see him doing anything to jeopardise his career or his partnership.

Anneke made for the bathroom, showered and washed her hair, then dressed in tailored shorts, added a cotton top. She cut up a selection of fruit, added cereal, then followed it with a poached egg on toast for breakfast.

She put a small load of washing through the machine, and after completing some essential housework she caught up her keys and drove into Byron Bay with the intention of browsing through the many craft shops, maybe taking time out to sip a cappuccino at one of several outdoor cafés before purchasing a selection of fresh fruit and a few staple vegetables.

The aroma of freshly baked bread was irresistible, and she entered the shop, purchased a baguette and a few savoury scrolls, then emerged out onto the pavement.

Some ham, a wedge of Brie, and a delicious salad would suffice as lunch. Then she'd curl up in the capacious cane chair on her aunt's porch and lose herself in a book until it was time to prepare dinner.

'Well, now, girl, what's that you've got there?'

She heard the voice, took in the thin face, the long, unkempt hair, the nose-stud, the eyebrow-ring, and a range of studs and earrings attached to each ear. The loose-flowing shirt looked as if it hadn't been washed in weeks, likewise the frayed and slashed jeans.

One glance at those eyes was enough for her to determine this was no peace-loving New Age devotee. They were dark, beady, and mean.

Trouble. Unless she handled him carefully.

Anneke lifted one shoulder in a careless shrug. 'Bread, fruit and vegetables.' She made to move past him, and saw the subtle shift of his body as he stepped close.

Damn. 'You're in my way,' she stated calmly.

'That's a problem?'

'It could be.'

'So, what you gonna do, pretty girl?' he mocked.

'Any one of a number of things.'

He leered at her, and ran the tip of his tongue over his lower lip. 'Such as?' His mouth parted in a sound-less laugh. 'Scream?'

'How's your pain level?' Anneke countered matter-of-factly.

An arm curved along the back of her waist while another deftly removed a carry-bag. '*Chérie*. My apol-ogies.' She felt the heat of Sebastian's frame as he leaned in close and brushed his lips to her cheek in a warm caress. 'Have you been waiting long?'

She turned her head and met a pair of steady dark eyes, glimpsed their warning flare, and controlled the unexpected flip her stomach executed as she became lost in the devastating warmth of his smile.

Only a fool would have ignored the hard-muscled body beneath the open-necked shirt and stonewashed jeans, or dismissed the ruthless intensity behind his deceptively mild expression.

Anneke had the distinct feeling he was poised for action. It was evident in his stance, the sharp stillness apparent in his eyes. For one infinitesimal second she almost felt sorry for her aggressor.

'Sebastian. *C'est opportun.*'

A split second to think. So, not fluent, he acknowledged. The accent was passable. His smile widened. Good. She would understand what he said when he made love to her.

His eyes were carefully bland. 'Should we effect an introduction?' He thrust out his hand and enclosed the young man's palm in a firm grip. 'Lanier. And you?'

'Go to hell.'

Sebastian's expression didn't change. 'What a shame, my friend,' he intoned with deadly softness. 'We're not going there.'

Anneke didn't blink at the blistering and very pithy response. 'Charming,' she murmured facetiously as her aggressor turned and ambled off along the pavement. 'Pity his suggestion was anatomically impossible.'

Sebastian's eyes narrowed fractionally. 'He intended to relieve you of whatever money you had in your wallet.' To fund the next fix.

'It would have been interesting to discover his threshold of pain.'

He cast her a sharp glance. 'What particular method did you have in mind?'

She told him, concisely, analytically, and had the satisfaction of evidencing a measure of respect.

'Reassuring,' he conceded, 'to learn you can take care of yourself.'

Anneke inclined her head. Dealing with the scruffy young creep wouldn't have posed a problem. However, she would have had to discard the carry-bags in a hurry, and to have her carefully selected purchases crushed or broken in a physical fracas would have been a terrible waste.

She turned towards him and raised an enquiring eyebrow. 'And your field of expertise?'

He had trained beneath a well-respected master, practised in many a *dojo*, and occasionally fought in places no civilised self-respecting person would consider while serving his country for a time.

It was simpler to name one. 'Karate.'

Anneke considered him thoughtfully. Most men would have launched into a string of achievements. However, Sebastian Lanier was not 'most men', and his simplicity intrigued her.

There was more to him than met the eye, she perceived. Entrepreneur, writer. What other vocation and skill did he possess?

Sebastian indicated the carry-bags. 'Anything likely to spoil in there for the next hour?'

'No. Why?'

He deftly turned her in the opposite direction. 'You can join me for lunch.'

She regarded him solemnly. 'It's polite to ask.'

His mouth curved to form a wolfish smile, and there was a gleam in those dark eyes she didn't quite trust. 'I feel it's the least I can do in light of the gastronomic feasts you've prepared for me over the past few nights.'

'Gastronomic' indeed. 'Feast' depended entirely on the interpretation, she decided with irreverent suspicion. 'Thank you.'

There were any number of cafés and restaurants from which to choose. Instead, he led her into a modern pub, the owner of which had gained recognition in the area for his brush with fame and the garnering of considerable wealth. A man's man, and one of the boys, local legend had it, who could sup beer at the bar with his friends equally as well as he'd cemented business deals in Hollywood and London.

'You don't object to a counter lunch?'

She searched Sebastian's features in an attempt to discern whether his choice was deliberate, and found nothing to indicate that it might be.

'It's ages since I had fish and chips.'

He cast her a musing glance. 'I think you'll find they manage something less basic.'

They did, and, although relatively simple fare, the freshly caught grilled schnapper was delicious, the salad superb, and it was obvious the licensee patronised the local bakery.

Sebastian noted her enjoyment, observed her healthy appetite, the precise but intensely feminine movements of her hands, the manner in which she sampled each mouthful.

Poetry in motion. There was no guile, no studied orchestration. He wondered what she would look like with her hair loose, and spread over his pillow as she slept. Or tossed and dishevelled in the throes of passion as she rode him hard and fast.

She possessed a beautiful mouth, even white teeth. Was she well versed in using both to drive a man wild and hold him on the knife-edge between pleasure and pain?

Confrontational, no artifice, he mused thoughtfully. What you saw was what you got.

Yet she wasn't above playing a diverse game. For the sheer hell of it, he suspected, as he mentally reviewed the exotic meals she'd delivered all three evenings. He'd expected unimaginative fare. Not the dishes she'd gone to a great deal of trouble to prepare.

His eyes acquired a gleam of dancing amusement. What did she have in mind for tonight?

Anneke sensed his gaze, caught the musing glint apparent, and spared him a level look. 'Nice to know I amuse you. Perhaps you could be specific?'

Sebastian banked down the laughter, broke off a piece of bread and ate it, then offered her a warm smile. 'How specific would you like me to be?'

She watched the powerful movement of his jaw, the way his facial muscles clenched and relaxed, the smooth column of his throat. His hands fascinated her. Broad palms, strong wrists, tanned skin stretched over fluid sinew, long, tapered fingers that belied their strength, clean, well-shaped nails.

'Oh, the whole truth and nothing but the truth will do.'

'I'm curious to know where you learnt to cook.'

She effected a light shrug. 'A young chef rented the apartment next to mine for a while. I helped him perfect his English, and in return he shared his culinary skills.'

'Among other skills?'

She didn't pretend to misunderstand his meaning. 'He wasn't my lover.' She replaced her cutlery, then carefully pushed her plate aside and stood to her feet. 'Thanks for lunch.'

He'd offended her. Interesting. 'Sit down.'

'No.' Her eyes flared, darkening to the deepest emerald flecked with gold. Without a word she turned and walked from the room, out onto the pavement and into the sunshine.

She lifted a hand and slid her sunglasses down from atop her head, and walked along the street towards her car.

'You left these behind.'

Anneke heard Sebastian's faintly accented drawl, paused, then turned and threw him a fulminating glare.

He had her carry-bags secured in each hand, but made no effort to pass them to her.

'I'll take them.' She reached out, only to scream in silent frustration as he fell into step beside her. 'Don't,' she warned in a deadly quiet voice, 'think you're safe, just because we're in a public place.'

He looked at her with studied ease, aware from the set of her shoulders, the slightly clenched fists, that she meant what she said.

'We're almost at the car park.'

'You don't need to play the gentleman,' she retaliated with heavy sarcasm.

'In this instance, I choose to.' He scanned the wide

apron of bitumen with its lines of parked cars, identified hers, and crossed towards it.

Anneke walked ahead of him and unlocked and opened the passenger door, then stood aside as he placed the carry-bags onto the seat.

He straightened, and she was suddenly intensely aware of his height, his proximity, and the faint musky aroma of cologne and man.

He looked down at her, saw the tilt of her chin, the residue of anger that tightened her expression. Without a word he lifted a hand and trailed the tips of his fingers down one cheek and splayed them along her jaw.

Then he smiled and lowered his head down to hers, capturing her mouth with his own in a gentle evocative kiss that was all too brief.

'Drive carefully.' Without a further word he turned and navigated a line of cars to his own powerful Range Rover.

Frustrating, *irritating* man, she accorded, adding a few descriptive and vividly pithy curses as she crossed round and slid in behind the wheel.

She reversed, then eased her sedan out onto the street. By the time she arrived at her aunt's cottage she had devised numerous ways to render him grievous bodily harm, as well as concocting the most bizarre series of menus that she could summon to mind.

Anneke unpacked the carry-bags, poured herself a cold drink, and checked her watch. Three hours until she needed to begin dinner preparations.

Housework, she decided. She'd clean and dust and polish. Busy hands, healthy mind. Well, hers was filled with vengeful thoughts, which somehow made a mockery of that particular saying.

When she'd finished, everything sparkled and the cottage was redolent with the smell of beeswax. And the richness of freshly baked fruit cake.

It was after five when her mobile rang, and without thinking she wiped her hands, then reached for the unit and activated it.

Nothing. Only an eerie silence echoed her customary greeting. Her fingers shook slightly as she disengaged the phone.

Rationale dictated it was just a crank call. She doubted it was Adam. Although she couldn't discount the possibility he might take a perverse delight in causing her a degree of nervous anxiety.

It was just after six when she delivered Sebastian's evening meal.

'Stay and have a drink with me.'

Anneke looked at him, saw the unbound hair and noted its unruly state—almost as if he'd raked his fingers through the length on more than one occasion.

Maybe the plot wasn't working out, or the characters weren't performing as they should. Or he was struggling through a bout of writer's block.

'Thanks, but I don't drink.' Not entirely true. She adored good French champagne, and reserved the partaking of it for special occasions. As this wasn't one of them, and she seriously doubted he had a bottle of Dom Perignon or Cristal on ice, it was simpler to decline. 'Your meal will get cold, and so will mine,' she said easily, and turned towards the door.

He made no attempt to dissuade her, and when the

door closed behind her he crossed to the table, removed the cover and examined the contents of the tray.

It could have been worse. He moved to the bank of cupboards, took out a skillet and reached into the refrigerator for a large T-bone steak.

When it came to the dessert, he scraped off the cream, took a tentative bite, then opted for fresh fruit. He washed it down with bottled mineral water, then spooned freshly ground beans into the coffee-maker, poured water into the cylinder and switched it on.

The glass carafe had just begun to fill when there was a crashing sound from the adjoining cottage.

He was out of the door and running, Shaef at his side, adrenalin pumping, his mind actively selecting one scenario after another as he covered the set of steps in one leap and pounded on the door.

CHAPTER FIVE

A MUFFLED and very explicit curse fell from Anneke's lips as she surveyed the mess at her feet.

Cut flowers were strewn in an arc across the floor, water pooled in a widening puddle, and Aunt Vivienne's prized Waterford crystal vase lay shattered in a hundred shards on the laundry's ceramic-tiled floor.

There was no one to blame but herself. Unless she counted a fractional second's distraction at the insistent and distinctive peal of her mobile telephone.

'Anneke.' Forceful, authoritative, *demanding*. Sebastian's voice penetrated the evening's stillness, accompanied by the heavy, insistent rap of knuckles on wood.

'OK, OK,' she responded in resigned exasperation. 'I'm in the...' Her voice trailed to a halt as he appeared at the screened laundry door.

'Hell,' he cursed quietly, taking in the scene at a glance. Her legs were bare, so were her feet.

'Apt,' she responded drily.

'Don't move. I'll be back.'

He was, within minutes, with a bucket, pan and brush.

'Don't throw out the flowers.'

'They're likely to contain hidden pieces of glass.'

'Crystal,' she corrected without thought, and incurred a dark, sweeping glance.

'Waterford, thirty-five years old, wedding gift. You want the pattern detail?'

'There's no need to be facetious.'

'Likewise, you don't need to be so particular.'

'Oh, go soak your head in a bucket!'

His smile held a certain grimness. 'Nice to have your gratitude.'

She wanted to burst into tears. She treasured beautiful things. Loved the art and symmetry of exquisite crystal and porcelain. To have a piece break by her own hand was almost akin to killing a living thing.

He glimpsed the momentary desolation, caught a flash of something deeper, and fought the temptation to pull her into his arms. Such an action, he knew, would only earn him the sharp edge of her tongue.

'Vivienne has plenty more flowers in the garden,' he offered mildly, ignoring her protest as he deftly swept everything into the bucket, then dealt with the water.

'Vacuum cleaner. Hall cupboard?' Had to be. Both cottages were similar in design.

Twice the vacuum hose rattled as the cleaner sucked up undetected shards of crystal, and she stepped onto a towel he spread on the floor while he completed the task.

'Thanks,' she added, aware she owed him that, at least. She could have coped, dispensing with the mess, but it was likely she'd have cut herself in the process.

Dammit, she didn't want to owe him. Nor did she

particularly covet his company. He made her feel…uncomfortable, she conceded reluctantly.

As if he was all too aware of the sexual chemistry between them, and content to wait and watch for the moment *she* felt it.

Well, she had news for him. She could pin it down to the precise moment she'd walked into Aunt Vivienne's kitchen the first night she arrived and found him there making tea. For her.

Sebastian watched the fleeting emotions chase across her expressive features, divined the reason for them, and kept his own expression deliberately bland.

She could tell him to go, or ask him to stay. There was always tomorrow, the day after that. And he was a patient man.

The tussle between politeness and impoliteness warred, and there was really no contest. 'Would you like some coffee?'

He studied her in silence for a few seconds. 'Thanks.'

In the kitchen she set the coffee-maker up, then extracted two cups and saucers, added a bowl of sugar, and took cream from the refrigerator.

Anneke was conscious of him as he leant one hip against the servery. His tall frame made the kitchen seem smaller, and she became aware of every move she made. Only sheer habit prevented the spoon clattering onto the saucer, and she was extremely careful with the glass carafe as she poured hot coffee.

Sebastian collected both cups and set them down on the dining room table, then he pulled out a chair and folded his length into it.

She crossed to the table and sat opposite him. Conversational skills were something she'd rarely lacked. Yet at this precise moment she had trouble summoning one topic to mind.

'How's the book going?'

An amused gleam momentarily lit his eyes before he successfully hid it by letting his eyelids droop fractionally. The inevitable question an author had to field from time to time. 'My answer would only seem a paradox.'

The dry response made it easy for her to resort to humour. 'You've hit a bad patch?'

He winced mentally. 'You could say I've dug myself into a hole and I can't see a way out.'

'Why not back up and avoid the hole altogether?'

Good point. 'I need to think about it a while.'

'So sharing coffee and conversation is really an excuse not to stare at a blank screen and curse beneath your breath?'

'Perhaps I couldn't resist your charming company.'

Icily polite. Furiously angry. Indignant, voluble, even sarcastic. At no stage could she recall being charming. Maybe it was time to try.

'Tell me why you write.'

'Curiosity, or genuine interest?'

'A bit of both,' she answered honestly.

'An obsessive need to create a story.' A statement which usually brought a non-committal response, indicating uninterest or lack of comprehension.

Anneke looked at him carefully. Glimpsed the fine lines fanning out from the corners of his eyes, the faint furrow creasing his forehead, as if he'd frowned in concentration too often in the past few hours.

'And the *how* of it?'

His mouth quirked. 'Matching the image in my head with words that allow the reader to capture my vision.'

An art form that wasn't always easy, requiring dedication and discipline, she perceived. There could be no doubt Sebastian Lanier possessed both qualities.

He waited for the inevitable comments relating to fame and fortune, the media circus he went to great pains to avoid. But none were forthcoming.

Inane questions weren't her practice. 'It must be a fascinating process.' Her eyes glinted with humour. 'And not without a degree of frustration when the words don't flow as you need them to.'

His smile held a warmth that made her stomach curl. And the eyes were dark, gleaming and steady. Assessing, analytical, almost as if he had calculated every move, every angle, and was waiting to see which one she would choose.

It gave her an uncanny feeling.

'Mind if I pour more coffee?'

His voice was husky and held a tinge of humour, almost as if he'd read her mind.

'Of course not. Help yourself.'

He indicated her cup. 'Want me to refill yours?'

It was strong, really strong. If she drank another, she'd be awake half the night. 'No, thanks. I'll have water instead.'

He crossed to the servery, helped himself from the coffee-maker, then reached into a nearby cupboard, extracted a glass and filled it with water. All with the ease of a man who was familiar with her aunt's kitchen.

She could almost imagine their easy friendship, and experienced a pang of envy.

He should get out of here. The computer beckoned, and he'd just had a fleeting but inspired flash as to how he could circumvent the current plot hole.

However, the coffee was good, really good. And Anneke's current mood intrigued him.

He placed the glass down onto the table in front of her, then slid into his chair.

'Your turn.'

Her eyes widened, the light, clear green darkening fractionally as comprehension hit.

Fascinating…eyes a man could drown in, and he discovered he wanted to, very much. Thread a hand through her silky hair and hold fast her head while he shaped her mouth with his own. Anchor her against him so she felt his need while he heightened her own. The slow erotic glide of hands, lips, until neither was enough and the barrier of clothes proved too much.

'You live in Sydney, and work in a legal office,' Sebastian prompted, banking down libidinous images.

'No longer work in one specific legal office,' Anneke corrected drily.

'Resigned?'

'Walked out.'

His eyes held a humorous gleam. 'Problems with the boss?'

She looked at him in measured silence. 'You could say that.' A statement she didn't intend to clarify.

At that moment the phone rang, its double peal insistent, and her eyes flared momentarily with apprehension.

Another nuisance call?

Sebastian unbent his lengthy frame and pushed in his chair. 'I'll let you get that.' He drained the remains of his coffee and carried the cup and saucer to the servery. Then he lifted a hand in silent salute and let himself out of the back door.

Anneke crossed to the phone, removed the receiver, and experienced relief when she discovered the caller was one of her aunt's friends.

A relief which proved short-lived when the phone rang again minutes later.

She tossed up whether to answer it or not, for she couldn't discount the possibility it might be a legitimate call. Indecision warred for a few seconds, then she took a deep breath and unhooked the receiver.

Her heart sank. No answer, only heavy breathing. She resisted the temptation to crash the receiver down on its cradle. 'Damn you,' she said fiercely. 'Try this again, and I'll contact the police and have them put a trace on the line.'

There was the faint click of a receiver being replaced, then the hollow sound of a cut connection.

'Problems?'

Anneke whirled at the sound of that deep, faintly accented voice, and saw Sebastian, tray in hand, standing just inside the kitchen door.

Her heart was thumping in her chest, and her eyes, she knew, were stark and wide. Control kicked in, and she forced her voice into even tones.

'You heard.' There was no point in pretending he hadn't.

With ease, he crossed the room and deposited the tray on the servery. 'You didn't answer the question.'

Why fabricate? 'Someone seems to be having fun at my expense.'

He leant a hip against the cabinet and regarded her carefully, noting a face devoid of colour, eyes that were far too dark. 'How many such calls have you taken?'

'That was the sixth call in three days, if you count my mobile.'

'He's persistent.' He waited a beat. 'Abusive?'

Anneke shook her head. 'So far he hasn't said a word.'

'Tomorrow we notify the phone company and arrange an unlisted number.' His eyes hardened, and he kept them partially hooded. 'Shaef stays with you.'

'*We?* I can take care of it. And I don't need Shaef.'

'It's Shaef or me. Choose.'

She shot him a look of disbelief. 'Aren't you going just a tiny bit overboard with this?'

His eyes were obsidian, his gaze hard and unblinking. 'No.'

Anneke drew in a deep breath, considered telling Sebastian to go take a running hike, then thought better of it.

'It's probably a random call by some idle teenager who, hearing a female voice on the line, has decided to play a stupid game.'

'Maybe.'

'You think it's my ex-boss? If he's caught, and I

press charges, the Law Society will suspend him from practice,' she qualified slowly. 'Why take the risk?'

Sebastian's gaze remained steady. 'Some men get their kicks skating close to the edge.'

'He already has my mobile number. Why not use that instead of the house phone?'

'It's too simple. He wants you to be aware he knows where you are.'

Her eyes darkened until they resembled the deepest emerald. Was Adam that cunning? That devious? She could recall telling him she had an aunt who lived in a cottage on a northern coastal beach, but she was willing to swear she hadn't mentioned Aunt Vivienne's surname, or *which* north-coast beach.

Get a grip, she mentally cautioned. You're not in any danger.

'Don't answer the house phone, and switch your mobile onto voice mail.'

'Any more instructions?'

'Don't be sassy.'

He loomed too close for comfort, and it took an effort not to step back a pace. 'You've done your good deed for the day. Twice over.'

'Is that a subtle hint for me to leave?'

'I'd hate to keep you from your work.'

'The computer can wait,' Sebastian drawled, moving forward a pace. 'This won't.'

'This' was his mouth on hers in what proved to be a devastating invasion. He possessed the touch, the instinctive mastery to make a kiss seem like an extension of the physical act itself.

Worse, to make a woman feel a kiss was nowhere

near *enough*. That there was more, much more to savour in the realm of sensual delight.

A demanding lover, Sebastian Lanier would take everything a woman offered, and encourage her to give more.

Anneke suppressed a slight shiver. The reward would be magnificent, she acquiesced. Electrifying.

Her heart pounded, and her pulse raced almost out of control as he trailed his mouth to the edge of her jaw. She cried out as he savoured the column of her throat, and she arched her head to allow him greater access.

His hands were warm against her clothing as they moulded her close, and the barrier was something to be dispensed with as the need arose for skin against skin.

Sebastian was the first to move, tugging her blouse free, his fingers deft with buttons as he freed each and every one.

Her own sought purchase on soft cotton, and yanked hard until the tee-shirt slipped out from his waistband.

Dear Lord, he felt good. Hard ribs, corded muscles, broad back, wide shoulders. Her hands curved higher, then clung as he crushed her to him.

His mouth claimed, *staked* a possession that brooked no denial, and for one brief second she almost threw common sense out of the window.

Sebastian was aware the exact moment she began to retreat, and he reluctantly and very slowly broke the kiss, allowing his lips to brush hers, savouring each corner, then he pushed her gently to arm's length.

'I want to take you to bed.' A faint smile curved his lips. 'But I have the feeling you'd only hate me in the morning.'

As well as herself. Twisted sheets and an energetic coupling wasn't on her agenda. With any man.

'I'll write down my phone number. Should anything go bump in the night, call me.' He slid a hand to her cheek, cupped it, and traced her lips with his thumb. 'OK?'

Anneke inclined her head fractionally.

'I'll whistle up Shaef.'

Five minutes later the Alsatian was instructed who he had to guard, and how. Both doors were securely locked, and Anneke settled herself in bed with a good book.

It was after eleven when she put out the light, and on the edge of sleep it was Sebastian's image which came to mind. His sculpted features, the piercing grey eyes that saw too much.

Someone who had experienced more than his share, and had dealt with it. Only a fool would surmise otherwise.

She thought of his kiss, the way his mouth felt on her own, the familiarity of his hands as they moulded her body. And hated herself for wanting more.

CHAPTER SIX

ANNEKE woke early, stretched, then slid out of bed and almost stepped onto a sleek-coated animal curled protectively on the floor. A very large animal.

Oh, my God. *Shaef.*

Memory surfaced in one fell swoop, and a soft curse fell from her lips.

With considerable caution she skirted round the dog and crossed to the bathroom. The dog followed.

Five minutes later she returned to the bedroom, filching her swimsuit from the shower stall where she'd hung it over the taps to dry.

It fitted snug over her slender curves, and she pulled on sweat-shorts and top, then made her way into the kitchen.

Fresh orange juice added a certain zing to her palate, and she looked at the dog with a degree of doubt.

'OK, I guess you need to go outside. Water,' she declared decisively, and hunted for a bowl. 'Food.' The dog's ears pricked at the mention of it.

Dammit, she was a cat person. Dogs gnawed on bones, ate meat, and munched on dry food. A goodly amount of each, she surmised, judging by Shaef's size. None of which she had on hand.

'Sorry, fella.' She placed a bowl filled with water onto the floor. 'This will have to do for now, then you can go home for breakfast.'

When she let him out of the back door, he promptly lolloped to the nearest tree, then, considerably more comfortable, returned to sit on the step.

'Divided loyalties, pal. I'm going for a run along the beach. You get to choose whether you guard me or the house.' She smiled and leant down to fondle one silky ear. 'Personally, I'd go for the house.'

He didn't, of course. She hadn't moved more than half a dozen steps when he fell in beside her. 'Well, there's no doubt you take after your owner,' she said conversationally. 'He's every bit as stubborn as you are.'

Anneke reached the beach and sprinted down onto the sand. And saw Sebastian engaged in callisthenics. Waiting to join her?

Sebastian *plus* his dog? She sprinted towards him. 'Been waiting long?' she queried sweetly.

He wasn't deceived by the mildness of her tone. She was angry. Well, he could handle it. He drew himself up to his full height with ease, placed a hand on one hip and offered her a warm smile.

'Beautiful day.'

She'd slept well. It made the fact that he hadn't seem worthwhile.

'Should I put this down to chance? Or is your appearance on the beach at this hour a forerunner of things to come?'

My, she possessed a sharp tongue. He had an urge to take her mouth with his own and change tart to something smooth and sweet.

'You object to my company?'

She placed a hand on each hip, taking defiance to

a new level. 'In the thinly veiled guise of bodyguard, *yes*.'

He had to work hard to prevent humour from entering his voice. 'Are you saying only one of us gets to share your run?'

Damn him, he was amused. 'Given a choice, Shaef wins out.' Her eyes searched his, saw the purposeful intent evident, and she released a deep sigh. 'But you're not going to give me a choice, are you?'

'No.'

'I just might have to hit you.'

'Think carefully before you do.'

There was a silkiness evident in his tone that sent a faint shiver down the length of her spine.

Without a further word she turned and broke into a run, aware of the moment he joined her, man and dog matching their stride to hers. Part of her wanted to set a punishing pace, but she knew she'd never outrun either of them.

A degree of resentment rose to the surface. Against Adam, if it was he who'd initiated a nuisance campaign, but primarily with Sebastian, for any number of reasons, she decided darkly. Foremost, for tugging at her emotions and turning them every which way but loose.

The sandy cove curved out to sea in a low outcrop of rocks, and Anneke turned when she reached that point and began retracing her steps without pause.

Shaef was having a wonderful time, bounding on ahead, then diverging down to the incoming tide to examine a shell or a piece of seaweed. Sebastian jogged steadily at her side.

It was a relief to draw level with her towel, and without saying so much as a word she pulled off her joggers, stripped down to her swimsuit, and sprinted lightly down to the water's edge.

She fully expected Sebastian to join her, and silently vowed as she dived into the cool sea that he'd regret it if he did. Quite *how* she'd ensure he regretted it, she wasn't clear.

Sebastian intuitively opted to engage Shaef in a game of throw-the-stick until Anneke emerged.

'Wise,' she muttered beneath her breath, and missed the amused gleam in his dark eyes as he called Shaef to heel.

'Share breakfast with me.'

She was sharing his dog, his protection. That was enough. She caught up the towel and wound it sarongwise round her waist. 'Thanks, but no, thanks. I have a heap of things to do.'

He snared her wrist as she turned to walk away from him. 'Lock the cottage securely if you go anywhere. Drive with the central locking system in place. And make sure you park the car on a main thoroughfare.'

She began to steam with indignation. 'Anything else?'

'Carry your mobile phone at all times.'

'I'm amazed you haven't mentioned Shaef.'

'That's a given,' Sebastian intoned hardily. 'Where you go, he goes.'

The steam changed to smoke. 'Now just a tiny minute, here.' Anneke lifted a hand and poked his chest. Hard. 'If my heavy breather is Adam, he's hundreds of miles south in Sydney. A nuisance, but not a threat.'

'And if it's not Adam?'

Ice chilled her veins. 'I intend to find out one way or another. Meantime, stay off my back.' She poked his chest again for good measure, then tugged her hand free and marched back to the cottage.

Impossible, dictatorial, *stubborn* man. Who did he think he was? And by what right did he imagine he could tell her what to do?

Sebastian watched her retreating form, and that of Shaef, who, at a click of Sebastian's fingers, had taken a few bounding strides to fall in at Anneke's side.

A woman who would give as good as she got, and be passionate in giving it... Be it anger, or making love. The former he could handle with one hand tied behind his back. It was the latter that bothered him.

He could have done with cooling down in the ocean himself, and he measured the time it would take her to shower, make coffee, eat whatever it was she had for breakfast, then begin making phone calls.

At the very least he had ten minutes, even if she messed up the order of things.

Anneke entered the cottage and headed straight for the shower, where she sluiced off the salt water and shampooed her hair. Then, towelled dry, she dressed in sapphire-blue shorts and a matching sleeveless top.

Coffee, hot, sweet, strong and black, then she'd fill a bowl with cereal and fruit.

It was after eight when she crossed to the phone. Aunt Vivienne was first on her list, and, after eliciting news that Elise was fine, she gave her aunt relevant

details and relayed the fact that until she contacted the
police she had no idea whether they'd put a trace on
the line or suggest she apply for an unlisted number.
Either way, Aunt Vivienne's permission was essential.

Next came a call to the phone company, who, on
receiving relevant details, promised to check their re-
cords and ring back.

Which left the police. Two 'on hold's and two
transfers later, she connected with a very informative
young man.

'Yes, ma'am. The complaint was logged in at
twenty-o-five hundred hours last night by a Sebastian
Lanier acting on behalf of Vivienne Sorrel, owner of
the property. The duty officer advised appropriate action, which I understand is being taken, pending authority this morning from Vivienne Sorrel. Perhaps
you might like to check with Sebastian Lanier?'

Check with him? She'd kill him! 'Thank you.' She
replaced the receiver with care, then turned and
marched from the cottage, closing the distance between both residences in swift, angry strides.

The back door was open, the screen door unlatched,
and she knocked once, then entered to find Sebastian
crisping bacon in the microwave while eggs simmered
in a pan atop the stove.

'What God-given right do you think you have to
log in a report with the police on my behalf?' Anneke
demanded wrathfully.

The toaster popped up crisped bread, and he
crossed to the servery, removed both slices and calmly
buttered them.

'You're angry.'

Emerald fire flashed in her eyes, and she had to clench her fists to refrain from lashing out at him. 'You bet your sweet life I am.'

He glanced up, and shot her a direct look as he extracted a plate from the cupboard. 'I thought it wise to instigate immediate enquiries.'

'Just *who* in hell do you think you are?'

He placed the toast onto the plate. 'I promised Vivienne I'd keep an eye on you.'

'Well, you can take your damned eye off me, as of now.'

Sebastian deftly removed the pan, slid eggs onto toast, collected the bacon, and carried both plates to the table.

'Want to share?'

'No, I don't want to share *anything* with you!' She drew in a deep breath and released it. 'Nothing, *nada*, *niente*. Do you understand?'

He filled a mug with steaming aromatic black coffee, stirred in sugar, and savoured a mouthful. His shoulders lifted in a deliberate Gallic shrug. 'That's certainly specific.'

Anneke flung her arms in the air in a gesture of enraged despair. 'You're not going to do as I ask, are you?'

His eyes pierced hers, dark, dangerous and lethal. 'No.' He picked up cutlery and cut a neat slice from the corner of his toast. 'Not until the nuisance calls stop.'

'I'm twenty-seven years old, not seventeen. I've lived alone for seven years in a city known for its high crime rate. I can take care of myself.'

Sebastian forked a mouthful of toast and egg into his mouth, chewed and swallowed it, then proceeded to cut another slice.

'You've forgotten one thing.'

The anger was still evident, simmering beneath the surface. 'And what, pray, is that?'

'I gave Vivienne my word.'

'And your word is sacrosanct,' Anneke declared with marked cynicism.

'Yes.'

'So get used to it?'

'I'm simply telling you how it is,' he said calmly.

'In that case, there's nothing more to say.'

'No.'

There were *several* more words she could have uttered, many of them blistering and not in the least ladylike. However, restraint in this instance was a favoured option.

'Fine.' She turned towards the back door and walked from his kitchen, then crossed the stretch of lawn and garden separating each cottage.

Her car stood in the carport, and, making a split-second decision, she went indoors, changed her clothes, caught up her bag and mobile phone, then locked up the cottage, slid behind the wheel and reversed down the driveway.

Within minutes she gained the main road leading onto the northern highway. The Gold Coast was only two hours' drive away. Shopping centres, movies, glitzy boutiques. Just the place to escape to, Anneke decided.

She had travelled less than five minutes when her mobile phone rang, and she automatically activated it.

'Tell me where you're going, and what time you expect to be home.'

Her stomach performed a backwards somersault at the sound of Sebastian's voice on the line. It sounded impossibly deep, his accent more pronounced.

Anneke took a deep, steadying breath. 'Go to hell.' Then she cut the connection.

It should have made her feel better. Instead, she felt more and more like an angry juvenile kicking out against authority.

Examining the situation analytically, she was allowing emotions to overrule common sense.

Damn. She thumped a fist against the steering wheel. This contrary ambivalence was ridiculous.

Without further thought she slowed down and pulled off to the side of the road. She caught up her mobile phone and prepared to punch in digits she realised she didn't have. Sure, he'd written down his number, but that was on a piece of paper tucked into a teletex in her aunt's kitchen.

OK, all she had to do was ring directory service. Two minutes later she de-activated the call, and groaned with frustration. Sebastian Lanier's phone number was ex-directory.

One car passed, then another. She didn't notice the Range Rover ease to a halt behind her, nor was she aware as the driver slid out from behind the wheel and trod the bitumen to the passenger side of her car.

A firm tap on the glass was the first indication she had of anyone's presence.

Anneke's head swung towards the window, and even as her elbow moved in automatic reflex to punch down the central locking device the passenger door opened and Sebastian slid into the passenger seat.

His eyes were dark, almost black, his expression grim and unrelenting.

'Careless,' he drawled. 'Very careless.'

'My knight in shining armour,' Anneke mocked. Her eyes were sheer crystalline emerald.

One day soon he would take that spitting tongue of hers and tame it. Was she aware just how close he was to doing it now?

His eyes seared hers as he placed an arm along the top of her seat. 'Co-operate, Anneke, and we'll get along fine.'

It was impossible to ignore the clean male smell of him, the faint aroma of aftershave. Just as it was impossible to dismiss the way her pulse tripped and raced to a quickened beat in his presence.

'The moment the police discover the source of your nuisance calls,' Sebastian assured her with a degree of cynicism, 'you're as free as a bird.' His expression hardened. 'Now, tell me where you're going, what time you expect to return.'

Her chin tilted and her eyes assumed a fiery brilliance. 'What if I don't?'

'That was the first option,' Sebastian said hardily. 'The second is for me to tag along with you.'

'Don't be ridiculous!'

'Choose, Anneke.'

'And if I don't have any set plans?'

'The second option applies.'

Why was she fighting him? She couldn't win. He wouldn't allow it.

She took a deep breath, then slowly released it and handed him her mobile phone. 'Press "redial", and you'll discover I was trying to reach you for the sole purpose of relaying my whereabouts on the Gold Coast and estimated time of return.' When he didn't take the phone, she hit the 'redial' button and pressed the unit to his ear. 'Except your number is ex-directory, and not even the citing of an emergency would reveal it.'

She delved into her bag, pulled out a piece of paper and a pen and thrust them at him, watching as he stroked a series of digits, then handed back the paper.

'Satisfied?' she demanded.

'Ring me when you leave the Coast.'

It wasn't negotiable, and she didn't even bother to refuse him. Although it was impossible not to resort to sarcasm. 'Do we synchronise our watches?'

Sebastian cast her a look that was more expressive than mere words, then he reached for the door clasp and slid out from the seat. 'Drive carefully.'

He closed the door, then covered the distance to his Range Rover.

Anneke watched him in the rear vision mirror, then she activated the ignition, eased the car onto the road.

It should have been a wonderful day. The sun shone brightly in a clear azure sky. The temperature soared to a midsummer high. With only two weeks to go before Christmas, the shops bore colourful decorations and there was an air of expectancy among the many shoppers filling the malls and walkways.

Christmas carols, and a store Santa handing out lollies and balloons to eager children added festive anticipatory cheer.

Anneke had thought to spend Christmas with Aunt Vivienne, but now it appeared she'd be spending it alone.

She could fly to Seattle, join her mother and stepfather for a 'yours, mine and ours' family Christmas.

Or, alternatively, there was her father, happily ensconced in London, who would welcome her into *his* extended family.

A small body careened into her legs, and she held onto the runaway child, soothing the little boy until a harassed and very pregnant young mother caught up to him.

Within minutes her mobile phone rang, and after a moment's hesitation she answered the call. There was a sense of relief to discover it was a friend from Sydney, wanting to exchange mutual news. Difficult in the face of that friendship not to reveal her whereabouts, although 'the Gold Coast' was hardly a fabrication. She simply didn't add that she was only there for the day.

Lunch comprised a salad sandwich washed down by mineral water in an upmarket café, and afterwards she selected a number of Christmas cards.

Her mobile phone rang again while she hovered in a specialist boutique specialising in imported toiletries, and she gave the sales assistant a helpless shrug accompanied by a faint smile, then moved to one side to gain a little privacy.

'Anneke.' The familiar male voice was quiet, almost restrained, but very clear on the line, and her stomach flipped as she gripped the phone.

'Adam.' Calm, keep calm. Act nonchalant, a tiny voice persisted.

'Bitch,' he hissed before she had a chance to disconnect the call. 'No woman runs out on me.'

'There's a first time for everything,' she said crisply. 'Chalk it up to experience.'

'Didn't think I could find you, did you, sweetheart?'

Relief, revulsion...both washed over her in realisation that Adam had been the source. 'Making nuisance calls wasn't very smart, Adam.'

'Payback time,' he dismissed. His voice lowered to a seductive drawl. 'You should have played with me; we could have had a ball.' He proceeded to explain his sexual preferences in graphic detail. 'Pity, but I value my skin, and you've proven to be way too much trouble. *Ciao*, darling. Have a good life.'

Anneke closed the phone and replaced it in her bag. She should, she silently castigated herself, have cut the connection as soon as she heard his voice. Now she simply felt angry, sickened, as his words echoed and re-echoed inside her head.

CHAPTER SEVEN

THE impetus to continue shopping was sadly lacking. She needed a different image, something to distract her from dwelling on Adam's bitter invective.

There was a multiple number of cinemas within the shopping complex. She'd go buy a ticket and choose a film to view.

A film about the *Titanic* was currently showing, and it was after six when she entered the car park, located her car and slid in behind the wheel.

Her mobile phone message-bank listed that two calls had been received during her cinema sojourn. One was from Sebastian, the other from the police. She contacted the duty sergeant at the designated number, who relayed the fact that trace on her aunt's telephone had been successful, then contacted Sebastian.

He picked up on the second ring. 'Lanier.'

A concise, deep voice that had the ability to raise goosebumps on the surface of her skin.

'Anneke.' She barely paused a second. 'I'm leaving now.' She cut the connection, then switched on the ignition and eased the car down several floors to street level.

The drive to Byron Bay was uneventful, and soon after crossing the Queensland-New South Wales border she passed paddocks high with mature sugar cane.

Banana plantations dotted the distant rolling hills, and there were avocado farms, and rich, fertile soil revealing row upon row of pineapples.

Dusk fell swiftly, the shadows lengthening and deepening as light gave way to dark, and it was almost nine when she pulled in beneath the carport adjacent her aunt's cottage.

She switched off the ignition, left her numerous purchases in the boot, then locked the car and trod the path to Sebastian's back door.

Five minutes, ten at the most, then she'd leave.

The screen door was unlocked, and Shaef stood on the other side, tail swishing back and forth in welcome.

Anneke knocked and entered the kitchen, then moved down the hall. Sebastian had had part of the wall between two bedrooms removed. A large executive desk complete with a state-of-the-art computer sat in the middle of one room, and the other was lined from floor to ceiling with bookshelves. In the centre of the room was a large antique buttoned leather armchair, with a matching ottoman, and a standard lamp. Combined, it made a large office-cum-library.

He looked up from the sheaf of papers he was studying, and leaned back in his chair.

'Take a seat.' He indicated one of two sited on the other side of the desk.

'I'd really prefer to keep this short.'

He noted the weary curve of her shoulders, the faint lines of strain marring an otherwise smooth forehead.

Shaef moved forward, nuzzled her hand, then slumped at her feet.

Sebastian sent her a long, considering look. 'Sit down.'

'Still giving orders?'

He ignored the sally, his eyes dark and far too discerning. 'Have you eaten?'

Food, in any shape or form, would probably make her ill. 'I had something earlier.' It wasn't exactly a lie.

'I'll make some tea.' He rose to his feet, crossed round the desk, then moved into the hall.

Anneke could hear the distant sound of water flowing from a tap, the faint hum of an electric kettle as it heated, the chink of crockery.

She closed her eyes. It had been a hell of a day. And it wasn't over yet.

Sebastian re-entered the room, saw the fringe of lashes touching each cheek, the pale, translucent skin.

She was beat, and without doubt emotionally exhausted.

He placed the cup and saucer near the edge of the desk, and watched her nostrils flare slightly as the aroma of bergamot teased the air. Her lashes lifted, then swept upwards in a slow, curving arc.

'Thanks.'

It was hot, heaven, and sweeter than she preferred. She took another appreciative sip, then put the cup carefully back onto the saucer.

'I guess you know the police scored a positive trace to Adam's mobile phone?'

Sebastian leaned one hip against the edge of the desk. 'Yes.'

She tilted her head and looked at him. 'Thank you for your concern.' He deserved that. 'And your help.'

'As I recall, you weren't too keen to accept either,' Sebastian said drily.

No, she hadn't been. 'You were very controlling.'

One eyebrow rose, and his mouth curved with a tinge of humour. 'I'm surprised you don't add "manipulative".'

'That, too,' Anneke agreed.

'Did it ever occur to you to question *why*?'

With just a few words their conversation had taken a subtle shift, and she wasn't comfortable with the change. 'Maybe we can continue this another time.' She stood to her feet, and immediately wished she hadn't, for it brought her much closer to him than she would have liked. 'Although it really isn't necessary, is it?' She took a backward step, and missed the faint gleam of amusement apparent in those dark eyes.

'You think not? Perhaps I'd better clarify it.' He reached for her shoulders and pulled her forward until she stood anchored between his thighs. Then he slowly lowered his head and brushed his lips against her temple. 'Are you beginning to get the picture?'

One hand slid down her back and cupped her buttocks, while the other slipped up to hold fast her head.

'Sebastian—'

His lips feathered down to the edge of her mouth, lingered there, then teased a trail of light kisses along the full lower curve.

'I don't think this is a—'

'Good idea?' He slid his tongue between her lips and felt rather than heard her breath catch.

'No,' Anneke whispered, as her heart raced to a faster beat, and heat flared through her veins.

His mouth was a soft caress as his hands moulded her close.

A kiss, she told herself. That's all it is. Why, she could even persuade herself that it didn't mean anything. Nothing at all. Men had kissed her before, in friendship, affection, and with a lover's passion.

She lifted her hands and linked them together at his nape, then leant in against him to enjoy the sensation of closeness. And came seriously unstuck when his mouth firmed on her own.

He'd kissed her before, as a questing, seeking experiment, and as a form of angry punishment.

This, *this* was different. Very different. It was both possession and promise. And it made her feel terribly afraid.

He had the touch, the instinctive skill of a man well versed in a woman's needs. His hands, his fingers, knew when to glide, where to caress, to drive her wild.

It was as if every sensitive nerve-end quivered in anticipation, then shrieked at each teasing stroke, every light pinch.

Dear God, she was silk, her skin satin-smooth, and each erogenous zone reacted like fire to his touch. He wanted to free her beautiful body of the restriction of clothes, to explore each indentation, each curve, until she moaned with delight, then begged for release.

That it would be him, only him she saw when he drove himself into her and made her his own. And him, only him, who had the power to take her to the brink, then tip her over the edge. He who held her tight and caught her when she fell.

His fingers sought the clip fastening of her bra and deftly released it, then he slid his hand to cup the fullness of her breast, teased its hardened peak, then trailed his mouth down her throat to the creamy crest. And felt her resistance.

What was she doing? This had gone way beyond mutual exploration, or mutual gratitude.

Anneke could feel the evidence of his arousal, the hard potent shaft beneath the zip of his jeans as it pressed high against his belt. Sensual heat emanated from his skin, and the beat of his heart was hard and deep.

His mouth settled on hers, persuasive, evocative and devastatingly sensual.

It would be easy, so very easy to let him take her wherever he wanted to go. To give in to the magic he promised and just enjoy whatever the night might hold.

Yet, no matter what the enticement, casual sex wasn't her style.

It took considerable effort to retreat, to drag her mouth from his and push herself to arm's length. More to quieten her fast-beating heart and attempt to regain her breath.

'I think,' Anneke enunciated unevenly, 'it would be best if I left. Now,' she added, dropping her hands from his arms.

'Best for whom?'

'Me. You. Us,' she added for good measure. 'I

mean, there is no *us*.' This was getting worse with every passing second. 'It's just—'

'Quit while you're ahead,' Sebastian advised gently, watching the fleeting change of expression chase across her features as she struggled for control.

He could pull her close, wreak havoc with that beautiful mouth, and take her here. On the desk, the floor. It didn't matter.

And that was the part that bothered him. He'd always displayed *finesse* with a woman. Wining, dining, flowers, pretty compliments. Sex by mutual consent, albeit that it might be wild or restrained. Rarely had he felt the urge to tear clothes from a female body, abrade her skin with his mouth, his hands, and join himself with her like a plundering conqueror.

He admired women…their strengths, their weaknesses, their passion. He respected their innate femininity. And he had enjoyed them. No serious commitment, no strings attached.

Until now.

Now he was captivated as never before by a smile, the way her mouth curved to tilt at the edges. The sweep of long lashes and the lure of a pair of green eyes which lightened or deepened according to mood.

She was fire and ice, passion and fury. And he wanted her in a way that he'd never wanted a woman before.

'Thanks for—' Her voice wasn't quite steady. 'Being there for me.'

He leaned forward and brushed a finger down the slope of her nose. 'My pleasure.'

'Really?' A faint smile teased the edges of her

mouth as she moved back a pace. 'We've been at daggers drawn most of the time.'

It was his turn to smile. There was a dangerous quality evident in the darkness of his eyes, a latent passion which, unleashed, would sweep her way out of her depth. It was there in his expression, the forceful set of his features, the stance that was studiously relaxed. Like the watching eye of a tiger, just waiting to pounce.

Go, a tiny voice taunted. Don't linger.

Without a further word she turned and walked from the room, traversed the hall and let herself out of the back door.

Shaef shadowed her steps as she crossed the path connecting the two properties, and she leant forward to fondle his ears as she unlocked the cottage, then sent him on his way before she stepped inside.

The house was quiet, and she took a long, cool shower, slipped on a robe, then she delved into the refrigerator for a light snack.

Television provided instant visual entertainment, but there was little that captured her attention, even less that held her interest.

It had been a long day, and she took time to examine each and every incident in the hope that reflection would bring peace of mind.

Fat chance. All it did was prove she was too wired to simply fall into bed and covet sleep.

In desperation she selected a book, settled into an armchair, and tried to lose herself in the characters and plot of a favourite author.

Five minutes later she thrust it down. On impulse

she went into the bedroom, discarded the robe and slipped into shorts and top.

Within seconds she left the cottage and made her way down onto the beach.

The moon was high in the sky, bathing everything with a pale opalescent glow. Shadows from a clump of palm trees cast long fingers over the sand, and the sea was a mass of silver and dappled pewter that stretched right out to the horizon.

Anneke walked along the damp sand left by an outgoing tide, and breathed in deeply of the clean night air.

There was a whimper, a short bark, then Shaef fell in step at her side.

'Unable to sleep?'

She should have known Sebastian would investigate Shaef's departure. Yesterday, even this morning, she would have resented his presence.

'I figured a walk might help.' It was impossible to detect his expression in the moonlight.

They walked in silence for a few minutes, and she was aware of him in a way she found vaguely frightening.

Somehow she'd known he was trouble from the moment she first caught sight of him.

At first she'd thought it was just chemistry. Sensual sexual magnetism at its most potent. An electric awareness that was both foolish and capricious.

'Want to talk about it?'

Anneke heard Sebastian's words, examined them, and took solace from the shadow of semi-darkness.

How could she say that it was *he* who was on her mind, *him* disturbing her thoughts?

'Adam rang me this afternoon.'

Sebastian's voice became a silky drawl. 'Foolish of him.'

'Very,' she replied in succinct agreement.

'I imagine the conversation went from bad to worse?'

'You could say that.' She turned her head and looked out over the silver sea. There didn't seem to be any need to fill the gaps in between, or repeat the vicious personal attack. It was over. That was all that mattered.

By tacit consent they turned and began retracing their steps.

'Have dinner with me tomorrow night.'

Anneke directed him a faintly humorous glance. 'You want me to prepare a meal for two, then sit down at your table?'

'I had a seafood restaurant in mind, overlooking Byron Bay. Silver service, wine steward, waiters,' Sebastian indicated with unruffled ease.

'I get to wear stiletto heels, make-up?' She laughed, a delightful light sound that held genuine mirth. 'OK. You're on. What time?'

'Six.'

When they reached Aunt Vivienne's cottage he stood aside while she inserted the key into the lock, then he turned and cut a leisurely stride to his own home.

She tried to tell herself she wasn't disappointed he'd made no attempt to touch her.

CHAPTER EIGHT

ANNEKE'S wardrobe of formal and semi-formal wear was reasonably extensive. The only problem being that most of that particular range of her clothes hung in the closet of her Sydney apartment.

In her rush to escape her job, Adam and the city, she'd simply dragged down a suitcase and pulled clothes off hangers, out of drawers, and flung them willy-nilly into the case.

Her proposed sojourn on an isolated beach had lent itself to including casual shorts and tops, jeans. Not elegant after-five wear, or extravagant high-heeled pumps.

It was a clear choice between a classic black dress, or a long floral slip.

The black dress won out, and she tended to her make-up with care, left her hair loose, and was about to catch up her purse when she heard Sebastian's Range Rover pull into the driveway.

Anneke reached the door as Sebastian trod the path, and the breath caught in her throat at the sight of him.

Attired in dark tailored trousers, matching jacket, and white shirt and tie, he was the antithesis of the man she was accustomed to seeing every day.

The image unsettled her. It was crazy to feel nervous, but she couldn't prevent the heavy thud of her heart, or the unwarranted apprehension which curled round her nerve-ends.

'Hi,' she greeted brightly. Too brightly?

Polite conversation had never been more difficult, and she waited until Sebastian reached the highway before querying, 'How long have you lived next door to my aunt?'

'Five years.'

'Yet during each of my visits I've never caught sight of you.'

He turned his head and cast her a quick glance. 'I travel around a bit in between finishing one book and starting the next.'

'Publicity tours?'

'Yes. And research.'

'You'd represent a publishing promoter's dream. The height, the arresting looks, combined with more than a hint of the dark and dangerous. The women would flock to the literary luncheons, the book-signings.'

'A compliment, Anneke?' he queried with deceptive mildness. 'Or a condemnation?'

She subjected him to a detailed appraisal, and took her time giving a considered opinion. 'Oh, a compliment.' Her eyes travelled up and met his briefly. 'I don't doubt you handle it all with consummate charm.' Except there would be an absence of ego, she determined silently.

She watched as he entered town and eased the vehicle into a car park. He cut the engine and removed the key from the ignition. 'Shall we go?'

The restaurant Sebastian had chosen specialised in

seafood, and she ordered prawn cocktail as a starter, sea perch as a main course with vegetables, and she declined dessert.

Sebastian merely doubled her order, added prawns and scallops to his dish, then requested the wine steward bring champagne.

'We're celebrating?'

He dismissed the tasting ritual, and indicated both flutes be filled. Then he touched the rim of his flute to her own. 'To friendship.'

Friendship? Could a woman be *friend* to a man such as Sebastian Lanier? Somehow Anneke doubted there would be any half-measures. Sebastian might observe the courtship dance, with its seeking manoeuvres, but when he'd staked his claim it would be all or nothing.

She had the strangest feeling that dinner this evening in semi-formal surroundings was the first step he intended she take to…*what*? His bed?

Their starter arrived, and she bit into the first of three succulent prawns doused with a delicate sauce and set on a bed of shredded lettuce.

It was difficult to sit opposite a man at a dinner table and not subconsciously observe the way he ate. Whether he stabbed his food with the fork, how he employed the knife. If his use of the cutlery was precise, or merely utilitarian. Body language, despite an adherence to good manners, tended to be revealing.

'Where will you spend Christmas?'

Anneke lifted her head and was unable to discern much from his gaze. 'I haven't made any definite plans.' She lifted her flute and sipped some champagne, then replaced it down onto the table. 'What about you?'

He pushed his entrée plate to one side and leaned back in his chair. 'Paris.'

The city of love. The Arc de Triomphe, Champs Elysées, the Eiffel Tower, the Left Bank and the River Seine. Misty grey skies, drizzling rain, the cold. But the ambience…

Anneke stifled a sigh. 'You have family there?'

'Grandmère.' His expression softened, his mouth relaxed and his eyes held reflective warmth. 'Her eightieth birthday falls on Christmas Day.'

She could imagine the gathering, and felt vaguely envious. To be involved, to be part of it… The laughter, love. Gifts and giving.

'When do you fly out?'

'Friday week.'

A lump settled inside her stomach. In eight days he would leave, and when he returned she'd be gone.

The waiter appeared with their main course, and she viewed the grilled sea perch with its artistically displayed vegetables with perfunctory interest. All of a sudden her appetite seemed to have fled.

How long had she known this man? A week? Yet, while his presence had alternately annoyed and inflamed her, there was a pull of the senses, almost as if something was exigent, forcing recognition on some deep, primal level.

There was a part of her that urged compliance, a devilish spontaneity uncaring of anything except *now*.

And that was dangerous. Infinitely dangerous. Somehow she couldn't imagine it being easy to sample what Sebastian Lanier had to offer, then calmly turn and walk away.

It was better, far better not to engage in anything at all. Besides, what could happen in a week?

Anneke picked at the fish, sampled each of the vegetables, returned to the fish, then replaced her cutlery down onto the plate.

'The fish isn't to your liking?'

She glanced up and met Sebastian's perceptive gaze. 'No, it's fine. I'm just not that hungry.'

He speared a small scallop from his plate and held it temptingly close to her mouth. 'Try this. It's perfection.'

There was an implied intimacy in the gesture, and her eyes widened slightly, then stilled as she was held mesmerised by the sensual warmth apparent in the dark grey eyes of the man seated opposite.

Anneke felt as if she was damned if she took the morsel, and equally damned if she didn't.

'It's easy,' Sebastian said gently. 'Just open your mouth.'

She hesitated another second, then leant forward and took the scallop from his fork with her teeth.

Act, a tiny voice prompted. 'Superb texture,' she commented, and glimpsed the latent humour apparent.

'More?' The query was a soft, sensual drawl, and she shook her head as she reached for her glass.

What was the matter with her? Even the champagne tasted different.

The waiter appeared and removed both plates, queried their preference for tea or coffee.

'Tea—Earl Grey,' Anneke qualified, while Sebastian chose black coffee.

There was music, and a small dance floor, with two couples moving together as a slow ballad emitted from strategically placed speakers.

'Dance with me.'

She looked at him carefully, and knew she should refuse. There was something evident in his expression she couldn't quite define. Sensuality, intoxicating and mesmeric. Bewitching chemistry at its zenith.

Anneke gathered her napkin and placed it on the table, then stood to her feet and allowed Sebastian to lead her to the dance floor.

He caught her close with natural ease, his steps fluid as he led her slowly round the small square.

She could close her eyes and pretend there was no one else around. Slide her hands up over his shoulders and link them together at his nape. Undo the leather clasp that bound his hair, then thread her fingers at will through its length.

The image remained with her of how he'd looked the first night she'd caught sight of him in her aunt's kitchen. A five o'clock shadow that had deepened into dark stubble, his hair loose and tousled. Even then she'd thought him lethal. *Shameless*, when he'd captured her head and bestowed a plundering kiss.

One ballad led on to another, and it was more than five minutes before the pace changed to something upbeat.

Sebastian led her back to the table. 'More tea?'

'No.' It was after ten. They'd eaten a leisurely

meal, enjoyed a dance. There was no reason to linger. 'Would you mind if we leave?'

Sebastian settled the bill, and they walked to the car park. Within minutes the Range Rover eased its way onto the road, then picked up speed as they left the town behind.

Headlights shone twin beams into the encroaching darkness, and Anneke leaned her head back and focused on the road.

At this time of night there wasn't much traffic, and all too soon Sebastian reached the turn-off leading down to both cottages.

Anneke reached for the door-clasp as soon as he switched off the engine.

'Come in and share a drink with me.'

Every nerve in her body screamed an emphatic *no*. 'It's late, and I'm tired.' Did she sound as breathless as she felt? Dear heaven, she hoped not!

He caught hold of her hand and lifted it to his lips. 'You can sleep in tomorrow.'

'Sebastian—'

He stilled her voice by the simple expediency of pressing a hand over her mouth. 'Anneke.' His voice held a teasing quality. 'Are you afraid of me?'

She hesitated a fraction too long. 'No, of course not.'

His smile was warm and infinitely sensual. 'Then come share a coffee with me.'

Ten minutes, she compromised. She'd drink the coffee, then she'd go home.

Shaef greeted them at the door with restrained delight, and sank down at Anneke's feet as she chose the informality of the kitchen in preference to the lounge.

Sebastian shrugged off his jacket and discarded his tie, then he crossed to the sink and filled the coffee-maker with water, ground fresh beans and spooned them into the filter, then depressed the switch. 'Milk or cream?' He crossed to a cupboard and extracted two cups and saucers.

'Milk.'

He opened the refrigerator door, and she saw what looked suspiciously like her *bombe au chocolat*. Beside it was the sponge stuffed with strawberries and cream.

'You should throw them out.'

He shot her an amused glance. 'Not yet. I like to look at them.'

Her voice came out as a strangled sound. 'Why?'

He extracted a carton of milk and closed the refrig-erator door. 'Because it reminds me of how much trouble you went to trying to kill me with indigestion.'

Of course he knew. How could he not?

'I was intrigued to know what you'd dream up to serve me next.'

The coffeemaker completed its cycle, and Sebastian took hold of the carafe and filled both cups.

'It was a challenge,' she conceded with a tinge of humour. She spooned in sugar, stirred, then sipped the contents. 'I owe you a meal. A decent one,' she quali-fied.

'An attempt to redeem yourself?'

'I'll go one better,' she said solemnly. 'Give me a

menu, and I'll prepare the food. Do you prefer vegetables or salad?'

'Vegetables. Buttered baby potatoes in their jackets, asparagus with hollandaise sauce, honeyed carrots.'

'Dessert?'

'You.'

Anneke's eyes flew wide. 'Sorry, I don't decorate body parts. Suggest something more conventional.'

He replaced his cup, removed hers, then captured her hands and pulled her towards him. 'Will this do?'

She didn't have a chance to answer. His mouth closed over hers in a gentle exploration that melted her bones.

Hands moulded her close as he deepened the kiss, and she opened her mouth to him, slid the tip of her tongue beneath the hardness of his own, and felt his breath catch.

Anneke wasn't quite ready for the long, sweeping response as he took her from pleasure to possession, then staked a claim.

It was all she could do to hang on and ride the storm of his passion.

No one had kissed her with quite this degree of hunger, and her whole body throbbed beneath his explosive touch as he began a trail of discovery of each and every pleasure pulse.

His mouth left hers and sought the vulnerable column of her throat, the delicate hollow, the edge of her neck, before slipping low to the soft curve of her breast.

Somehow the zip fastening at the back of her dress

slid free, and the tiny shoestring straps were eased over each shoulder.

An indistinguishable moan died in her throat as deft fingers teased a sensitive peak to hardness, then rendered a similar supplication to its twin.

He took her to the brink between pleasure and pain, then trailed his mouth down to suckle each tender nub until she moved restlessly against him.

It wasn't enough, not nearly enough, and a soundless gasp escaped her lips as one hand slid to the apex between her thighs, teased the thin silk barrier of her briefs, only to retreat.

Anneke whimpered in protest, then she caught hold of his head and brought his mouth to her own in fierce possession, testing his control.

She'd thought to delight in his loss of it, but nothing prepared her for the deep, penetrating invasion that took hold of her emotions and tossed them high.

Her hands reached for his shoulders and she simply clung to him until the storm inside began to diminish. Slowly, ever so slowly, he lightened the kiss until his lips merely brushed against her own, then he linked his arms at the base of her spine.

His eyes were dark, so dark they were almost black, and there was a waiting quality evident beneath the sensual warmth.

The next move was hers. He was giving her the option to move away from him, say any words by way of excuse, then leave.

If she stayed, it would be because she wanted to, not due to any unfair persuasion on his part.

Indecision warred temporarily as she fought desire with sanity.

How could you know a man for months, a year, *longer*, yet not really know him at all? Then meet another, and see almost at once the heart of the man beneath the many layers fashioned by time and experience?

She could turn away and never know the joy he offered, or the depth of emotion they could share. Yet what was the price she might have to pay?

Sadly, she had the feeling it would be way too high.

'I think I'd better go.'

Sebastian leaned forward and brushed his lips against her forehead. 'I could tell you not to think. Just to feel.'

She lifted her head and met his steady gaze. There was a depth apparent that frightened her. Not out of a sense of threat, but something she was too afraid to define.

'I know.' Her voice came out as a husky whisper. She even managed a shaky smile. 'But you won't.'

He let his arms fall to his sides, and watched the fleeting emotions chase across her expressive features.

Then he watched as she took a backward step, then turned and walked to the door.

'Be ready at nine.'

Her hand froze as she reached for the latch, and she cast him a startled glance over one shoulder.

'Our picnic, remember?' A slow smile spread his mouth. 'I'll organise the food.'

Anneke recovered quickly. 'Nine.' Then she opened the door and closed it quietly behind her.

She'd left a light on inside her aunt's cottage, and it provided a welcoming glow as she crossed the path.

Sleep didn't come easily. Nor did peace of mind. But then she hadn't expected it to.

CHAPTER NINE

ANNEKE woke at dawn, opened one eye, groaned, then rolled over and tried to capture sleep. Two hours would be great, but she'd settle for one.

Ten minutes later she gave up on it and slid out of bed. An early-morning swim, then she'd shower, have breakfast, and package the small Christmas cakes designated as gifts ready to consign to the postal services tomorrow.

She expected to see Sebastian on the beach, but he was nowhere in sight. She ran the length of the cove, then stripped down to her swimsuit for a leisurely swim.

It was almost eight-thirty when Aunt Vivienne rang to report that Elise was progressing so well the doctors were confident she'd go close to full term.

'How are you getting on with Sebastian, Anneke?'

Oh, my, now there was a question! What would her kindly aunt think if Anneke went with total honesty and said she was on the verge of going to bed with him?

'Fine.' That covered a multitude of contingencies.

'Why don't you fly up and join us for Christmas, darling? I know Sebastian is going to Paris, and I don't like to think of you at the cottage alone.'

'That's thoughtful of you,' Anneke declared

warmly, grateful for the option of spending the festive
season with family.

It was almost nine when she smoothed a hand down
the seam of her designer jeans; then slid nervous fingers along the ribbed hem of the skinny top she'd
chosen to wear.

A knock on the door heralded Sebastian's arrival,
and she caught hold of her bag, collected her sunglasses, then crossed to open the kitchen door.

Clad in dark blue jeans and a black shirt with the
sleeves rolled part-way up each forearm, he looked
far too vibrant for any girl's peace of mind.

'Good morning.'

Sunglasses made it impossible for her to detect his
expression, and she matched his smile with one of her
own.

Sebastian headed the Range Rover north when they
reached the open highway.

'Where are we going?'

'The Gold Coast hinterland. Lamington National
Park, O'Reilly's.' He spared her a warm glance.
'We'll feed the lorikeets, have lunch, then maybe
head down to Surfers Paradise for an hour or two.'

The sun was hot, tempered by a slight breeze, and
Anneke was delighted by the friendly lorikeets.
Feeding time was something else as the brightly coloured green and red plumed parrots settled on her
arms then walked up onto her shoulders. Some even
settled on her head, and she laughed when one became over-curious with the band confining her hair.
His claws became tangled in the single thick plait, and
his squawking brought Sebastian to the rescue.

'Hold still.'

'Believe me, I wouldn't think of doing anything else,' she assured him as he moved in close.

Too close. She was intensely aware of his shirt-clad chest and shoulders only mere inches from her cheek. Clean fabric mingled with the faint musky tones of his aftershave, and played havoc with her senses.

'He won't hurt you,' Sebastian murmured. 'He's just frightened.'

That makes two of us. But it wasn't the parrot she was afraid of.

'There,' Sebastian reassured. 'He's free.' He caught hold of her chin and lifted it. 'His claws didn't scratch you?'

'No.' Her mouth was inches away from his, and she had to control the temptation to reach up and pull his head down to hers.

'Hungry?'

'Yes.' It was true. The mountain air had given her an appetite.

'Come on, then.' He caught hold of her hand and tugged her towards the path leading to where the land cruiser was parked.

Sebastian unlocked the rear door and opened up a portable cooler. *'Voilà.'*

There were fresh steaks, crisp lettuce, fresh fruit, mineral water and a bottle of wine.

'You came prepared.'

His eyes challenged hers. 'Always.'

She doubted if anyone had managed to gain the element of surprise with this man. He was intensely vital, acutely alert, and far too discerning to be caught unawares.

Gas-fired barbecues were positioned at intervals on a grassed area adjacent the car park, and there were tables with fixed umbrellas to shade picnic-makers from the sun.

Sebastian took hold of the cooler. 'Let's grab a niche over there. I'll cook the steaks while you mix the salad.'

They drank a glass of superb Lambrusco with their meal, and washed the fruit down with mineral water.

Anneke rose to her feet and stacked plates and cutlery into a plastic bag ready to place in the cooler.

'Feeling energetic?'

She lifted both shoulders in a light shrugging gesture. 'Not particularly.'

So she hadn't slept much either. After an hour of tossing and turning, he'd pulled on a pair of jeans, booted up the computer and worked until three.

He collected the cooler and stored it in the rear of the Range Rover. 'Then let's head down to the Coast.'

More than an hour later they were seated at one of many tables overlooking the broadwater, savouring cappuccinos. It was a relaxed atmosphere, with numerous people wandering the boardwalk, admiring the many craft moored at the adjacent marina.

The physique, the hair, the dark, attractive features earned Sebastian more than a few covetous glances from the women who passed by their table.

'Oh, my,' Anneke declared, *sotto voce*. 'I think you have made a conquest. That's the second time one particular blonde has walked this way. Perhaps I should go powder my nose and leave a clear field?'

'Do that, and I'll take evasive action,' Sebastian drawled.

'You'll go powder *your* nose?'

He tipped his sunglasses further down his nose and speared her a level look over the rims. 'Kiss you in such a manner there'll be no doubt *you* are my only interest.'

'Wouldn't you be taking an enormous risk?' Anneke queried sweetly. 'I might push you over the railing into the water.'

'Then we'd both look foolish,' he intoned lazily as he leaned forward and trailed light fingers down her cheek.

Her eyes dilated fractionally at his featherlight touch, and her lips quivered as he traced their fullness with his thumb.

'You've been treading on eggshells all day,' he said gently. 'Waiting for me to pounce?'

She held his gaze. 'I think you have a strategy,' she said with innate honesty. 'I just need to figure out which ploy you intend to use.'

Sebastian laughed, a soft, chuckling sound deep in his throat. He stood to his feet, anchored a ten-dollar bill beneath one saucer, then reached for her hand. 'Come on, let's walk.'

They explored the upmarket shopping complex, then wandered to the wharf market where fresh seafood was sold direct from the fish trawlers.

Anneke examined the prawns, the many varieties of crustaceans. They looked succulent, mouthwatering. 'I promised you dinner.' She shot him a teasing grin. 'Are you willing to trust me?'

'You want to take some of these home?'

'I'm buying,' she insisted as he extracted his wallet. 'I mean it,' she said fiercely.

He lifted both hands in the air. 'OK.'

She chose carefully, with the expertise of a market haggler, selecting, rejecting, until she was satisfied she had the best of the best.

'Let's get this into the cooler and head home.' Her mind was already busy with the preparation she needed to make, the time factor, a mental rundown of salad makings in the refrigerator.

It was almost seven when they reached the cottage. 'Give me an hour,' Anneke said as she extracted the seafood from the cooler. That would give her time to shower and change, and have the food ready on the table.

'I'll bring the wine.'

She managed it with five minutes to spare, and spent four of those minutes wondering if she should change blue jeans for black dress jeans, add blusher and eyeshadow or just stick with lipstick. Perfume?

A knock at the door precluded the necessity for either, and she crossed the kitchen and let him in.

Sebastian took the bottle of chilled white wine to the servery. 'Shall I open this?'

Anneke handed him the corkscrew. 'Please.'

He'd showered, shaved and changed into casual dark trousers and a pale blue shirt. Aunt Vivienne's kitchen wasn't large, and he seemed to fill it.

She extracted two glasses and set them on the table as he eased the cork out from the neck of the bottle.

'Anything I can do to help?'

'It's all done.' Did she sound as nervous as she felt?

He leaned forward and covered her mouth with his own, taking advantage of her surprise by bestowing an erotic tasting. He lingered a few seconds, then lifted his head.

She looked…momentarily startled, and her slight confusion pleased him. 'Shall we eat?'

Oysters mornay, chilli prawns, and crustaceans in their shells, split in half and the flesh coated with a delicate sauce and grilled. Fresh salad greens, and a baguette she'd heated to crunchy perfection in the oven.

'Magnificent,' Sebastian declared, with the pleasure of a man who had eaten well. 'More wine?'

'No,' Anneke refused quickly, and earned a slight smile.

'The need for a clear head?'

She didn't answer, didn't dare. 'I'll make coffee.'

Her movements were mechanical as she set up the coffee-maker, and when she turned to open the cupboard he was right there.

'Sebastian—' His lips settled over the vulnerable hollow at the edge of her neck, and she lost track of whatever it was she'd intended to say.

His mouth was warm, his tongue an erotic instrument as he teased the pulsing cord, savoured it, then used the edge of his teeth to take delicate nips from the sensitive hollows.

She made one last-ditch effort at protest, only to

have it die in her throat as he turned her fully into his arms and covered her mouth with his own.

One hand lifted to cup her nape while the other slid down her back and pressed her close against him.

His arousal was a potent force, and she felt her bones begin to melt as liquid fire coursed through her veins. Each sensory nerve-end was heightened to acute awareness, and her body leaned in close to his as he deepened the kiss to an imitation of the sexual act itself.

Anneke wanted to feel his flesh, taste him in a tactile exploration that would drive him wild. Her fingers slid to the opening of his shirt, freed each button, then she trailed butterfly kisses across his chest, tangled her tongue in the whorls of hair, took possession of one male nipple, and suckled.

His body shuddered, then tautened as firm hands clasped hold of her waist, and it was she who cried out as he lifted her onto the servery, then parted her thighs and positioned himself between them.

His eyes were dark and impossibly slumberous as he tugged her top free from her jeans, then pulled it over her head. The bra clip slipped open with ease, and he slid the straps down her arms and dispensed with the scrap of silk and lace.

Then he buried his face in the valley between her breasts and caressed the soft curves, tormented and teased each roseate peak, then trailed a path down to her navel.

Her jeans were a barrier he dispensed with with ease, tugging them free and dropping them onto the floor.

He kissed her, gently at first, then with an increasingly demanding possession, and when he at last lifted his head she could only look at him in shaken silence.

Sebastian didn't have to ask. The unspoken question was apparent in his stance, the liquid darkness of his eyes, the curve of his mouth.

A slight shudder ran through her body. If she turned away now, she'd never know his touch. And she wanted to, badly.

Not just the physical. She wanted more, much more than that. His heart, his soul. Everything.

Maybe, just maybe, she should take the gamble and run with it. Let emotions take her wherever he led.

A week could be a lifetime. And better to experience a week of heaven than never to experience it at all.

Slowly she reached out and slid her fingers to his nape, where a clip fastened the leather strip that bound his hair. Her eyes never left his as she slipped it free. Then she forked her fingers through the silken river of black, and spread it out so that it flowed onto his shoulders.

It gave him a rakish look that was pure pagan, primitive, and it was a gesture she'd wanted to make ever since she'd first stepped into this kitchen and found him making tea.

His smile was slow and infinitely sensual as he copied her actions, releasing the thin elastic band at the base of her plait, then threading his fingers through the length of her hair.

It was the expression in his eyes that made her

catch her breath and caused her pulse to quicken to a much faster beat.

'I think,' she said shakily, 'you'd better take me out of the kitchen and into the bedroom.'

He played the game, teasing her gently. 'You think so?'

'Otherwise I may never be able to cook or serve food in here again.'

Sebastian laughed. A deep, husky sound that curled into the recesses of her heart. 'Put your arms round my neck.'

Anneke did as she was told, and he kissed her long and deep, then he carried her through to the bedroom, switched on the light, and let her slide down to her feet.

In one easy movement he sought the pocket of his jeans, extracted a slim foil square and slipped it beneath one pillow.

Mesmerised, she stood still as he popped the studs on his jeans, then shucked them off. The thin covering of black silk sheathing his manhood followed, and her eyes widened at the sight of him.

His was a savage beauty. Primal, powerful. A man who could show great strength, even cruelty. Yet there was a tenderness apparent, an acute caring for those who were sufficiently fortunate to win his trust, his love.

Sebastian reached for her, pulling her in close as he tumbled them both down onto the bed. He was hungry for her, wanting, needing to sheath himself in the silken sweetness of woman. Not just any woman. *This* woman.

He needed to show her the difference. Knew, hoped, that she would *know*.

Anneke let her fingers splay over taut muscles at his shoulders, trailed them to explore his ribcage, then slid down over his flanks to urge him close.

'*Non, mon ange.* We are just beginning.'

He took pleasure in the tasting of her skin, every inch of it, with the pads of his fingers, his lips. And felt her pulse quicken, her breath become erratic and fast.

Her body began to feel like the strings of a finely tuned violin, his touch creating magic that reverberated along each nerve fibre until her whole being *sang* to a tune that had never been played.

The feeling was so intense she could hardly bear it, and her hands became more urgent as she began to plead with him to ease the ache deep within.

He soothed her as she arched against him, caressing the moist heat with a touch that brought her to one explosive climax after another.

It wasn't enough, not nearly enough, and she became a wild wanton in his arms, pliant, bewitching, *his*.

He entered her slowly, allowing the silken tissues to stretch to accommodate him, then he drove forward with one powerful thrust.

Anneke gasped at the level of penetration, absorbed it, then met and matched his rhythm, unable to prevent the soft guttural cries that escaped her lips as he took her higher and higher to the brink, held her there, then caught her when she fell. And kissed the light tears as they trickled from her eyes.

Sebastian curled her close in the circle of his arms, and she dozed for a while, then stirred at the movement of a hand sliding low over one hip.

He was asleep. His breathing hadn't changed. She began a slow, tactile exploration of her own, skimming over warm skin, strong muscle and sinew to his pelvis, lightly examining the faint hollow, the keloid puckering of a surgical scar.

She let her fingers trail up over his ribcage to the dark smattering of hair on his chest. Hair that was light and springy, and different in texture from the glossy length he wore bound at his nape.

More than anything she wanted to explore the angles and planes of his sculpted features, the chiselled cheekbones, the hard jaw, the sensitive lines of his mouth.

Most of all she wanted to wake him. To feel again the power of his body as he joined it with hers. The acutely intense spiral of sensation that mixed pleasure with pain, then transcended both to rapturous ecstasy.

He'd shown her remarkable *tendresse*. Now she wanted his passion, unbridled, shameless and primitive.

A hand reached for hers, caught it, and brought it to his lips. Her heart almost stopped, then quickened to a faster beat as she raised her head and met a pair of dark eyes lambent with molten desire.

'You're awake.'

Without a word he kissed each finger in turn, savoured her palm, then grazed the fragile veins at her wrist.

One slight tug, and she lay sprawled across his chest.

She gained purchase on his shoulders and leant forward to kiss him, loving the feeling of power as he let her take control.

The sensual tasting tested his strength, and just when he thought he could stand it no longer she slid down onto him. Her movements were deliberately slow as she completed one erotic circle after another until it drove him wild. His hands bit into her waist, then splayed over her hips, holding her still as he drove into her again and again, until it was she who cried out, and their voices mingled in a mutual expression of wild, untamed passion.

Afterwards, when the spiralling subsided and their breathing returned to normal, he pulled her close and held her there.

Her hair was a mass of tangles from where he'd raked his hands through its length, and he soothed it gently, feeling its texture, the long silken strands that fell in a cloud over her shoulders.

He kissed her, long and deep, then he buried his mouth in the soft hollow of her neck as she slept.

Again and again they turned to each other in the night. As the light fingers of dawn filtered through the windows they rose from the bed and showered, only to return to bed to sleep until the shrill peal of the phone sounded loud in the morning stillness.

Sebastian kissed her briefly as she lifted her head and groaned. 'You'd better answer it, *mon amie*.'

Who could be ringing at this hour? She spared a

glance at the bedside clock, and jolted upright. My God, *midday*!

She scrambled out of bed, grabbed the sheet and wrapped it round her naked form, then stumbled as the tucked-in portion stubbornly refused to part from the mattress.

Sebastian chuckled as she swore, and leaned forward to wrench it free.

Anneke raced into the kitchen, lifted the receiver and heard her aunt's anxious tones on the other end of the line.

Thinking quickly on her feet after a long night of loving and very little sleep was difficult. 'I was in the shower.' A necessary untruth, and she shivered as she felt Sebastian's lips nuzzle her neck. When his hands unbound the sheet, there was little she could do except shake her head at him in silent remonstrance.

'Is everything all right, darling?' Aunt Vivienne queried. 'You sound a little...strange.'

His lips sought her breasts, savoured the swollen peaks, then bit gently into the tender softness.

On a strangled note she ended the call, replaced the receiver, then allowed herself to be pulled into his arms.

'You're insatiable,' Anneke said unsteadily as his teeth nipped an earlobe.

'In a minute, I'm going to collect my clothes, go home, and spend what's left of the day at the computer.' His lips trailed to her temple, caressed the fast-beating pulse there, then travelled down to the edge of her mouth. 'I have a deadline to meet before I leave for Paris.'

She turned her mouth to meet his, and wondered if she'd ever be able to survive after he left. 'I'll bring dinner.'

'And stay.'

'Sebastian—'

'Stay, Anneke,' he repeated insistently. 'My bed, or yours. It doesn't matter.'

No, it didn't. To deny him was to deny herself.

CHAPTER TEN

THE days ran into each other, each one seeming more poignant than the last.

Sebastian rescheduled his work pattern from mid-morning to seven in the evening. Dinner was extended by an hour, and the nights were something else as their lovemaking took on a new dimension.

Anneke told herself she was happy, happier than she'd ever been. And she was. Except the dawn of each new day brought her one day closer to the time she'd have to bid Sebastian goodbye.

Wednesday they drove into Byron Bay township and consigned Sebastian's manuscript to his American agent via courier. Then they celebrated with champagne and dinner at the town's finest restaurant.

'Tomorrow we'll fly down to Sydney.'

Anneke heard the words, but didn't absorb them. 'What did you say?'

Sebastian's smile held a combination of humour and sensual warmth as he repeated the words.

Her heart flipped, then raced to a painful beat. 'We?'

'We,' he gently mocked. 'That will give you time to gather some clothes together, do any necessary shopping, and pack.'

'Pack?'

'You're coming with me to Paris.'

Her mind whirled at the implication, and her stomach began to compete with the erratic beat of her heart. 'What about a passport, visa—'

'Your passport is valid.' His eyes gleamed with humour as her mouth opened, then shut again. 'Vivienne,' he revealed succinctly.

'You've spoken to Aunt Vivienne?'

'I needed to check on your passport, make arrangements for both cottages, Shaef.' He paused for a second. 'And tell her you wouldn't be spending Christmas with her in Cairns.'

Christmas. She'd need to get gifts for his family; she couldn't possibly go empty-handed...

A strangled laugh rose and died in her throat with the realisation she didn't know any details at all, with the exception of his grandmother.

Sebastian caught each fleeting expression and accurately defined every one of them. He reached across the table and caught hold of her hand. 'It'll be fine,' he reassured her. 'Trust me.'

They arrived in Paris mid-morning on a cold, wet, typically grey mid-winter day, tired after a long international flight.

Sebastian collected their hire car, and drove to the gracious old home on Ile Saint-Louis where his grandmother had resided since the day she was born.

A very beautiful home, with exquisite carpets, antique furniture, and *objets d'art* worth a small fortune.

Anneke wasn't sure what she'd expected. Certainly it hadn't been a very stylish and sprightly woman who could easily pass for fifteen years younger than her eighty years, and whose command of the English language was more than impressive.

'Your rooms are ready. I know you must want to shower, then change and rest.'

'Room, Grandmère,' Sebastian corrected. 'We share.'

'So.'

Anneke couldn't imagine such a little word could convey such meaning.

'Are you not going to introduce me to this young woman you have brought to meet me?'

'Grandmère...Anneke Sorrel.' His arm remained at Anneke's waist. 'Anneke...my grandmother, Madeleine Lanier.'

'Come here and let me look at you.'

'You will frighten her,' Sebastian declared with amusement.

'Indeed.' Madeleine Lanier drew herself up to her full height and glared at her grandson. 'I frighten no one. And if she belongs to you, she belongs to this family.'

A faint smile teased Anneke's lips. 'So you get to pass judgement.'

'She speaks.' Madeleine placed a hand to her heart.

'Indeed she does.' Sebastian leaned forward and gently brushed first one paper-thin cheek, then the other. 'And be warned, she also speaks passable French.'

'I think,' Madeleine declared, 'we should go into the conservatory and take coffee.'

'Tea,' Anneke said gently. 'Earl Grey, if you have it.'

'Has a mind of her own, hmm?'

'Yes, I do.'

'Good. I could not have borne it if Sebastian had brought me an airhead with designs on his money.'

'I do not think Sebastian would have dared do such a thing.'

That earned a quick glance from sharp brown eyes, and the beginnings of a musing smile. 'He has dared many things in his short lifetime. But crossing me is not one of them.' She moved forward and batted her grandson's arm away from Anneke's waist. 'Let her go. We shall get along very well, she and I.'

Madeleine Lanier was a pussycat. An aged, very fiercely loyal lady, who guarded her family with her life. But a pussycat, nonetheless.

Anneke spared Sebastian a mischievous smile, and met his gleaming gaze, saw the faint shrug of resignation that accompanied it.

'You are going to marry her, of course.'

'Of course, Grandmère. I just haven't got around to asking her yet.'

Madeleine stopped in her tracks, turned and directed her grandson a baleful glare. 'And why not?'

Anneke didn't know whether to smile or cry, for there was a very strong possibility jet lag had caused her to imagine the entire conversation.

The glare shifted to Anneke. 'You do *want* to marry Sebastian?'

This was the craziest discourse she'd ever entered into! 'If he asks me, I'll give it some thought.'

'Indeed!'

They took coffee in the conservatory. And tea.

With tiny *petits fours* and dainty sandwiches. Then Madeleine shooed them upstairs.

'Your luggage will be in your usual suite, Sebastian. Breakfast,' she declared regally, 'is served at eight. Don't be late.'

The staircase was wide and curved gently upwards in a sweeping arc to the upper floor central landing, from which a wide corridor stretched in both directions.

Sebastian turned to the right and traversed the corridor to its end, then opened the door to an elegant suite with views out over the Seine.

Anneke slipped out of her shoes and crossed to the window. It was drizzling, and what she could see of the city was shrouded in damp mist.

In spring, in summer, it would be clear, the skies a delicate blue, and there would be colour instead of the grey of winter.

Hard, masculine arms closed round her waist and linked together over her stomach, and she leaned back against him.

She felt weary almost beyond belief. She wanted nothing more than a long, hot shower, and a comfortable bed.

'I love you,' Sebastian said gently. 'I planned to ask you to marry me over a candlelit dinner on Christmas Eve, with champagne, a single red rose, the gift of my mother's ring. To introduce you to the family on the day we present and open gifts. Noël.'

His lips touched the vulnerable spot just beneath her ear, and she turned to meet his mouth.

'Yes,' she said simply.

It had been that easy. His arms tightened fractionally. 'No qualifications?'

'Two. We do the Christmas Eve thing, and you bring me back to Paris in the spring.'

His smile stole her heart. 'You're beautiful, *mon ange*. My life.'

Anneke reached up and brought his mouth down to hers. *'Je t'aime, mon amour. Je t'aime.'*

Family, Anneke reflected as she stood within the circle of Sebastian's arms after breakfast on Christmas morning.

The elegant lounge was filled with various aunts and uncles, cousins. And children. Madeleine Lanier's great-grandchildren. Beautifully dressed, exquisitely groomed, and extremely well behaved. Madeleine would not have tolerated it otherwise.

She glanced across the room and met the eyes of the gracious old lady, and smiled.

Everyone together in peace and harmony. Sharing, caring. Hopes and dreams. Gifts and giving.

For Madeleine Lanier, this house, her family, represented a lifetime of memories.

And Anneke had gifted and been given the greatest gift of all.

Love.

MIRACLE ON CHRISTMAS EVE

Sandra Marton

Dear Reader,

I remember the Christmases of my childhood with special fondness. I grew up in New York, where chimneys and shingled rooftops were few. Still, on Christmas Eve I hoped to hear sleigh bells and the clip-clop of reindeer hooves.

Santa isn't real. There's no old gentleman in a red suit, no sleigh, no goodie-filled sack...but what if there were? What if Santa could reach into that sack and pull out a miracle, just when you needed one?

That's my Christmas wish to you, dear reader. A miracle, just when you need it most.

With love,

Sandra Marton

CHAPTER ONE

NICK BRENNAN figured that Scrooge had gotten it right.

Christmas was definitely the most overrated holiday of the year. He'd had plenty of time to think about it, considering that he'd been stalled in a barely-moving line of traffic for the past forty-five minutes.

A horn blared angrily behind him, setting off an answering chorus from a dozen other cars.

Nick smiled thinly. Right. As if that would change anything. This was New York traffic. Friday afternoon New York traffic, the Friday afternoon before Christmas. Anybody dumb enough to be trapped in it deserved what he got.

Including him.

'Stupid,' Nick muttered, tapping his fingers impatiently against the steering wheel.

That was the only word for it. He'd been living in Manhattan for almost a decade. He knew the score. Even his PA, who was just a few years out of some Iowa cornfield, knew that leaving New York today wasn't terribly bright.

She'd tried to talk him out of it.

'Why don't you let me phone around, see if I can't book you onto a flight to Vermont?' Ellen had said.

He'd given her a bunch of reasons, all of them logical. Because she'd never find a seat for him at the last minute. Because not even the charter service Brennan Resorts employed would be available at the eleventh hour. Because even if she lucked out, who knew for how much longer anything would be able to take off? The weatherman, as usual, had gotten it wrong. The predicted light snow was about to turn into a major storm.

Nick had told Ellen all those things. The only thing he hadn't told her was the truth. He was driving to North Mountain because he hoped the six hours on the road would give him time to talk himself out of reaching it.

Oh, he'd come up with practical reasons for going. After all, he owned the mountain now, most of it, anyway, the same as he owned the cabin that stood on its crest. And, as soon as the details were settled, his people would bring in the equipment necessary to demolish the cabin and start work on the newest Brennan resort. Nick was a hands-on kind of guy. He always looked a site over before work began. It was, according to Wall Street, one of the reasons for his success.

But nobody was going to bring in any kind of equipment, until the harsh New England winter ended in April, or maybe even May.

No matter how you looked at it, there wasn't a reason in the world to make the trip now.

Nick blew out his breath.

A couple of months ago, he hadn't even known he owned North Mountain. His people had brought him an estate deal that contained several prime parcels of land in New England. Nick had moved fast, as he always did, and quickly given them the okay to make the buy.

He'd had no idea the mountain was part of the package. Not that he'd have cared, if he'd known. The mountain was perfect for development, and no amount of sentimental claptrap would change that. No, it wasn't sentiment that was sending him to Vermont.

Vermont, in December.

Christmas carol time. Horse-drawn sleigh time. Cold, star-studded night time...

Holly time.

Seven years ago come Monday morning, he and Holly had been married. One year later to the day, they'd agreed to a divorce.

And all of it had begun on North Mountain, in a cabin a million miles from anywhere.

The horn behind him blasted Nick into reality. He shot a nasty look into his mirror and inched the Explorer forward.

Okay. So, the realization that he'd bought the mountain, and the cabin, had hit him hard. That had surprised him. He didn't think about his once-upon-a-time marriage anymore. Hell, why would he? Nick's jaw tightened. He'd made a mistake. So what? Life was like that. You made a mistake, you rectified it and moved on. The one thing you never did was look back.

Then, what was he doing, sitting in this God-awful traffic, heading for the place where he'd made his biggest mistake? It made no sense.

Maybe it did. Maybe it would help him get rid of the memories.

Memories of Holly, wearing a flannel nightgown instead of the silky one she'd bought for their honeymoon, because the cabin had been so cold that first night...until he'd slowly stripped her of the gown and warmed her with his body. Memories of Holly, laughing after he'd tumbled her down in the snow, shrieking when he threatened to wash her face in it...her smile fading, turning soft and sexy as she became aware of the sudden pressure of his aroused flesh against hers.

Nick's hands tightened on the steering wheel.

Memories were all they were, foolish shadows of a dead past, and they made no sense because he wasn't in love with the woman in those memories. Not anymore. Not ever, when you came right down to it. Holly, herself, had been an illusion. A fantasy, conjured up by the lonely kid he'd once been.

He needed closure.

Nick almost laughed. Closure. The most popular word in the good old U.S. of A. Every two-bit TV talk show, every tune-in-and-spew-your-guts radio shrink, went on and on about closure. And, yeah, dumb or not, maybe that was what he needed. No point pretending that the seventh anniversary of his failed marriage hadn't affected him. How could he not be affected by the death of a dream?

Nick shifted his long legs. Okay. He'd go to the mountain, spend a few days, and find 'closure.' He'd bury his memories the same way his crew would bury the cabin, once Spring came, once his attorneys got things sorted out. The mountain was Nick's, but there'd been a rider attached to the deed, a 'no commercial construction' clause the owner had tacked on before he'd sold.

No problem. His people would find a way around the stipulation, and he would find a way around the memories. He'd see the cabin, walk the mountain one last time—and then a construction crew would come in, level the place and start building the most luxurious ski resort in New England. It would be the newest, finest Brennan resort in the chain and all the 'closure' a man could possibly want.

And, in the process, he'd have himself a weekend off. Time to unwind, enjoy a break. No boardrooms. No meetings. No desk heaped with memos. Not that he'd be cut off completely. A three-room cabin high on top of a Vermont mountain, no matter how plush, was not an eight-room penthouse, or three floors of office space on Fifth Avenue, but Nick had come prepared. He had his cellular phone in his pocket, his portable computer on the seat beside him, and his wireless fax on the floor.

The guy behind him honked again.

Nick felt his blood pressure zoom. For one sweet moment, he thought about getting out of the Explorer, marching back to the jerk's car, banging on the window and asking the guy if he really, honestly thought things would go any faster with him leaning on his horn...

The breath hissed from his lungs.

Closure was what he needed, all right.

He was angry at Holly, angry at himself, and he

had been for six long years because he'd never had the chance to tell her the truth, that he'd never loved her, not really, that she wasn't the only one who'd made a mistake.

Not that he'd ever get the chance to tell her anything. But going to the cabin, to the mountain, would be the next best thing. He'd feel better, afterwards. He wouldn't snarl at Ellen, bark at his staff, sit in traffic with his adrenaline pumping as if he were a boxer waiting for round one to begin.

The tail lights ahead of him winked. Slowly, miraculously, the line of vehicles began moving. Nick downshifted. It was one of the great mysteries in New York, how you'd be creeping along, measuring your success in inches and all of a sudden, the road would open up. It was like life. You'd plod along and then, wham, wings would sprout on your feet and you'd find yourself flying, measuring your success in millions of dollars instead of the twenty bucks still in your pocket after all the bills were paid...

Measuring it alone. Always alone, no matter how many well-wishers crowded around, no matter what the papers said or how many gorgeous women you were with, because the only woman you'd ever wanted to share your success was gone, had been gone for six years, would always be gone...

The horn sounded. Nick shot a look at his mirror and glared at the guy in the Chevy. Then he shot into the fast lane, poured on the gas, and let the Manhattan skyline fade into the fast-gathering darkness of the winter night.

*   *   *

Holly Cabot Brennan figured she'd reach the top of North Mountain in two or three millennia.

She frowned, bit down lightly on her bottom lip, and tried to see through the whirling snow.

At the rate she was going, even that might be too much to expect.

The old guy at the gas station had tried to warn her. He'd looked at her, her rented car and the sullen sky through rheumy eyes and announced that she'd need more than a full tank to get much further.

'Gonna be a bad 'un,' he'd said, in the clipped, Down-East twang she hadn't heard in years.

Holly had smiled politely. 'The weatherman says the storm's not going to hit until after midnight. Besides, I'm not going very far.'

'Weathuhman's wrong,' the old gent replied. 'How far you goin'?'

'Not very,' Holly said, looking over at the battered ice machine that stood beside the gas station office. 'Does that thing work?'

'Aye-up, it works, though why you'd be wantin' ice in the dead of winter is beyond me.'

Holly thought of the big ice chest she'd crammed into the trunk. It was stuffed with shrimp, lobsters, lobster tails, butter, clams, oysters and assorted other goodies. Then she thought of trying to explain all that to the old man.

'I've got some stuff in an ice chest,' she said, leaving off the details. 'And I figure, just in case they forgot to clean out the freezer and turn it on, up in the cabin...'

'Cabin on North Mountain?' The old guy looked at

her as if she were certifiably insane. 'Is that where you're goin'?'

'Uh-huh.' Holly popped open the trunk, dropped coins into the ice machine, then marched back to the car with two bags of cubes. 'You just about finished there?'

'Won't have much worry about the freezer bein' on, Missy. Storm like the one that's comin', you won't have no power at all. Assumin' you'll make it to the top, that is, which you most likely won't.'

Holly shut the ice chest, then the trunk, and wiped her gloved hands on her wool slacks.

'Ever a font of good cheer,' she said brightly. 'Okay, how much do I owe you?'

'Chains.'

'I beg your pardon?'

'Chains,' the old guy said. Holly held out a twenty-dollar bill, and he took it from her hand. 'Bettah still, you ought to have a cah with four-wheel drive.'

'I've driven up the mountain before,' Holly replied politely. 'I'll be fine.'

'Aye-up, most times, mebbe.' He cocked an eye towards the sky. ' But there's a storm comin' in.'

'Not really,' she said, even more politely. 'The weather reports say—'

The old man's lip curled. 'Don't care what they say.' Carefully, he plopped Holly's change into her outstretched hand. 'Storm's comin'. Bad one. You at least got them new-fangled brakes in that car?'

What new-fangled brakes? Holly almost said. She hadn't owned a car in years. What was the point, when you lived in the heart of Boston? Besides, she'd spent the past six months in a Tuscan farmhouse, up to her elbows in olive oil, plum tomatoes, and garlic, and the last three weeks on a whirlwind tour across the States, signing copies of *Ciao Down With Holly*, the book that had come out of her stay in Tuscany. She knew all there was to know about the differences between the cuisines of Northern and Southern Italy, but brakes were something else entirely.

Not that it mattered. She'd be at the cabin before the old doomsayer's prophecies came true. So she'd smiled pleasantly and said her brakes were just fine, thanks, and then she'd driven off, watching in her rear-view mirror as he'd stood looking after her, shaking his head mournfully.

'Ridiculous,' Holly had muttered to herself, as she'd made the turn onto the road that led up North Mountain. As if some old man in the middle of nowhere could do a better job predicting the weather than the CNN meteorologists…

Halfway up the mountain, the snow started falling.

At first, the flakes were big and lazy. They settled prettily onto the branches of the tall pine trees that clung to the slope on Holly's left while sailing gracefully off the precipice to her right. But within minutes the wind picked up and the snow went from lazy to fierce, changing direction so that now she was driving headfirst into an impenetrable cloud of white. And there was no way to turn back. The road was too narrow and far too dangerous for that.

She was driving blind, trapped in the heart of what seemed to be the beginning of a blizzard. All she could do was hunch over the steering wheel, urge the car forward inch by slippery inch, and try not to wonder whether or not she had the 'new-fangled' brakes she'd pooh-poohed just half an hour ago.

The old man had been right. She'd been stupid not to have rented a car with four-wheel drive. Who was she kidding? She'd been stupid to have decided to come to the cabin at all.

Everyone had tried to tell her that. Not just the guy at the gas station. The clerk who'd rented her the car. The traffic cop in Burlington, when she'd asked for directions. Even Belinda, her agent, who knew as much about New England as a vegetarian knew about a pot roast, had blanched when Holly had said she was taking off for a few weeks in Vermont.

'Where?' Belinda had said incredulously—but Belinda figured that civilization ended once you took the Lincoln Tunnel out of Manhattan.

'It's a place called North Mountain,' Holly had replied. 'I've rented a cabin.'

'You're going to spend a few weeks in a cabin?' Belinda repeated, the way someone else might have said, 'You're going to spend a few weeks on the Moon?'

'That's right. It's very luxurious. There's a Jacuzzi, a huge stall shower, a big fireplace in the living room...'

Belinda snorted. 'Try the Waldorf. It's got all that, plus room service.'

Holly did her best to offer a cheerful little laugh.

'I need a change of routine,' she said. ' A real one, before I start on the next book. You know how hard

I've been working this year, and there's a whole bunch of ideas I want to try before I begin writing...'

And then she stopped, because she knew she was babbling, because she could tell from the look on Belinda's elegant face that she knew it, too.

'Poor darling,' Belinda crooned. 'You really do sound exhausted.'

'Oh, I am,' Holly said quickly, because it was true. She *was* stressed.

That was what she told herself, at first.

She'd been working hard. She had been for the past seven years—well, six years, ever since she and Nick had been divorced. Her parents had wanted her to come home and pick up her life as if nothing had happened but something *had* happened, and Holly wasn't about to pretend otherwise. The last vestiges of girlhood had fallen away the day she took off her wedding ring. So she'd explained, as gently as possible, that going home just wasn't possible. She'd refused her father's offer of financial support the same as she'd refused Nick's, and set out to create a life for herself.

And she'd done it.

The little column for the *Green Mountain Daily* had blossomed into a monthly feature for *What's Cookin'?* magazine, and it led to the contract for her first cookbook. Holly had found herself on the fast track, and she loved it. She could put in six hours in the kitchen, another two at the computer, tumble into bed and wake up the next morning, eager to start all over again. At least she had, until a couple of weeks ago.

The first time she'd awakened in the middle of the

night with a knot in her belly and another in her throat, she'd figured it was a sign she'd put too many capers into the *Putanesca*.

By the fourth time, though, she knew it wasn't a recipe gone wrong that had awakened her.

It was her dreams.

She was dreaming of Nick, which was ridiculous. She hadn't done that in almost six years, hadn't seen him in almost six years, hadn't thought about him in almost six years…

It was a long time. The realization hit at three o'clock on a cold December morning, when she awakened with Nick's name on her lips. That wasn't heartburn she was feeling, it was anger. And why not? She was coming up on the seventh anniversary of what had begun as a marriage and had ended as a disaster.

Holly rose from bed, wrapped herself in her robe and padded out to the living room. She clicked on the TV and surfed through a bunch of movies that had been old before she was born. She zipped past a pair of talking heads that were deep in what she'd thought was a discussion of ghosts, then zipped right back when she realized the 'ghosts' they were discussing weren't spooks at all but memories, unwanted ones, of people in a person's past.

'So, Doctor,' the interviewer chirruped, 'how does one put these memories to rest?'

Holly, with one hand deep in a bowl of leftover gourmet popcorn, paused and stared at the set.

'Yes,' she murmured, 'how?'

'By facing them,' the good doctor replied. He pointed his bearded jaw at the camera, so that his bespectacled eyes seemed to bore straight into Holly's. 'Seek out your ghosts. You know where they lurk. Confront them, and lay them to rest.'

Pieces of nut-and-sugar-encrusted popcorn tumbled, unnoticed, into Holly's lap as she zapped the TV into silence.

'North Mountain,' she'd whispered, and the very next morning she'd phoned her travel agent. Was the cabin on the mountain still available? The answer had taken a while but eventually it had come. The cabin was there, it was for rent, and now here she was, about to face her ghosts...or to turn into one herself, if she didn't make it up this damned mountain.

There! Off to the left, through the trees. Holly could make out the long, narrow gravel driveway. It was still passable, thanks to the sheltering overhang of branches.

The car skidded delicately but the tires held as she made the turn.

She pulled up to the garage, fumbled in the glove compartment for the automatic door opener the realtor had given her. The door slid open. Holly smiled grimly. So much for the old man's predictions about a power outage, and thank goodness for that. Night had fallen over the mountain and for the first time it occurred to her that it wouldn't be terribly pleasant to be marooned here without electricity.

Carefully, she eased the car into the garage. Seconds later, with the door safely closed behind her, she groaned and let her head flop back against the seat rest.

She was safe and sound—but what on earth had

she thought she was doing, coming to this cabin? You didn't bury your ghosts by resurrecting them.

'You're an idiot,' she said brusquely, as she pulled her suitcase from the car and made her way into the kitchen.

She switched on the light. There was the stove, where she'd prepared the very first meal she and Nick had shared as husband and wife. There was the silver ice bucket, where he'd chilled the bottle of cheap champagne that was all they'd been able to afford after they'd blown everything on renting this place for their honeymoon. There was the table, where they'd had their first dinner...where they'd almost had it, because just as she'd turned to tell Nick the meal was ready, he'd snatched her up into his arms and they'd ended up making love right there, with her sitting on the edge of the counter and him standing between her thighs, while their burgers burned to a crisp.

The lights flickered. Deep in the basement, the heating system hesitated, then started up again. Holly sighed in gratitude.

What on earth was she doing here? She was an idiot, to have come back to this place.

'Worse than an idiot,' she said, in a voice blurred with tears—not that she was weeping with regret. Why would she? Marrying Nick had been a mistake. Divorcing him had been the right thing to do, and she didn't regret it, she never had. She was crying with anger at herself, at the storm that was going to make it impossible for her to turn around and drive down the mountain...

The lights blinked again. In a moment, the power

would go out. She'd never be able to open the garage door without it; the door was old, and far too heavy. The power had gone out for a couple of hours when they'd stayed here years ago, and not even Nick—muscular, gorgeous, virile Nick—had been able to wrestle the door open.

Holly swallowed dryly. She couldn't, she wouldn't, be trapped here, with her memories. She had to get out before that happened, and never mind the raging storm and the treacherous road. She could manage the drive down. She'd be careful. Very careful. Nothing was impossible, when you put your mind to it. Hadn't life taught her that?

'I am out of here,' she said, exactly at the moment the lights went out.

CHAPTER TWO

BY THE time he reached the turn-off for North Mountain, Nick was almost driving blind.

He had the windshield wipers turned up to high but the snow was falling so thick and fast that the wipers could barely keep up.

At least the Explorer was holding the road. That was something to be grateful for. And so was the gas station, just ahead. The last few miles, the needle on the gauge had been hovering dangerously close to empty.

Nick pulled beneath the canopy, stepped from the truck and unscrewed the cover to his gas tank.

'Hey there, Mister, didn't ya see the sign? Station's closed.'

A man had come out of the clapboard house beyond the pumps and jerked his thumb at a hand-lettered sign tacked to the wall. He had the raw-boned look of an old-time New Englander and the accent to match.

'No,' Nick said, 'sorry, I didn't.'

'Well, ya do now.'

'Look, I need some gas. And you're probably the only station open for miles.'

'Ain't open. Told ya, I'm closed.'

Nick flashed his most ingratiating smile.

'My truck's just about running on fumes,' he said. 'I'd really appreciate it if you'd let me fill up.'

'Ain't no need for gas,' the old man said, 'seein' as there's no place to go in a blizzard.'

Oh, hell. Nick took a deep breath and tried again. 'Yeah, well, the weatherman says it's not a blizzard. And by the time it is, I'll be where I'm going, if you'll let me have some gas.'

The old fellow looked him up, then looked him down. Nick found himself wishing he'd taken the time to exchange his black trench coat, charcoal suit and shiny black wingtips for the jeans, scuffed boots and old leather jacket he'd jammed into his suitcase. He'd almost given up hope when the guy shrugged and stomped down the steps to the pump.

'It's your funeral.'

Nick grinned. 'I hope not.'

'Where you headed?'

'Just a few miles north.' Nick peered towards the office. 'You got a couple of five-gallon gasoline cans you could fill for me?'

'Aye-yup.'

'And maybe a couple of bags of sand?'

'That, too.'

'Great.' Nick pulled out his wallet as the old guy screwed the cover back on the gas tank. 'If you have some candles you'd be interested in selling, I'd be obliged.'

'Well, at least you're not a fool, young man, wantin' to buy ice in Decembah.'

Nick laughed. 'No, sir. No ice. Just the gas, the

sand, the candles… Better safe than sorry, isn't that what they say?'

'The smart ones do, anyways. North, ya say. That's where you're goin'?'

'Yes. To North Mountain.'

The old man turned around, a red gasoline can in each hand, and looked at Nick as if he were demented.

'Ain't been a soul come through here in months, headin' for that mountain, and now there's two of you, in one day.'

Nick frowned. 'Somebody went up to the cabin?'

'I suppose. Couldn't tell 'em naught, either. Had the wrong car, wrong tires, wrong everythin'. Didn't have no business on that mountain, I tell you that.'

That was for sure, Nick thought grimly. Vagrants, even damn-fool kids with nothing better to do than go joy-riding, could get into trouble in country this isolated.

On the other hand, vagrants didn't drive cars, and kids around here had more sense than to be out in this kind of weather.

'Hunters, maybe?' he asked.

The old man guffawed. 'Hunters? Naw. I don't think so.'

Nick slid behind the steering wheel of the Explorer. 'How many guys were there?'

'Jest one, but—'

'Thanks,' Nick said. He waved, checked for the non-existent traffic, and pulled out onto the road.

'But it weren't guys a-tall, Mister. It were just this one pretty little woman…'

Too late. The truck had disappeared into the whirling snow.

The old man sighed. Crazy people, these city folk, he thought, and clomped back inside his house.

It took twice as long as it normally would have to make it up the mountain.

The drifting snow had buried the road in many places and at times the visibility was just about non-existent. Nick kept an eye out for another car but there were no signs any had come this way. Of course, with the snow falling so heavily, there wouldn't have been much chance of seeing tire tracks.

Still, when he finally reached the turn-off that led to the cabin, he scanned it carefully for signs of a trespasser, but there was nothing to see.

He pulled up outside the garage and got out to open the door. The snow, and the wind, hit him with enough force to take his breath away but he bent his head against it and grasped the handle of the garage door.

'Damn!'

How could he have forgotten? The door was electric. It wouldn't move an inch no matter how much muscle you applied and, of course, he'd forgotten to have somebody send him the automatic opener.

Well, that was life. He'd have his work cut out for him, digging the truck out from under umpteen inches of snow tomorrow morning. He trudged back to the Explorer, opened the door and stuffed his cellphone and his wireless fax into his pockets, hung his carry-on and his computer case from his shoulders, and hefted a box of supplies into his arms. Steak, potatoes, a couple of onions and a bottle of single-malt Scotch. The basic food groups, enough to hold him through the weekend. He slammed the door shut with his hip, dug the key to the cabin from his pocket, and made his way to the front porch.

Damn, Nick thought as he climbed the wooden steps. He'd forgotten to bring coffee. Well, he'd have to make do with a shot of the Scotch to warm his bones, and then he'd fall straight into bed. It sounded like a mighty fine plan.

He wedged the box against the door, fumbled for the lock and turned the key. The door wouldn't open. He scowled. Was there an unwritten law that said doors had to stick when a man was freezing his ass off on the wrong side of them? Nick grunted, shoved hard, and almost fell into the cabin as the door groaned noisily and swung open on a yawning blackness.

'Idiot,' he muttered.

He had a flashlight, but it was inside the box. And to put the box down without walking into something, he needed to be able to see.

There had to be a light switch on the wall. He seemed to remember one, to the left...

'Come on,' he said impatiently, as he felt for the switch. 'Where are you hiding? I know you're there.'

Something swished past his face. He sensed it coming just quickly enough to duck before it connected with his skull.

'Hey! What the...?'

A creature flew at him from out of the darkness,

shrieking like a banshee. Nick yelled, threw up his arms to ward the thing off, and went down in a heap, box, carry-on, computer and all.

The creature was right on top of him.

Talons dug into his shoulder, went for his eyes. Warm breath hissed onto his face. Was it a bobcat? A lynx? A mountain lion? No, not that. There were no big cats here, weren't supposed to be, anyway. A wolf? Gone for at least a hundred years, but people said...

'Perfume?' Nick whispered.

What kind of cat wore perfume?

The thing began trying to scramble away from him. Nick grunted. His hand closed on something fragile and bony. An ankle? A wrist? Did cats have ankles and wrists?

Perfume. Delicate bones...

Nick's eyes widened against the darkness.

'Bloody hell,' he said. 'You're a woman!'

And then something hit him hard, in the back of the head, and he slipped down and down into deepest, darkest night.

Holly stood over the unconscious intruder and trembled with fear.

Was he dead? Had she killed him?

At first, she'd thought she was dreaming. She'd been lying in bed, still shaking with cold despite wearing her long johns, wool socks, a hat and her New England Patriots sweatshirt, buried to the tip of her nose beneath half a dozen quilts, busily telling herself there was nothing the least bit spooky about being alone on the top of a mountain with no lights and a blizzard raging outside, when she'd heard something.

A sound. An engine.

Good, she'd thought. The snowplows were out.

Snowplows? Back home, in Boston, yes. But here? On the top of this mountain?

Holly'd shot up in bed, her heart pounding. The night was so still. Every sound seemed magnified a hundred times, and each had sent a wave of terror straight through her.

The thud of a car door. The scrunch of footsteps in the snow. The thump of booted feet mounting the steps, crossing the porch. The sound of the front door being battered open.

That was when she'd moved, jerking out a hand for the portable phone on the night table, remembering even as she put it to her ear that the damned thing wouldn't work with the power out. Petrified, almost breathless with fear, she'd looked around desperately for a weapon. Something. Anything.

The phone. It was a weapon. It didn't have as much heft as she'd have liked but she was in no position to be choosy.

Now what? Should she hide and hope the intruder wouldn't find her, or should she tiptoe down the steps, see what he was doing, slip up behind him when he wasn't watching and knock him over the head?

Whatever she did, she'd be quiet. Oh, so quiet. Super quiet, like a little mouse, so that he wouldn't so much as suspect there was a woman in the house. A lone woman...

And right then, just as she was tiptoeing to the top of the stairs, trying to hear herself think over the thud of her heart, the intruder had spoken in a low, angry voice.

'Come on,' he growled. 'Where are you hiding? I know you're here.'

Terror had impelled her, then, terror and the realization that he knew she was here. She'd raced downstairs, tried her damnedest to bash his brains out right away and, when that hadn't worked, she'd screamed the way Belinda had once said she'd been taught to scream in a martial arts class and hurled herself straight at the intruder.

He was huge. Seven feet, for sure. Eight, maybe. Three hundred pounds, no, four hundred, and all of it muscle. And he was strong as an ox. He'd struggled mightily, grunting and shoving and trying to dislodge her, but she hadn't given an inch. Then his hand—a hand the size of a house, and as powerful as a steel trap—had closed around her wrist.

'Perform,' he'd said, in a voice as deep as a bass drum, and just as a hundred terrible explanations for that command swept into Holly's mind his grasp on her wrist had tightened. 'Blood,' he'd snarled, 'you're a human!'

Perform? Blood? Human?

Holly hadn't hesitated. She'd swung the phone again and that time she'd hit him on the top of his miserable head.

Now he lay sprawled at her feet, face-down and motionless.

She poked him with her toe. He didn't move. She poked again. Nothing happened.

Holly's heart was in her throat.

'Oh, God,' she whispered.

Had she killed him? Had she killed this—this escapee from a funny farm? Her teeth banged together, chattering like castanets. What about all that stuff she'd always laughed at? The tabloid headlines that screamed about visitors from outer space? Did an alien lie at her feet, looking to perform some bloody human sacrifice?

Holly forced out a laugh. 'For heaven's sake,' she said shakily, 'get a grip!'

This was no alien. It was a man, and even if he was a certifiable loony who thought he'd been hatched on Mars, the last thing she wanted was to have his blood on her hands.

She had to turn him over, see if he was alive or dead. And to manage that, she needed light.

There were candles in the kitchen; she'd used one to see her way upstairs an hour or two ago. Was it safe to turn her back, leave the room, leave this—this creature lying here? Suppose he awoke? Suppose he stood up? Suppose…

'Ooooh.'

Holly leaped back. He was moaning. And moving. Very, very slightly, but at least he was alive. She hadn't killed him.

The man groaned again. It was a pitiful sound. Her heart thumped. How badly had she injured him? She couldn't see. Couldn't tell. For all she knew, he might be lying there, bleeding to death.

'Mister?'

There was no response.

'Hey, Mister!'

Holly took a tentative step forward. She poked him with her toe, then poked him again. Carefully, she squatted down beside the still form and jabbed him with a finger.

Nothing happened.

Holly heaved a sigh of relief. Good. He was still unconscious. As for his wounds—that could wait. Right now, she needed to find something to tie him with.

The man groaned and rolled onto his back, one arm thrown over his face. Holly leapt to her feet and scrambled into the shadows.

'Don't move!' she said. Oh, that sounded pathetic! She cleared her throat, dropped her voice to what she hoped was something raspy and threatening. 'Don't move another inch, or so help me I'll...I'll shoot.' And she brandished the portable phone before her.

Move? *Move?*

Nick would have laughed at the idea, if he hadn't been afraid that laughing would make his skull crack open. The last time his head had felt like this was in fourth grade when Eddie Schneider, excited at the prospect of striking out the last guy up, had managed to bean him with a fastball.

'You hear me, Mister? Don't even think about moving.'

It was a boy's voice, young and unsteady. Well, hell. Nick felt pretty unsteady himself. On the other hand, the last thing he wanted to do was lie here, at the mercy of a dangerous kid armed with a gun and some kind of animal that attacked people.

He had to sit up, if he was going to get out of this in one piece.

Nick forced another groan, which wasn't very difficult, all things considered.

'Gotta sit up,' he said thickly. 'My head…' He swallowed. 'If I don't sit up, I'm liable to toss my cookies.'

'No!' The kid's voice cracked. 'I mean…okay. Sit. But no fast moves. You got that?'

Nick nodded. A huge mistake. His head felt as if it might fall off. On the other hand, that might not be such a bad idea.

Carefully, he eased himself up with his back against the wall.

'Damn,' he said, 'what was that thing?'

'What thing?'

'That animal. The cat.'

'Cat?' Holly said. She swallowed dryly. Oh, boy. This was bad. He was hallucinating again. First blood, and humans. Now cats…

'Yeah. You know, the one wearing the perfume.'

Holly took another step back. 'Cats don't wear perfume,' she said carefully.

'This one did, when it attacked me.'

He was crazy, all right. And you didn't argue with a crazy man, you just acted as calmly as you could.

'There's…' Her voice slipped up the scale, and she cleared her throat. 'There's no cat here, Mister.'

'Dog, then. Was it a dog? I hope to hell you've locked it in another room.'

On the other hand, what could it hurt to let him think she had an attack dog by her side?

'It's a, uh, a…' *Think, Holly, think. What kind of dog was big and tough?* All she could come up with was an image of the cocker spaniel that had lived in the house next door, in Tuscany. 'It's, uh, a Rottweilder.'

'A what?'

'A Rottweilder.'

Nick hesitated. 'You mean, a Rottweiler.'

Holly shut her eyes, then opened them again. 'That's what I said. A Rottweiler, and don't you even breathe funny or I'll turn him loose on you.'

What she'd said was Rottweilder. Nick was sure of it. And a very well trained one it must be, for it not to be making a sound, not even a growl or a pant.

'Where is it?'

'Where is what?'

'The dog?'

'It's—it's here, right beside me. You want a close-up look? I'll let go of its collar.'

'No,' Nick said quickly, 'no, that's okay…'

There was no dog beside the kid, not a Rotter or even a poodle. The kid was standing in the shadows but his outline was visible and there was nothing beside him, except for a chair.

Slowly, ever so slowly, Nick brought up one leg and then the other.

'Don't move, I said!'

'I have to. My head's bleeding.'

'Are you sure?'

'Positive.' Nick touched his scalp gingerly, expecting to feel the warm ooze of blood, but all he found was a huge bump. 'Yeah, it's bleeding, all right. Listen, I've got to get to a doctor.'

'No! I mean...' What? What did she mean? 'I mean, I'll get you a compress. After I call the...' *Oh, Lord. She couldn't call anybody. She couldn't even tie the intruder up, without rope. And how was she going to search for rope? Was she going to ask him, politely, to just lie still and wait until she made a circuit of the cabin?*

Nick's eyes narrowed. Call whom? Did the kid have an accomplice?

'Look,' he said carefully, 'I'm willing to forget this, okay?' Slowly, holding his breath, he shifted his weight again. 'I don't know who you are and I don't care. You just turn around, walk out the door, and we'll pretend this never happened.'

'Me? Walk out the door? You must think I'm crazy. I'm not turning my back on you for one second, Mister. And I'm not going out into that blizzard, either.'

'Think it over, kid.' Carefully, ever so slowly, Nick began lifting himself from the floor. How clearly could the guy see him? Not very. He'd have to bet on that. 'I'm willing to give you my word that I won't press charges if you—'

'*You* won't press charges? For what?'

'For breaking and entering. For putting a hole in my skull. For menacing me with a gun.'

'You really are crazy! I didn't break or enter anything. As for menacing...you're the one who's doing the men—'

A scream broke from Holly's throat. The man had come to his feet with a blinding burst of speed. She turned to flee but he was across the room and on her before she'd had the chance to take a step.

'Okay, kid,' he snarled.

The phone went flying as he wrapped his arms around her and lifted her, kicking and screaming, from the floor. They lurched across the darkened living room in a grotesque two-step, crashed against a table and careened into the sofa. The man went down and she went down with him, falling across his body and into his lap.

'The police are coming,' Holly panted. 'I called them, as soon as I heard you breaking in.'

'You didn't call anybody, punk.' Nick wrestled the kid's hands over his head, rolled over and pinned the slight body beneath his. 'And why would you, when you're the one who's done the breaking in?'

'Get off me!' Holly jerked her hips up and tried to wriggle free of the hard body above her. The hard, masculine body that seemed—that seemed strangely familiar...

'Forget it, kid,' Nick growled.

'Get off!' Holly twisted beneath him again.

'Hey.' Nick scowled. 'Don't—don't do that.'

Holly fought harder. Her body brushed his, and a flash of heat shot through her blood, which was not just crazy but sick. 'Get off, dammit,' she yelled, and shoved against him again.

Bloody hell. Nick caught his breath. What was happening here? His anatomy was reacting to the shifting motions of the kid's. That was nuts. Worse than nuts...

...Except, this wasn't a kid trapped under him. And it certainly wasn't a boy. It was—it was...

'Holly?' he whispered.

The body beneath his became rigid. 'Nick?'

'Holly,' he said again. It was all his brain seemed capable of managing.

'Nick,' she murmured, on a rising breath.

'Yeah,' he said. 'It's me.'

And then he did the only thing a man could do, under the circumstances.

He bent his head, breathed in the soft, floral scent of his ex-wife, and kissed her.

CHAPTER THREE

WAS this a dream, or was it real?

Holly couldn't tell.

Nick's arms were around her. His mouth was warm and firm against hers. It felt so good, so familiar, to be in his embrace.

If it was a dream, she wanted it to go on for ever.

Nick groaned softly as he kissed her. It wasn't a sound of pain; it was a sound of pleasure, one she'd heard many, many times during the months of their marriage. Holly's heartbeat quickened in response. She knew what would happen next, how his hands would slip beneath her, how he'd cup her bottom and lift her closer so that she could feel the heat and hardness of his arousal against her belly...

Desire, swift and electric as a flash of lightning, shot through her blood. Her arms rose, wound around his neck. Her fingers tangled in his hair.

'Nick,' she said in a broken whisper.

'Yes,' he said, 'yes, baby, it's me.'

She gave a little moan as he kissed her again, more deeply this time, parting her pliant lips with his. His tongue was hot silk as it slipped into her mouth.

'Oh, Nick,' she whispered, 'Nick...'

His hands slid down her body, cupped her, lifted her, brought her hard against him. Holly gasped at the feel of him. Her body felt liquid, eager and ready for his possession.

'Baby,' he said, against her lips.

Holly arched against him, mindless with pleasure. This was Nick in her arms. Nick, whom she'd always loved, Nick who had once been her husband…

Nick?

Oh my God, she thought, and she slammed her hands against his shoulders at the same instant she bit down on his lip.

Nick yelled, rolled off her and jammed his hand against his mouth.

Holly shot to her feet.

'Light,' she snapped. 'We need light!'

'There's a flashlight in that box,' Nick said sullenly, jerking his head towards the upended carton.

Holly glared at him. Then she stalked to where the box had disgorged its contents and plowed through the stuff until she came up with the flashlight.

'If you had this, why on earth did you come stumbling in here in the dark?'

'Because I didn't expect the lights to be out.'

'You could have used this flashlight.'

'You attacked me before I could get to it. Why didn't *you* turn on the lights?'

'Oh, right,' Holly said coldly. 'I'm supposed to turn on the lights when I hear somebody breaking in? Why not just hold up a flashing neon sign that says "Hey, here I am"?' She switched on the beam and shone it at Nick. 'Anyway, I couldn't. The storm knocked out the power.'

'Hey.' Nick ducked away from the bright light.

'Take it easy, will you? My head hurts enough as it is without you drilling that thing right into my eyes.'

'You—you…' Surely, there was a word that suited the occasion, and the man, but Holly was too angry to think of one.

Nick stood up slowly. He took his hand from his lip and peered at it. There was a blur of something dark on his fingertips, something warm and sticky.

He looked at Holly in disbelief.

'You bit me,' he said.

'You're lucky that's all I did!' Rage bubbled through her, at him, at herself, at whatever unholy combination of forces had brought them together this night. 'You—you sneaky, scheming, miserable, lying, cheating…' She ran out of words but not out of anger. 'I hate you, Nick Brennan,' she yelled, and just to make sure he got the message she kicked him.

'Hey!' Nick danced back out of range. 'What are you, nuts? First you give me a concussion, then you try to bite off my lip, now you're treating my shins as if I'm a soccer ball.'

'Don't make me laugh!' Holly folded her arms over her chest. 'All you've got is a little bump on your head.'

'I'm glad you think it's little!'

'And your lip's still attached to your face.'

'No thanks to you,' he said indignantly. He pulled a handkerchief from his pocket and dabbed at the cut. 'Dammit, I'm bleeding buckets!'

'You aren't…' Holly frowned. 'Where? Let me see.'

'Right there,' he said, pointing to his mouth.

'Where? I can't—'

Nick took her hand. His fingers were warm, the tips calloused, just as she remembered. It surprised her that they would be, after so long. Nick Brennan had made a success of himself. His was the quintessential tale of Boy Makes Good. She saw his name and his photo in the papers, from time to time. Not that she looked; it was just that he was hard to miss. Nick in black tie, at the opera. At charity benefits. At the opening of his newest hotel. No way he'd ever be seen in jeans and workboots again; no way he'd ever wield a jackhammer or drive a big Cat, or work up a sweat...

'Here,' he said softly, and touched her fingertip to his mouth.

It was like touching a hot stove. Heat sizzled through her bones and through her blood. Nick felt it, too. She could hear it in his quick, indrawn breath.

His hand tightened on hers. His lips parted. He drew her hand further across his mouth, until she could feel the whisper of his breath, the softness of his flesh...

Holly snatched her hand back.

'You're fine,' she said briskly. 'There's hardly anything there.'

Nick stuffed his handkerchief back into his pocket. 'Yeah, well, it feels like it's going to be swollen for a week.'

'Good,' Holly said self-righteously. 'What made you figure you could bust in here, scare the life out of me and get away with it?' She pointed at the door.

'You turn around and get out of this house this minute, Nick. You got that?'

'My head hurts.'

'Good. Now, get out!'

'I need a compress. And some aspirin.'

'You need a night in a jail cell,' Holly said coldly.

'For what? Nobody's going to arrest a man for using his key to open his very own door.'

'What do you mean, your very own door?' Holly slapped her hands on her hips. 'Don't tell me that realtor screwed up! I rented this cabin for four weeks of peace and quiet.'

'You couldn't have. This cabin isn't—'

'Isn't what?'

Isn't the realtor's to rent, he'd almost said...but some inner voice warned him that now was not the time to tell her that, or to go into details about his ownership. Besides, there was always the faint possibility he'd screwed up, misread the date on which Brennan Resorts assumed ownership of North Mountain.

'Isn't what?' she demanded again.

Nick shrugged. 'It must be a mix-up,' he said. 'I, ah, I made rental arrangements, too. One of us must have gotten the date wrong.'

Holly stared at him. Nick had decided to spend time at the cabin? But why? She couldn't think of a single reason. Nick Brennan was Brennan Resorts. He had half a dozen of the world's classiest hotels to stay in, if he wanted to get away for a few days.

'My company is thinking of buying property in the area,' he said, as if he'd been reading her mind. 'I decided to come up and take a look around. I figured I might as well arrange to spend the weekend in a place I knew rather than take my chances on some dinky motel.'

'Oh.' His explanation was logical, and yet it disappointed her...not that there was any reason it should have disappointed her. Nick wouldn't be here to bury his ghosts. Why would he, when he didn't have any? Holly smiled coolly. 'Well, that makes sense. I mean, Mr Hotshot Brennan certainly wouldn't want to spend his time in a place that wasn't up to his standards, would he?'

'Cheap shots used to be beneath you, Holly.'

'And pretentiousness used to be beneath you.'

'Oh, for God's sake! What are we arguing about?' Nick stalked across the room, then swung around and faced her. 'Look, there's obviously been some sort of mistake made.'

'You can say that again!' She bent and scooped the portable phone from the floor. 'And you should consider yourself damn lucky. If this stupid thing worked, the sheriff would be here by now, clapping you in leg-irons.'

'Leg-irons?' Nick laughed. 'You've been watching too many bad movies. Besides, the only guy liable to show up here this time of year is going to be riding in a sleigh pulled by eight tiny reindeer.' His grin faded as he took a second look at the thing in her hand. 'A phone? Dammit, Holly. You said you had a gun.'

'What did you expect me to tell a lunatic who breaks into my home in the middle of the night? Stop, or I'll shoot you with my portable?' Holly tossed the telephone onto the sofa. 'You're lucky it wasn't a gun, or you'd be complaining about a lot more than a teeny bump on your head.'

'Yeah, well, you're lucky I didn't decide the only way to take out a guy with a gun was to beat the hell out of him.' Nick put his hand to his head and winced. 'And the bump isn't teeny, it's the size of a grape-fruit.'

'That's a pathetic untruth.'

'You're right.' Nick turned and marched away. 'It's really the size of a cantaloupe.'

'Where are you going?' Holly demanded, stalking after him.

'To the kitchen, to get a cold compress for my lip before I bleed to death.'

'Oh, stop being melodramatic. You're not going to bleed to death.'

'And to get some ice for my head.'

'Didn't you hear what I said before? I want you gone!'

'Yeah, yeah,' Nick said wearily. The long, difficult drive, the shock of the confrontation a few minutes ago—hell, the shock of finding Holly here—were all catching up to him.

He paused in the center of the kitchen. The room was dark but he could make out the hulking shapes of the stove, refrigerator and sink. If he remembered right, there was a paper towel holder just above the sink, and he headed for it. What he really needed was a shot of Scotch, assuming the bottle wasn't shattered, but he had the feeling Holly wouldn't appreciate waiting while he went back to the living room to find out.

'I know what you told me,' he said, as he tore a handful of sheets from the roll, folded them into a square and pressed it to his lip. 'But mmf mff mffer.'

Holly snatched the improvised compress from his hand.

'I can't understand a word you're...' She frowned. 'You're bleeding.'

Nick gave a hollow laugh. 'I told you that twenty minutes ago. Heck, baby, that's what tends to happen when you sink your fangs into somebody's face.'

'Don't call me that,' Holly said quickly. She turned on the faucet. It made a gurgling sound, spat out a few drops of water, and went dry.

'Don't call you what?'

'Baby.' She grasped his chin, put the folded paper towel to her lips to moisten it, and dabbed at the cut on his mouth. 'I don't like it. I never did.'

'Seems to me there was a time you liked it a lot.'

Her gaze flew to his. His eyes were locked on hers, and what she saw in their hazel depths—the shared memory of nights, and days, of breathtaking passion—made her heartbeat stumble.

'Well,' she said, lying through her teeth because he was right, there'd been a time his nickname for her, murmured in that soft, gravelly whisper of his, had been enough to make her melt, 'you were wrong.'

Nick's jaw tightened. 'Yeah.' He jerked the compress from her hand, balled it up and tossed it into the sink. 'I was wrong about a lot of things.' He looked at her again. Even in the near-darkness, she could see the arrogant little smile that tilted across his lips. 'But not about what happened a few minutes ago.'

'That I beat you up, you mean?'

'That you were mighty cooperative for a woman who thought she was in the grip of a guy who'd just broken into her house.'

Holly felt the colour bloom in her cheeks. 'I'm sure you'd like to think so. But I wasn't cooperative, I was shocked.'

'Shocked,' he said, folding his arms.

'Of course. You took me completely by surprise.'

'You're telling me that if a stranger comes along, scares you senseless, then grabs you and kisses you, shock will make you kiss him back?'

'No! Certainly not.' Holly glared up at him. 'I mean, as soon as you kissed me, I knew you weren't a strange...' She stopped and cleared her throat. 'Look, you're twisting this thing around to suit yourself. All I'm saying is that you can't compare a man forcing a woman to kiss him to what happened just now.'

Nick gave an evil chuckle. *Oh, hell.* Holly had all she could do to keep from slugging him again. He'd set her up, and she'd gone for it. She'd walked right into that one.

'Okay,' she said coldly, 'your lip's stopped bleeding. It's time to say goodbye.'

'Goodbye,' he said, and opened the freezer.

'Dammit, Nick—'

'We've only dealt with one wife-inflicted wound. There's still another to go.'

'Ex-wife, if you don't mind.'

'I don't mind at all.' Nick slammed the freezer door shut. 'There's no ice.'

'There's plenty outside,' Holly said sweetly.

He touched his hand to his head, hissing when his fingers came in contact with his scalp.

'What'd you hit me with, anyway? A brick?'

'Did I hit you really hard?'

'Did you...?' Nick gave a sharp laugh. 'No, of course not. I just rolled up my eyes and passed out for kicks.'

Holly felt a tiny twinge of guilt.

'Let me see your head,' she said.

'Why? So you can check the damage and cheer?' He took a step back as she lifted a hand towards him. 'Don't bother. I don't need—'

'Don't be such a coward, Nick. Bend down and—'

'I wasn't a coward.' His hand clamped down on her wrist; his tone was chill and hard. 'It wasn't me who was afraid of change.'

'It wasn't change,' Holly said quietly, 'it was destruction.'

They looked into each other's eyes for a long minute, and then Nick's hand fell from hers.

'Forget the bump,' he said. 'I'll take care of it.'

Holly clucked her tongue. 'Stop being a baby and let me see it.'

'I am not a baby. I am a sensible man who knows better than to offer my skull to the woman who just whacked it.'

'You are a baby.' She rose on her toes. Her fingers moved lightly in his hair, and he held his breath, wondering how in hell the impersonal touch of a woman he hadn't seen in years could be sending chills down his spine. 'Or did you hope I'd forgotten the time you got that tetanus shot and passed out?'

Nick rolled his eyes.

'I don't believe this! A woman takes a couple of isolated incidents, puts her own spin on them and wham, she comes up with her own version of the truth. I was working on that old house—'

'The Shelby place.'

'Yes. And I managed to put a rusty tenpenny nail through my hand.'

'Because you were careless.'

'Because I had the damned flu, and a fever.'

'All the reasons you should have been home, in bed, instead of parading around on a construction site.'

'Oof.'

'Does that hurt?'

'Of course it hurts,' Nick growled. 'And I wasn't "parading around", dammit, I was working because we needed the money.'

'You were working because you were too damned stubborn to let *me* work.' Holly stepped back. 'You'll live. Your Everest-sized bump is no bigger than a *petit pois*.'

'A what?'

'A tiny pea. And the point of my story was that you went out like a light when you got to the emergency room and they gave you that shot.'

'I passed out because of the shock. And the fever.

The doctor said so. And because when you came flying into the emergency room you looked as if—'

'As if what?'

As if you couldn't bear it, if something happened to me. As if you really did love me as much as I loved you...

'As if you were afraid you'd barf at the sight of blood,' he said briskly, 'and who could blame you? Well, thanks for the first aid. You're right. I'll be fine.'

'You know, maybe you should put some ice on—'

'I will. I'll follow your advice.' Nick forced a smile to his lips. 'I'll dump some snow on my head, when I get outside.'

'Oh.' Holly nodded. She ran the tip of her tongue over her lips. 'Well, then...'

'Yeah.' Nick cleared his throat. 'Well...' Merry Christmas. That was the thing people said, this time of year. But he hadn't said those words in six years, and he sure as hell wasn't going to say them now. 'Take care of yourself, Holly.'

'You, too.'

They stood in the darkened kitchen, looking at each other, and then Nick cleared his throat again.

'It was good seeing you.'

Holly nodded. That was all she seemed capable of doing. She wasn't about to risk speaking, not when her throat suddenly felt tight.

Nick raised his hand, as if he might touch her, and then drew it back.

'It's been...interesting.'

'Interesting?' she said, in a croak.

'Uh-huh.' His smile tilted, and he lifted his hand first to his lip, then to his head. 'For lack of a better word.'

'Oh.' Holly gave a quick little laugh. 'I, ah, I'm sorry about that, but—'

'No. No, that's all right, I understand. There you were, figuring you were tucked in bed, safe and sound...' His gaze drifted over her, then returned to her face. 'You *were* in bed, weren't you? When I came in?'

'Yes. Yes, I was.'

'Yeah, well, as I said, it's understandable.'

They stared at each other for another few seconds and then Nick drew a breath.

'Well...'

'Well,' Holly said.

'Goodbye.'

He turned and started towards the door. She followed him in silence, watching as the man she had once loved, the man who had once been her husband, collected the stuff that lay scattered all over the floor and then put his hand on the doorknob.

No, she thought desperately, oh, no...

'Nick!'

He swung around quickly, his eyes on hers.

'Yes?'

The space between them seemed to hum. Holly swallowed dryly; Nick took a step forward.

'Nick,' she said again, this time in a whisper. 'It's—it's late. And the road must be awful. Where...where will you go? How will you find a place to stay? What will you do...?'

Her words trailed away. Nick's eyes burned into hers, and he answered the only question that mattered, the only one she hadn't asked.

'Are you asking me to stay?' he said softly.

Holly stared at him. There was no point in pretending she didn't know what he meant. The kisses they'd shared just a little while ago, the flame that had ignited when he'd taken her in his arms... The memories held within these walls made pretence impossible.

'Holly?'

Nick's voice was husky. Holly could feel the heat of it burning through her skin.

'No,' she said, after a minute. She blinked her eyes against a sudden sting of tears and wrapped her arms around herself. 'No,' she repeated, very softly. 'I'm not.'

He nodded. Then he turned, opened the door, and stepped out into the night.

CHAPTER FOUR

THE moon had risen. It sailed the dark sky like a ghost ship playing hide-and-seek with the clouds.

The wind had died down, leaving the snow in fanciful drifts. The mountain lay cocooned in silent, white radiance.

It was a beautiful scene but a dangerous one. And that, Nick figured, was just as well. It was a lot better to devote his attention to making it down the driveway to the road than to think about whatever it was that had happened back in the cabin. The way he'd felt, seeing Holly. The hunger in the kiss they'd shared, and the question he'd asked her, before he could stop himself from asking it.

He really didn't want to think about any of it. Not tonight.

The snow was deep. Eighteen inches, at least. But the Explorer had four-wheel drive and, by some minor miracle, the wind had almost scoured the driveway clean. Still, it was slow going.

At last, he reached the end of the narrow gravel drive. Ahead, he could see the road that would take him down North Mountain.

The hair rose on the back of his neck.

'Bloody damn,' he whispered.

The road, tortuous on a nice day, was a treacherous

white ribbon now. One wrong move, and he'd end up in the yawning blackness of the valley.

Nick cursed and eased to a gentle stop.

What was the matter with him, thinking he could get down this mountain tonight?

He *wasn't* thinking, dammit. That was the problem. Seeing Holly again must have fried his brain.

He glowered out of his windshield. He'd come looking for closure, not for the opportunity to become a statistic.

'Damn,' he whispered, and then he blew out his breath, folded his arms over the steering wheel and laid his forehead against them.

He was behaving like a fool, doing things that made no sense, and all because of an unexpected encounter with a woman who'd ceased to mean anything to him a lifetime ago. It was late. The temperature was probably someplace around zero, there were snowdrifts the size of igloos all around, and what had he been doing?

Heading for a joy ride down Suicide Mountain, for Pete's sake. And Holly had been so glad to get rid of him that she'd never even considered that it might be the last ride he ever took. Nick sat up straight, shifted into reverse, backed to a handkerchief-sized space that constituted a wide spot on the roller-coaster of a road, made a careful U-turn and headed back the way he'd come.

The cabin was his. Even if there'd been a screw-up, even if it had been at his end, what did it matter? Not even Scrooge would send Tiny Tim out on a night like this.

His grip tightened on the steering wheel.

On the other hand, Scrooge had never been faced with spending the night in a cabin built for two with his ex. His gorgeous, sexy, desirable ex. The tension between them, those last couple of minutes, the way Holly had looked at him...

If he'd gone to her then, taken her in his arms, they'd have ended up in bed.

Nick squirmed uncomfortably in the leather seat. Well, so what? All that proved was that the old physical thing was still there, the same as when they were kids. She'd been eighteen, he'd been twenty. They'd met at a shopping mall. Not 'met', really; they'd bumped into each other, and almost the second they'd looked into each other's eyes the attraction had been...

Attraction? Nick snorted. They'd been hot for each other's bodies, that was what they'd been, so hot that nothing else had mattered, and because they'd been young and naïve, they'd ended up convincing themselves it was love.

But it hadn't been. Holly had come to her senses, just as her old man had said she would. She'd realized that sex wasn't, couldn't ever be, love, which was fine with Nick because *he'd* realized that only a spoiled little rich girl could think that a run-down apartment and second-hand furniture and a mountain of unpaid bills added up to domestic bliss. Twelve months later, they'd done the civilized thing and agreed to a divorce.

End of story.

He'd kissed her tonight. Well, so what? He'd been

so damn surprised to see her and yeah, she was still a good-looking woman.

A beautiful woman. But the world, as he'd spent the past years discovering, was filled with beautiful women. Holly was hardly unique. Yes, the old appeal was still there, but they were both adults. They'd have no trouble sharing the cabin for the night. Then, tomorrow, after the sun came up and the snowplow did its job, he'd do the gentlemanly thing and split. And it would be easy to do. He'd come for closure, and now he had it. In spades.

Nick frowned. There was just one thing.

Why had Holly come to the mountain?

She'd said something about needing a few weeks of peace and quiet, but from what? What could be stressful about the life of a rich woman who had everything she wanted? Unless...

His mouth became a thin line.

Unless it had to do with some guy. Unless she was getting over some guy. He couldn't think of any other reason for a woman like Holly to deliberately hide herself away in such an isolated place, where there wouldn't be a servant within calling distance.

Or—or maybe she wasn't going to be alone, all those weeks. For all he knew, a lover could be joining her.

Or a husband.

Nick's hands tightened even more on the steering wheel. Why not a husband? There was no reason Holly wouldn't have married again. She was still young, still beautiful, still everything any man could possibly want.

A muscle bunched in his jaw as he pulled up outside the cabin. He'd made such a fast exit that he hadn't asked any questions. Now, he would.

Gingerly, he touched his mouth and then his head. Damn right, he would.

She at least owed him an explanation.

Holly sat in the middle of the bed, snug under layers of blankets. Her knees were up, her arms were wrapped around them, and she was warm. Well, warm enough. And safe.

Nick was neither. How could she have let him drive that road on a night like this? The snow. The ice. The wind, and the dark.

She shuddered.

Nick was a good driver, sure. He'd been into motorcycle racing when they'd first met but sending him out into a snowstorm, on North Mountain...

'Are you asking me to stay?' he'd asked.

She sighed. If only he hadn't asked it the way he had, in that low voice she remembered all too well, with desire for her etched into every hard plane of his face. She could have said yes, she wanted him to stay, that he could sleep on the sofa because it would be foolhardy for him to risk his neck on the road.

And that *would* have been all she meant...

Wouldn't it?

She sighed, closed her eyes, and let her head droop against her upraised knees.

Absolutely. The invitation would have been an act of kindness, nothing more. They were adults, and adults could surely share three rooms and a bath for one night, especially when whatever it was that had drawn them together years ago was long since dead...

She groaned and fell back against the pillows.

Who was she kidding? She knew exactly what it was that had drawn them together. Sex. Sex, plain and simple. She'd been almost painfully young, and incredibly naïve. No boy had ever done more than kiss her goodnight, before Nick. But, with him, kisses weren't enough. Touching wasn't enough. She'd wanted him, begged him to take her...

It was still embarrassing to remember her abandon. No wonder she'd convinced herself that what she felt for Nick was love, not lust. Nick, in his faded jeans and his black leather motorcycle jacket, with that look of defiance on his gorgeous face...

Holly drew a ragged breath.

The Nick who'd shown up tonight was a different man. The custom-made suit, the pricey trench coat... She smiled to herself. He'd found what he'd always wanted, and it certainly hadn't been her.

Nick had figured that out first. He'd been out in the world. He'd realized that they'd been wrong for each other, and they'd parted like two civilized people. No accusations, no fights, no regrets, only the bittersweet realization that sex hadn't been enough.

But it was still there. The heat. The excitement. The desire.

Holly shivered, and burrowed deeper into the blankets.

It was probably a good thing he'd left. What was there to worry about? He'd make it down the mountain just fine. Besides, if he'd had any doubts about the road, he'd never have...

What was that?

Holly's head came up sharply. She'd heard something. The throaty growl of an engine.

'Nick?' she said.

She tossed aside the blankets and leaped from the bed. The wind and the cold had rimed the window with snow but...

Yes. Oh, yes. It was Nick.

Had he come back for her?

She put her hand over her breast. Her heart was thumping so hard it felt as if it were going to ram against her ribs.

Nick rummaged inside the Explorer, took out his carry-on bag. When he straightened up, she could see his face clearly in the moonlight. Her heart thumped again. He was so handsome. Big, and masculine, with those hazel eyes that never seemed quite certain if they were green or brown, that proud nose, that wonderful, sexy mouth.

He looked up. Holly knew he couldn't see her but she fell back against the wall anyway. Her breathing quickened. Would he knock? Or—

He used his key. She heard the door open, then slam shut. Heard his footsteps on the stairs.

Holly's knees felt rubbery. Nick was in the house, and he was coming for her. In seconds, he'd be standing before her. There'd be no decisions to make, no weighing of right and wrong. Nick would open the bedroom door, look at her as he had a little while ago, the way he'd always looked at her, and she would run to him, go into his arms.

Footsteps sounded on the steps. Holly trembled. Waited.

The door swung open.

'Nick,' she whispered, 'you came back.'

'Damn right, I came back.' He dropped his carry-on bag to the floor and folded his arms over his chest. 'Get this straight,' he growled. 'No way in hell am I going to drive that road tonight.'

She blinked. 'What?'

'You heard me.' He unbuttoned his trench coat, slipped it off and tossed it on a chair. 'I'm no happier about this arrangement than you are. You, me, this cabin... Believe me, this is not my idea of a good time.'

'No.' She cleared her throat. 'No, it's not mine, either. But you're right.'

'And before you put up a fuss...' Nick frowned. 'I am?'

She nodded as she began stripping half the blankets from the bed and piling them in her arms.

'The storm's bad. And that road must be a nightmare.' She plucked a pillow from the bed, too. With the stuff in her arms piled high enough to almost hide her face, she maneuvered past him. 'It was bad enough when I drove up, hours ago.'

'Well, yeah. I just thought—'

'Do you remember where the linen closet is?'

'No. Yes. I...' *He was right? How could that be? He'd never been right, not where Holly was concerned.*

'It's next to the bathroom. Grab a couple of sheets and bring them down with you.'

He watched, bewildered, as she made her way to the stairs. The bedlinens were piled higher than her head.

'Hey! Holly, wait a second. I'll take that stuff. You can't see...'

'I can manage fine, thanks. You just bring the sheets.'

Holly dumped the blankets on a chair near the sofa. Her hands trembled as she took the throw pillows and tossed them aside.

What on earth had she been thinking? She'd *never* have made love with Nick, not even if he'd begged! She was done with all that, done with wanting him—

'Are these okay?'

She looked up. Nick was holding out a pair of flannel sheets.

'Fine,' she said, and took them from his outstretched hands.

'Can I help?'

She shook her head. 'No,' she said briskly. 'I can manage just fine.'

Nick frowned. He had the feeling she was right: she *could* manage fine. Something about her had changed, but what was it?

Maybe he'd been right, and there was a man in her life. It wasn't his business. It was just that he was curious.

She bent over the sofa and smoothed down the bottom sheet. She was wearing an outlandish outfit—he hadn't really noticed it before but now he took in the details. Sweatshirt, long johns, heavy socks. He'd never seen anything less feminine. No. That was a lie. The sweet curve of her back was—

'Toss me the other sheet, will you?'

His eyes followed her every movement. The heavy sweatshirt disguised her breasts, but he didn't need to see them to remember their conical shape or silken perfection. The rest of her was outlined clearly by the clinging long underwear. Her gently rounded bottom. Her long legs—legs that had once locked around his waist to drive him deeper as they'd made love...

Nick swung away and walked to the fireplace.

'Heck of a thing,' he said gruffly. 'A fieldstone hearth, plenty of kindling and matches...'

'And no firewood. I know. It was the first thing I checked, after the electricity went out. Well, the second thing, after the candles.' She plucked a blanket from the chair, shook it out, then laid it across the improvised bed. 'Too bad. I've gotten really good at building fires.'

'Yeah? I'd have figured it took a small army to get anything started in those walk-in fireplaces at Pinetops.'

'Oh, it pretty much does.' She straightened, blew a strand of wheaten hair out of her eyes. 'I meant in my place, in Boston.'

Nick nodded, his face a perfect blank.

'Nice town, Boston.' He bent down, stared intently into the fireplace. 'Live alone?'

Holly hesitated. The desire to tell him that she lived with a man was almost overpowering, but what was the point? He wouldn't care. Not that she wanted him to.

'Yes. I live alone. And you?' She knew the answer, knew that he hadn't remarried, thanks to the media's interest in him, but why tell him that? 'Do you live in New York?'

'Uh-huh.' Alone, too, he almost said...but she didn't ask. Why didn't she ask?

'I don't know how anybody stands the pace.' Holly added the other blankets, smoothed them neatly and folded back a corner. 'I mean, whenever I fly down to visit Belinda, my agent, or my publisher—'

'Your what?' he said, as if she'd suddenly told him she paid visits to a psychic.

'Belinda, my agent, or my publisher.' She turned towards him, her hands on her hips. The look on his face said it all. He knew nothing about her career. Well, why would he? Just because she knew all about his... 'My publisher,' she said again, with a little smile. 'I write cookbooks.'

Nick's brows lifted. 'You?'

'Me.' Holly folded her arms. 'I know you never figured I could do more than boil water—'

'That's not true. You were great.' He grinned. 'All those ways you came up with to cook hamburgers.'

'Be honest, Nick. You hated every last one of them.'

'That's not true. I just figured—'

'You figured I was playing house.'

'Look, I knew you'd never been inside a kitchen in your life, until we got married. It wasn't fair to ask you to take on--'

'No.' Holly's tone was polite, but her eyes were cool. 'You're right. It wouldn't have been fair to ask. But I didn't need to be asked. I was your wife, Nick. And wives cook. They clean. They iron. Wives do lots of things…but not *your* wife.'

'I don't believe this.' Nick folded his arms over his chest. 'Six years, and it's still the same old thing. Well, you're right. I didn't marry you for free maid service.'

Holly picked up the pillow and hurled it onto the sofa.

'You know something?' She spun towards him again, her eyes dark with anger. 'I never really figured out why you *did* marry me. I used to think it was for sex, but it wasn't that, was it? It didn't have to be, considering that I fell into bed with you days after we met.'

'Are we back to that, too? Listen, baby—'

'*Don't* call me that! I am not your baby. I am not anybody's baby.'

'One argument at a time, okay?' Nick slapped his hands on his hips. 'I married you, dammit, because I loved you! Because I wanted to give you everything you deserved, everything you wanted…'

'Bull! What an incredible ego you have, Nicholas Brennan! How could you possibly have known what I wanted?'

'A man knows, that's all. When he loves a woman—'

'On the other hand,' Holly said coldly, 'what *you* wanted was no secret.'

'Oh, yeah?'

'Yeah.'

'Well, I'm waiting.' Nick's jaw shot forward. 'Tell me what I wanted, since you know so much about it.'

'You wanted success. Recognition.' She threw her arms wide. 'You were determined to show them all that they were wrong!'

Nick laughed. 'Who's this "them"? What in hell are you talking about?'

'You know exactly what I mean, Nick. You wanted just what you got. Your name in headlines. A fat bank account.'

'Ah, the horror of it all.' He shook his head and put on a mournful face. 'To think of it, that a guy would want to make good in this world. Lord, what a tragedy.'

'Don't laugh at me!' Holly stamped her foot. 'You and that— that monster-sized chip you wore on your shoulder—'

'Chip?' His voice rose as he stomped towards her. 'Hey, baby, I'm not the one with the chip. While I was out there, working my butt off, there you were, just waiting for me to come in the door at night so you could pounce on me and tell me about all the mistakes I was...Holly? Holly!' Holly had turned and was striding away. Nick followed her to the foot of the stairs, watching as she began climbing them. His voice rose, along with his temper. 'Where do you think you're going?'

She swung around and glared at him, cheeks pink with anger.

'I never pounced on you when you came through the door, and you know it!'

'You damn well did. Everything got the Holly Cabot Brennan vote of disapproval. The people I knew. The places I went. The things I did...'

'You know, I used to think we never quarrelled. Even just a little while ago, I was thinking about how—how civilized our divorce had been. Some tears, some polite conversation, and it was over.'

'What's your point?'

'My point,' Holly said bitterly 'is that I lied to myself all these years and never realized it until this minute.'

'Well, you're realizing wrong. We didn't fight. Never.'

'You're the one who's wrong, Nick. We fought. I did, anyway. It's just that I never let the anger out. I kept it all bottled up because I was this—this good little girl who wanted to please you. To make you look at me the way you... Oh, this is stupid! It doesn't matter anymore. The past is dead, and our disaster of a marriage with it.' She turned away, her back rigid. 'And I can't begin to tell you how glad I am for that!'

'Holly, wait a minute—'

'Goodnight, Nick. If we're lucky, and they plow the road during the night, please have the decency to be gone before I get up.' Her voice trembled. 'Actually, if you really had any decency at all, you'd—you'd take those blankets and that pillow and make your bed in a snowbank!' She stormed up the stairs and slammed the bedroom door behind her.

Nick stood there for a long minute, staring blindly at the empty hall and the closed door. Then, very slowly, he made his way to the sofa, sat down, and buried his head in his hands.

CHAPTER FIVE

MAN, it was cold!

And late, too. At least three or four in the morning, Nick figured. No question but that he had to have been tossing and turning for hours, ever since Holly had stormed out of the room.

He lifted his arm and peered at the lighted dial of his wristwatch.

Midnight? It was only midnight?

Nick groaned and fell back against the pillow, except the pillow wasn't there. The arm rest was, and he managed to connect it perfectly with the bump on his head. He winced, mouthed an oath, and rubbed his skull with the tips of his fingers.

'Great,' he muttered. 'Just great.'

What a night this had turned out to be! The laugh of it was that he'd come to North Mountain for a break. Considering how things were going, he'd have found more relaxation if he'd decided to camp out in the middle of Times Square.

And the weekend was only just beginning.

Nick rolled over, picked up the pillow and punched it into shape.

The room lay in total darkness. Not a good sign, he thought sourly. If the clouds had rolled in again, if it snowed...who knew when the road would get plowed? With his luck, he might be marooned here until New Year's.

The thought made him shudder.

No way.

'No way at all,' he said, as he flipped onto his back, folded his arms over his chest and glowered at the ceiling.

Plow or no plow, he was getting out of here at sun-up. Holly could keep the cabin and her distorted memories of their marriage all to herself. The way she'd talked, anybody would think he'd been the one who'd screwed up their relationship.

'And it wasn't,' he growled into the silence. 'She knows damn well it wasn't!'

When he'd married Holly, she'd been everything he'd wanted, every dream he'd ever dreamed. She was beautiful. Bright. Kind. Caring. He'd wanted to put down roots, build a marriage, a family, a life they'd both be proud of.

What he hadn't figured was that she'd only wanted to play at being married. Either she still hadn't realized it or she wouldn't admit it, even now. All the self-righteous accusations she'd hurled at him tonight, accusing him of fighting with her and then turning her back on him before he'd had a chance to respond…

Damn, but she'd made him angry!

Angry, hell. He'd been furious. After she'd slammed the bedroom door, he'd paced the living room, muttering to himself, until, finally, he'd run out of steam, peeled down to his shorts and climbed under the blankets on the sofa.

Sofa? Nick grimaced. This wasn't a sofa. It was a

slab of concrete, with an occasional steel bar built in for effect. Only an Indian fakir would call it suitable for a night's sleep. It was short and too narrow. His feet dangled over the arm and hung out from under the blankets. And every time he rolled over he risked getting dumped onto the floor.

To top it all, he was freezing. He felt as if he'd curled up on a shelf in a walk-in freezer for the night.

What he needed were his thermals, his wool shirts, sweats and heavy socks, all the stuff still packed in his carry-on, which he'd thoughtlessly left upstairs.

'Another brilliant move in a night of brilliant moves, Brennan,' he muttered in disgust, and dragged the blankets up over his shoulders—a *truly* brilliant idea, since all he accomplished was to leave his shins hanging out in the cold.

Nick sighed.

Amazing, that a fight with a woman who didn't mean a thing to you anymore could be so upsetting.

Holly's rage had caught him off guard. He could hardly recall her so much as raising her voice, during their marriage. They'd never quarrelled, not even at the end. Sometimes, when he'd found her looking at him with that hurt-little-girl expression, he'd had all he could do to keep from demanding that she tell him what was wrong. He could have dealt with that, with some yelling and anger, even with some flying crockery.

But there'd been none of that. Holly's silence had damn near killed him. That, and the pained look in her eyes.

'What do you want from me?' he'd said to her once. Okay. He hadn't said it, he'd shouted it.

'If you don't know,' she'd said in a broken whisper, 'I can't tell you.'

That was the night he'd finally admitted defeat. He'd packed his things and moved out, and the lawyers had taken it from there. He'd never set eyes on his wife again.

His ex-wife. How come he kept forgetting that?

Now it turned out that Holly had just been waiting for the chance to tell him off. And tell him off she had. The clipped words. The flashing eyes. The regal posture, when she'd walked away.

Holly had changed, all right. Changed a lot.

The Holly he'd married had been a girl who'd spent her life in a world of fairy-tale privilege. And he'd taken her away from all that. Holly the Princess had tied on an apron and become Holly the Housewife.

At first, he'd thought it was sweet. After a while, he'd realized there was nothing sweet about watching his beautiful wife transformed into a drudge, and knowing he was the cause.

She'd baked. She'd cooked. She'd made curtains for their hovel of an apartment. Curtains, by God, when she'd probably never so much as sewn a button on a blouse in her entire life. And the way she'd stood at the door each night, those first few months, breaking into a big smile as he came in filthy and tired and irritable from a day spent building houses for rich people who'd never done a thing in their lives to deserve them, lifting her face for his kiss as if he weren't dirty, and smelly, and her old man's worst dream come true...

Not that her housewife act had lasted. Just about the time he'd finally gotten a handle on how to go from wielding a hammer for the rest of his life to finding the pot of gold at the end of the rainbow, Holly had come to her senses. Instead of smiling when he came in at night, she'd sulked. No. That was the wrong word. She hadn't sulked. She'd seemed...hurt. As if he'd somehow let her down when, dammit, what he'd been doing was working his ass off to give her the life she deserved.

Holly the Princess had become Holly the Silent.

It was anybody's guess who she was now, and none of his business.

Nick sat up, pummelled the pillow a little, jammed it behind his head and lay down again. He turned on his right side, turned on his left...

And rolled right off the sofa, in a tangle of blankets.

'That's it,' he snarled. He shot to his feet and began pacing.

Sleep was not a possibility. He had to do something or go crazy, but what could you do in a cabin without electricity in the middle of the freaking night, with the temperature someplace around zero and your ex in the bed upstairs...?

Bloody damn!

He came to an abrupt halt. He'd been so busy counting his own miseries that he'd forgotten that Holly had to be freezing, the same as he was. Worse, probably. She'd given him half her supply of blankets. And she'd never dealt well with the cold. He used to tease her about it, when she'd curl up against him at night, those first months of their marriage, with her hand spread across his chest and her thigh over his.

'I don't know what I'm gonna do with you, baby,' he'd say, as he drew her to him, and she'd give a sexy little laugh and say that if he couldn't think of something she certainly could...

'Stop it, Brennan,' Nick growled. What was he trying to do? Drive himself crazier than he already was?

To have come to this cabin in the first place was crazy. To find your ex-wife inside and come back after she all but tossed you out was certifiably loony. Forget the snow. He'd have been better off taking his chances with the road. It couldn't be any more dangerous than where his thoughts were heading but it was only logical to think about waking Holly and suggesting they share the blankets.

Oh, yeah. That was just what he needed, all right. Snuggling down under the blankets with Holly was definitely the way to go.

Nick sighed. He was losing it. What he needed was to do something constructive. Like build a fire in the fireplace, to throw some warmth into the room.

He squatted down before the hearth and looked it over. Somebody had cleaned it, laid out kindling, made sure there were two boxes of safety matches within easy reach—and then forgotten to arrange delivery of firewood.

That didn't make much sense.

There'd been wood waiting, the last time he and Holly had come here. A whole cord of it. Well, no. There'd been some logs stacked here, beside the hearth, but the rest had been neatly stored in a little shed that was built onto the back of the garage…

A grin spread across his face. Hastily, he pulled on his trousers, his shirt and his shoes. Then he made his way through the silent cabin to the kitchen, opened the back door and stepped outside.

Ten minutes later, Nick's soaked clothing was draped over the back of the sofa. And he had a big, beautiful fire glowing on the hearth.

He held his hands out to the flames and smiled with satisfaction. Then he looked back up the stairs. Holly had all but told him never to darken her doorway again—but she'd change her mind, when she saw the fire.

He ran up the steps, then stood outside her room, listening. At first, he heard nothing but then, after a moment, he thought he could hear something. The sigh of the wind in the eaves, perhaps…

Or the sound of a woman, weeping.

He hesitated, then rapped lightly on the closed door. 'Holly?'

There was no response.

'Holly?' he said, and knocked again.

The noise, whatever it was, stopped.

'Holly? Are you okay?'

Silence. Nick frowned and put his hand on the doorknob.

'Holly, answer me!'

'What do you want?' Holly said, in a muffled voice.

Nick leaned his forehead against the door and heaved a sigh of relief.

'Are you okay in there?'

Holly grabbed a tissue from the box on the night-stand, wiped her eyes and blew her nose.

'I'm fine,' she said. Tears spilled down her cheeks and she rubbed them away with the back of her hand. 'Just—just a little chilly.'

'That's what I want to talk to you about. Can I come in?'

She hesitated. If Nick saw her like this, what would he think? She'd been crying for so long…her eyes and nose were probably pink and swollen.

'Holly?'

He'd undoubtedly misinterpret her tears and think they were for him. They weren't. She'd done with crying over Nick a long time ago. She'd been crying out of anger, that was all. Anger, plain and simple.

'Dammit, Holly, what's wrong?'

But he couldn't see her, not unless he had the flash-light and he didn't, or she'd have been able to see the beam of its light shining under the door.

'Nothing's wrong,' she said, and sat up. She ran her hands through her hair, fluffing it away from her face. 'Come on in.'

Nick stepped into the room. Holly's face was a pale ivory oval against the pillows.

'Hi,' he said, and cleared his throat.

'Hi,' she said, and smiled.

'I, uh, I…' *What was the matter with him? He'd come upstairs to tell her that he had a fire going in the fireplace, not to stand at the foot of the bed in tongue-tied oblivion.* But it was hard to think straight, when he looked down at the beautiful face of his wife.

'Nick?'

'Yes?'

'You said you wanted to tell me something.'

'Oh. Oh, right. Right...' He frowned. 'Your voice sounds strange. Have you been crying?'

'Crying?' She gave a gay little laugh. 'Me? Of course not. I mean, it's cold, yes, but I wouldn't cry over that. I, uh, I think I might be catching a cold.'

She'd drawn the blankets to her chin. And there were so many blankets that her body was shapeless beneath them. But his memory supplied all the details. Her graceful throat, with that place just at the juncture of neck and shoulder that always seemed to smell like spring rain. Her silken breasts, and the way they filled his palms...

Nick's body clenched like a fist. That didn't surprise him. What did was the sudden clenching of his heart.

Holly, he thought, baby, where did it all go? What happened to us?

'Nick? Are you okay?'

'Sure.' He smiled. 'Better than okay. That's what I came to tell you.'

He sounded pleased with himself. Not smug. Just pleased, and eager to share the pleasure with her. Holly's heart surged with delight. This was the Nick she remembered. The easy laughter in his voice. The beautiful, tautly-muscled body....

'On second thought, I'd rather surprise you.' He moved to the side of the bed and held out his hand. 'Come on.'

'Come on, where? It's freezing cold—'

'Exactly.'

'It's the middle of the night—'

'Yeah, that's what I thought, too. But it's only...' He lifted his hand, checked his watch. 'It's only twelve-thirty.'

Only twelve-thirty? Her spirits dropped like a stone sinking into a pond, but she kept her tone perky.

'All the more reason for me to stay put.'

Nick sighed. 'Okay,' he said, 'if you're going to be stubborn...'

Holly shrieked as he scooped her into his arms, blankets and all. 'Nick! What on earth are you doing?'

'If Mohammed won't come to the mountain...' He grunted as he rearranged her in his arms. 'Just hang on tight. I don't want to trip over these blankets.'

What choice was there? Holly put her arms around his neck and hung on as he headed for the stairs.

'Really,' she said, 'Nick, this is silly.'

Except, it wasn't. It was wonderful, just like the dreams she'd been having. She was in Nick's arms, where she belonged.

Where she'd once belonged.

She shuddered, and Nick drew her closer. 'Cold?'

'Yes,' she said. What else could she say? Not the truth, that she was engulfed in sensation, almost painfully aware of Nick's masculine scent. The sexy rub of his unshaven jaw against her cheek. The strength of his embrace, and how good it felt to lie, secure, within it.

Her heart was beating like a drum.

'Here we go,' he said, as he carried her into the living room...and she saw the flames, leaping on the hearth.

'Oh, Nick!' Her voice rang with delight. 'You built a fire. But how?'

He gave a wicked chuckle as he sank to the floor before the fireplace and settled her in his lap.

'Well, I was going to tear the sofa apart with my bare hands and feed it to the flames—and then I remembered something.'

Holly knew she ought to move. It was wrong to be here, snug in her ex-husband's arms. But being snug—being warm—was what this was all about, wasn't it? Finding warmth, against the deadly cold of the cabin?

'What did you remember?' she asked.

'Where we found the firewood the last time we were here. It was in the shed, remember?'

'No.' She frowned. 'No, I don't— Oh. Of course! How could I have forgotten? The wood-shed, out behind the garage.'

'That's the place.' He leaned back against the sofa, so that her head lay against his shoulder. 'Do I get a merit badge for this one or not?'

Holly laughed. 'My Eagle Scout,' she said softly.

'Feels good, doesn't it?'

'Wonderful,' she murmured, shutting her eyes and burrowing even closer.

They sat without talking, soothed by the warmth of the fire. Nick dipped his head and inhaled the fragrance of Holly's hair. Her skin. She smelled like a morning meadow, fresh and new and touched with the scent of wildflowers. And she felt—she felt wonderful, here in his arms.

The feel of her was new, and yet it wasn't. How

could it be? Every inch of her body was imprinted on his. He remembered each curve, each sweet line. He knew what would happen if he kissed her throat, where it lay bare. If he breathed against her skin. If he raised her sweatshirt and bit gently at the straining flesh of her breast.

His body turned rock-hard. It was sudden and unexpected, and so unnerving that he shot to his feet while Holly gasped and clung to his neck. He deposited her on the sofa, swung away, grabbed for the poker and stabbed blindly at the burning logs.

'Okay,' he said briskly, 'here's the plan. We'll spread a couple of blankets on the floor, in front of the fire. Then we'll dump the rest of them over us. That ought to keep us warm enough so we can be sure of waking up in the morning with fingers and toes still attached.'

When it was safe to turn around and face her, he saw that her face was flushed with color. Her eyes were dark, almost the color of the night crowding in at the windows. Had she felt the pressure of his arousal? Or was she wary of spending the night lying so close to him?

'It's the only sensible thing to do,' he said softly.

She nodded. 'Yes. I agree.'

'Good.'

She cleared her throat and forced a little smile to her lips. 'It's certainly better than turning into an advertisement for the wonders of cryogenics.' Her smile broadened, and she touched a finger to the tip of her nose. 'Or for freezer burn. I do still have a nose, don't I?'

Nick grinned. 'Definitely.'

'Good. For a while there, I was pretty sure I was going to lose it.'

'That's right. It wasn't just your hands and feet that used to turn icy, it was your nose, too. I remember nights when we'd turn over in our sleep so that you'd end up holding me, and I'd wake up because that cute little ice cube was pressed into my back…'

His words trailed off. Their gazes met, held, then slid away.

'Okay,' Nick said briskly. He plucked some blankets from beside the sofa and laid them before the hearth. 'Ah, the wonders of nature. I don't recall anybody doing this in *The Sound Of Music*, do you?'

Holly laughed. 'No.'

'Yeah, well, maybe they don't have power failures in the Alps.' He grabbed the pillow, placed it at one end of the improvised mattress. 'Ready when you are, Frosty.'

Holly laughed again. She knew what he was doing, making a joke of the fact that they were about to sleep together, but it wasn't helping. Her mouth was dry; her heart was doing a crazed two-step.

'Holly?'

She raised her head and focused on Nick's face. One look told her that he knew what she was thinking.

'You'll have your half of the bed, and I'll have mine. I promise.'

'Of course,' she said, and before she could feel like too much of an idiot she scooted off the sofa, onto the blankets he'd arranged, and lay down with her head on the pillow.

Nick layered the remaining blankets over her. Then he lifted one corner, edged beneath the stack, and lay down so that no part of his body was touching hers.

'Okay?'

'Fine.'

They lay in silence for a few minutes, and then Nick sighed. 'We should have brought down that other pillow.'

'Here. You can use—'

'No, don't be—'

They rolled against each other, caught their breaths, and instantly pulled apart.

'I'll be fine,' he said gruffly.

'You sure?'

'Positive.'

Silence enveloped them. They lay on their backs, staring at the ceiling, watching the shadows cast by the fire.

All I have to do is reach out my hand, Holly thought...

All I have to do is touch her, Nick thought...

'Nick?'

Holly's whisper was tenuous and soft as a sigh. Nick felt his heartbeat accelerate.

'Yes?'

'I'm sorry for what I said before. About the chip on your shoulder.'

'No, that's okay. You were just being honest.'

'Yes, but...' She sighed again. 'You were a good husband, Nick. It's just that I...'

'You wanted somebody else,' he said, trying not to let the pain show in his words. 'I understand.'

'No! Not somebody else. Some*thing* else. Something I'd thought you—you and I... Never mind. I just wanted you to know that I didn't mean to hurt you.'

'Yeah. Me, too.'

'You, too, what?'

'I'm sorry if I said anything that hurt. All that stuff about the Holly Brennan stamp of approval...it wasn't true. I mean, that's how it sometimes felt, but...' He cleared his throat. 'You were a good wife, Holly. It's just that I—'

'I wasn't the wife you wanted.'

No, he thought, hell, no. It was me. I couldn't measure up. I wanted only you, Holly. I still want...

'Here,' she said, and moved closer. 'The pillow's big enough to share.'

'Are you sure?'

'I'm sure.'

They lay side by side, sharing the improvised bed and the pillow but as far apart as two human beings who'd once shared their lives with each other could possibly be. The moments slipped past and then Nick thought, The hell with it. He reached for Holly's hand and clasped it in his.

'Goodnight,' he whispered.

Holly blinked hard. Tears burned behind her eyelids.

'Goodnight, Nick.'

She shut her eyes. He shut his. The fire burned. The wind sighed.

After a while, Nick murmured in his sleep and rolled to his side. He reached out for Holly. For his wife. Lost ·in her dreams, Holly went straight into his arms.

CHAPTER SIX

NICK awoke alone, in a heap of blankets that still carried Holly's scent.

His shoulder felt just a little stiff, the way it used to in the mornings when they'd been married. In the days when Holly had still slept the night through with her head tucked just beneath his chin.

That was how she'd slept last night, with her hand splayed over his chest and her leg draped over his...

God, it had felt wonderful.

His smile faded. What good did it do to think such things? She'd probably gone into his arms out of long-remembered habit, nothing more.

He sat up and ran his fingers through his tousled hair. The fire was still burning on the hearth. He'd fed it a couple of times during the night, each time slipping carefully from under the blankets so as not to wake Holly. The last time he'd crept back into their warm bed, he'd yielded to temptation, bent his head and brushed his mouth gently over hers. Holly had sighed and murmured something that might have been his name and he'd drawn her close, tucked her head beneath his chin, and fallen into a deep, peaceful sleep.

Nick glanced at the window. The storm was over. The sun was rising into a cloudless sky.

His heart constricted.

The plows would come through this morning. There'd be no excuse for him to stay. Not that there'd be any use in staying...

'Good morning.'

Nick looked around. Holly was standing halfway between the kitchen and the living room, wearing jeans, hiking boots, and a heavy ski sweater. Her long wheaten hair was pulled back in a French braid, and her face was shiny and as scrubbed as a schoolgirl's.

He smiled. He'd almost forgotten that his wife—his former wife—was a wonderful sight to wake up to.

'Good morning,' he said. 'I seem to have overslept.'

Holly grinned. 'You're a regular lazybones. How about some caffeine to get you started?'

'Caffeine? You mean...' Nick lifted his head and sniffed the air. 'I thought I was hallucinating. Is that really coffee I smell?'

'I was wondering how long it would take you to notice. Just wait there one second...' She disappeared into the kitchen and popped out a minute later with two mugs in her hands. 'You still take it with cream and one sugar?' she asked as she came towards him.

Nick nodded. 'Yeah.'

Holly reached down to the warm ashes in front of the fireplace and removed a grey and white speckled coffee pot.

'Damn,' Nick said with pleasure. 'I never noticed.'

She filled both mugs, smiled, and handed one over. He took it and buried his nose in the fragrant steam.

'A miracle. Thank you.' He took a sip, sighed, and

looked at Holly, who'd sat down, cross-legged, opposite him. 'How'd you manage it?'

'Well, I decided to poke through the pantry.'

'And you found a coffee shop?'

Holly laughed. 'I found coffee, and a pot. And we already had the fire...'

'Hey, that's terrific! I've been sitting here, thinking about the stuff I brought with me, wondering if I'd really managed to forget to bring along some coffee.' He winced. 'My stomach kept insisting it wasn't up to starting the day with half-raw steak.'

Holly laughed. 'I remember. You had two ways of grilling steak over an open fire. Burned to a crisp, or raw.'

'Hey, give a guy a break. Call it steak tartare and the price goes up, babe...' Nick shook his head. 'Sorry. I didn't mean to—I know you hate it when I call you—'

'It doesn't matter,' she said quickly.

'It does. There are so many things—'

'Nick.' Holly ran the tip of her tongue over her lips. 'Let's not do this, okay? The snow's stopped, the sun's out, and before you know it they'll clear the road and you can leave.' A smile seemed to tremble on her lips. 'So why don't we declare a moratorium on the recriminations and apologies for the next couple of hours?' Holly shifted her coffee cup to one hand and extended the other. 'Just two old friends, enjoying breakfast together. How's that sound?'

Impossible, that was how it sounded. They'd been lovers, not friends...

'Nick?'

Friends. It wasn't a bad idea. Maybe that was the way to find closure, once and for all.

Nick clasped Holly's hand in his. 'It sounds fine. Just give me a couple of minutes and I'm all yours.'

He wasn't all hers, not anymore.

Holly stood at the kitchen counter, cracking eggs into a blue ceramic bowl and listening to Nick's footsteps overhead.

What was he doing? Dressing, she hoped. One more look at his bare chest and she'd be lost.

One more minute in his arms, in front of that fire, and she'd have been worse than lost. She'd awakened, when he'd crept out from under the blankets to stoke the fire during the night, stunned to find that she'd been sleeping in his arms. She'd been on the verge of telling him she was awake, that she was going to make a bed for herself on the sofa, but then he'd put his arms around her, given her the most tender of kisses...

It had left her shaken, and silent.

A flush rose in her cheeks. You didn't exorcise the ghost of a dead marriage by sleeping with your ex-husband, no matter how sexy he was. And Nick was sexy, all right. She didn't have to be in love with him anymore to recognize that. Still, it wasn't desire she'd felt last night, lying in his arms. It was much more. Warmth, and comfort, and a sense of rightness and such deep well-being that—

'Hi.'

Holly swung around. Nick was standing in the doorway. Her heart tripped at the sight of him. This was the Nick she remembered, not a sophisticated man in an expensive trench coat and custom-made suit, but a guy who looked like an ad for outdoor living. He was wearing a turtleneck under a worn flannel shirt, faded jeans and leather hiking boots that looked even older than hers. There was a day-old stubble on his jaw, and a beat-up leather jacket hung over his shoulder from his thumb.

It was as if no time had passed. He looked gorgeous and just a little dangerous, the way he'd looked the first Christmas they'd come here…

And the last.

That last Christmas was the one she had to remember, when they'd finally admitted what each had known for months, that their marriage was not dying but dead, and that the only decent thing to do was give it a quick burial.

'Hi,' she said, and flashed a quick smile. 'I made some more coffee and the eggs are ready to go.' She smiled again, even more brightly. 'No bacon, I'm afraid, so you'll just have to make do with whatever I can whip up.'

'Over easy is okay with me.'

'Well, I have some cheese. And some cream. If you're feeling adventuresome…'

'That's right, I almost forgot. Cookbooks, you said.' Nick shrugged. 'What the heck? Surprise me.' He shrugged on his jacket and pulled a toothbrush from his pocket. 'Just give me five minutes to use the facilities…'

Holly laughed. 'You'll be back quicker than that.

I've already used the facilities. It's probably ten below zero outside.'

Nick grinned. 'Thanks for the words of warning, but you'll see. This is guy weather. I can handle it.'

'Yeah, yeah, yeah.' Holly grinned. 'That's what they all say.'

He came bursting through the door minutes later, snow sparkling on his hair and on his shoulders, with a pile of wood in his arms.

'You weren't kidding! Ten below is right.'

'Told you so.'

'Let me just dump this wood and then I'll set us up for breakfast on the coffee table, so we can stay warm beside the... Hey. You already did.'

He dropped the wood, straightened up, and put his hands on his hips. Holly had moved the coffee table so that it stood before the fireplace. She'd set two places, complete with linen napkins. A small basket stood centred between the settings, heaped with...

'Biscuits?' Nick said, looking up at her in amazement.

Holly blushed. 'I brought some leftover stuff, from home.'

'Leftover biscuits?'

'Uh-huh. I've been trying out new recipes, trying to zero in on what I want to do in my next book... Oh, for Pete's sake.' She sat down, cross-legged, before the table. 'Stop looking at me as if I'd just invented penicillin or something. Let's eat, before we both collapse from hunger.'

She served him something that looked like a cheese

omelette but tasted like heaven. It was either almost
as good as the light-as-air biscuits or maybe the biscuits were almost as good as the egg stuff. Nick
couldn't tell and besides, it didn't much matter. The
meal was incredible, all the more so because it had
been cooked over an open fire by a woman whose
only claim to culinary fame had been...

'*A Hundred and One Ways to Cook Hamburger.*'
Holly folded her linen napkin and smiled at him.
'That was my very first book.'

'You're joking.'

'Cross my heart. I'd been doing a column for a
magazine, and I'd done some pieces on inexpensive
meals for couples just starting out—'

'Dining on the Cheapside,' Nick said. 'Wasn't that
what we called it?'

Holly laughed. 'Yes. I mentioned that, to my editor,
and she really thought it would make a good title,
but—'

'But?'

*But I knew that I'd never be able to look at the
book without thinking of you...*

'But I was afraid it would sound too, ah, too flip.'
Holly reached for the coffee pot and refilled both their
cups. 'So, we went with something more straightfor-
ward.'

'And the cookbook was a success?'

She nodded. 'More than we'd expected. They'd
done an initial print run of 25,000 and they'd have
been happy with a fifty per cent sell-through, but—'

'Wait a minute!' Nick smiled and held up his hand.
'Can you translate that into English?'

'Oh. Sorry. Well, print runs can range from—'

She explained. Print runs. Sell-throughs. Wholesalers, and distribution, and dealers. And he listened. Tried to listen, anyway, but it was tough. This astute woman—this knowledgeable businesswoman—was the same girl who'd never balanced a checkbook in her life, until he'd shown her how.

'I never had a checkbook before,' she'd said, when he'd almost gone crazy the first time the bank had phoned to say their account was overdrawn.

'That's unbelievable,' he'd snapped. 'How could you never have written a check?'

'I charged things. I mean, I had accounts wherever I needed them.'

That was the first time he'd really understood how different they were. They weren't just a rich girl and a poor boy trying to make a marriage work, they were people from planets at the opposite ends of the galaxy, struggling to find a common language.

'I'm boring you.'

'What?' Nick blinked. 'Boring…? No. Not at all. I'm just fascinated by, you know, how you've changed.'

'I'm not eighteen anymore,' she said quietly.

He nodded. 'Seven years is a long time.'

'A lifetime.'

Nick cleared his throat. 'Are you—are you happy?'

'Yes.' Or, at least, she'd thought she was happy. Until the dreams. Until last night. 'Yes,' she said, and smiled brightly. 'I'm very happy. I love my work. And I love Boston. I've made lots of friends, and I've got this wonderful apartment... What about you? Are you happy?'

Nick hesitated. He hadn't hesitated a month ago, when a reporter on *This Week* had slyly posed him the same question. 'Of course I am,' he'd said.

'Nick? Are you happy?'

'Sure.' He smiled. 'Life's been good to me.'

'I know. I see the Brennan name everywhere. In fact, I stayed in a Brennan hotel the last time I was in Dallas on a book-signing tour.'

He grinned. 'And? Did it win the Holly Cabot seal of approval?'

His smile made it all right; there was no anger to the words this time, the way there'd been last night.

'Absolutely. Fresh flowers in the room, chocolate on my pillow at bedtime. Nothing was missing...' *Except you.*

The cup slipped from Holly's hand and clattered against the table. Coffee oozed over the polished wood.

'Here,' Nick said, 'let me—'

'No. That's okay.' She stabbed at the spill with her napkin, then got quickly to her feet. 'Well. I guess it's time to clean up. Why don't you take a pot of water from the kitchen and heat it over the fire so we can do the dishes?'

He nodded. 'Sounds like a good idea.'

He stood up, his gaze following Holly as she walked to the kitchen. There'd been something in her eyes, a moment ago. Regret? Pain? No. He was seeing what he wanted to see—and what did *that* mean, anyway? There was nothing to see, nothing to look for except that which he'd come for in the first place.

Closure. And, thanks to the storm, and the enforced intimacy of the long night, he had that.

He could leave today, knowing he'd made peace with his past, and with Holly.

Holly. Once she'd been his wife, and his lover. Now, at long last, she might just have become his friend.

And that would have to be enough.

'What've you got in this thing, anyway?' Nick grunted as he heaved the ice chest from the trunk of Holly's car. 'Rocks?'

'Supplies,' she said, hurrying ahead of him to open the door. 'Here. Put it on the counter.'

'Supplies, huh?' He groaned as he set the chest down and turned towards her. 'I brought "supplies", too. They didn't weigh enough to give a guy a hernia.'

'Well, I told you, I'm going to be staying a while. And I'm going to be working up some recipes. I've got a new book to write.'

Nick leaned back against the counter and folded his arms. 'One Hundred and One Ways to Cook Chicken?'

Holly laughed. 'More like a hundred and one ways to cook lobster.'

His brows lifted. 'People can dine on the cheap eating lobster?'

'I write for a different crowd now.' Holly wrinkled her nose. 'Two-income households, lots of money but no time to cook during the week, so they go all out on Saturday and Sunday.'

'Ah. Yuppies.'

'Or whatever they're called today. How about you?'

'How about me, what?'

'You said you had some stuff, too. Don't you want to bring it in?'

He shrugged. 'Is isn't much, just a couple of steaks. I left the box in my car. It's cold enough to keep and besides...'

'Besides, you'll be leaving soon.'

They looked at each other for a long moment, and then Nick smiled.

'Remember when we were here before?'

'Which time?'

'The first time,' he said quickly. 'There's nothing about the last time that's worth recalling.'

Holly nodded. 'I remember.'

'It snowed that first time, too.' His smile tilted. 'We had a snowball fight. And you said I cheated.'

'You did! You sneaked up behind me—'

'I hit you, fair and square.'

'Didn't.'

'Did.'

'Didn't! The rules were—'

Nick walked casually to the door and opened it. Holly saw what was coming, shrieked and feinted, but it was too late. He grabbed her, and the handful of snow he'd gathered slid icily down her collar and along her spine.

'That's a declaration of war, Brennan,' she gasped.

'Marquess of Queensberry rules,' he yelled, as they grabbed their jackets and ran outside.

'Street rules,' she yelled back.

'Give me a break, Cabot.' Nick dodged her first snowball. 'What does a poor little rich girl know about the street?'

'Plenty,' Holly said, and set out to prove it.

Half an hour later, they'd fought their way almost to the road.

Nick ducked behind a pine tree. A snowball whizzed by his nose.

'Enough,' he said, laughing. 'I give up, Cabot. You win.'

Holly stalked towards him. 'You'd better not be trying to fool me, Brennan.'

'Me?' he said, eyes wide and innocent.

She bent, scooped up a handful of snow, and kept on coming. 'I haven't forgotten how this started, with you jamming ice down my collar while we were still in the kitchen.'

'It was snow, not ice, and that was different.'

'Different, how?'

'Different, because I saw an opportunity and took it.' Holly yelped as Nick grabbed her and hoisted her up in his arms. 'Like now,' he said, laughing, and they tumbled down into a deep white drift.

She struggled to get away, but he caught her, rolled her on her back and straddled her.

'Give up?' he said, holding her arms above her head with one hand, while he scooped up snow with the other.

Holly gasped. 'No fair,' she sputtered.

'You called it war, Cabot. Anything's fair, in love and in war.'

'You're no gentleman, Nick Brennan.'

'And you're no lady, Holly Cabot.' He leaned forward. 'Say "uncle" or get your face scrubbed with snow.'

'Never!' Holly stuck out her tongue. 'I don't give up that easily.'

'Okay. You asked for it—'

Holly bucked as he leaned towards her. 'Nick. Nick, you rat...'

She laughed, and he laughed...and suddenly they were in each other's arms and their mouths were clinging together.

'Nick,' Holly whispered, 'oh, Nick!'

'Baby,' Nick breathed, 'my sweet, sweet baby.'

He flattened his hands on either side of her flushed, snow-chilled face and kissed her with all the bottled-up passion and desire of the endless years that had separated them. Holly wound her arms around his neck, kissing him back as she had so many times in her dreams.

'Kiss me,' she sighed, against his mouth. 'Kiss me...'

The sound was faint, at first, and had no meaning. It was a distant rumble, but it grew louder and louder.

No, she thought, no, please!

Nick heard it, too. He raised his head, listening. 'What in hell is that?'

Holly tucked her face against his shoulder.

'It's the plow,' she said, in a broken whisper. 'They're clearing the road.'

'No.' The word burst from his throat, harsh with anger and disbelief. He rolled over, sat up, and glared around him. 'I don't—'

'Look. Through those birches. Do you see it?'

Nick's breath left his lungs in one long rush. He saw it, all right. The plow had come, the road was clear.

It was time for him to leave, unless...

Holly reached out and touched her hand to his cheek. 'It's for the best,' she said softly. Her eyes glittered with unshed tears, but she smiled. 'There's no going back, Nick. We both know that.'

The hell we do, he started to say...but she was right. Time machines existed only in the movies, not in real life.

So he nodded, got to his feet and held out his hand. Holly took it and stood up beside him.

'You've got snow in your hair,' she said, and gently brushed it away.

There was a catch in her voice. He knew there'd be one in his, too, if he tried to speak. So he took her hand, instead, and brought her palm to his mouth. Hands clasped, they walked slowly to the cabin.

'I'll get my things,' Nick said.

Holly nodded. 'I'll wait here.'

He reached the top of the porch steps and looked around. Holly's back was to him but he knew she was crying.

'Get it over with,' he muttered, and reached for the door.

What was the sense in prolonging this? She'd spoken the truth. It was too late to go back. Miracles only came around once in a lifetime. They'd had theirs, and they'd tossed it away.

Determination got him through the door and halfway up the stairs to the bedroom—and then he stopped.

How could he leave her? They had just found each other again. Sure, they'd had their miracle, but who said you only got one in a lifetime?

Wasn't Christmas all about miracles?

Nick's jaw tightened. He'd never run from anything in his life, except his marriage. Now, he had a second chance. Okay, maybe it wouldn't work. Maybe by the time the weekend was over he'd be more than ready to admit that what they'd had was really gone for ever.

But how could he know that, if he left now?

He took a deep breath. All he had to do was convince Holly. And, dammit, that was what he was going to do...

'Nick?'

He turned at Holly's whisper. She was standing in the open doorway, looking up at him, her hair wet with snow, her lashes spiky with tears.

'Holly.' He came down the steps slowly, searching for the right words, for the right way to say them.

'Nick,' she said, 'oh, Nick, please, please, don't go!'

And then they were in each other's arms.

ability to think. Pleasure as Holly cup cucumber wine
Licking drop after drop and easing her through the first
mount. Her hands lifted behind his head... she on of
her feet against the back and kissed his chest, and he
felt tremor and

CHAPTER SEVEN

A MOMENT ago, Nick had been searching for the
words that would convince Holly to let him stay with
her.

Now, with her in his arms, words had no meaning.

At the beginning of their marriage, they'd never
been able to get enough of each other. Need had fed
on need; coming through the door at night, seeing
Holly waiting for him, he'd been gripped with such
hunger that there'd been times they hadn't even made
it to the bed before they were in each other's arms,
loving each other.

What he felt now transcended even that.

Desire hammered in his blood and roared in his
ears, until the universe was reduced to this moment,
and this woman.

His wife.

Nick cupped Holly's face and lifted it to his.

'Do you know what you're asking?' he said, his
voice a rough whisper.

Color flew into her cheeks. She slid her arms
around his neck. He felt her fingers curve into the hair
at the nape of his neck. She swayed forward, rose
towards him, so that they were breast to breast, hip
to hip.

'Yes. Yes, I know,' she said, as she kissed him.

The kiss drove away whatever remained of Nick's

ability to think. He swung Holly up into his arms, kicked the door shut and carried her through the silent house. Her hands linked behind his head; she buried her face against his neck and kissed his throat, and he told himself to hang on, hang on.

He took her to the blankets that had been their bed throughout the long night. The fire still burned on the hearth; the flames flickered and cast their soft glow over Holly's lovely face as he lowered her to her feet.

'I couldn't have left you,' he whispered, framing her face in his hands.

She caught his hand in hers, turned it to her lips and kissed the palm.

'And I couldn't have let you go.'

Nick bent his head and kissed her mouth. 'It's been so long, baby. And I've been so lonely without you.'

'Tell me.' Her eyes were dark, and deep enough to drown in. She laid her palms against his chest, letting the rapid beat of his heart pulse through the tips of her fingers. 'I need to know that I haven't been the only one—'

He silenced her with a long, deep kiss. She tasted just as he remembered, as sweet as honey, as dazzling as champagne. She made a soft, whimpering sound and pressed herself to him, fitting the soft curves of her body to the hard planes of his. He groaned, slid his hands down the length of her spine and under the waistband of her jeans, under her panties, cupping her warm flesh in his hands.

'Nick,' she whispered, 'Nick, please...' He curved his hands around her, sought and found the heat between her thighs. She gave a broken sob and said his name again.

'Tell me,' he said, because he needed to hear the words. 'Tell me what you want, baby.'

Holly caught her lip between her teeth. He was killing her with the touch of his hands, with the heat of his kisses. She was shimmering, glowing, turning into a flame more radiant than any that blazed on the hearth.

She drew back in his arms and looked up at him. 'Make love to me,' she murmured. 'Touch me. Kiss me, taste me…'

The primitive sexuality of her words shot through him like a pulse of flame. The girl he'd been married to would never have said such a thing. Sex had been incredible between them, but he'd always been the one who'd initiated it, who'd whispered words that had brought a blush to Holly's cheeks. She had been responsive, yes, but she'd never asked for anything.

Instinct warned him that she would not hesitate to ask, now. It made what lay ahead all the more exciting.

He unzipped her ski jacket and slipped it from her shoulders, doing it slowly, dropping his head to kiss her arched throat and brush his mouth over hers. Then he knelt before her and unlaced her boots. He slid them from her feet, one at a time; stripped off her socks; lifted each foot and kissed the tender arch, the delicate toes.

He undid her jeans, and they fell in a rough tangle at her feet. She stepped free of them, and he reached forward and drew her sweater over her head.

Now, she was almost naked.

Almost naked, before a man for the first time in so many years. Holly trembled at the realization. There'd been opportunities, but never the desire. What would Nick say, if he knew she hadn't been with a man since him?

Her own vulnerability terrified her.

Nick was just standing there, looking at her. Why didn't he say something? Do something? Once, he'd never been able to keep from touching her. Had the years wrought so many changes? Was she a disappointment, after all this—?

Her breath caught as he reached out and stroked his hand down her cheek, her throat, her shoulder…her breast.

'Holly,' he whispered. 'Holly, my love.'

Slowly, he opened the front clasp of her bra. Her breasts tumbled free and he saw her reach, automatically, to cover herself.

'No,' he said, and caught her wrists. 'Let me look at you.'

He could look at her for ever, if she'd only let him. She was so beautiful.

Creamy skin. Perfect, rose-tipped breasts. The cambered slope that led to the gentle rise of her belly.

He hooked his thumbs into her panties, slowly slid them down her hips. And he looked at her again, his eyes feasting on her breasts, on the graceful curve of her waist, the roundness of her hips, the golden delta between her thighs.

Need for her raced through him like a flood through a ravine. He whispered her name and gathered her into his arms, lifting her, cradling her, as she put her hands on his shoulders and opened her mouth to the heat of his.

'Yes,' she said, against his lips. 'Nick, please, oh, please…'

He wanted to slow down. For her sake. Hell, for his. It was just the way it was when they were kids, on that hot summer day they'd ridden his old Honda to Gailey's Pond and he'd undressed her, seen her, touched her for the very first time.

This was different. There was no rush…

With a ragged groan, Nick tumbled down to the blankets with Holly in his arms.

'Now,' he said, and his hands and hers fumbled at the zip on his jeans, freed his hot, aching flesh, guided it to hers…

He entered her on one long, hard, heart-stopping thrust.

She cried out and arched against him. His head fell back and he thrust deeper.

And, after so many years of being alone and apart, they were one.

When he figured he had enough energy to stand, Nick got up and took off his clothing.

Holly watched through half-lowered eyelids.

'Mmm,' she said. A smile played across her lips. 'Very nice.'

He flushed. She'd seen him naked a thousand times before. Still, there was the feeling that this was their first time together.

'All testimonials welcome,' he said, with a smile.

He came down beside her and took her into his arms. 'You're even more beautiful than I remembered.'

'Thank you.'

She said it so seriously that Nick's brows lifted. 'Thank you?'

'Well…' Holly blushed. 'Six years is a long time. I haven't gotten any younger, you know.'

'Ah. Well, that's true. I suppose a man can't expect too much from an old broad of twenty-five… Hey!' Grinning, he rolled her onto her back and pinned her hands gently over her head. 'You've got sharp elbows, you know that?'

'You haven't gotten any younger, either,' she said indignantly.

'Oh, yeah, I know it. My joints creak, my bones ache…it's a hell of a thing, to be pushing thirty.'

'You won't be pushing it for another three years,' Holly said, trying not to laugh. 'And, if it makes you feel any better you look pretty good for an old codger.'

'Just, "pretty good", huh?'

'Well, not bad.'

'You could try being a little more specific.'

'You're pathetic,' Holly said, lips twitching.

Nick waggled his eyebrows. 'A couple of minutes ago, you were whistling another tune, m'dear.'

'I don't know what you're talking about. For starters, I do not whistle.'

'Whistle, applaud, sigh…what's the difference?' He grinned. 'The point's still the same. You were pretty well pleased a little while ago.'

'What would you like, Nicholas Brennan?

Applause? You'll do anything to get me to stroke your ego!'

'Well, you can stroke that, too,' Nick said, with an evil leer.

Holly burst out laughing. 'You're impossible.'

His smile faded. 'And you're so beautiful you make my heart ache,' he said softly, and kissed her again, with sweet deliberation. 'I love you, Holly.'

Holly felt her heart turn over. She clasped his face and brought his mouth down to hers.

'Nicky,' she sighed, 'my Nicky...'

His mouth closed over hers, and the sweetness of their kisses yielded to the fierce hunger that they'd never forgotten.

'Nick,' she whispered. 'Oh, Nick, how I love you!'

The words, those sweet, sweet words he'd never let himself dare hope to hear again, shot through him like a flame. Nick rolled her beneath him, sheathed himself in her.

'Forever,' he said.

Holly's eyes fixed on his. 'Forever,' she whispered, as he began to move.

How could it be any other way? He was part of her, and she was part of him. That was the way it had been, the way it would always be.

Nothing would ever separate them again.

They slept, awoke long enough to make love again, and slept some more.

When they awoke next, the fire had begun to die. Nick fed it some wood while Holly, dressed in his flannel shirt and her wool socks, made a dash for the kitchen. She raced back, carrying a box of crackers, a jar of peanut butter, and a knife.

'I am freezing!' she squealed, burrowing under the blankets, and proved it by putting her icy feet against Nick's thigh.

'By God, woman, are you trying to freeze me to death?' Nick reached down, caught hold of her feet, and rubbed them briskly. 'I'd almost forgotten that you have no heating system of your own.'

'Complaints, complaints.' Holly bit into a peanut-butter-laden cracker, then held out the remaining half. 'Here. Maybe some food will improve your disposition.'

Nick grinned, bit into the cracker, and chewed. 'You're just trying to keep my energy levels up.'

'Oh, right.' Holly licked peanut butter from her fingertips and flashed him a smug grin. 'As if you have any energy levels left, now that I've had my way with you...' Her smile faded. 'Nick? It's as if the past six years never happened.'

'I know. We must have said these same things to each other a thousand times, and laughed whenever we did.' Nick leaned over and dropped a gentle kiss on Holly's lips. 'We had some good times, babe,' he said softly. 'Didn't we?'

'Yes.' She nodded. 'Yes, we did.'

'I have to be honest and admit that I'd pretty much forgotten the good times.'

'Well, so did I.' Holly shrugged her shoulders. 'I suppose that's only natural. I mean, when two people get a divorce...'

Her voice cracked. Nick frowned, hooked his arm around her neck, and pulled her close.

'That's all behind us,' he said.

'Is it?'

He felt, rather than saw, Holly's sudden hesitancy. 'Damn right it is.' His tone was gruff, almost harsh. 'What kind of question is that to ask?'

'A reasonable one,' she murmured, and looked down at her lap.

'The hell it is!' He clasped her chin. 'Look at me,' he said and, when she finally did, he glowered at her. 'I love you. You love me. What else matters?'

Holly shrugged. 'We loved each other the last time around, too,' she said, after a minute.

'Yeah, but we were young. Just a pair of kids.'

'We had problems, Nick. I don't think they had to do with our being kids.'

'Sweetheart.' Nick reached out and drew her into his arms. 'We got married without your parents' blessing.'

'They didn't try to stop us.' Holly shut her eyes and laid her head against Nick's chest. 'You know that. They even came to the wedding.'

'Yeah.' Nick gave a sharp laugh. 'Some wedding. You and me, standing in the office of a Justice of the Peace, you clutching a bouquet of supermarket flowers—'

'They were beautiful flowers,' she said softly.

'They were the only thing I could afford. Me in my one and only, super-shiny, too-short-in-the-pants, too-tight-in-the-shoulders blue gabardine suit.'

Holly smiled against his chest. 'You looked gorgeous.'

'Oh, yeah. I'll just bet. I know how 'gorgeous' I looked, baby. I could see it reflected in your old man's eyes.'

Holly pulled back and looked into Nick's face. 'My father's approval—'

'His disapproval, you mean.'

'Whatever you want to call it, Nick, that was never a problem for me.'

Nick sighed and drew her close again. 'Look, the bottom line is that everything was stacked against us. We were young, we came from different worlds, I was broke...' He lifted Holly's face and smiled at her. 'Fast-forward seven years. Here we are, young but not wet behind the ears. And I am a long, long way from being broke. As for those different worlds...' He grinned. 'Would you believe I've learned to eat raw clams without turning green?'

Holly smiled. 'I remember that. You were so sick afterwards.'

'Well, sure. Your parents invited us to dinner, your father ordered for us... How could I have told him I'd never in my life seen a clam outside of a can of chowder?'

Holly's smile faded. 'You could have. It wouldn't have mattered.'

'Not to you, maybe.'

'Not to him, either. I admit, he wasn't thrilled when I said I was marrying you—'

'An understatement, if ever I heard one.' Nick's smile was forced. 'Not that I blamed him. President of the biggest bank in town, member of the Chamber of Commerce... Hell, why would a guy like that want to see his daughter hook up with a loser?'

Holly pulled out of Nick's embrace. 'He never called you that,' she said fiercely. 'And I wouldn't have let him! You were never a loser.'

A muscle tightened in Nick's jaw. 'I know what I was then, baby. And I know what I am now.'

'Nick—'

'I know what I want now, too.' In one easy motion, he caught Holly and gently drew her down beside him. 'You, sweetheart, ' he whispered, and kissed her. 'You, in my arms, in my heart, in my life.'

The words were sweet, but all too painfully familiar. Nick had said them before, when he'd proposed all those years ago. Then the words had been filled with dreams and promise.

Where had it all gone wrong? When had the dreams died?

'Nick,' Holly said, 'we need to talk.'

'Later.'

'Nicky. I think—'

'I love it when you say my name that way.' His lips teased hers. His hands moved over her body, cupping her breasts, stroking her skin. 'I used to lie awake at night, after we split up, and sometimes I could swear I'd hear you whispering my name in the dark.'

Holly's breath caught as he bent his head and kissed her breasts. His lips closed around the nipple of one, then the other; his fingers drifted between her thighs.

Don't do this, a voice sighed inside her. Talk about what went wrong, or you'll be right back where you started seven years ago.

But this was Nick. Her husband, as much today as ever, because she had never stopped loving him. And she never would.

CHAPTER EIGHT

HOLLY didn't want to wake up.

The dream—this dream—was too sweet. The comforting weight of Nick's arm around her waist. The heat of his body against hers...

Nick stirred, murmured in his sleep. His arm tightened and he drew her back against him, closer into his embrace.

Holly smiled. She wasn't dreaming. Nick, the man she'd never stopped loving, was real.

Carefully, not wanting to wake him, she turned in his arms and studied his face. Everything about him was just as she remembered. The dark hair, tousled now by sleep. The black lashes, so full that they lay against his cheek. The nose, with its sexy little bend. The high cheekbones, so prominent in the pool of light cast by the lamp on the table beside the sofa...

Holly's eyes rounded. Lamplight? *Lamplight?*

'Nick!' She shot upright in their improvised bed.

'Mmm.' Nick reached up and lightly cupped her breast.

'Nicky. Come on, wake up.'

'I am awake, baby.' He clasped her shoulder and he drew her face down to his. 'Want proof?' he whispered, his voice raspy with sleep and desire.

'You're incorrigible,' she whispered back, but her smile belied her words.

225

Nick kissed her again, rolled onto his back and drew her close. He caught her hand, guided it to him. 'Is that the medical term for this condition, Doc?'

'Nick.'

'Mmm. That feels nice.'

It did. It felt wonderful. What she was doing to him, what he was doing to her…

'Nick.' Holly pulled free of his embrace, sat up, and gave him the sternest possible look. 'Here you are, fooling around—'

'Another medical term?'

'Fooling around,' she said severely, gently slapping his hand away, 'while I'm trying to give you important news.'

Nick sighed. 'We've landed men on Mars?'

'Nick, for goodness' sakes—'

'The power's back.'

'No! Honestly, you'd think…' Holly blinked. 'You know?'

'Uh-huh.' Nick grinned. 'The heating system went on with a roar about an hour ago.'

'And I slept through it?'

'Yup.' He sat up and threaded one hand lazily into her hair. 'C'mere and give me a kiss.'

'Why didn't you wake me?'

'What for? Besides, I doubt if anything could have wakened you.' He gave her a grin so sexy it made her pulse quicken. 'I can't imagine why, but you were out to the world.'

Holly blushed. 'Exhaustion,' she said primly. 'From that drive through the storm yesterday. You know. Delayed reaction.'

'A likely story.' Suddenly, his smile faded. He swept her hair behind her ears, then captured her face between his hands. 'It was incredible,' he said softly. 'Making love with you again…it was everything I remembered, and more.'

Holly smiled. 'I love you.'

'Again.'

'I love you. I love you. I—'

Nick kissed her. When he drew back, he was smiling.

'Do you remember the first time we made love?'

'How could I forget? We drove up to Cape Cod.'

'It was a moonlit night, in early fall. And the beach was deserted.'

'We went for a walk, down by the water.'

'And then into the dunes.' Nick's voice roughened. 'You said you were cold, and I put my arms around you.'

'You kissed me,' Holly whispered. 'And kissed me again.'

'And you slipped your hands inside my jacket, up under my shirt…'

Holly put her arms around Nick and kissed him. 'I've never forgotten that night.'

'That was the night I told you how much I loved you.' He looked into her eyes and smiled. 'I love you even more now, sweetheart. And I don't want to lose you again.'

'I don't want to lose you, either. But—'

'No "but"'s. We'll make it this time, baby.'

'Will we?' Tears glistened in her eyes. 'I couldn't bear it if we failed again, Nick. I couldn't!'

Nick kissed her mouth, her eyes, her tear-stained cheeks.

'We won't,' he said. 'I promise.'

She knew he meant it, but she knew, too, that a thousand things could go wrong between a promise and reality. They had to talk about what had separated them the first time…

But Nick was touching her, caressing her. After a while, there was nothing to say that couldn't be better said with kisses.

Nick shouldered open the front door. His arms were full of things: the carton of groceries he'd taken back out to his truck, his computer, his cellphone, his wireless fax. He dumped the stuff on the hall table, took off his jacket and ran his fingers through his hair.

It had started snowing again. He wondered if another storm might be rolling in, and smiled. Actually, he didn't much care. What could be better than getting snowed in with Holly? Ellen expected him back at the office first thing Tuesday morning, and yeah, there was business to attend to, but nothing—nothing—would ever be as important as the miracle that had happened here this weekend.

He'd come to North Mountain for closure, and he'd ended up winning back the only woman he'd ever loved.

A grin lit Nick's face. He peeled off his jacket, turned on his computer and set up the fax machine. Then he picked up the carton, and strolled into the kitchen. He had a feeling this wasn't quite what the radio shrinks had in mind when they talked about closure, but it sure as heck was good enough for him. Perfect, if you wanted to be accurate.

He paused in the doorway and looked at Holly. She was standing at the stove, stirring something in a skillet that was sending up clouds of fragrant steam. God, she was lovely.

And she was his.

He put down the carton, propped one hip against the table edge, folded his arms, and happily observed his wife.

She had the same effect on him today as she'd had when he was still a kid. She'd been so sweet and innocent…from the first minute she'd walked into his life, he'd wanted nothing more than to cherish her and protect her.

Now, at least, he could.

He knew why their marriage had failed. It was his inability to accept his guilt over having taken his beautiful Holly from a life where she'd had everything, to one where she'd had nothing. That was why he'd accused her of trying to play house, because it had killed him to see the change in her—a change that was his fault. Her graceful hands, reddened by housework. Her midnight-blue eyes, shadowed by worries over money. Her back, achy after hours spent hunched over the ancient sewing machine she'd rescued from God only knew where.

Oh, yeah. It had damn near killed him, all right, especially since he knew he'd stolen her from the life she deserved, one of grace and beauty and wealth.

It was guilt that had made him work a thousand hours a day, that had driven him to school at night so he could improve himself and improve their lives. It was his fault she'd lost her old friends, and been too weary to make new ones. No wonder she hadn't been as excited as he'd wanted her to be about his successes. What could he possibly have expected the night he came home all excited about winning a contract and she'd said she really didn't give a damn?

He'd thought it meant she didn't give a damn about him.

Nick shook his head. He understood now. What she'd really meant was that he'd neglected her. Well, he'd never neglect her again. Hell, he'd pamper her as she'd never been pampered, fill her life with luxuries, see to it that she had everything she could possibly want.

Love, swift as an avalanche, swept through him.

'Holly,' he said, and when she turned to him, her face lighting with as much joy as surprise, he was lost. He crossed the room with quick, purposeful steps, took the spoon from her hand and pulled her tightly into his arms. 'I love you,' he whispered, and kissed her.

'Wow,' she said, laughing when he let her breathe again. Her eyes were bright with happiness. It thrilled him to know he'd put that glow on her face. 'What did I do to deserve that?'

Nick grinned. 'It's not you,' he teased, 'it's whatever you're cooking up in that pan.' He leaned past her and took an exaggerated sniff. 'Man, oh, man, what is that? Some secret French sauce?'

'Oh,' Holly said with a coy smile, 'it's just something I whipped up.' She laughed, gently shoved him away, and turned off the gas under the skillet. 'It's drawn butter, you big jerk. For the lobster.'

'Ah.' Nick laughed. 'Well, that's pretty exotic.'

Holly smiled. 'You're right. After all, this is a special occasion.'

'Yeah.' He grabbed her around the waist, spun her towards him, and kissed her again. 'Darned right it is.'

An hour later, Nick stared in amazement at the pile of lobster shell fragments heaped on the plate between them.

'Tell me we didn't eat all that,' he said.

'Okay. We didn't.' Holly grinned. '*You* ate most of it.'

Nick slapped his hand over his heart. 'The woman's trying to hurt my feelings! Me? Eat all that lobster?''

'You liked it, hmm?'

'Liked it? I loved it.' Nick reached for her hand and twined his fingers through hers. ''Fess up, babe. That wasn't just plain old butter.'

Her smile broadened. 'You're right.'

'So, what was it?'

'It's a secret.'

He laughed. 'A secret?'

'Uh-huh.' Holly batted her lashes. 'You want to know what it is, you'll have to buy a copy of my next cookbook.'

'Which comes out…?'

'A year from July. Of course, I have to write it first, but—'

'No, you don't.'

'Sure I do.' Holly smiled and lifted Nick's hand to her lips. 'I have a contract that says so.'

'Contracts,' Nick said, dismissively. 'My lawyers will get you out of that.'

Holly's smile grew puzzled. Gently, she disengaged her hand from his and sat back.

'Why would they do that?'

'Because I'll ask them to. You won't have time to do that sort of stuff after we're married.'

'What sort of stuff?' she asked, after a pause.

'You know. This stuff. Mucking around in the kitchen.'

'Mucking around in the…?'

'Yeah.' Nick shoved back his chair, stacked the plates, and rose to his feet. 'I know you didn't do this for the money,' he said, as he scraped the leavings of their meal into the trash. He looked back and flashed her a smile. 'As if there could possibly be much money, playing around with cookbooks.'

Holly folded her hands tightly in her lap. 'Really?' she said, very calmly. 'And how would you know how much money there is, playing around with cookbooks?'

'Well, I don't know. Not exactly. But I figured—'

'You figured wrong,' she said, in that same calm voice, and then told him exactly how wrong he was.

Nick's eyebrows shot towards his hairline. 'Really?' He laughed and shook his head. 'Wow. I had no idea—'

'As for doing it for the money…do you build hotels for the money?'

'I don't build them, baby, I own them.'

'It was a figure of speech.'

'I know, but—'

'Answer the question, please. Do you build them for the money?'

Nick licked his lips. He had the sudden feeling that he was heading into deep water in a leaky rowboat.

'Well, sure. I mean, I like what I do. Hell, I love it. But—'

'But you like being paid, too. Surprise, Nick. So do I.' She smiled tightly. 'And, while we're on the subject, I've always liked what you'd probably call "mucking about" the house. Sewing. Cooking. Fussing.'

'Yes. I know that. I—'

'No. No, you don't know that.' Holly kicked back her chair and got to her feet. 'You never understood that I liked contributing what I could to our marriage.' She grabbed the salt shaker and pepper mill from the table, marched to the counter and slammed them down. 'Not money, but things that I hoped would make our lives more pleasant and take some of the burden, the worry about money, off your shoulders.'

'Sweetheart, that was generous of you. I'm only trying to point out that none of that is necessary anymore.'

Holly swung towards him, eyes flashing. 'I *hate* it when you use that condescending tone with me!'

Nick stared at her. What the hell was happening? 'Holly, baby—'

'My name is not Hollybaby! I might have been young when you married me, but I was a grown woman, not a—a starry-eyed Rapunzel, living in a tower, waiting for a man to come along and rescue me.'

'Hey.' Nick held up his hands. 'How about we take a deep breath and calm down?'

'I hate it even more when you patronize me!'

Holly spun back towards the sink and plunged her hands into the soapy water. Six endless years had gone by but nothing had changed. Oh, they were arguing, yes, instead of sulking in silence, but Nick still saw her as a helpless, spoiled little rich girl. All that was left, if time really was going to spin backwards, was for him to end this scene by saying he had work to do...

'Do you want help with the dishes?' he said, after the silence had become almost unbearable.

'No.'

He sighed. She didn't want anything, not from him. He could read it in the set of her shoulders. Damn if he didn't feel as helpless as he'd felt years ago, wanting to go to Holly and either kiss her or shake her until she understood that all he wanted was her happiness.

The only solution was to get himself out of here before one of them said something they'd regret.

'Fine,' he said. 'In that case...I'm going to get my computer. I have some work to do.'

Holly dumped a pot into the sink. Soapy water sloshed over the edge.

'Important work, I'm sure.'

'Yes. Of course it's—'

'Important. I know. After all, you don't deal in cookbooks.'

'Holy hell,' Nick roared. He stalked to the sink, clasped his wife's rigid shoulders, and spun her towards him. 'You're right. I don't deal in cookbooks. I run a Fortune 500 company, baby, and I'll be damned if I'll apologize for it!'

'Why would you? I'm sure the world turns at your command.'

'You never gave me any credit for what I did, Holly. Well, try this on for size. I've got the biggest deal ever in the works right now.'

'Imagine that,' she said politely. 'I'm just amazed a man of your importance would have chosen to rent a cabin like this for a weekend.'

'I didn't rent it. I own it.'

He saw, with bitter satisfaction, that that stopped her.

Her eyes widened. 'You own North Mountain?' she said incredulously.

'Damn right I do. I'm going to build a resort right here, where this cabin stands, that'll dwarf anything you've ever imagined.'

'You mean...you mean, you're going to take down this cabin?'

No. Hell, no! He knew it instantly. He wasn't. That was the reason he'd come to the mountain, to admit to himself that he'd never tear the cabin down...

Holly wrenched free of his hands. 'Good. That's wonderful news.'

'Holly, wait—'

'Burn it down, why don't you?' Her heart felt as if it were breaking in pieces, but she'd be damned if she'd let him know that. 'That's the best way I know of to get rid of ghosts.'

'Ghosts?' he said in bewilderment.

'That's why I came here, Nick. Because, lately, I was plagued with memories. I couldn't seem to stop thinking about us. About our marriage.'

'I know. Holly—'

'No. You don't know. You *never* knew.' She spoke quickly, running her words together, despising herself for letting herself think she still loved him, knowing she'd despise herself even more if she let him see her cry. 'Our marriage was a mistake. I always knew that but I guess I just needed reminding.' She lifted her chin and forced a smile to her lips. 'Thank you for providing it.'

Her words knifed through his heart. 'No.' He pulled her into his arms, though her body was stiff and unyielding. 'You don't mean that. Think of how it was between us, just a little while ago. The things we said, the things we did…'

'Sex,' she said. Her voice trembled, but her eyes were steady on his. 'That's what it was, Nick. And it's not enough. It doesn't make up for a lack of love.'

Nick's face whitened. His hands slid from Holly's arms and fell to his sides.

'Closure,' he said softly.

'What?'

He didn't bother answering. What was there to say, when the woman you loved confirmed your most painful suspicions? She'd never said she didn't love him before, not even when they'd agreed to divorce. But he'd always known there'd come a time she'd look at him and realize that their marriage, that *he* had been a mistake.

That time had finally arrived, and there was nothing more to say.

He made his way into the living room, unplugged his computer, snapped it shut and tucked it under his arm. Then he slung on his jacket, stuffed his cellphone and the fax into his pocket and glanced up the stairs. His suitcase was up there, but he didn't give a damn about something so trivial. A couple of more minutes in this place and, despite his pain, he'd do something stupid, like telling Holly that he still loved her, would always love her, whether or not she'd ever loved him.

He heard Holly's slow footsteps behind him.

'Nick.' Her voice was low and shaky. 'Nick, I'm sorry…'

'Yeah.' He pulled the door open. 'Me, too.'

The door swung shut, and Holly was alone.

CHAPTER NINE

NICK took a hard right as he came down off the mountain and swung into the gas station with tyres squealing.

The station looked deserted. He got out of the Explorer and put his hands on his hips.

'What kind of a place is this?' he growled. 'You can't sell much gas if you're never open for business.'

A bell jingled behind him. Nick spun around and his mouth dropped open. An old man was coming down the steps from the office. But it wasn't the owner of the station. Hell, no. This bozo had white hair down to his shoulders, a big moustache and a bushy white beard. His red cap was trimmed with a perky white tassel; he had on shiny black boots and a bright red suit.

'Santa Claus?' Nick said, with an I-don't-believe-it laugh.

'Aye-up.' The old guy swaggered towards Nick. 'It's Christmas Eve, you know.'

'Is it?' Nick shrugged. 'I guess I forgot.' He looked the old man over from head to toe. Just went to prove that you could never trust anything. Who'd have figured this character would go in for Christmas hype? 'What's with the outfit?'

'Been doin' it for near onto twenty years. You want this thing filled up?'

'No, the gas is fine. But I've got a long drive ahead of me and the light on my dash says my oil's running low.'

'Don't want that to happen, especially with a new storm comin' in.'

'Yeah, that's what I thought.'

Santa cocked an eye skyward as he opened the hood of the Explorer.

'Storm'll be here late tonight. Good thing you came down from the mountain or you'd have been snow-bound for a week.'

'Yes, I know. I...' Nick frowned. 'You remember me?'

'Oh, aye-up. Remember you well. Bought extra gas, some bags of sand...didn't need any of it, I take it.'

'No. No, the road was passable.'

'And you decided not to stay, hmm?'

'That's right. I...' Nick looked at the old guy. 'I never said I was going to stay.'

'Aye-up, that's true enough. Let's see...you're a quart down. Regular, or the extra-expensive stuff?'

'The extra-ex...' Nick laughed. 'Regular. Regular's fine.' He tucked his hands into his pockets. 'So, you put on this outfit every Christmas?'

'Just about.'

Nick smiled. 'And does it sell extra gas?'

'Does it...?' Santa shook his head. 'Don't do it for that. I'm headin' over to the home down on East Main. Been turnin' up there every Christmas Eve for the past—'

'Twenty years,' Nick said slowly. 'You mean the Hunter Home for Boys, right?'

'Aye-up, that's it.'

'Man, but it's a small world! I grew up there. You used to show up at Christmas and give us each a toy.'

'Uh-huh.'

Nick smiled. 'Wow. You were the best thing that happened to me all year.'

Santa shut the hood of the vehicle and wiped his hands on a bright red rag. 'Thought as much, from the way you climbed up on my knee one time when you were maybe five or six, and whispered your one wish in my ear.'

Nick blanched. 'You couldn't remember that... Oh. Oh, of course. It's what all the kids did, right?'

'"Give me somebody to love,"' you said. Remember?'

There were a couple of seconds of silence, and then Nick gave a little laugh. 'Amazing,' he said, 'that we'd all have made that same wish.'

'Then, when you got too big to climb on my lap, you said you had another wish.'

Nick's smile faded. 'I suppose you remember that, too.'

'"I want to make lots of money when I grow up,"' you said.' The old man looked into Nick's eyes. 'Well,' he said softly, 'your wishes came true, son. I just hope you managed to figure out that money can't buy happiness but it sure as heck can get in the way of it.'

Nick stared into Santa's blue eyes. They'd seemed

faded with age yesterday but now—now they were bright, and clear, and bottomless.

'I found happiness,' Nick said in a choked voice. 'But I lost it.'

'Lost it, or misplaced it? There's a big difference.'

Nick shook his head. 'Lost it. I was a damn fool. I let the woman I loved—the only woman I'll ever love—think that my becoming successful was the most important thing in the world.'

'Wasn't it?' Santa asked softly.

'No! Hell, no. She was the most important thing. She still is. She'll always be. It's just that...' He swallowed dryly. 'I wanted to give her everything she'd given up, to marry me. It killed me to see her doing things she'd never had to do in her life, scrimping, sweating, counting pennies just to keep us going...'

'Ah. I see.' Santa nodded thoughtfully. 'So, while she was supposed to be grateful you were knocking yourself out to give her everything, she was also supposed to understand that you didn't want her to give you anything in return.'

'You don't understand. I'm not talking about turning away her gifts. I'm talking about not wanting to watch her work. She sewed, she cooked, she cleaned...'

'She made you a home,' Santa said quietly. 'And you didn't want it.'

'No!' Nick's hands knotted into fists at his sides. 'God, no! Of course I wanted it. I wanted her. I wanted...I wanted...'

And suddenly, after all the years and the sorrow, he saw it all. How Holly had tried to give him tangible proof of her love and how his own stiff-necked pride, his damnable ego, had made him blind to those tokens of the heart. How he had rejected her offerings again and again...

How he'd rejected them tonight.

Nick whisked his wallet out of his pocket and peeled off a bill. He pressed it into Santa's mittened hand.

'Does that cover the oil?'

Santa looked down at the bill and his bushy brows lifted. 'Ten times over. Just wait a minute while I get change.'

'No. I don't want change. In fact...' Nick opened his wallet again, pulled out half a dozen bills, and stuffed them into Santa's hand, too. 'Buy some more toys for the Boys' Home. How's that sound?'

Santa grinned. 'Sounds just fine.'

'Good. Great. Terrific.' Nick grinned, too. Then he patted the old man awkwardly on the back. 'Thank you,' he said, as he slid behind the wheel of his Explorer. 'For everything.'

'You're welcome.' Smiling, Santa watched as Nick pulled out onto the dark, deserted road. His smile broadened when the vehicle suddenly stopped, then roared into reverse.

Nick put down his window. 'Santa?'

'Yes?'

Nick smiled. 'Merry Christmas.'

The old man chuckled. 'Merry Christmas to you, too, son. And to that sweet young woman you left up on North Mountain.'

Nick's brow furrowed. 'How did you...?'

'Got to get goin',' the old man said, and just at that moment a sudden snow flurry swept through the station, obliterating everything in a whirl of white. When it had passed, the old man was gone, and the station lights had winked out.

Nick stared at the darkened gas pumps. Then he took a deep breath and swung the Explorer across the highway, back towards North Mountain.

Holly sat, cross-legged, in the middle of the bed.

The wind was howling wildly around the cabin; snow pattered against the windows. It was the kind of night to curl up by the fire, to lie in the arms of your lover...

She blinked back her tears.

What an idiot she'd been, to have thought she and Nick might have had a chance at being happy. He was so full of himself, of his plans, his successes...

She jumped at the sudden, piercing shrill of the telephone, then stared at it as it rang again. Who'd call her here, especially tonight?

Her heart thumped and she snatched up the phone.

'Nick?' she said.

'Holly?' It wasn't Nick. The voice was too deep. 'Holly,' it said again, and then the instrument went dead.

Great. This was just what she needed. Another storm building, a telephone that wouldn't work...

The phone rang again.

'Hello?' Holly said, jamming it against her ear.

A chorus of metallic shrieks and whistles poured

through the receiver. Holly winced and held the thing away from her ear.

'Is anybody there?' she shouted. 'You'll have to speak up, whoever you are. I can hardly hear you.'

'Holly? It's...linda.'

'Who?'

'It's me. Bel...'

'Belinda?' Holly frowned and switched the phone to her other ear. 'I don't think this connection's going to last. Why are you calling? Is there a problem?'

'No. No prob...' Static crackled like lightning. '...hello. And to tell you...idea.'

'An idea? What kind of idea? Listen, this phone's going to die any second. If you called for a reason, you'd better get to it.'

'I just...wonderful new recipes yet?'

'No. But I will.' Holly frowned. 'Belinda? Your voice is so deep. Are you okay?'

'I'm fine. Just...flu. There's...going around.'

'Well, you sound awful. Not at all like yourself. You ought to make yourself a toddy. Hot, buttered rum is—'

'Holly. Listen to me. I've had...book.'

'What?' Holly shouted. 'I can't hear you.'

'I said, I have an idea for your next book.'

Holly blinked. That was certainly unusual. Belinda didn't know a thing about cooking, or cookbooks. The success of their relationship had to do with Holly's talent and Belinda's contacts, not her expertise. But then, this entire conversation was unusual. The static. The howling wind. The surprising depth of Belinda's voice.

The faint hint of a New England accent?

Holly swung her legs to the floor and sat up straight. 'Belinda? Belinda, is that really—?'

'...book for...marrieds.'

'Marrieds? What does that mean?'

'...cookbook. For...newly-weds.'

A cookbook. For newly-weds? Holly rolled her eyes. Of course, this was Belinda on the phone. Who else would come up with an idea that had been done to death?

'There are a hundred books like that,' she said. 'One-dish meals, quick meals, easy meals... I really don't think there's a market there.'

'...with advice. Know what I mean?'

'No, I don't know what you mean.' Holly's frown deepened. 'You really should see a doctor. Your voice is so strange, it's, well, almost masculine. It's kind of spooky.'

'Holly. About the book—'

'Belinda.' Holly pinched the bridge of her nose and took a deep breath. 'Look, it isn't that I don't appreciate your efforts. It's just that I've had a long day. It snowed up here, and—and you were right, I shouldn't have come at all, and—'

'A recipe on one page, a bit of advice on the other,' Belinda said.

Holly sighed. 'What kind of advice?' she said wearily, because it was becoming obvious she'd never get Belinda off the phone until she heard her out.

'Are you sure you can hear me clearly now, Holly? I want to make sure you get all of this.'

'Yes. Actually, for some reason, you're suddenly coming through just fine.'

'Good. As for the sort of advice you could offer— how's this? You'd ask your readers, "Is your husband working longer hours than you think he should? Is he less appreciative of the things you do around the house than you think he should be?"'

'Honestly, Belinda…'

'"If he is, perhaps you need to consider things from his viewpoint. If he grew up poor, and you grew up rich, he probably feels guilty about taking you away from that lifestyle."'

Holly got off the bed. 'Belinda? What is this?'

'"Maybe he's overcompensating. Maybe he's working harder than he should to try and give you the things he thinks you deserve."'

'Wait a minute. Wait just a darned minute! Who is this?'

'"Maybe, when he sees you sewing curtains, and cooking hamburger in a zillion different ways, he sees only that he's condemned you to a life of drudgery."'

'Who *is* this? I know it isn't Belin—'

'Aye-up, maybe he's behaved badly, Holly, but if he has, it's only because that boy loves you with all his heart.'

There was a gentle click, and then a buzz, and Belinda's voice—someone's voice—was gone.

Holly stared at the phone and then, very carefully, put it down. Who could have known so much about her? About Nick?

Her throat constricted.

Who could have been so right?

Why hadn't she seen it? It wasn't that Nick was self-centered, it was that he blamed himself for not having been able to give her the things she'd grown up with.

'Things,' Holly said bitterly. As if 'things' mattered, as if Nick weren't the only thing that mattered, the only man, the only love of her life.

'Holly?'

Holly's head came up. 'Nick?' she whispered.

It couldn't be. She had to have imagined his voice.

'Holly. Where are you? Holly, sweetheart...'

She raced from the bedroom and through the hall. Oh, it was true! It was Nick, coming up the stairs.

'Nick,' she said, and when he looked up and saw the joy on her face he knew everything would be all right.

'Holly,' he whispered, and a second later they were in each other's arms.

A little before midnight, the snow stopped. The stars came out, burning fiercely against the blackness of the sky, and a big white moon hung over North Mountain.

Holly, snug in her husband's arms, turned her face to his.

'I love you, Nicholas Brennan,' she said.

Nick kissed her. 'And I love you, Mrs. Brennan. For richer, for poorer, in sickness and in health...'

'Forever,' Holly whispered, and they kissed again. After a moment, she put her head on his shoulder. 'Will it bother you? My career, I mean.'

'Bother me? Sweetheart, I'm proud of you. I can't wait to tell everybody I know that my wife writes cookbooks.' He grinned. 'I might even buy a couple, and learn how to cook—if you'll agree to give me private lessons.'

Holly laughed softly. 'Absolutely—if you'll take me along on some of your business trips.'

'Come with me on all of them—although there won't be so many, now. I've got some damn good people working for me. I don't have to be involved in every detail of running Brennan Resorts.' His arms tightened around her. 'I don't want to be, baby…I mean, sweetheart. Not anymore.'

'Actually,' Holly said dreamily, 'I love it when you call me "baby".' She touched her fingers to his lips. 'It's sexy. And it makes me feel protected.' She snuggled against him, and then she cleared her throat. 'Nick?'

'Hmm?'

'I know this sounds weird, but—did you call me on your cellphone this evening? Before you got here?'

Nick shook his head. 'I tried. I wanted to tell you how much I loved you, and what an idiot I've been…'

'What idiots we've both been,' Holly interrupted.

'But your line was busy.' He sighed. 'It's probably just as well. I might have said the wrong thing and you'd have told me not to bother showing my face.'

'No. I'd never have told you that. Not after I spoke with— with…'

'With whom?'

Holly frowned. It was a good question. Who'd telephoned her tonight? Belinda? In her heart, she didn't think so. But if it hadn't been Belinda or Nick…

'Somebody who gave me some good advice,' she said.

'I had a conversation I'm grateful for, too.' Nick laughed. 'You'll never believe it, but this old guy was all dressed up as--'

'Nick! Nick, look!'

Holly and Nick turned towards the window. Something was moving across the face of the moon. Figures. Tiny figures. One, two, three, four...

'...five, six, seven, eight,' Nick said in hushed tones.

Holly stared, transfixed. 'And that,' she whispered, 'that looks like a sleigh. Nick, do you see it? And—and there's someone driving it. He's waving to us...'

A cloud swept in, obscuring the moon. When it passed, the silhouette was gone.

Nick gave a shaky laugh. 'Snow geese. That's what it probably was. Snow geese, flying across the night sky.'

'Snow geese,' Holly said, letting out her breath. 'Definitely.'

Nick smiled. 'Merry Christmas, wife.'

Holly smiled, too, as she went into his arms. 'Merry Christmas, husband.'

'Aye-up,' the wind whispered, as it curled around the snug little cabin. Off in the distance, the sweet, haunting sound of sleighbells rang out across the mountain.

YULETIDE
REUNION

Sharon Kendrick

Dear Reader,

Think of Christmas and images come crowding in fast as an express train. Gifts and mince pies; carols and midnight mass; glittering tinsel and the scent of pine. The wondering faces of children searching the night sky, looking for Santa.

But mostly Christmas is about love.

Whether you're by a log fire while snowflakes fall outside, or eating a turkey on a blazing beach—everyone wants somebody to share the joys of the season with.

And falling in love at Christmas has its own special kind of magic....

Merry Christmas!

Sharon Kendrick

CHAPTER ONE

THE first time Clemmie saw Aleck Cutler, she knew she had to have him.

There was only one tiny obstacle in the way—he just happened to be dating someone else at the time.

Worse. He might only be eighteen years old, but apparently he was serious about the girl. Everybody said so. Very, very serious.

Clemmie didn't believe them. Not at first. People didn't get married at eighteen, for goodness' sake, so it couldn't be *that* serious, could it? Okay, people could fall in love at eighteen, but they didn't generally get *married*. What would be the point?

And anyway, Clemmie thought, staring hard at her fountain pen. He couldn't possibly be in love with Alison Fleming, even if he thought he was. Because that wasn't part of Clemmie's life plan. He was going to fall in love with *her*, just as she had fallen love with him the first time she saw him. When he had held the door open for her and said, 'Hi,' his greeny-blue eyes crinkling at the corners as he gave her the most irresistible smile imaginable.

It was like being touched by magic—there was no other way to describe it. And if Aleck hadn't realised yet what was as obvious to Clemmie as the writing on the wall—namely, that they were made for each other—well, he soon *would*!

Clemmie gave a great sigh as she glanced down at the open textbook in front of her. She was bored; that was the trouble. She had been bored for a whole month—ever since she had joined the sixth-form of Ashfield High. A month of trying to get used to a new house, a new town, new school, new stepfather...

Clemmie bit her lip and picked up her pen to write, but found herself unable to concentrate and put it down again almost immediately. She stared out of the window across the school playing fields. It wasn't as though she didn't *like* her stepfather— she did. Dan was a good man, who loved her mother, and her mother deserved that love. Clemmie's father had died when she was little, and it had been a real struggle for her mother. It was just...

Clemmie sighed once more as she retied the ribbon at the end of one thick, shiny plait. Did the two of them have to be quite so ecstatic about each other all the time, and in front of *her*?

It wasn't that they were constantly pawing at each other, or kissing, or anything like that. Just that sometimes the way her mother gazed at Dan, and the way that he gazed back at her—well, it just made Clemmie think she shouldn't even be in the same building, let alone the same room!

The school was fine, too, if she was being honest, and much more relaxed than the city school she had been used to in London. It had a good academic reputation and it wasn't too big, though it had lots of playing fields where you could walk at lunchtime and lose your soul up into the sky. And the other girls in her year were friendly. The boys, too, thought Clemmie, wincing; some of them had been *very* friendly.

Except for Aleck Cutler, of course.

Apart from that one blinding smile on her first day, he had remained cool and polite and indifferent.

He was in the year above Clemmie, and the unrivalled star of the school. He was the kind of person you wanted to hate because he was so perfect, but ended up sighing over. He loved sport and hated books, but he had the best grades in his year. He never showed any personal vanity whatsoever—in fact, he never seemed to bother what he looked like—yet he never looked anything other than thoroughly delectable, whatever he was doing. Covered in mud and wearing a pair of short-shorts, he attracted large audiences of swooning schoolgirls who normally couldn't tell one end of a rugby ball from the other!

He lived on his parents' farm on the edge of Ashfield, and he worked there every weekend and all through the holidays—and the hard, physical work made him fitter and tougher than anyone else of his age.

He was wonderful in just about every way, Clemmie had decided. In fact, there was only one blot on the landscape, and that was Alison Fleming, his girlfriend.

Clemmie had found out as much as she could without seeming too obvious. The facts were simple. Aleck had been going out with Alison Fleming for six months, and in that time he had not looked at another female. Worse was to follow. Alison Fleming was very beautiful, with pale, turquoise eyes and a mass of honey-coloured hair which always hung in an immaculate gleaming bell to her shoulders.

Clemmie did everything in her power to get Aleck to notice her, motivated by a deviousness she'd been unaware she possessed. She hung around unobtrusively until she saw him leave the building—with or without Alison—and then she would saunter along home on the opposite side of the road, with her long red-brown hair flying wildly and her skirt rolled over twice at the waistband so that it showed yards of long, stockinged leg.

She joined the School Debating Society, of which he was the Chairperson. The only problem being that whenever he was in the room all Clemmie's brilliantly thought-out arguments went straight out of her head, and she stared at him, totally tongue-tied. It certainly put her off a career in public speaking!

But as time went on, and the end of the year approached, Clemmie gradually began to accept that maybe the love affair she longed for just wasn't meant to be. Aleck would be leaving soon, and going off to university. And not alone either—but with Alison. He obviously just wasn't interested in any other girl. Although sometimes, *sometimes*,

Clemmie could have sworn that she had seen him giving her a hard, slanting look from beneath the dark lashes which shaded those amazing blue-green eyes of his.

It might have all died a quiet death had it not been for the night of the Summer Ball on the last night of term, which was thrown in honour of all those who were leaving the school. Clemmie didn't particularly want to go—seeing Aleck for the last time, with his arms draped around Alison, would be like subjecting herself to the most awful form of torture.

In the end, she was persuaded to go by her mother.

'You *must* go, Clemmie.' Hilary Powers frowned at her daughter. 'You're always complaining that there's nothing to do around here, and now you're turning down the opportunity to go to a really nice dance!'

Clemmie turned her mouth down. What could she *say*? That she'd fallen hook, line and sinker for a man who was besotted with someone else?

'And I'll give you money for a new dress,' smiled Dan. 'How about that?'

Clemmie couldn't win.

She bought a dress which was absolutely beautiful but left very little to the imagination. A black silk slip dress, beneath which she could wear only the briefest of black lace thongs.

'Do you like it?' she asked her mother.

Her mother screwed her face up and looked at her daughter. Pale face, too many freckles, dark hair spilling down like mahogany satin—gorgeous! But

the *dress*? 'I'm not sure, darling. It's a bit revealing.'

'Gee, thanks, Mum!' scowled Clemmie. 'You do
wonders for my confidence!' What *was* it with
mothers, sometimes?

'Are you wearing a bra?'

'I *can't* wear a bra—it shows!'

'Then I'll lend you my black chiffon wrap,' said
her mother briskly. 'You can throw that round your
neck and look slightly more decent.'

Clemmie got ready with Mary Adams from her
year, the two of them standing giggling and shaking
with nerves as Clemmie swept unfamiliarly thick
mascara onto her dark lashes. She was so nervous
that she accepted a glass of wine from the cask in
Mary's fridge, and then another. By the time she
arrived at the dance she was floating, *floating*—and
danced with every single boy who asked her.

Too giddy and too excited to eat, she glugged
back a glass of the fruity punch she was given and
tried not to look at Alison Fleming, who was de-
mure and stunning in virginal white. While Aleck
looked like the only real man in the room, his height
and build and bearing making him seem like warm
flesh and blood, while the others all looked like
cardboard cut-outs.

Clemmie was on her way back from the rest
room, moving slightly unsteadily along the corridor
with her eyes glittering darkly against the dead-pale
of her cheeks, when she saw Aleck.

He was standing with his back to her, standing

perfectly still by the window of an empty, unlit classroom. His old classroom.

Clemmie drew in a deep breath of longing. She should go straight past. He wasn't interested. He had a girlfriend.

But the wine and the punch had loosened her tongue and this was probably the last time she would ever see him.

'Hi,' she said recklessly, standing illuminated in the bright light of the corridor.

Aleck turned round slowly, his eyes flickering over her in a way she didn't quite understand. If he was surprised to see her, he didn't show it. But then, his face rarely showed anything, and it certainly didn't now.

'Hi,' he said coolly.

Clemmie gulped and walked over to stand beside him at the window, which overlooked the tennis courts and the soccer pitches beyond. She wondered what this school would be like next year, with no Aleck Cutler to gaze at, to think about, to fantasise over... It didn't really bear thinking about.

'So,' she said, and stared out into the night as her eyes grew accustomed to the darkness. 'What are you looking at?'

He gave a small laugh, then shook his head. 'Nothing.'

Clemmie felt bold. 'Yes, you were!' she teased. 'I saw you.'

He found himself smiling reluctantly. She was as exuberant as a puppy. 'Okay, then,' he admitted. 'I was just looking out at that old house. See?'

She followed the direction of his eyes but she knew which house he was talking about. The tumbledown house which dominated the town. From her bedroom window in Dan's house, Clemmie would look down at the overgrown lawns, the flowerbeds which were choked with weeds. In autumn, the fruit fell from the apple and pear trees, lying ignored and rotting on the ground. It was a sad house, she had often thought. A neglected house. 'You mean the old grey one? Isn't it supposed to be haunted?'

He shook his head. 'I don't believe in all that stuff! It's only spooky because no one's lived in it for years.'

'I wonder why?' she queried softly.

Aleck looked at her, finding her ridiculously easy to talk to and yet sensing some unknown danger in the air. 'Because it's big. And it's run-down—you'd need serious money to update it and run it. People with that kind of money don't generally want to live in a small town like Ashfield.'

'But you do?' she asked perceptively.

He shrugged. 'Maybe.'

There was silence for a moment, though Clemmie could hear her heart booming out in a muffled thud. She saw the pensive set of his profile. 'Feeling sad?' she asked softly.

He narrowed his eyes suspiciously, like a man not used to being quizzed about his feelings. 'Sad?'

'About leaving.' She noticed that he wasn't looking into her eyes any more, just staring very hard at her silky black dress, and that a tiny muscle had begun to work in one cheek.

There was a pause. 'A little. Closing a chapter of your life is always sad.' He gave a low laugh, and abruptly turned his attention away. But not for long. He looked back into her eyes then, and Clemmie felt drawn in by the magnetism of that cool, mocking gaze. 'Though maybe nostalgic would be a better word.'

'Yes.' Clemmie giddily swept her fingers back through her thick red-brown hair, so that it spilt in mahogany streams all the way down over her silk-covered breasts. Dizzy with wine and longing, she tried to think of something interesting and original to say, and failed dismally. 'Will you be sorry to leave?' She leaned back to perch her bottom on the wide window-ledge and smiled at him.

The movement distracted him as much as the invitation in her eyes, and Aleck found his eyes drawn once again to the pale gleam as her breasts thrust heavily towards him. He felt the slow, insistent throbbing of desire start to build up, felt it begin to pulse powerfully through his veins. 'Sure, I'll be sorry,' he said, in a husky voice that didn't sound like his own at all. 'There's a lot I'm going to miss.'

Drunk with the heady delight of his proximity, with the obvious appreciation in his eyes, Clemmie found herself purring like a parody of a sex-symbol. 'And what are you going to miss most?'

Aleck felt his muscles tense as she lounged back negligently on the window-ledge. She might as well have been naked for all that dress was covering her up, the two inverted vees of the bodice taut and stretched as they struggled to restrain the lush

young breasts. The silk lay smoothly against her
flesh, except for where he could quite clearly see
the outline of some outrageously flimsy G-string.
Aleck swallowed. 'Well, I'll miss seeing you,' he
told her, in a throaty whisper.

Clemmie opened her dark eyes even wider, her
surprise completely genuine. '*Will* you?'

'Sure, I will.'

'I didn't think you'd even noticed me,' she told
him honestly.

He gave a hollow guilty laugh, as Alison's memory slipped from his mind like sand through his fingers. 'Not *notice* you?' he demanded unsteadily.
'Oh, come *on*. You'd need to be blind or pretty stupid not to notice *you*, Clemmie…'

His face gave him away.

Clemmie could see the fight that was taking place
within him, yet she was too trapped by desire to
heed it. Too flattered by the look on his face which
must have mirrored her own. A look she had
dreamed of, night after night, but never thought she
would see in the flesh. Compelled by a need she did
not recognise, she put her hands up behind her head
to cushion her head on her palms, and the action did
even more to accentuate her breasts. 'You do say
the nicest things,' she smiled.

Appalled at his behaviour, and yet unwilling or
unable to stop himself, Aleck took a step towards
her. Why not just give her what she so obviously
wanted? What *he* so obviously wanted, too. 'Do I?'
he murmured. 'I don't just *say* the nicest things,
Clemmie, I do them as well…'

He moved his lips towards hers, and Clemmie wondered if she had imagined the dark note of warning which had coloured the throaty whisper of his response. But then his mouth was covering hers and the effect was like lighting touchpaper.

He showed none of the finesse of the Aleck of her dreams, just pulled her into his arms and began a kiss which was so shockingly intimate and so unbelievably sensual that Clemmie felt she should have been outraged by it. Yet she found herself kissing him back as though she had been born for just this moment.

He pulled her closer, so close that her lush silken-covered breasts were crushed against his chest. God, he could feel those nipples digging into him like tight little rocks. He couldn't help himself, and just briefly brushed his fingertips over each straining mound, expecting her to slap his face. But she didn't.

She couldn't. The moment he touched her, she was lost. His. Submerged and drowning in silky-dark erotic waters. She knew that she shouldn't be letting him do this, that she should be pushing him away, insulted—but instead Clemmie nearly died with pleasure when he touched her breasts. The wine and her loneliness and the overwhelming emotion she had felt for Aleck Cutler since the moment she'd first laid eyes on him, all combined to become the most potent, sensual cocktail of her young life.

His mouth was still on hers as his thigh pushed its way insistently between hers, his fingers now straying beneath the silk of the bodice itself until they alighted on each exquisitely aroused nipple and he circled the bare skin of each painful peak with erotic triumph.

'Clemmie,' he moaned into her mouth.

'W-what?'

'God, you're so *beautiful*,' he managed to get out, from between gritted teeth.

Her head tipped back as he kissed her neck. 'No, I'm n-not...'

'Beautiful,' he contradicted, still in that dazed kind of voice. 'And I want you. Do you know that? So badly.'

'I want you, too,' she gasped in wonderment, and laced her fingers into his thick dark hair.

His hand moved to the pert curve of her bottom, cupping each silk-covered buttock with a groan, and he was just about to slide the slithery material up, so that he could touch her legs and beyond, when the brief and rapid sound of footsteps heralded a third person's arrival and the room was thrown into bright light.

Bedazzled, they sprang apart—just in time to see the Head of Science standing by the light switch, with a whole gaggle of giggling fifth-formers just behind him.

'Good evening, Cutler,' he said stonily. 'Perhaps you and Miss Powers would like to come to my office. I think that a little talk is probably long over-due. Don't you?'

Clemmie looked up into Aleck's face. For a split second their eyes connected, and in his she could read the unmistakable message of self-disgust and outraged recrimination.

And she knew then why mothers always warned their daughters about being too easy. Because Clemmie would have done anything to be able to remove that look of seething contempt from Aleck Cutler's beautiful eyes.

CHAPTER TWO

'MOM, Mom—*Mom*! Is this really, *really* our new home?'

Clemmie laughed and looked up from the packing case she was hunting through. Where *was* the wretched kettle? She smiled into the excited face of her ten-year-old daughter. 'Yes, Justine,' she smiled. 'It really, really is!'

'And did I come here when I was very little?' Justine sat back on her heels and looked up at her mother.

'Yes, you did. You wouldn't remember. It was where Grandma used to live—'

'With Grandad Dan?'

'That's right.' Clemmie lifted the bright blue kettle out of the packing case with a look of triumph. 'There—found it! Why don't you go and get your sister and bring her down, and then we'll all have a break?'

'Is there any cake?'

'Ginger cake, if you're very good!'

'Whoopee!' shrieked Justine, and scooted off to find Louella.

Clemmie looked around her at the empty room, still trying to take everything in, wondering why her life never seemed to chug along comfortably like everyone else's. Not that she was complaining. Not now. Not with this lovely house to call her own. A home at last, after a long time searching.

Clemmie sighed, remembering the man who had brought her and her mother so much happiness. *Dear* Dan. Because he'd been her stepfather she had not expected him to love her. But he *had* loved her, loved her as much as if he had been her own father. And yet...

When he died, she had somehow expected him to leave the house to one of his blood relatives, not to her. There had been a nephew somewhere, an elderly aunt somewhere else. And it wasn't as though she'd seen a lot of him. Her visits from the States had tended to be when she could afford them, which hadn't been very often. And after her mother had died she hadn't had the heart to come back to Ashfield at all.

Clemmie's mother had died six years previously, and—judging by his letters—Dan had never seemed to get over that. Yet when they'd rung Clemmie in America, to tell her that Dan himself was seriously ill, she had damned the expense, jumped on a flight and come straight over. He had died that same day, gratified that the woman he had looked on as a daughter should have been there to hold his hand while he slipped away...

Clemmie had flown back to the States—to her two beloved daughters and the realisation that she could no longer live in the small American town where her life had broken down so dramatically. Something was going to have to change...

Dan's legacy had come like a bolt out of the blue,

and a welcome one. The house and enough capital
to live on for a little while. A life-saver. A new
beginning. A new life in England.

Clemmie's divorce had left her even more broke
than she'd been before, scrubbing around to make
ends meet in a country where suddenly, without her
American husband, she was a foreigner. A foreigner, moreover, with foxy dark eyes and a curvy
body. The kind of woman universally feared by
other, not-so-happily-married women...

So she had packed the three of them up, lock,
stock and barrel, and moved them back to Ashfield.
Back to the town where she had spent two fractured
years before going off to college, her whole view
of the place coloured by her ill-advised passion for
Aleck Cutler. What a gullible little fool she had
been!

Part of her had wondered about coming back at
all, but it had only been a small part. Women in her
position had little choice about where they lived.
She was happy, and grateful for Dan's legacy, and
strangely drawn to Ashfield. In spite of her youthful
mistakes, it was the only place where she felt some
affinity with the past. And with such an uncertain
future lying ahead of her, Clemmie needed to hang
onto that feeling right now.

Clemmie boiled the kettle and made tea, then cut
slices of dark, sticky gingerbread and laid them out
in a pattern on the plate. The frantic thump, thump,
thump of feet on stairs heralded the arrival of her
two daughters, and as Clemmie carried the tray into

the sitting room she gave them a slow smile of contentment.

They looked as fresh as daisies, she thought proudly, and not as though they'd stepped off a transatlantic flight just hours earlier. They were, quite simply, the lights of her life.

For, no matter what else she achieved in her life, she had done this—and mostly on her own, too. Produced two beautiful, intelligent and charming little girls—though she conceded that she might be a little biased! Now she had to raise them to be happy. Nothing else really mattered.

'Mummy, I've chosen my bedroom!' sighed Justine. 'It's *really* cool!'

'Why does she always get to choose first?' complained Louella, scowling.

'Because I'm ten and you're only eight!' crowed Justine.

'But it's not fair!'

Clemmie bit back the temptation to inform her younger daughter that life often *wasn't* fair—she didn't want to turn her into a cynic at such a tender age! 'Don't you like *your* bedroom, Louella?' she asked softly. 'It's the one that *I* used to have when I lived here. It isn't the biggest, but it has the best view in the house, in my opinion.'

'It's neat,' nodded Louella, so that her waist-length brown plaits jiggled up and down. 'I can see right over the wall to that big garden at the back— the one with the swimming pool. And there was a girl there, playing on a *swing*.'

'Was there?' asked Clemmie absently, pouring out the tea.

'I waved at her—and she waved back!'

'That's nice, darling.'

'So would she be our nearest neighbour?'

'Yes, she would.' Clemmie handed over a thick slice of cake and watched while Louella took a bite. 'It's good that someone's living there at last—it was empty for years and years.' And then fragments of a long-ago conversation swam up to the surface of Clemmie's memory, and Aleck Cutler's perfect eighteen-year-old face imprinted itself there.

She shook her head, trying to get rid of it, wondering why the recollection still had the power to shake her. Because there could be nothing more pathetic than a woman of twenty-nine carrying a torch for a man who was married to someone else.

And Aleck had married Alison.

'It's not *really* like moving somewhere completely new, is it, Mom?' observed Justine slowly. 'Since I guess you must still know lots of people here?'

Clemmie shook her head. She still wore her thick, red-brown hair long, but most days, like today, she didn't have time to do any more with it than drag it back into a ponytail. 'Not really, honey,' she said softly. 'I left when I was eighteen, so I kind of lost touch. Friendships don't thrive unless you invest time in them, and I never really had the time. I went away to college and then—'

'Then you met Dad?' asked Louella brightly.

'That's right,' agreed Clemmie steadily, and kept

her face poker-straight. It was difficult, she had decided, to be a mature and generous human being where her ex-husband was concerned, but she was trying. Oh, Lord, how she was trying! She understood that it was in a child's nature to love its parents absolutely, as Justine and Louella loved their father. But Bill had let the girls down so many times over the years, whittling away at that love every time he did so, that Clemmie had to force herself to say anything positive about him.

'And once I went to the States to live with your dad, then I didn't get to visit very often at all.'

'So you don't know very much about Ashfield, Mom?' asked Justine thoughtfully.

'I know where the church and the shops and the schools are—but that's about it! I'm relying on you two to find out where all the excitement is—think you could do that for me?'

'You bet!' grinned Justine.

The three of them sat on the floor, drinking their tea and eating cake. Clemmie was reluctantly thinking about unpacking another case when there came the sound of a girl's voice, calling, 'Hello?'

Justine and Louella looked at one another excitedly before springing to their feet and running into the hall.

'Our first visitor!' smiled Clemmie, as she followed them out, and then her mouth dried as she stared at the young girl who was standing on their doorstep.

She looked about ten, the same age as Justine, but she was tall for her age, with pale hair which fell neatly to her shoulders and pale, creamy skin. But it was her eyes which made Clemmie's mouth fall open in an unconsciously shocked reaction.

Greeny-blue mesmeric eyes, fringed with thick dark lashes. There could not be another pair of eyes in the world which were that beautiful. Clemmie swallowed. This was Aleck Cutler's daughter, she realised, with a certainty which astonished her almost as much as her own heart-racing reaction.

'Hello,' said Clemmie, hoping that her voice didn't betray her shock. 'Are you our new neighbour?'

'I am,' answered the girl politely, in a remarkably grown-up voice. 'I live in the house at the back. I'm Stella Cutler.'

So she had been right! Clemmie felt her nails, concealed in the back pockets of her jeans, dig hard through the denim into the soft flesh of her buttocks, while the world threatened to sway intolerably before righting itself once more. Aleck's daughter! *Here!*

'I'm Clemmie Maxwell. I used to be Clemmie Powers. And this is my daughter, Justine.' Clemmie swallowed as she indicated both her daughters. 'And her sister Louella. Say hi, girls!'

'Hi!' the two chorused shyly.

'We were just having a tea break, Stella,' continued Clemmie, trying to behave as she would normally behave if a young neighbour came to call. 'Can you stay for a while and join us? Or do you have to get back?'

'Oh, I can stay,' said Stella quickly.

'Shouldn't you check with your parents first?' Clemmie forced herself to ask.

Stella shook her blonde head, her face curiously lacking in emotion. 'No, that's okay. I was home alone—so there's no one there to ask. But I'd *love* some tea,' she added winningly.

'Well, then, tea it is!' Clemmie led the way into the sitting room and wondered if she had suffered some kind of emotional block all those years ago. Why on earth was she feeling so disorientated just because Aleck's daughter had come to visit? He was a guy she had had a mad crush on and they had shared a kiss *twelve* years ago! Nothing more than that. So why was she making such a big deal out of it?

'Our mom makes *fantastic* cake! You should see what she does for our birthdays! She makes rainbow frosting that tastes like heaven!' Louella was confiding to Stella, her freckly face so like Clemmie's as she babbled away excitedly.

'Are you American?' asked Stella curiously.

Justine shook her head. 'Our dad was—*is*,' she corrected herself hurriedly. 'But he still lives in America, with his new girlfriend and their baby, and we live here now! But that's where we grew up, and that's why we've got accents. Do you suppose we'll get teased by the other kids?'

Stella shook her head. 'No way! All the girls will be jealous! If you speak with an American accent everyone thinks you're a movie-star over here!'

'You're kidding?'

'No, I'm not!'

Clemmie left them chattering while she went to refill the kettle, but before it had begun to boil she heard footsteps on the stairs and Justine shouting, 'We're taking Stella upstairs to show her round. Is that okay, Mom?'

'Okay, that's fine!' Which would give her time to tackle some of these boxes...

Clemmie began to unpack the cases which were stacked haphazardly all over the kitchen floor, humming to herself as she did so. She had been torn—wanting to bring every single stick of furniture with her, mainly so that the girls would feel safe and surrounded by the familiar, but there had also been a side to her which had wanted to throw everything away. To start anew—without any objects which would remind her of Bill and the marriage she had struggled so long to sustain.

In the end she had just brought their favourite things—the good set of china which had been a wedding present, the rocking chair which Bill had carved for her in the early, happy days, and some small Shaker knick-knacks she had collected over the years. Amazing, she thought, as she pulled a jug out of the case and carefully peeled away the protective paper from it. You could spend ten years of your life in another country, and come back with very little to show for it.

Just two gorgeous daughters and a fierce determination to steer clear of men! Men were nothing but trouble and heartbreak. Men chewed you up and spat you out.

Even so, it seemed a rather cruel irony that

Clemmie was now faced with the prospect of having to confront Aleck and Alison Cutler over the garden wall!

Still, she told herself briskly, as she placed a vase on the window-ledge. She had survived isolation and desertion and infidelity in a foreign country— she was damned sure that she could endure seeing her schoolgirl crush and the woman he had courted and married!

The morning seemed to fly by, so that Clemmie was able to accomplish plenty. She spent much of it wiping down the walls and the paintwork. She might think about giving each room a lick of paint once the girls had gone back to school.

Having Stella certainly helped keep them out of Clemmie's hair, and she seemed like a very self-contained child. She had organised Justine and Louella into tidying up their giant doll's house, and when Clemmie had stuck her head round the door a couple of minutes ago it had been to see three heads bent over it in industrious play!

At one-fifteen Clemmie washed her hands, put the kettle on, and was just thinking about getting some lunch for them all when there was a loud and peremptory knocking on the front door.

She stole a quick glance at herself in the mirror and grimaced at her jeans and old yellow tee-shirt, wishing that she'd made a bit more effort. She wasn't best dressed to impress any of her new neighbours! Her dusty hair could do with a wash, and her face was completely bare of make-up, which only drew attention to the freckles which spattered her nose and cheeks and which were the bane of her life.

She pulled the front door open and the welcoming smile froze on her lips as she realised the identity of the man who stood so tall and so broodingly on her doorstep. Clemmie stared up at Aleck Cutler.

Twelve years was a long time in anyone's life—particularly the years between eighteen and thirty, when adolescents became adults—but all Clemmie could think about was how the essential characteristics of the man remained unaltered.

He was even taller, yes, and he had filled out, that was for sure. The snake-hipped teenage Aleck had been transformed into a big, strong man with hard, firm flesh and shoulders so wide you felt you could have rested the world there. Just a few silver strands ran through the abundant thickness of his dark hair, but the eyes were as remarkable and as mesmerising and as vibrant as they had been all those years ago, and Clemmie felt her face suddenly grow heated...

'A-Aleck!' she stammered. 'Aleck Cutler!'

He stared at her, but made no greeting in response. Just clipped out coldly, 'So it's true. You're back.'

If his eyes hadn't been spitting unfriendly fire, Clemmie might have smiled. As it was, the hostile vibrations she was getting from him made her stiffen her shoulders defensively. 'Obviously,' she responded, her own voice chilly.

'Have you got my daughter here?'

'Y-you mean—Stella?' she managed, stung and confused by his combative air.

'Since I only have one daughter—yes, I *do* mean Stella,' he told her with icy emphasis.

Clemmie could tolerate all kinds of things, but rudeness was not one of them. Years of being insulted within a failing marriage had reinforced her determination never to let a man treat her that way again. She stared at him. So he could wipe that disdainful look off his face right now!

'Yes, she's here!' she snapped back. 'And how was I supposed to know that you only have one daughter? Telepathy isn't one of my particular talents!'

He looked at her properly then, the green-blue eyes taking their time as they slowly surveyed her from head to toes, and Clemmie was left feeling as though they had stripped her bare.

'No,' he said carefully. 'As I recall you had many talents, Clemmie, but telepathy wasn't one of them.'

'Just what are you implying?' she demanded, furious at that critical look on his face, and even more furious at the unconscious quickening of her heart when she realised that he *did* remember her name.

He gave a disparaging smile. 'Oh, you surely don't need me to spell it out for you, do you?'

'Oh, I do,' she mocked sweetly. 'I can't *stand* innuendo! So if you've got something to say, Aleck, why don't you just go right ahead and say it?'

He raised his dark brows so that they slanted in arrogant surprise. 'You mean relate the simple fact that if we hadn't been discovered, then we probably would have ended up making love—with you straddled over one of the classroom desks, your panties down by your ankles?'

All the heat drained from Clemmie's face—she was so shocked and horrified by his crude portrayal of what had actually happened. What a way to *put* it! 'How can you say something like that?' she whispered, in a hollow voice. 'How *can* you?'

He shrugged, apparently not bothered by her white face, nor her trembling mouth. 'How can I not? It's what happened, isn't it, Clemmie? Or would you prefer to define the episode as true *love*? Maybe that's how you usually justify your behaviour to yourself—I don't know.'

He managed to make the word 'love' drip with such venomous sarcasm that Clemmie stared at him in horror. 'But it was just a kiss!' she protested.

'Really?' His eyes narrowed alarmingly. 'Is that what it was? Some kiss! Do you normally let men who kiss you for the first time touch your breasts like that, Clemmie?'

She wanted to hit him. Because at least hitting him would detract from the way her body responded when he said 'touch your breasts'. How could he? How *could* he? Her fingers itched to claw at him in some frighteningly primitive way, but to do that would be to compound his opinion of her as some emotional loose cannon.

'Why are we discussing something which happened twelve years ago?' she demanded, swallowing back her lust and her anger and attempting to transform them into dignity.

'I thought that was what you wanted,' he observed. 'You were the one who persisted with the subject, weren't you? After all, I came over simply to fetch my daughter—'

'Then I'll go and find her,' said Clemmie tonelessly.

'Before you do, Clemmie...' He lifted his fingers and, annoyingly, Clemmie found herself halting in her tracks. 'Didn't it occur to you that I might be worried? Didn't you consider ringing me to say that Stella was here?'

'Of course I did!' she defended. 'And Stella *told* me that it was okay! She told me that she was home alone—'

'She was *not* alone!' he shot back repressively. 'I was working in my study, and she was probably bored and saw you arrive. She's ten years old, for God's sake—didn't it occur to you to check with me first?'

The trouble was that he was right. She *should* have checked, should have got Stella to ring her father, or should have done so herself. She hoped that he would have done the same if her girls had turned up unexpectedly at *his* house. And she wondered if she would have been so reluctant to ring if the father in question had been anyone other than Aleck Cutler...

He threw her a look that was distinctly insulting. 'Though maybe you decided that it would suit you to have her stay so long.' His eyes glinted. 'Was that it?'

'And why would I do that?' she queried steadily,

her heart pounding away in her head as she began to realise just what he was getting at.

'Maybe you were hoping that I would come looking for her and...'

'And what?' she goaded, needing to hear him say the unbelievable.

'And maybe you wanted to finish off what we started all those years ago?'

Clemmie came closer to hitting someone than she had ever done in her life, but she fought the feeling as if she was fighting for her life. She was not about to start brawling like a fishwife! She managed a tight, supercilious smile. 'I don't think so, Aleck. I grew out of teenage fumblings a long time ago. Besides, even if I *was* still turned on by heavy petting—I've always made it a rule not to fool around with married men.'

His eyebrows disappeared into the thick, dark hair as he feigned surprise. 'Really? Then you *must* have changed, Clemmie, because you had no qualms about flinging yourself at me then, did you? Knowing all the while that Alison was waiting for me.'

Clemmie swallowed, acknowledging that he was speaking the truth, and yet... 'You're very good at abdicating responsibility, aren't you? You could have just said no, Aleck,' she told him coldly. '*You* were the one in a relationship—not me! And you were the one who made the first move, as I recall. You kissed *me*!'

He smiled, but his eyes were Arctic-bleak. 'So I did, but who wouldn't, in the circumstances? There are very few men who would pass up the chance of a beautiful, scantily clad girl offering herself on a plate the way you did, Clemmie.'

Clemmie finally snapped; she couldn't help it. She raised her hand and flew it at his face. But if she was fast, then Aleck was even faster, and he imprisoned her wrist with his hand, bringing her right up close to him in the process so that his eyes were a viridian haze away. They blazed fire and desire, but something else, too. Something very like animosity.

She could feel his breath on her face, warm and sweet, while her own was being sucked into her lungs in short, rapid bursts, as if she had been drowning and had suddenly found air. Just the touch of his hand where he held her wrist was enough to make her heart thunder with excitement, and Clemmie knew then that Aleck Cutler still had a unique and frightening physical dominance over her.

And she was *not* going to give in to it!

Men had tried it on again and again since her divorce, each and every one of them assuming that if she hadn't got a husband then she must be desperate for sex. So desperate for it, in fact, that she would accept a quick grope in the back of a saloon car from men whom she thought looked as though they'd landed from Mars.

But Aleck was not like that, she recognised...

Aleck was different.

Aleck was a temptation, but he was also a married man.

'Let me go,' she said quietly, and to her astonishment he did exactly that. Dropped her hand quite unashamedly, a look of mocking combat in the blue-green eyes. And Clemmie realised that it was all a game to him.

'Does your wife know you tantalise women like this?' she taunted, on a whisper. 'Your eyes promising them all kinds of alluring things? Will you rush home to finish what you started here?'

His face went deathly white, his mouth narrowing into a thin, angry line. She saw his fists whiten with tension, saw the stiffening of his powerful frame, and Clemmie suddenly felt wary, wondering what he was about to do next. And she wondered how she would respond...

'Get Stella,' he ordered in a low voice. 'Get her *now*!'

'Oh, I'll get her, don't worry,' said Clemmie, swallowing down the panic of her reaction to him and squaring up to stare at him proudly. 'And you just stay away from me in future, Aleck Cutler—do you hear?'

Their eyes met.

'Yes, I hear,' he said softly. 'But this is a small town, Clemmie, you know that. You'll be seeing me around the place—that's unavoidable. You shouldn't have come back to Ashfield if you can't stand the reality of that.'

'I can't stand the reality of married men who come on as strong as you just did!' she snapped, and saw the light in his eyes wither contemptuously.

'I'll wait outside,' he said abruptly, his face as cold as stone.

Clemmie watched as he roughly pulled the door open, and slammed it hard behind him.

Three pairs of feet clattered down the stairs behind her. Startled out of the disturbing nature of her thoughts, Clemmie turned round to see the three girls, their faces alarmed as they jumped the last few steps to land beside her.

'Was that my father?' Stella asked, chewing anxiously on her bottom lip. 'Is he angry? Why did he storm out like that?'

'What's the matter, Mum?' asked Justine, frowning. 'Why has your face gone so pale?'

'I...I felt a little tired, th-that's all,' said Clemmie quickly, before bending down to look at Stella. 'You'd better go and find Daddy. He didn't know you were here, did he?'

Stella shook her head, close to tears. 'I didn't tell him! I thought he might not let me come.'

'Why would he not have let you come, Stella?' asked Clemmie in a low voice.

The child shook her blonde head distractedly. 'Because he swore when he heard you were coming back!'

'Oh, did he?' queried Clemmie softly.

'I should have told him that I was coming over!' babbled Stella.

'Well, yes, you should—and you always will in future, won't you? Now go on,' said Clemmie gently, straightening up to open the front door. 'Go and sort it out with him. It'll be fine—you'll see.'

'Th-thanks,' said Stella, and ran outside to find her father.

Clemmie bit down on her lip to urge a little colour back into her face, then pinned on a bright smile before facing her daughters, hoping that she didn't look as freaked out as she felt. Explanations were the last thing she felt she could cope with right now. 'So did you have a nice time playing with Stella?'

Justine screwed her nose up, recognising that Clemmie's question was intended to change the subject and ignoring it completely. 'Mommy, why *did* Mr Cutler storm out like that?'

Louella turned her little face up, her clear blue eyes innocent and curious. 'Yes, Mummy, why did he?'

'It's—er—difficult to explain,' Clemmie hedged, as she struggled desperately to think of something suitable to tell them. 'I knew him vaguely years ago, and we didn't really get on that well then. Seems like nothing has really changed!' she finished, her face one of bright determination.

'Was he upset about his wife?' asked Justine.

Guilty colour rushed to her neck. 'His *wife*?'

'Yes,' said Louella. 'His wife died. Didn't he tell you? He hasn't got a wife, and Stella hasn't got a mummy.'

CHAPTER THREE

CLEMMIE could hardly believe what Justine and Louella had just told her. She stared at them very hard.

'Mr Cutler's wife is *dead*?' she repeated, as though saying the words aloud might make them seem more believable. 'Are you *sure*?'

Justine gave her a look which made her appear far older than her ten years. 'Mummy,' she said reprovingly, 'people don't usually lie about things like *that*, do they?'

Clemmie shook her head distractedly. 'No, no— of course they don't,' she agreed. 'It's just that it's...it's...'

'What, Mummy?' asked Louella.

'Such a shock, that's all. She must have been very young. When did she die? Did Stella say?'

Justine looked uncomfortable. 'Well, no. And we didn't like to ask—'

'Of course you didn't!' Clemmie flung her arms round both girls and hugged them both extra tightly. Poor Alison, she thought sadly. To miss out on her daughter growing up. Oh, why on earth hadn't Aleck *said* something?

Clemmie's stomach churned with embarrassment as she remembered the way she had taunted him

285

about his wife at home. Why hadn't he told her then? Had he been too angry? Or too hurt?

She shuddered as she recalled the things she had implied, and was half tempted to run straight after him, to pour out her apologies to him now, while the wounding things she had said were still fresh. But she forced herself not to act impulsively. She was a grown woman now, not a kid of seventeen. It would only confuse her girls, and probably upset Stella into the bargain, and that was the last thing she wanted to do.

Instead, she resolved to say something quietly to Aleck when she next had the opportunity to see him on his own. She would tell him that she was genuinely sorry that Alison had died. And he could make of it what he wanted.

With a fierce determination fuelled by the need for survival, Clemmie pushed all thoughts of Aleck out of her mind while she spent the next few days settling in. In a way, it was good that there was so much to do. The phone to be connected. The post redirected. She had to sign on with the doctor and the dentist, and register the girls at the local junior school. She was fortunate that there were places for them both, and they would enrol next week, at the start of the new term.

The leaves on the trees were already beginning to turn golden, and the air held the tang of woodsmoke and the sharp bite of early autumn. Clemmie looked around the house which Dan had left her, realising just how much needed doing.

Every window in the place needed new curtains.

Dan had obviously let the place go after her mother had died. It wasn't as though Clemmie wanted new curtains simply because the pattern of the old ones didn't appeal—just that they were so old and moth-eaten they didn't really serve any useful function at all! Fortunately she could sew, so all she needed was to hunt around for some cheap material.

She also needed to decide the best way to earn them some money—Bill was sending the barest minimum towards his daughters' upkeep, and Clemmie knew her ex-husband well enough not to hold her breath if it didn't arrive...

And when she had sorted out their immediate needs, she also needed to make some friends in the town—for her daughters' sakes as much as her own. As they grew older, the last thing they wanted was a lonely mother who relied on *them* for company! Clemmie winced as she remembered her encounter with Aleck. She hadn't got off to a very good start, had she?

She used the last of her savings to buy Justine and Louella their school uniforms. Clemmie thought how gorgeous they looked as they stood in the out-fitters, giggling excitedly in the brand-new green and gold clothes. They had not had to wear uni-forms to school in the States, and the novelty factor had a lot to do with their approval of the bottle-green pinafore dresses, the pale lemon shirts and the green and yellow striped ties.

She could have bought them second-hand, but a stubborn pride made her refuse to even consider it. The girls had enough stacked against them in any case. They were children of a broken marriage, living in a strange country and having to start a new school. The last thing Clemmie wanted was for them to stand out like sore thumbs in hand-me-down clothes. She would sooner go without herself than allow that to happen...

She was just waiting for the girls to get changed when she heard a hesitant voice behind her. 'Clemmie? Clemmie Powers?'

Clemmie turned round, frowning as she stared at the woman in front of her who had spoken. She looked about the same age as Clemmie, her face vaguely familiar through the fine lines of age.

'It *is* you! I heard you were back!' the woman said. 'You don't remember me, do you? I'm Mary Adams, and we—'

'Got ready for the end of year dance round at your house?' smiled Clemmie. 'Of course I remember you! How *are* you, Mary?'

Mary smiled. 'I'm fine. Married with a seven-year-old son who keeps growing and growing—hence all these new school clothes!' She held up several bulging carrier-bags as illustration. 'How about you?'

Clemmie kept her face cheery, despite the inevitable feelings of failure that her marriage had not survived. But time and time again she told herself that it was not her *fault*. She had tried her best, but her husband had liked other women and hadn't seen why a wife should cramp his style! For the sake of her daughters, she had swallowed her hurt pride and suggested counselling, but Bill had told her emphatically that counselling was for 'suckers', and that had been the end of that.

'I have two beautiful daughters,' she told Mary proudly. 'But no husband—he's in America and we're divorced. I inherited my stepfather's house, and here we are—to stay!'

Mary looked rueful. 'Well, at least you've travelled further than I have and seen a bit of the world!' she said. 'I never moved out of Ashfield.'

'Well, there's a lot to be said for continuity,' observed Clemmie wistfully. 'And you've put down good, solid roots.'

They looked at one another and laughed.

'We sound like a mutual admiration society!' smiled Mary.

'Strong case of the other man's grass always being greener?' giggled Clemmie.

'You've got it in one!'

A car drew up outside the shop front and tooted its horn, and Mary looked over her shoulder. 'Typical! That's my husband—why do men always turn up when you don't want them to? And there's a double yellow line outside, so I'd better run! Listen, why don't I give you my number?' She took paper and pen out of her shoulder bag and scribbled down some figures. She handed the piece of paper to Clemmie. 'Why don't you come over for a drink one evening?'

'Oh, I'd love that,' said Clemmie fervently. 'I don't really know a soul in Ashfield!' Unless you counted Aleck Cutler, of course. And Aleck didn't really count...

Clemmie dropped Justine and Louella off at school on the Monday morning. She stood at the school gate watching them go in, thinking how young and vulnerable they looked in their brand-new uniforms. But they waved their hands at her in an exaggerated fashion and she was gratified to see excitement rather than apprehension on their faces. She watched as a teacher took them off to the playground to join the others, and soon they were lost among a sea of bobbing heads. Their new life in England was beginning...

The bell rang and the noisy playground emptied, and Clemmie swallowed back the mixture of emotions she felt—the inevitable sadness and pride that her children were growing up.

But she was free! Free to do exactly as she pleased until three-thirty, when she came to pick them up again.

And yet Clemmie's heart felt heavy, and it wasn't difficult to pinpoint why. A sense of guilt hung over her like a blanket—and no matter how hard she tried she just couldn't seem to shake the feeling off. She knew that she owed Aleck an apology, yet couldn't work out how to go about it without him immediately leaping to the conclusion that she wanted to see him for all the wrong reasons.

Then her breath froze in her throat as she saw a tall, familiar figure just leaving the playground, and she blinked rapidly, wondering if her mind was playing tricks on her. Had she somehow managed to magic him up in her thoughts?

But when she opened her eyes again he was still

there, dressed very casually, his long legs encased in faded jeans worn with a thick navy sweater.

Dare she face him?

He began to walk up the hill, and Clemmie watched him, lost in an agony of indecision. If she left it much longer, he would be gone, and when might she get another opportunity like this?

She began to follow him. She walked at a normal pace at first, because she didn't want to look as though she was running after him, and pretty soon he had disappeared round the corner and she had lost him.

But she knew where he was heading. To the big old house that they had stood and looked at out of his classroom window, all those years ago.

It took her about fifteen minutes to reach it, and several times she nearly lost heart and turned back, but something kept her going until she had reached the house, deserted except for a battered old Jeep which stood at the far end of the driveway.

Clemmie stared at the house properly for the first time in twelve years.

The first thing she noticed was that it didn't look as big as she remembered. Oh, it was big enough, certainly in comparison to most of the houses in Ashfield, but it wasn't the huge, sprawling mansion it had seemed to her dazzled eyes when she was a teenager.

The second thing Clemmie noticed was how the building and the land around it had been utterly transformed.

Aleck, and presumably Alison too, must have either worked day and night or spent an absolute fortune changing the tumbling-down monstrosity into the elegant building it was today. Crumbling bricks had been righted, decaying windows replaced. The lawns were smooth and weed-free, and the hedges neatly clipped. The holly-bright berries of a pyracantha blazed scarlet against the soft grey stone—and the dark, groomed elegance of Cypress trees, gave the garden a curiously Mediterranean feel.

Feeling scruffy and flustered and out of place, Clemmie smoothed a hand nervously over the crown of her head and yanked up the elastic band which held her hair back. Then, before she could change her mind, she went up to the wooden front door and knocked.

It was opened almost immediately by Aleck, his face so impassive that it occurred fleetingly to Clemmie that he might almost have been expecting her...

He said nothing at first, not a word, just stood looking at her, his blue-green eyes unreadable, and Clemmie found herself admiring and resenting his self-possession in equal measures.

'Hello, Clemmie,' he said at last, and gave an exaggerated frown. 'My memory may be growing defective, but I could have *sworn* that you told me to stay away from you.' His eyes glittered. 'Well, it's going to be pretty difficult keeping to my side of the bargain if you're going to turn up like a waif and stray on my doorstep.'

She had rehearsed several openers on her walk up here, but her nerves had blitzed them away and now, gazing into those unbelievable eyes, she found herself saying the predictable. 'Aren't you going to ask me why I've come?'

His mouth flattened. 'I presume you're about to tell me.'

Clemmie nodded, unwilling to just blurt it out, and wondered if he was going to leave her standing on the doorstep like a salesman—until he obviously took the hint and said heavily, 'I guess you'd better come in.'

'Thanks,' she said drily. 'Unless I'm keeping you from work?'

He shook his head. 'I'm an architect,' he said, as if that explained everything.

Clemmie blinked in surprise. It was the last thing she had imagined him doing. She thought of architects as pale, slender aesthetes, delicately sipping tea out of bone-china. Not rugged-looking men with ruffled hair, wearing old jeans. 'You didn't carry on with your parents' farm, then?'

He shook his head. 'The farm was sold years ago, and they bought a place in Spain; the climate suits them. Milking cows was never my idea of fun, and one of the beauties of being an architect is that you get to work from home—and you can please yourself about when you actually do it.'

'Lucky you,' she said, before biting her lip and wishing she could unsay it. He was widowed with a child, for goodness' sake—what was lucky about *that*?

His eyes narrowed as he took in her embarrass-

ment, and when he spoke his voice sounded almost
gentle. 'Come on—this way.'

She followed him along a passageway crammed
with interesting things—sumptuous oils, a carved
chest, a suit of armour—and Clemmie was tempted
to say it was too bright and messy to be an *architect's* house.

But then he led her into a light and sterile-looking
sitting room which Clemmie decided should be re-
named—since it looked as though no one had ever
sat in it! It was the neatest and most soulless room
she had ever seen, with stark white walls and metal
lamps which looked like surgical instruments. She
would have bet her last penny that no one had ever
sprawled here, toasting marshmallows in front of
that elegant and unfriendly marble fireplace.

It was the kind of room which would have looked
good in the window of a department store, but not
in a *home*. It looked more like a stage set, with two
pale ice-blue leather sofas facing one another.

The room was almost empty apart from the photos. Clemmie shivered. There were photos everywhere, and each one featured Alison—an eternally
young and beautiful Alison.

Clemmie's heart clenched, and she thought that
this was the last thing she had expected. It was all
so *contained*, somehow. And this cool, watchful attitude of Aleck's—that was not what she had been
expecting, either. When they had met last week
there had been fireworks when he had fought with
her and touched her. Today was somehow…
different.

Glancing at one of the photos, Clemmie cleared a throat which suddenly felt as inhospitable as sandpaper. 'I just wanted to say how sorry I am about your wife—'

'Oh, *please!*' He shook his head impatiently.

Clemmie screwed her eyes up. 'Please, what—?'

'Please don't lie to me, Clemmie,' he interrupted her softly.

'*Lie?*' Clemmie stared at him, her mouth falling open in confusion. 'W-why would I want to lie about something like that?'

'Come on—get real.' He scowled. 'It's pretty obvious.'

'Not to me, it isn't.'

'You never cared for Alison, so why should you suddenly start professing to care now that she's dead? Alison was superfluous to you. You wanted me, Clemmie. Badly. You always wanted me. I could read it in your eyes all those years ago and I read it there again last week. And I wanted you, too...' he finished, on a bitter note of self-reproach.

Clemmie forced herself to respond logically. After all, she wasn't still a schoolgirl, flying off at the deep end when someone said something she didn't want to hear. And maybe Aleck's grief was still raw enough for him to want to lash out at other people. But, even so, his entirely justified criticism of her behaviour made her heart sink with remorse.

'Okay, I wanted you!' she agreed, sounding more calm than she was feeling. 'But so what? It was a schoolgirl crush that got slightly out of hand, nothing more! Or do you really think that I've spent the last twelve years reliving that rather squalid little episode in the classroom, Aleck?'

His eyes flickered like the first flames of a fire. 'You mean you haven't thought about it? Not even once, Clemmie?' he quizzed softly.

Muddled by her desire to lie to him, Clemmie tried to speak, but no words came.

'Because I know damned well that I have,' he finished silkily. 'It's one of those memories which stubbornly refuses to die.'

Both thrilled and threatened by his words, Clemmie forced herself to meet his piercing gaze, feeling the betraying scrape of hardened nipples against the lace of her bra as her body instinctively responded to his powerful sexual aura. 'Why?' she questioned proudly. 'Was it so very wonderful?'

'It was left unfinished. Thwarted at its peak.' His eyes glittered. 'So it never had the chance to become destroyed by familiarity. And unfulfilled passion never leaves the memory, didn't you know? It's the sweetest fruit on earth.'

'You cynic,' she whispered.

'Cynic?' he questioned shortly. 'Or simply realistic?'

Clemmie swallowed. This kind of talk was getting her nowhere except hot and bothered. 'I'm sorry about Alison,' she said again. 'Really, I am.' And maybe this time she got through to him, because some of the wariness left his eyes.

He nodded, then gestured rather awkwardly towards one of the powder-pale sofas, like a man unused to playing polite games in parlours. 'Why don't you sit down?'

Clemmie had planned to say her piece and go, but she was stunned by this unexpected thawing. Stunned and more than a little curious. So she perched gingerly on the very edge of one of the sofas, afraid that her denim jeans would leave some muddy mark behind! 'Thanks.'

Aleck remained standing, his back to the marble fireplace, and Clemmie suddenly thought that in *his* casual jeans and sweater he didn't seem to fit into this pale, elegant room, either. She focused her eyes on some of the silver-framed photographs behind him. Alison cradling a baby. Alison with a toddler Stella. Alison and Stella sitting in a formal studio portrait, both mother and child in elegant cream silk, their faces fixed into professional smiles. Alison misty in pearls.

Clemmie stared up at Aleck, her heart going out to him as she imagined what he must have been through. Did he want to talk about what had happened? He could easily say if he didn't. And didn't every bereaved person she'd ever spoken to always say the same thing? That people were always too embarrassed to mention the dead, so it was as if they had never lived…

'When did Alison die?'

He looked at her, his eyes widening fractionally, as if he *was* used to people pretending that it had never happened. 'Five and a half years ago now,' he said slowly.

Clemmie stared at him. 'But I thought—'

He jerked his head up to look at her, his eyes now narrowing intently. 'Yes? What exactly did you think, Clemmie?'

She wriggled her shoulders uncomfortably, feeling like a butterfly caught on a pin, unable to escape that piercing stare. 'That it had happened much more recently than that—'

'And what gave you that idea?'

'I don't know. Just the way you reacted when I...when I mentioned your wife over at my house the other day. You just looked so *raw*.' She saw him flinch and took her courage in both hands. 'What happened, Aleck?' she asked him quietly. 'How did Alison die?'

'Didn't anyone tell you?' he demanded. 'You mean, no one bothered to fill you in on the facts? Hell, local gossip must be falling short of the mark!'

'There wasn't anyone to ask,' she answered. 'Don't forget, there are very few people I know round here. I came here when I was sixteen and left again two years later. And even if there *had* been someone to ask, I'm not into tittle-tattle.'

'Aren't you?'

'No.'

He let out a long, painful sigh. 'We were in Switzerland,' he told her baldly. 'Alison was killed by an avalanche—'

Clemmie clapped her hand over her mouth as she tried to take in the full horror of his words. 'But that's terrible, Aleck,' she whispered. 'So sudden! So cruel!'

He didn't react to her sympathy, just carried on

with his story, as if telling it would diminish the first awful impact. 'We were on a skiing holiday. Alison loved skiing. It was our second to last morning, and she decided to go out with the guide. Stella was young, and not very well, so I'd stayed back at the hotel to look after her. Alison was very excited. She was a good skier—better than me, in fact—and the guide had promised to take her down one of the black runs which aren't available to your average punter. It was one of those things—they called it a freak accident. When they came to tell us, Stella took it very badly.'

'Oh, the poor, poor baby!' breathed Clemmie instinctively, and saw the sudden guarding of his expression. He did not want her pity, she realised. What good would her sorrowful words do now, years later—words that Aleck would probably regard as meaningless if they came from her? Why not stick to what was relevant?

'I just wanted to say that I'm sorry for the things I said the other day, and for the things I implied,' she told him softly. 'That's the reason I came today, Aleck, only everything came out the wrong way. I was angry and I struck out at you.'

But Aleck shook his head. 'I'm partly to blame. I said some pretty cruel things myself. I deliberately stirred you up, Clemmie. I just didn't realise how easy it would be.'

She met his darkened stare while doing her level best to resist it. What was it with her and this man? The allure he had held for her as a teenager did not seem to have diminished with the passing of the years. And refusing to acknowledge that would be immature, surely? 'You mean—you couldn't believe that I'd still behave like a complete pushover?'

'I don't know if that's how I would describe it.' He frowned. 'Let's just say that there seems to be an extremely strong chemical reaction whenever we're around one another. Even now.'

'I think it's called lust,' she answered slowly, and braved his blazing stare. 'Nothing more than that.'

'Is that all it is?' He gave a sardonic laugh. 'Oh, you *do* disappoint me, Clemmie. And here was me, rather hoping that what we were experiencing was unique.'

Unfortunately, as far as Clemmie was concerned it *was* unique. But imagine if he knew *that*, she thought grimly. He was talking about sex, and she was thinking about something entirely different. Women were always confusing sex with love—that was the biggest mistake they made in relationships. And she had vowed never to make that mistake again. 'You flatter yourself,' she told him softly.

'Do I?' he mused. 'I wonder.' And he let his eyes drift over her in a cool, unhurried look.

She *tried* to resent it, but instead Clemmie found herself dazzled by that stare, unable to move from its focus. It was like being caught in a powerful spotlight which revealed her every fault and weakness. And she found she was *glad* she had come on the spur of the moment, and not bothered getting changed, because at least he wouldn't think she had come here dressed for seduction.

Yet some stubborn, feminine side to her character wished that she *had* worn something a little more becoming. Her denims were neither old nor faded enough to be fashionable, and neither did they cling tightly to her bottom. Her sweater was a pretty shade of russet, which made the most of her shiny red-brown hair, but it was old and bobbly now from too many washings, and her blue suede moccasins were old and scuffed. In fact, she looked exactly what she was—a twenty-nine-year-old divorcee whose face was beginning to show the signs of age.

She licked her lips nervously, wondering what she was still doing here. She had said what she had set out to say, and in the process she had learnt that she was still at the whim of this most inconvenient longing for Aleck.

'What about you?' he asked suddenly. 'What brought you back to Ashfield?'

'I was left the house by my stepfather.'

'And that's the only reason?'

Clemmie threw him a scornful look. 'You think it had something to do with you being here?'

He smiled. 'Hardly. My ego may be healthy, but it isn't insufferable.' He was watching her closely. 'So what happened to your husband?'

'Nothing happened to him. He's in America.'

'And?'

'We're divorced. And that's all you need to know, Aleck.'

'How intriguing.'

'It's nothing of the sort—it's just a common-or-garden marriage break-up story,' she said briskly,

because his eyes had lightened with a luminous softness so that Clemmie found herself wanting to tell
him. She, who hadn't confided in a soul, was now
inexplicably gripped by a desire to pour all her trou-
bles out. To *Aleck*, of all people! 'The sort you've
heard time and time again.'

'You sound very cynical,' he observed quietly.

'Well, that's what divorce tends to do to you,'
she told him bitterly, realising that if she didn't get
out of here soon he'd have her blurting even more
out. 'I think I'd better go, Aleck.'

'The girls are at school, aren't they?'

'You know they are.'

'Well, then? What are you rushing back to?'

'It's not what I'm rushing back *to*,' she amended
wryly. 'It's what I'm running away *from*.'

'And that is?'

He knew damn well! 'You,' she answered softly.
'Why?'

She made no mention of the fact that she was
tempted to reach out and touch the faint shadowing
around the curve of his jaw, trace it with first her
finger, then her mouth... 'Because you have trouble
written across your forehead in large letters—and
because I'd like to take a raincheck on trouble! I've
had enough to last me a lifetime, Aleck!'

'I see!' Faint laughter lifted the corners of his
mouth in the ghost of a smile. 'So there's nothing
I can do to make you stay?'

It was a deliberately provocative question, and
Clemmie could hear the subtle note of desire which
coloured his voice. A desire which she could have

all too easily matched. She became aware of the silence in the house, and of the fact that they were alone. And aware, too, that there was plenty he could do to make her stay. It seemed that her feelings for him hadn't changed very much in all these years.

But she had come back to Ashfield for a quiet life, not to lay herself wide open to having her heart broken by a man like Aleck. Because instinctively she recognised that he could inflict wounds far deeper than any Bill had made...

Reluctantly, she shook her head. 'I don't think so somehow, Aleck. I think the best thing we could do for each other would be to stay well away.'

He stared deep into her eyes. 'What a pity,' he mocked softly, and stood up. 'In that case, I'd better see you out.'

CHAPTER FOUR

SEPTEMBER blended into October, and the leaves fell in a blaze of glorious autumn colours from topaz and gold right through to copper and cinnamon. Clemmie crunched through great heaps of them on her way to dropping the girls off at school in the morning in what soon became a comforting and familiar routine.

Aleck she'd hardly spoken to—not since she had been up to his house that morning. She saw him most days in the playground, when he dropped Stella off, and he would give her a cursory nod—sometimes even say good morning, but nothing more. Clemmie felt oddly dissatisfied—she had asked him to stay away, but now that he had she found herself wishing that he wouldn't. Contrary woman that she was!

To distract herself from thinking about him, she poured all her energy into straightening up the house as best she could. The windows now gleamed as brightly as diamonds, and she had wiped every single grubby mark from the walls. In the evenings, once the children had gone to bed, Clemmie began making curtains.

To her relief, she had also managed to find herself a job, working mornings at Ashfield's general store, which sold everything from newspapers and balloons to carrots and nutty brown bread. She was hired by Mrs Humphries, the shop's owner, a rounded woman of around fifty who sucked so many sweets that Clemmie was surprised the shop made any profit at all!

True, it wasn't the most high-powered job in the world, or the best paid, but it suited Clemmie's needs since it would be only four hours a day and she could be there to drop the girls off every morning and pick them up every afternoon.

And Mrs Humphries took an instant shine to her. In fact, she seemed to have only one reservation about giving Clemmie the job.

'What about school holidays?' she asked. 'Have you thought about how you'll manage then?'

Clemmie had thought long and hard about this. 'I'm going to put a notice in the school magazine,' she told her. 'And find out if I can share childcare with someone who works in the afternoon. Lots of women with children job-share these days, so it shouldn't be difficult. But don't worry, Mrs Humphries, I'll find something.'

'Nice to be so confident.' The other woman smiled.

Clemmie shook her head. 'Needs must. And I need this job.'

She told the children about it that night, when they got home. They sat round the kitchen table, cutting out orange masks like pumpkins, in preparation for Hallowe'en, and Clemmie made them all hot chocolate and sat down at the table to drink it with them.

'You mean you're going to be working in a *shop*, Mummy?' asked Justine, askance.

'And what's wrong with working in a shop?' asked Clemmie sharply.

Justine shrugged. 'Nothing, I suppose.'

'Oh, come *on*, Justine—it must be something!'

'Just that you make fantastic cakes of your own. Why can't you sell those or something?' Justine added sulkily.

'What, from here?' laughed Clemmie, and counted off on her fingers. 'Point one—I have no capital to start up in business on my own. And point two—celebration cakes don't provide a steady income, and that's what we need right now. There are very few weddings or big parties in the autumn, darling. We can't rely on my cake-making to put food in our mouths.'

'When do you start?' asked Louella.

'No time like the present,' smiled Clemmie. 'I start tomorrow.'

Justine spread a little more bramble jelly onto her crumpet, and took a thoughtful bite. 'Stella Cutler's having a Hallowe'en party,' she said. 'She has one every year. Can we go?'

Clemmie's heart raced. 'Have you been invited?'

'Well, obviously, Mom! Or did you think we were going to just turn up?'

'What time,' Clemmie asked quickly, 'is the party?'

'Stella said her dad would ring you—'

'Why?' Clemmie questioned immediately.

'Because I said you would want him to, so you could hear all about what kind of party it would be.'

'Oh, Justine! Why did you have to do that?'

Justine looked at her mother in bemusement. 'Because that's what you're *like*!' she protested. 'You always used to check up when we were invited to parties in America. You know you did!'

'Y-yes,' said Clemmie slowly, thinking that Justine was absolutely right, and then the telephone began to ring.

She picked it up. 'Hello?'

'Clemmie?' said a deep voice.

She briefly contemplated feigning ignorance of the velvety voice on the other end, but only briefly. She had an idea that Aleck Cutler was perceptive enough to see through girlish ploys like that one! 'Hello, Aleck,' she said calmly.

'How are you?'

'Fine,' she answered stiffly. As if he cared!

There was a pause. 'Stella usually has a party for Hallowe'en—did your girls mention it?'

'About two minutes ago!'

'Well, it's on Friday night. Starts at seven—here. Would Justine and Louella like to come?'

'I'm sure they'd love to come.'

There was a pause. 'And how about you?' he asked quietly. 'Would you like to come along, too?'

'Me?' Clemmie laughed, flattered to be asked, in spite of everything. Too flattered. 'I'm a little old for apple-bobbing, Aleck!'

'I invite all the parents,' he continued doggedly.

'And at the end they just take their children home. It means that the party finishes when I want it to!'

'Smart thinking.'

'So will you come, Clemmie?'

'Do I have a choice?'

'Of course you do.'

'Well, in that case...' Clemmie glanced at herself in the hall mirror and scowled at her washed-out appearance, knowing that a sensible woman would have turned the invitation down. 'I'll come.'

'Good. See you on Friday.'

Clemmie forced herself to act as if he was just any other father inviting her to a kids' party. 'Would you like me to bring anything? Some dessert, maybe?'

'Just bring yourself,' he said, and rang off.

To Clemmie's annoyance, the days until Friday dragged like examination week. Every morning she put on the pale pink overall which Mrs Humphries gave her, tied her dark hair back neatly in a velvet bow, and went to work at Ashfield Stores. She sold newspapers and doled out little bags of boiled sweets to small children, weighed out mushrooms and cut portions of cheese from a big wedge.

As jobs went, it wasn't demanding—Clemmie felt she could have done it blindfold with her hands tied behind her back! What made it bearable was chatting to the customers, especially the elderly ones, who never seemed in too much of a hurry and were often glad to talk, if the shop was quiet. Some of them had known her mother, and Dan, and made Clemmie understand why she had leapt so eagerly at the chance of living in Ashfield again. It was the nearest she'd ever come to having a real home, she acknowledged sadly. And real roots.

Justine and Louella arrived home from school on the Friday, babbling with excitement as they dressed in the outfits which Clemmie had made for them. Louella was a ghoul, in an adapted white sheet and with her face painted to match, and Justine, resplendent in orange tee-shirt and black jeans, was dressed as a pumpkin.

'What are *you* wearing, Mummy?' asked Louella.

Clemmie shrugged, looking down at her blue denims and the bobbly russet sweater. 'I thought I'd come as I am.'

Justine frowned. 'Mummmy, you *can't*! You're *always* wearing that! You *have* to dress up! And can't you put some make-up on for a change? You never bother to wear it any more!'

'Don't I?' She smiled indulgently.

'You know you don't!'

It was true. Clemmie had grown out of the habit of putting make-up on. It seemed too much trouble to slap it on her face every morning when she was simply going to take it off again at night! And it was not—as she had told herself, time and time again—as though she was trying to attract anybody.

But Justine's words made her take a closer look at herself. She peered in the mirror—where she saw only the blemishes on her face, the faint laughter lines around her mouth and the slight shadowing beneath her eyes.

Maybe Justine was right. Maybe a woman of

twenty-nine should no longer allow her face to go bare. A bit of camouflage might be just what she needed!

'Give me ten minutes,' she told the girls.

She put on a pair of slim-fitting black jeans and a black sweater and brushed her hair out, letting it stream all the way over her shoulders and down her back in a style which she rarely wore any more since it was so impractical. She hunted around until she found her old make-up bag and applied pale foundation and lots of dark eyeshadow and mascara, so that her dark eyes looked sooty and enormous. She finished off the look with over-the-top shiny crimson lipstick and painted a large black beauty spot on one cheek.

When she walked back into the kitchen, the girls squealed with delight. 'Will I do?' she asked.

'Oooh, Mummy!' gurgled Louella. 'Are you a witch?'

'Don't be *stupid*, Lou!' said Justine witheringly. 'She's a vampire!'

'Maybe I'd better go and scrape it off!' said Clemmie, feigning alarm.

'Don't you dare!'

Bundled up in their warmest coats, the three of them walked through the wind and darkness to the Cutler house, where orange lanterns had been strung in the trees to light their way. As they neared the house, Clemmie could see a large pumpkin with a candle burning inside it in front of an uncurtained window, and black and orange balloons fluttered outside in the chill October air.

When Aleck opened the door to them Clemmie thought that he looked amazing—dressed in black jeans and a sweater very like her own. She stared up at him, her breathing almost as erratic as her heartbeat, and for a moment she despaired that she still seemed to be locked into an attraction for a man who even her worst enemy would tell her was a bad bet.

He smiled down at Justine and Louella. 'Ah! A pumpkin and a ghoul come to join us. Welcome! All the children are in the games room, getting covered in flour! Know where it is? No, of course you don't. *Stella!*' he yelled, and moments later his daughter came running up, dressed as a devil, and gave them all a wicked grin. 'Take Justine and Louella with you, sugar, and give them both a drink. I'll be along in ten minutes to check that you're behaving yourselves!'

The girls ran off, squealing with excitement, and Clemmie was left alone with Aleck, feeling oddly displaced, and wishing that she could run after them.

'I didn't know if you'd come tonight,' he said quietly.

'I said I would.'

'Yes, I know you did.' His eyes searched her face. 'But I thought that maybe I'd frightened you off last time.'

'I've been living on my own for a long while now,' she told him quickly, wishing he wouldn't look at her like that. 'And I think I can just about deal with men who come on strong to me.'

'That's comforting,' he remarked, and Clemmie could have sworn that was mocking laughter in his eyes. And humour, she suddenly realised, could be awfully seductive.

'Here—' She awkwardly held out the tin she was holding, glad for something to do with her hands. 'I know you said not to bother bringing anything, but I made you this in any case.'

'That's sweet of you. What is it?'

'A Hallowe'en cake.'

'A *Hallowe'en* cake?' His eyes glinted as he prised the lid off and peered inside at the lavish-looking confection, which was iced to look like a spider's web. 'Mmm. Best-looking cake I've seen in a long time!'

'You'd better wait until you've tasted it before you tell me that!'

'I'm sure it won't disappoint,' he answered softly. 'Come on through and meet the others.'

The kitchen was crowded, with about twenty adults standing around chatting and drinking hot punch. Some of them Clemmie had seen up at the school; several she had chatted to while she was waiting to pick up the girls. She smiled at those she recognised and waited for Aleck to pour her a drink.

He fetched her some gluhwein and she drank the spiced punch quickly, grateful for the warmth and the instant buzz of the alcohol, which steadied her nerves a little. Aleck introduced her to several of the parents, although it took Clemmie a little by surprise to hear herself greeted as, 'Oh, hello!

You're the woman who works in the shop, aren't you?'

Aleck flicked a quick glance at her as he led her away. 'Sorry about that.'

'What?'

'The shopgirl comment.'

'Well, it's true enough. That's what I do. I'm not ashamed of my work, Aleck,' she told him proudly. 'It may not be high-powered, but it's satisfying in a funny sort of way. I just want to earn my keep and disrupt the children as little as possible.'

'Bravo,' he whispered, and Clemmie looked at him sharply.

'Are you making fun of me?'

He shook his head. 'No, I'm not. I wouldn't dream of making fun of you.'

Her mouth gave a reluctant twitch. 'Now why do I find that difficult to believe?'

His eyes crinkled with laughter as their gazes clashed. 'Because you're a cynic?' he suggested softly.

She was grinning now, in a way she hadn't done for years. 'Oh, am I?'

She looked bloody gorgeous tonight, Aleck thought, suddenly wishing that his house wasn't full of other people. 'I'd better go and supervise the children for a while,' he said unenthusiastically. 'Check that they haven't wrecked the house. Ah! Come and meet Miss Cummings.'

A vivacious redhead with a mass of curls burst out laughing as she heard him. 'Don't you dare call me that, Aleck Cutler!' she scolded. 'You make me

sound a hundred and one, at least! Hi! My name's
Maggie,' she added disarmingly to Clemmie.

Maggie Cummings was not only fun, but pretty,
too. The kind of woman that Clemmie might have
felt a little jealous of if she hadn't been so nice. As
they chatted she told Clemmie that she had been
Stella's teacher the previous year. It also became
rapidly clear to Clemmie that Maggie thought Aleck
Cutler was the best thing since man had landed on
the Moon.

They watched in silence while he left the room,
and Clemmie felt that if she *didn't* ask her question
soon she would burst with curiosity. 'Have you
known Aleck for very long?'

'Oh, about three years,' said Maggie, giving her
a wry look. 'Which is quite long in *my* books—
though I can't say how *well* I know him, even
though...' Her voice tailed off and she shrugged
rather helplessly in response to the question in
Clemmie's eyes.

Clemmie swallowed, praying that she had misread all the signs but fearing they were deadly accurate. She drew a deep breath. 'Are you his—girlfriend?'

Maggie gave a rather hollow laugh and swallowed the last of her gluhwein. 'Heavens, no! That's
far too grand and proprietorial a title—and it's one
that I imagine Aleck would detest. I never felt
happy about calling myself that—even when we
were lovers.'

The word hit her like a fist in the guts, and
Clemmie felt sick.

'L-lovers?' she echoed, as though she had mis-heard. 'Y-you and Aleck were lovers?'

'Uh-huh. Amazing luck, really. He fought off every single woman for ages after Alison died—but I must have done something right, because he didn't fight me.' Maggie blinked rapidly, as if trying to keep tears at bay, then picked up another glass of the punch and drank most of it in one draught. 'I kept dropping enormous hints about where our relationship was going, but it seemed that Aleck was quite happy for it not to go anywhere. I suppose that isn't surprising, really.'

'Oh?' Clemmie sipped her gluhwein, her lashes deliberately shielding her eyes, terrified that Maggie would read the envy there.

'Well, no girl can compete with a dead, beautiful wife.' She stared very hard at Clemmie. 'Can she?'

'I guess it would be stupid to try,' said Clemmie thoughtfully, picturing the sitting room, crowded with portraits of Alison.

'Did you know her?' Maggie asked suddenly. 'Alison, I mean? Didn't I hear Aleck say that you were all at the same school?'

Clemmie shook her head guiltily. 'I was only there for a year before Alison and Aleck left. I didn't...*know* her, not to speak to. Not really. I knew *of* her, of course. She was very beautiful.'

'I thought she was a cold fish,' said Maggie ve-hemently. 'As cold as ice.'

The last thing that Clemmie wanted to do was to get into a slanging session over her host's dead wife, so she excused herself and circulated, trying

to chat to everyone in the room. And she was good
at circulating. When Bill had walked out, in a place
where she knew no one, it had been sink or swim,
and Clemmie had quickly learnt that if she didn't
go out and make friends they wouldn't necessarily
come flocking to *her*.

Even so, she was glad to help hand out baked
potatoes and sausages and mugs of hot tomato soup.
She chewed unenthusiastically on a hot dog as the
noise in the kitchen grew and grew, and then a small
voice said, 'I'm tired, Mummy.'

'Now watch them all catch the sleepy bug,'
laughed Clemmie to the woman she had been chatting to, and Aleck heard her and turned his head.

'Including yours?' he asked.

Clemmie shook her head, something in his eyes
making her heart pound deep in her chest. 'Mine
have enough stamina to keep going until dawn.'

'Stella, too,' he replied easily, and Clemmie was
left feeling as though she had in some way compromised herself. Maybe he thought that a single,
smouldering look from him would be enough to
have her hanging around on the off-chance!

Consequently, she was determined to be among
the first to leave, but fate—in the form of her two
daughters—conspired against her, and by the time
she found them using an ancient exercise bike in
the attic everyone else had gone home. She marched
them straight downstairs and into the hall.

'But, Mom, Stella's got to go around fetching all
the crisp packets and paper cups!' objected Justine.
'And me and Louella promised we'd help her.'

'Louella and *I*,' corrected Clemmie automatically, and looked down at Justine's pleading face, knowing in her heart that she wasn't being fair. Stella was the first friend that Justine had made in England and she seemed a really nice girl. And if Stella was anyone other than *Aleck's* daughter she would be delighted for her to stay and help. Clemmie shook her head, impatient with herself. When was she going to stop letting her life be governed by men?

She gave Justine her biggest smile. 'Of course you can go and help, darling. And Louella, too, but keep her with you, will you?'

'Yes! Oh, *thanks*, Mom!' And Justine ran off before her mother could change her mind.

'So,' came Aleck's deep voice from behind her. 'Since you appear to have successfully delegated all the clearing up to the children, I think you deserve a reward, don't you? Which would you prefer—wine or coffee?'

Clemmie turned round to see that he was bearing a tray containing both. 'Oh, coffee, I think.'

He raised his eyebrows. 'Sure? You haven't got work tomorrow, have you? Or school?'

'No, I haven't,' she agreed equably. 'But I do have two very noisy daughters, and I don't want to listen to them with a splitting headache.' And she had already drunk enough of his gluhwein to make her the wrong side of vulnerable.

'Then why don't we go and make ourselves comfortable?' he suggested.

It was a line which, if it had come from someone else, Clemmie might have found herself refusing.

Coming as it did, from Aleck, she found that she was following him like his shadow into the sitting room.

Sitting perched once more on one of the ice-blue sofas, surrounded by the stark and harsh lighting, Clemmie again had the uneasy sensation of being on a stage-set. Or, she thought suddenly, as her eyes alighted on the silver-framed photographs of Alison which were crammed onto every available surface—in a *shrine*.

Yes, that was it—a shrine. Maggie Cummings's words came back to mock her. 'No girl can compete with a dead, beautiful wife.' Her stomach clenching, Clemmie brushed a tiny fleck of dust off the arm of her black sweater and willed herself to toughen up.

Aleck noticed the jumpy gesture, noticed the up-tight way she was sitting. 'Is something wrong?'

She took the coffee he handed her, observing how big his hands looked. Big and capable. Gorgeous. She wondered if she would be able to drink her coffee without spilling it. 'I don't find this the most relaxing room in the world, if you must know.'

He nodded thoughtfully. 'Because of Alison's photos?'

'Not especially. Although—' She bit her lip.

Aleck was a powerful man in Ashfield; he had lived there all his life and done very well for himself materially, and consequently a certain mythology had grown up around the tall, handsome widower who lived up at the big house. Not many people told Aleck Cutler what was really in their hearts. He looked now at Clemmie with interest. 'Although what—?' he prompted softly.

'I think you've *overdone* it on the photos a bit. There are so many of them, Aleck, that it looks like some kind of...' She saw the question in his eyes and pushed the word out bravely. 'Shrine.'

He didn't deny it, or even flare up at her. Instead he simply nodded again. 'Yes.' He expelled a breath slowly. 'This room hasn't been touched since Alison's death. She had just decorated it; it was the first room in the house she had attempted. That was her job, you see, she was an interior designer. When she...' His voice hardened. 'After her death, when we came home, just the two of us, Stella wanted the room to stay exactly as it was. She brought down every photo of her mother she could find, and I agreed to put them in frames for her.'

Clemmie's eyes were very bright. 'I know you'll probably think I have no right to say this to you, but don't you think it's time that you both moved on from that, Aleck?'

He leaned back in his chair and studied her for a long moment, his hand resting against the side of his face, eyes narrowed in study. 'And how do you propose I do that?' he demanded. 'Just suddenly get rid of all the photos? Wipe out her memory? How do I explain *that* to Stella?'

Clemmie stared at him, her mind working overtime. Was Stella a convenient scapegoat? Maybe the truth was simpler than he maintained—maybe *he* was the one who was clinging onto the photographs, like a man obsessed. Perhaps the photos were a tangible warning to other women to stay away. To let them know precisely what Maggie had said: that you could never compete with a dead, beautiful wife.

'Nothing can ever wipe out Alison's memory,' she said quietly. 'She'll exist for ever in her daughter.'

'Yes.' He looked at Clemmie thoughtfully. Generous. A lot of women would have had difficulty coming to terms with that. Like Maggie. Maggie had just wanted to pretend that his other life, his married life, had never happened.

His hard, handsome face took on a fleeting trace of vulnerability, and Clemmie caught a glimpse of the teenage boy she had so adored. He settled back comfortably into the sofa and she found that a simple movement like that could drive all rational thoughts clean out of her head, to be replaced by a growing awareness of how much she wanted to physically *touch* him.

'You've tensed up again,' he commented. 'Is it me, I wonder?'

'Why? Do women often get tense around you, then, Aleck?' she queried, only half teasing.

'Not like you do,' he replied truthfully.

Clemmie forced herself to sip her coffee, wondering how truthful she dared to be. Hadn't she said enough for one day? 'Maybe that's because I still feel there is so much unfinished business between us.'

His blue-green eyes were very watchful. 'Such as?'

'Such as, I never knew whether Alison found out about...' Her words tailed off as she wondered how best to phrase it.

'That stolen kiss?'

Put like that, it sounded absurdly romantic, and so very innocent, and yet it had been neither. Not really. One of the least innocent actions of her life, and she wasn't proud of it. Not at all. 'Yes.' Clemmie's voice was quiet.

'Oh, yes,' he said slowly. 'Alison knew all about it. Her friends made sure of that.'

'And was she angry?' Clemmie breathed, then clamped her lips together, hard. 'Gosh, that was a dumb thing to say. Of course she must have been angry. She must have been furious.'

'I guess you could say that it focused her thoughts,' he replied, in an odd kind of voice, which made Clemmie wonder whether it was just too difficult for him to think about.

He dropped two lumps of sugar into his coffee and slowly stirred it, before lifting his head to look at her, and Clemmie was caught in the full force of that blue-green gaze. 'Tell me what you did when you left Ashfield,' he said suddenly.

She was caught off-guard. Perhaps if she hadn't been she might have been less honest than he deserved, because the truth, even now, was painful. She shrugged, aiming for the kind of shrug which hinted at nonchalance, but suspecting that she'd ended up with just the opposite.

'I went away to college in London, to study catering, and it was there that I met Bill.'

'Your husband?'

'Ex-husband,' she corrected, pushing down the feeling of defeat which always rose up to haunt her whenever she thought about the father of her children. 'Yes. He was spending the long vacation "doing" Europe, and we…we…' Her words trailed off helplessly.

'You fell in love?'

She looked at him sharply. Was he mocking her? But his eyes did not ridicule her—instead, Clemmie read in them something that she had never associated with Aleck Cutler before.

Understanding.

'Yes, we fell in love—whatever love is.'

'You doubt its existence, then, do you, Clemmie?'

'At barely nineteen I think that all kinds of feelings can be mistaken for love. Anyway, we both experienced that "can't-bear-to-be-away-from-you-for-a-second" kind of feeling.'

'Heady stuff,' he commented drily.

'Yes. It came as a bit of a relief, actually—' Then she closed her mouth as she realised just what she had been about to say.

'Relief?'

A relief to discover that Aleck Cutler was not the only man who could make her feel as if she was walking on air. That was what she had meant. But she wasn't giving his ego a free massage by telling him *that*! 'Just that when you both feel like that, and you decide to make your future together, it gives you a feeling of security.'

'And your life had been pretty short on security?'

She nodded. So he could be astute as well as understanding, could he? 'My father died when I was tiny—maybe you knew that? We lived in London, and Mum had to go out to work to support us. I was the original latch-key kid,' she added self-deprecatingly. 'When Mum met Dan I was delighted for her, of course—but it meant the upheaval of moving here. And sixteen is a bad age to move. I never really settled.'

'No,' he commented, his expression thoughtful. 'I don't expect you did.' He poured them both a second cup. 'So what happened next? With Bill?'

'Oh, we got married. In secret.'

'For romantic reasons?' he queried.

Clemmie shrugged. 'Not really.' At the time it had seemed the perfect solution, but the hasty ceremony, performed in front of two unknown witnesses, had seemed shabby. As though it didn't matter. 'Because Bill's parents were in the States, and it didn't seem fair to invite my mother and Dan if Bill had no one there for *him*. Justine arrived pretty soon after that. Then we had to wait for my papers. After that we went to America.'

'Whereabouts?'

'Oh, everywhere—or it seemed like everywhere! Florida first. Then Idaho. New York for a while.' She widened her dark eyes at him. 'Want me to continue?'

Aleck watched the way that her black sweater clung to the swell of her breasts, and he was invaded by a sexual hunger which was quite alien to him in its intensity. There was really only one thing he wanted right now, but he didn't feel it prudent to say so. And even if he did, he doubted whether he would get it... 'Yeah. Finish your story, Clemmie,' he prompted, quashing the stifling throb of desire.

'Bill had the original itchy feet. He couldn't hold down a job once he was bored with it. And he had a pretty low boredom threshold,' she added wryly.

'So you decided to leave him?'

Clemmie's face was rueful, her lips puckered with resignation. 'Oh, no! Quite apart from the fact that I was living in a strange country, we had two children by then. I really *wanted* my marriage to work.'

'But Bill didn't?'

'Bill wanted all the things which ultimately wreck a marriage—personal freedom to the detriment of everyone and everything else around him.'

'And what exactly does that mean, Clemmie?'

She swallowed down the revulsion. 'It means that Bill was a good-looking man with an eye for firm, young flesh—the younger the better.'

'Hell—'

'*No!*' she interrupted vehemently, the word spilling out like poison, but maybe the reason for that was that she had never told anyone the whole story before. Not a soul. So why choose Aleck Cutler? 'I want to finish! Maybe I have no right to criticise Bill? Do I? Not when you think about it. After all, all those girls he went with probably behaved the same way that I behaved when you were with

Alison. They probably threw themselves at him in the same way that I threw myself at you—'

'I'm not going to let you carry on with such misplaced condemnation,' he told her calmly, shaking his dark head to silence her. 'And I seriously doubt whether you would have let me make love to you.'

'That isn't what you said the other day!' She blushed as she remembered his cutting taunt. The deliberately crude way he had phrased it, insulting her and exciting her at the same time. Panties round her ankles...

Aleck sighed as he saw her cheeks colour. 'I know it isn't. But the other day I was angry, confused.' And too hot with desire to think straight. Like now. 'Besides, I wasn't even married to Alison at the time. Stop beating yourself up about what happened all those years ago, Clemmie. It's all in the past now.'

But the past had long tentacles which reached into the future. They were touching her now. And dangerously.

Clemmie stood up, her legs as wobbly as if she'd spent the evening at sea. 'Time I was going, I think.'

Aleck rose to his feet unenthusiastically, wanting her to stay but anticipating what kind of reaction he would get if he asked her to. 'I guess it is.' She walked right by him then, to get to the sitting room door, and impulsively he reached out for her, pulling her into his arms, staring down at her upturned face, at the freckles which spattered her cute little nose.

'Sure I can't persuade you to stay?' he murmured.

Clemmie made a half-hearted effort to struggle free. 'You said that last time—and I thought then that it was the corniest line I'd ever heard!'

'I know. So, can I?' he persisted, tightening his arms around her waist, just itching to capture her mouth with his.

'You can try!' she challenged. 'But I must warn—'

She got no further. Aleck did what he had been wanting to do ever since she had arrived here tonight, with those snaky hips in the lean black jeans and the soft sweater hugging her luscious breasts. He bent his head and took her lips by storm.

It was like being roller-coastered back through time, only better. Much better. Clemmie was older—and hopefully a little wiser. Aleck had been the first man she had ever kissed, but there had been others since, and every one—Bill included—faded into insignificance when compared to *this*.

For Aleck kissed like no other man. Made her feel like a different kind of woman. She melted against him, swaying as he tangled her hair between his fingers, sighing his pleasure deep into her mouth. As he pressed his body hard against hers, she could feel a tension building in him which matched her own. A special kind of tension which could only be released in the way that nature had intended.

And the children were just along the passage…

Gasping, Clemmie pulled away from him, wondering if her eyes were as black with passion as his,

wondering what it was with this man which made
her want to give in so easily.

'Oh,' he groaned, on a low note of disappointment.

Her breathing slowed. She could feel the heat between her legs, the warm rush of desire where she
ached so sweetly, and she could have wept. One kiss
and he could have her in such a compliant state?
Would he do the same with anyone? 'Maybe you
should have asked Maggie to stick around,' she
lashed out.

His eyes narrowed. 'And just what is *that* supposed to mean?'

'Just that I know she was your lover—she told
me.'

He didn't react. 'And?' He gave a hollow laugh.
'Surely you aren't outraged or shocked at *that*, are
you, Clemmie? We were two consenting adults,
without any ties at the time, just like you and I are
now. It isn't a crime to want to make love, you
know.'

He made it sound like an exercise session in the
gym, Clemmie thought indignantly! Where was all
the tenderness in *that*? 'Well, maybe you should
have chosen Maggie tonight—she might have
proved more responsive to your attentions.'

His face darkened. 'That's a pretty cheap re-
mark.'

'Well, it was pretty cheap behaviour, wasn't it?'
she breathed, her breasts tingling fiercely beneath
the black sweater. 'The kind we always seem to in-
dulge in whenever we're together!'

They were facing each other like boxers squaring up for a fight when they heard a muffled yelp from outside the open door, and Aleck frowned. 'Who's that?' he called out.

There was silence for a moment, and then the sound of a sob being stifled, and Aleck and Clemmie both rushed to the door in alarm.

Outside, rubbing her eyes with her fist, stood Stella, her shoulders shaking with sobs.

Aleck was crouched by her feet in an instant. 'Darling, what is it?'

'It's L-Louella,' she cried. 'She—punched me and kicked me! She was horrible to me, Daddy— and I don't like her!'

CHAPTER FIVE

JUSTINE and Louella came flying down the corridor to glare at Stella, and for a moment accusations and counter-accusations were hurled across the room.

'*She* started it!' yelled Louella.

'No, *she* did!' shouted Stella. 'You hit me first!'

The angry words Clemmie had exchanged with Aleck evaporated. She had rarely seen her younger daughter look quite so hurt or so furious. She tried to take some of the fire out of the situation. 'Shh, Louella,' she whispered. 'What on earth is the *matter*?'

'I hate her!'

'Louella!'

'It's not just Louella's fault, Mummy,' said Justine stolidly.

'What happened?' asked Clemmie steadily.

The three girls all clamped their mouths together and stared at nothing in particular.

Clemmie threw Aleck a resigned glance, and he gave her a 'search me' kind of look in return. He was standing with his arm around Stella, his face serious, but he had not started dishing out any blame and for that Clemmie was grateful. She strongly suspected that tempers were too frayed to get any sense out the girls tonight.

It seemed that Aleck thought the same way. 'Why

don't we sleep on it?' he suggested quietly. 'Go up-stairs and get ready for bed, Stella, and I'll be up in a minute.'

Stella's mouth trembled, her blue-green eyes fill-ing with angry tears as she turned and ran up the stairs.

'I'd better get my two home as well,' Clemmie said, and gave them both a squeeze. 'It'll all look completely different in the morning—you'll see!' But the looks on their faces remained mutinous.

'I'll fetch your coats,' said Aleck heavily, and he went to the cupboard to find them, feeling more raw than he'd felt in a long time. What the hell was going on with the kids? And what were all these mixed messages which Clemmie was sending out to him? She had wanted him to kiss her—he *knew* she had. She'd kissed him back, stirred his blood, left him wanting more. And *she* had wanted more, too. Yet all of sudden she had started rebuking him, as if he had overstayed his welcome.

He handed Justine and Louella their coats and they put them on in stony silence. Then he held Clemmie's open for her, a question in his eyes.

She hesitated. It had been a long while since a man had helped her on with her coat, and she was feeling emotional enough to overreact—the kiss and then the ensuing drama had seen to that. But she didn't want to add to the atmosphere by grabbing it out of his hands and insisting on putting it on her-self. So she slid her arms in, feeling stupidly cos-seted and protected as he shrugged it on over her shoulders.

Aleck found himself touching the worn cuff with the tip of his finger, finding its old shininess oddly moving. 'You need a new winter coat,' he said slowly.

Clemmie grimaced. 'I need a lot of new things—so does the house and so do the girls. And I'm afraid that a new coat is right at the bottom of the list! Come on, Justine, Louella—say goodnight to Mr Cutler, would you?'

She was half afraid that they would stomp out in a huff, but years of having good manners drummed into them had obviously paid off.

'Goodnight, Mr Cutler,' said Justine politely.

'Goodnight,' piped up Louella, in a small voice.

'See you!' said Aleck cheerfully, but more with hope than conviction.

The girls went out onto the porch, but Aleck signalled to her with his eyes and Clemmie held back a little.

'Disaster averted,' she said in a low voice.

He frowned. 'What do you suppose that was all about?'

'I'll find out,' she promised, and hesitated. She had turned him on, and then turned away and acted as if he was behaving outrageously. And there was no excuse for that kind of behaviour. When she spoke her voice was so quiet that Aleck had to strain his ears to hear. 'Back then, I didn't mean to be—you know—the kind of woman who—'

But he shook his head, her faltering little speech making him feel like some kind of marauding brute. 'You carry on doing exactly what you feel like doing, Clemmie,' he told her huskily. 'There's no book of rules to say how we should behave with one another—and if there was, I think I would have torn it up by now!'

Amazingly, Clemmie laughed, even with two woebegone daughters looking on as though she had no right to.

'We'll sort it out,' he promised her. 'Whatever this thing is—we'll sort it out.'

She nodded, believing him, tempted to reach up and touch his face with her hand, but she didn't dare. For the girls' sake. For her sake. 'Goodnight, Aleck.'

The girls didn't say a word on the way home, and when Clemmie had let them in to the house she sent them straight upstairs. 'Go and put your pyjamas on, will you, Justine? Lou? I'll heat some milk and bring it up—so scoot!'

By the time they were tucked up in their beds in the warm, pink glow of their Mickey Mouse night-light, Clemmie thought how impossibly innocent they both looked. She put the two mugs of milk down on the locker and sat on the end of Louella's bed.

'So,' she began, 'want to tell me about it tonight? Or we can talk about it tomorrow morning, if you're too tired?'

They exchanged worried glances and then Justine spoke.

'Stella said you'd been kissing her daddy!'

Clemmie felt colour steal up the side of her neck. She swallowed. 'And?'

'Were you, Mummy?' asked Louella.

Clemmie swallowed. She had vowed never to lie to her daughters, but right now she wished she hadn't made herself such a foolish promise. 'Yes, I was,' she agreed calmly.

'Do you love him, then, Mummy?' asked Justine, quite seriously.

Clemmie thought about this. How much more uncomplicated it would be if she could look her daughters in the eye and tell them truthfully that Aleck Cutler meant nothing to her. 'I...like him,' she admitted carefully, though she might have added that she had no idea *why* she liked him so much. 'And I'm attracted to him. I can't deny that. But love is different. Love takes time. And trust.'

'Did you love Daddy?' asked Louella plaintively, and Clemmie could have wept at the naivety of her question.

She struggled to contain her emotions, and to honour their father as best she could. 'Of course I loved him, darling, but I was very, very young at the time—much too young to know what love really meant. And to marry young and go and live in a different country—well, that places a lot of strain on a marriage.'

'Is that why you split up?'

Clemmie drew in a deep breath, knowing that she couldn't protect them for ever from the cruelty of the truth. She had decided a long time ago that keeping the truth from them was the only way of keeping their father's image relatively untarnished. For what child could cope with the fact that their father was an unrepentant womaniser? One day she might tell them more, but not now. 'In a way,' she prevaricated. 'I guess you could say that we weren't getting along, and we just couldn't live together any more.'

'But why doesn't Daddy come to see us any more?'

'Because his home is a long way away, darling. You know that.'

'But he didn't come very much when we were living in the next State, did he, Mummy?'

Clemmie bit her lip. It was one of the things which had finally given her the courage to leave the States—the fact that Bill might as well have been residing on another continent for all they saw of him. 'Well, Daddy's got a new baby now, and a new girlfriend...and they make demands on his time...which is perfectly natural. And I expect he's saving up to come here to visit you. H-he told me that he was.'

Anxious to change the subject, she turned to Justine. 'So is that what all the row was about? The fact that Stella saw her daddy kissing me?'

Justine looked down.

'Justine?'

Justine twiddled with her plait.

'She said that even if he *did* kiss you it didn't mean anything. She said you could never take her mummy's place, because her mummy was beautiful and Mr Cutler loved her more than anything in the world.'

Maggie's words came floating back, adding fuel to what Justine had just said. 'No girl can compete with a dead, beautiful wife.' And Clemmie felt ashamed at the sharp pang of jealousy which ripped through her belly.

'I'm sure he did,' Clemmie said steadily. 'And she *was* very beautiful. I used to see her at school. She had turquoise eyes and pale hair and looked exactly like a princess. And Stella is right, you know—no one could ever take her place. What is more—I don't want to.' She picked up the mugs of cooling milk and handed one to Justine and the other to Louella. 'Now, drink this and sleep on it,' she advised. 'It'll all look better in the morning.'

'I'm sorry, Mummy,' said Louella in a small voice.

'Do you think Stella will still want to be friends?' asked Justine plaintively.

'I expect so. But we'll have to wait and see,' said Clemmie as she bent down to kiss them. 'Won't we?'

The morning brought rain, lashing loudly against her window-pane like an animal banging to get inside. Clemmie woke up shivering. She had worn a baggy tee-shirt and a pair of thick socks to bed, but she could see that she was going to have to invest in some warm pyjamas. The house was *freezing*—and she certainly couldn't afford to have the heating on all the time.

She glanced at the clock on her bedside table. Getting on for ten o'clock—now that *was* a lie-in! She would go downstairs and make a pot of tea.

She popped her head round the girls' door, but they were sound asleep—sprawled out beneath their duvets with all the abandon of the young, oblivious to the world. Late night and too much emotion, she thought wryly, and went downstairs.

The pale, rain-soaked light of morning meant that it was bright enough to see by, and Clemmie didn't bother to switch the light on as she sat on the kitchen table, swinging her legs and waiting for the kettle to boil. Then she heard a faint tapping at the window, and she looked up to see a rain-soaked figure there.

Aleck!

She wished she could admit that she was surprised to see him, but she wasn't. Or that she was dreading seeing him, except she wasn't.

Swallowing down the anticipation and excitement which had caused some kind of tingling restriction in her throat, she padded barefoot to the back door and opened it, and a sudden gust of wind brought raindrops and leaves whirling into the kitchen.

Clemmie's eyes were huge. 'What are you doing here?'

'Getting wet!' came his terse reply.

'Then you'd better come in.' Tugging the tee-shirt right down to mid-thigh, so that it camouflaged her bottom, and wishing that she had bothered to put a brush through her sleep-tousled hair, Clemmie stood back to let him pass.

'Where's Stella?' she asked, trying to sound as normal as possible. As though it was nothing out of the ordinary for a man to be standing in her kitchen while she was still in her nightclothes.

'I dropped her off at the stables—she goes riding

on Saturday mornings. It was a bit of a struggle getting her out of bed this morning, but I figured that fresh air and exercise might be just what she needed.'

'Yes.'

His gaze flicked around the kitchen and settled on the open door leading to the hallway. 'And your girls?'

'Fast asleep. Or rather they were, when I checked a minute ago.' The kettle began to steam. 'Would you like some tea?' she asked, a trace awkwardly.

'Love some.' He removed his dripping waterproof jacket and hung it over the back of one of the chairs. He sat down without being invited to, stretching his long legs out in front of him, and made a pretence of looking around the kitchen with interest, when really his eyes kept being drawn to Clemmie and the sexy sight she made in her tee-shirt and bedsocks.

Clemmie tried to tip boiling water from the kettle without her hands shaking, tried to act as though she made tea for long-legged men with dark, brooding faces every day of the week. She wished she'd put a dressing gown on. Or jeans. Maybe she should excuse herself and do just that. But if she went up-stairs to change now, then not only might she wake the girls, but wouldn't it also draw attention to her semi-clothed state? And the fact that she was self-conscious about it?

She put the cosy on the teapot, asking, 'Would you like any toast? Or cereal?' Then could have kicked herself for sounding so eager to please. As though she couldn't wait to start waiting on a man!

He shook his head, a faint smile touching his lips. 'Just tea, thanks.'

She poured them both a mug, watching while he immediately cradled his for warmth between his large hands. She sat down at the table opposite him with her knees tucked in, keen to keep her bare legs hidden. It hadn't exactly escaped her notice that he had been watching her. And it wasn't that she *minded*—it was just so...so...*distracting.* 'Did you talk to Stella?' she asked.

He watched the steam rise from his mug—anything to keep his mind away from the infinitely more absorbing glimpse of her thighs. 'Yeah.'

Clemmie looked at him expectantly. 'And?'

He stared at her oval face, with the freckles standing out in relief, like stars against the paleness of her skin. Her big eyes were velvety-dark and startled—like a fawn's—and her hair was mussed and messy, as if she hadn't bothered brushing it. She looked, he decided, as he picked up the mug again and sipped some tea—nearly burning his mouth in the process—all rumpled from bed and as sexy as hell.

'And she's jealous,' he said bluntly. 'Simple as that.'

'But there's nothing to be jealous of!' protested Clemmie.

'Isn't there?' His eyes mocked her.

Clemmie studied her hands. Her ringless fingers, the neat, unvarnished nails. 'What did she say?'

Aleck shrugged. 'That she didn't want another mummy.'

Clemmie stared at him. 'One kiss doesn't put me up for the role of stepmother, does it?'

'Maybe in a child's eyes it does.'

'But this must have happened before, Aleck. Doesn't she know that you had an—affair—with Maggie?'

His eyes narrowed. 'How do you have the knack of making something which is perfectly natural sound in some way sordid?'

'You're guilty of the same,' she reminded him quietly. 'You made my slightly drunken antics as a schoolgirl sound like I was a nymphomaniac! But does she? Know about Maggie, I mean?'

'I don't think so.' He shrugged. It wasn't something he particularly wanted to talk about—his short-lived affair with the pretty schoolteacher. Certainly not to Clemmie. But she was just sitting there, looking at him expectantly, with her lips pursed together and that inquisitive look on her face. What could he do other than tell her? If he didn't, it would look as though he had something to hide. And there was nothing.

'We kept the affair very quiet,' he growled reluctantly. 'We thought that best, since she worked at the school. It lasted less than six weeks and ended amicably.'

'Did it?'

'Yes. We've stayed friends.' He met her questioning gaze unflinchingly. 'Which is why she was at my party.'

In Clemmie's experience, an 'amicable' break-up usually meant that one person was pretending like crazy not to mind! 'Really? So Maggie was happy with the outcome?'

Aleck sighed. 'You can be a very persistent woman, Clemmie Powers,' he observed wryly. Not the sort of woman you could fob off with a vague reply. 'Okay,' he admitted. 'Maggie may have thought she was in love with me—'

'Well, if Maggie *thought* she was in love, then presumably she knew her own mind,' Clemmie corrected acidly. 'She's an intelligent woman, after all. Maybe she *was* in love with you, Aleck, have you thought of that?'

'Well, maybe she was, but it wasn't reciprocated—and for God's sake, don't look at me like that, Clemmie! I can't help it if all I felt for Maggie was a deep affection.'

'And sexual attraction, presumably,' she pointed out. 'You aren't forgetting that, are you, Aleck?'

'No, but I wasn't actually going to spell it out in words of one syllable,' he said, in a voice which was tempted to snarl.

'So Stella knows nothing of the relationship?'

He shook his head. 'A child of seven, which is what Stella was at the time, is a lot less curious about human behaviour than a ten-year-old. She knew we were friends, and that's probably as far as it went in her eyes. Now she's older she's more switched on. Kids today tend to know more than we did at their age. And…' He wondered how honest he dared be.

She met his eyes. 'And?'

'And she probably can't bear the thought of us being a couple.'

'Which I suppose you're using as a euphemism for having sex?'

His sigh was midway between admiration and exasperation. 'Do you always say exactly what's in your head, Clemmie?'

Only to you, she was tempted to say. Only to you. Except that it wouldn't be the whole truth. She was only outspoken about topics she had no reason to fear. And so far she had successfully managed to avoid talking about what was uppermost in her mind. Not the woman he'd had a brief, uncommitted fling with. Not Maggie.

Alison. The woman he had loved, whose child he had fathered. The dead, beautiful wife that no one, including herself, could ever compete with.

'I'm too old for games,' Clemmie said instead. 'I had enough of them in my marriage to last me for life.'

His mouth tensed as he thought about his own marriage. 'Yes,' he agreed roughly.

'And who said anything about us being a couple?'

'It seems I just did.'

'Is that why you're here now?' she whispered to him, as if someone was listening.

'I don't *know*,' he whispered back. 'Maybe. Probably. Why did you come up to see me the other day, Clemmie? Turn up at my party when you clearly didn't feel you should? Is it because something powerful draws you to me as much as I am drawn to you? What *is* it between us, Clemmie?'

The schoolgirl Clemmie would have cited love as the reason for their confused feelings, but the older Clemmie was a lot more cynical about relationships. She tried to order her words so that Aleck wouldn't think she was building happy-ever-after fantasies about him. 'I told you before that it was lust.'

'So you did.'

His mouth turned down at the corners. For a moment, Clemmie thought disbelievingly, he'd looked almost *disappointed*.

'But I was wrong.'

His eyes narrowed. 'Oh?'

'I think it's a combination of things. You were right—our youthful attraction was thwarted. Unfulfilled. We never got those feelings out of our systems.'

'Sounds like there's only one sensible solution, then,' he murmured, in a voice of velvet, as rich as Turkish delight.

Clemmie's skin turned to ice, her stomach to mush at the way he was looking at her, the blue-green eyes travelling slowly up her legs, looking as though he would like to…like to… Clemmie swallowed.

He was the sexiest man she had ever met, and that was the truth. And it had been a long, long time since she had tumbled into bed joyfully with anyone. There had only ever been Bill, and towards the end sex had been nothing but a mechanical chore. Then, when she'd had proof that there *were* other women, that her fears weren't just the product of an over-active imagination—well, then she had sought the sanctuary of the single bed in the spare room.

But now she felt the sweet, unaccustomed ache of desire piercing her, and appreciated how easy it would be to open her arms to him and be caught in his, be welcomed there. But at what price?

'I want you,' he said deliberately.

'I know you do.'

'And you want me, too.' It was a statement, not a question.

'I know that, too.'

'Well, then?'

'Well, then, what, Aleck?' Her voice reflected her disbelief that he could be so naive. 'I'm a mother, remember? I'm a role model for my daughters! I'm not into red-hot short-term affairs—it would confuse the life out of them! Me too, if you must know. And I can't just leap into bed with you because we both happen to feel the urge! I can't compartmentalise sex like that.'

'But I'm not asking you to.'

Clemmie frowned. 'Then what exactly *are* you asking?'

'That we take things one step at a time.'

She screwed up her eyes in bemusement. 'Oh?'

He swallowed down the last of his tea and thumped the empty mug onto the table. 'Stella doesn't want to fall out with Justine and Louella; she likes them—'

'And they like her!'

'I like you,' he said softly.

She read the question in his eyes. 'Snap!'

He smiled, biting down the urge he felt to pull her into his arms and kiss her, because now was not the right time. 'Well, then, why don't we all try being friends?'

'Do you think we can?'

'I think we could accomplish absolutely anything,' he told her teasingly. 'Unless you think that I'd be unable to keep myself from laying a finger on that delicious body of yours.'

'I'm not *that* conceited!' she told him primly.

Well, you should be, he thought hungrily, but didn't say so. 'So. Friends?'

'Just friends?'

'For the moment,' he agreed, and picked up his empty mug to drain it unnecessarily, so that she wouldn't see the glint in his eyes. 'How about we start with the five of us having Sunday lunch tomorrow?'

'Do you think Stella will want to?'

'I'm sure of it.'

'Shall I...?' She hesitated, not wanting to come over as Little Ms Domestic.

'Mmm?' He loved the way her mouth softened into that cute little pucker when she was uncertain.

'Cook? The lunch, I mean.'

Aleck imagined a warm kitchen full of good smells. Imagined watching Clemmie move around in it, all relaxed and easy. 'Oh, yes, please,' he said softly.

CHAPTER SIX

LUNCH the following day was a success, judging by the plates scraped clean and the second helpings of apple crumble and custard which were demolished. Clemmie beamed at the children like a mother hen, then glanced up to find Aleck watching her so intently that she could scarcely meet his eye and immediately began stacking dishes as though her life depended on it.

Aleck's eyes were thoughtful. 'So now we walk it off?' he suggested, as he finished his coffee.

'Oh, Dad—*no*!'

Justine pulled a comical face. 'Mom, do we *have* to?'

Clemmie risked another look at Aleck and found that she wanted to walk beside him, outside, with the wind on her face and the freedom to talk without the girls listening. Four walls could hem you in sometimes. 'We most certainly do!'

They went up through the woods just beyond his house, where most of the leaves now lay in great drifts beneath the trees.

He told her about the school which had just been built—a school he had designed—in the nearby cathedral city of Salisbury. 'Best job of my life,' he sighed.

Clemmie scrunched a leaf underneath her boot.

345

She noticed the way his face lit up whenever he talked about his work. 'You sound so fulfilled by your job, Aleck.'

He smiled. 'I am. It's like a dream come true. You start out with an idea, you put it down on paper, and the end result is a beautiful, functional building. And buildings make such a difference to people's lives!' He looked at her closely. 'How about you, Clemmie?' His voice was soft. 'Do you like working in the general store?'

She shrugged. 'It's okay. I'd be lying if I said it was the job of a lifetime. It's certainly not demanding—but then it isn't stressful, either. And my priority is the children—and jobs which fit around them are hard to find. It's the eternal problem facing working mums. And besides—' she wrinkled her nose at him as she smiled '—I enjoy chatting to the customers.'

Lucky customers, he thought as he watched a dark strand of hair catch her lips and stay there, wishing he could brush it aside and place his mouth there instead. 'Stella says you make the most fantastic cakes.'

Clemmie grinned. 'Does she? That's nice! Why don't you send her over on Saturday afternoons after riding, if she'd like to, and she can help bake?'

Saturday afternoon cake-making became a regular thing, and Aleck would join them afterwards to eat up what had been made. There had been no repeat of the arguments between the girls, and the baking sessions gave Clemmie the chance to get to know

Stella better. She was a sweet child—confident, but occasionally diffident. Like the first time Clemmie had piled the cake mixture into the tins and pushed the bowl across the table towards her.

'Want to lick it clean?' she'd smiled.

Stella bit her lip. 'Am I allowed?'

Clemmie was taken aback. 'Of course you're allowed!' she said gently. 'Why wouldn't you be?'

Stella shrugged. 'Mummy never let me. She said it was messy.'

Clemmie nodded, and busied herself with putting the tins in the oven. It was not her place to criticise. 'Well, everyone's different,' she conceded. 'I expect that there's things I won't let my girls do that you're allowed to.'

'Like *what*, Mom?' asked Justine, who had been listening.

Clemmie searched for inspiration. 'Like horse-riding!'

'You mean you'll let us go horse-riding?' queried Justine doubtfully.

'We'll discuss it in the warm weather,' said Clemmie firmly, and then her face lit up like a Christmas tree as she looked outside and saw Aleck on the doorstep. 'Here's your father, Stella!'

He was carrying a big bunch of mauve Michaelmas daisies in his hand.

'Oh, you shouldn't have done,' she protested, burying her nose in their musky scent when he gave them to her.

His voice was casual. 'Maybe there's something else you'd prefer to flowers?'

Their eyes met in a long, silent message of longing, and Clemmie hid her blush in the blooms. He knew damn well there was! She wanted him so badly she couldn't sleep nights, and yet some instinct kept telling her that this thing between them was much too precious to rush.

He had said 'friends,' and 'friends' was clearly what he had in mind. And it was an education for Clemmie. She had never been friends with a man before. Not like this. Had never experienced this warm feeling of camaraderie with a member of the opposite sex. Bill's friends had been men; women were for sex and housework. His attitude had made her feel like an object, not a person.

But with Aleck, Clemmie began to relax. To unfurl. Like a cat stretched out before the blaze of a fire, she started to bask in the warmth of his affection. For the first time in her life she felt like part of the human race, instead of an outsider. She had been the latch-key kid, then the displaced stepdaughter, the young foreign bride, and finally the divorcee. Yet now she felt poised on the brink of something new and good.

Yes, she was still the divorced mother of two, but she no longer felt so isolated. And Aleck's friendship gave her an undoubted feeling of protection. In a small town where people tended to judge before they knew you, being close to a man like Aleck helped Clemmie regain the confidence which Bill had steadily chipped away at over the years.

But the downside of this patronage was envy. Maggie Cummings was now cool and distant whenever she and Clemmie met. And she seemed to take great pleasure in coming into the shop and asking for the most bizarre items. Lavatory brushes and bottles of air-freshener! Clemmie thought that she was being mischievous, but she didn't bother telling Aleck. The last thing she wanted to appear was weak, or spiteful. Particularly as she had—to some extent—what Maggie so obviously wanted.

Aleck.

Except…and she could have laughed if there had been any real humour in it…she didn't have Aleck at all. Not in the real sense, the biblical sense. She had him in the big-brother sense, and yet thirsted for him secretly, in the wasteland of her lonely bed at night. She had told him proudly that she wasn't into short-term affairs and she wished she'd had the sense to know when to shut up! Now she felt she would have him on any terms at all—and if three very impressionable little girls hadn't been involved, then she might have done just that.

And Justine had been very quiet of late. Clemmie had caught her hanging around waiting for the postman. Waiting for a letter from her father which never came. Clemmie sighed. She had written to Bill twice, pleading with him not to forget Christmas, but he hadn't even had the courtesy to reply. Soon, she realised with a sinking heart, she would have to telephone him.

One Monday lunchtime, in the last week of November, Clemmie trudged home up the hill from the shop in the driving rain. She let herself in, peeling off her raincoat and realising that the rain had soaked right through to her underclothes. She was just debating whether to run a bath when there was a knock on the door. She opened it slightly and stuck her nose round the crack, and there stood Aleck.

There was a moment's pause, a moment's hesitation. She didn't need to ask why he was here. She wasn't into playing games, not with Aleck, and she could read his intentions as clearly in his eyes as if he had written them on a placard and held it up in front of her.

'Come in,' she said.

He closed the door behind him. In the rain-darkened hall he seemed taller, more dominant and more vital than any man had a right to be. Clemmie sighed. He stared very hard at her, then reached out a fingertip to catch a raindrop which hung like a tear on her cheek.

'You're wet,' he observed huskily.

Clemmie felt the potent throb of desire as it hummed like a presence in the air around them. 'Then dry me,' she whispered shakily.

'Oh, *Clemmie*.' His voice shuddered softly as he took her by the hand and led her straight upstairs, as if he didn't trust himself to touch or kiss her properly until they had found the haven of her bedroom.

There was a big pink fluffy towel drying on the radiator, and he plucked it off and rubbed gently at her hair, so that the sodden strands began to puff out with static. His face was almost grave as he began to unbutton the little camel cardigan she wore, until it flapped open and the lushness of her breasts were revealed, straining uncomfortably against the shiny coffee-coloured brassière.

'Oh, *God*,' he breathed, and sucked in an almost agonised sense of longing. '*God*, Clemmie...'

The chill on her skin was forgotten. Her body felt alive and on fire, the look in his eyes promising her so much—promising her everything. He looked, she thought, with a dizzying sensation of recognition, almost as though this was his first time. The sense of wonder in his eyes was not feigned. The tremble in his fingertips no sham.

As he began to unbuckle the belt of her jeans, she lifted her own hands to undo the thick cambric shirt he wore, sliding each button through the hole until she found the hair-roughened chest, the flat, hard planes of his abdomen.

As he eased the denims over her hips she fleetingly wished that her underwear matched. She bent her head and covered one deep pink nipple with her mouth, and he gave a groan of pleasure.

'That's not fair!' he gasped. 'I haven't even touched you yet.'

Not *touched* her? Didn't he realise that she was on fire where his palms were sliding her black bikini pants down over her hips? And he might as well have been caressing her breasts, the way they were peaking and craving for his mouth.

The slow undressing became more frantic.

'I think we'd better get you out of these wet clothes as quickly as possible, don't you?' he murmured.

'Y-yes,' she managed, on a shuddering sigh, as she felt his nails scrape tantalisingly at the apex of her thighs.

By the time they were both naked the towel was dropped redundantly to the floor, since her skin had already dried in the heat his hands had produced.

He pulled back the duvet—a brand-new duvet, she thought fiercely. She had thrown all her marital bedding away on the very day her decree had become absolute. It was suddenly very important that Bill had no place here. This was Aleck's place—and his alone.

I love him, she thought, with the slightly stunned surprise of someone who had just recognised a simple truth.

I love him so much.

He drew her down beside him, the feather-filled duvet resting like a cloud on top of their seeking bodies. He tried to take things slowly, to explore every single centimetre of her as he had dreamed of doing, night after night, ever since she had come back into his life with all the light and beauty of a Christmas angel.

But it was no good. This time he just needed to claim her, impale her. Make her his. Make her...

Lifting his dazed head from her breast, where he had been licking voluptuously at her nipple, Aleck managed to formulate a half-coherent question.

'You're not on the pill?'

She shook her head.

'Damn!' He draped his arm over the side of the

bed and scrabbled around for his jeans until he had located the packet of sheaths in the back pocket.

Clemmie was caught between blush and giggle. 'Seems like you were planning this,' she observed. 'Want me to put it on for you?'

But Aleck shook his head violently. One touch of those slender white fingers *there*, and he suspected that he would possess all the control and finesse of a teenage boy. 'Next time,' he promised, as he slid it down. 'Or maybe the time after that.'

'How many have you brought with you?' she teased.

'Not enough!' he growled, and turned her onto her back.

He rose over her, proud and hard as a stallion, looking with pride and lust at her flushed cheeks and sparkling eyes. 'God, Clemmie,' he groaned. 'You are something else.'

With a stroke he possessed her, filled her, shot her with a fire which burned in her heart, and she found herself shuddering and clenching around him with a speed and an intensity which made her cry out.

He saw the tears which spilled like rain down her cheeks just as he closed his eyes, and he moaned out his own disbelieving pleasure in a cry which sounded loud in the silence of her bedroom.

And then, though they both fought against it like children, they fell sound asleep, the experience too shattering for either to lie awake and sane after it.

Clemmie woke to the sound of raindrops drumming against the window and the feel of a man's arms wrapped tightly round her, the warmth of his breath on her neck. She felt no shame, no regret, just an impression of something being overwhelmingly *right*. She savoured the sensations for a quiet moment—not moving, not opening her eyes—but something must have made him aware that she was no longer asleep, for he said softly, 'Hello.'

Clemmie let her eyelids flutter open, and she was caught and dazzled by the lancing blue-green light from his eyes.

'Hi.'

He moved slightly away from her, positioned himself so that her whole face was exposed to his searching gaze, as if seeking there the answer to an unspoken question. He nodded, as if satisfied. 'So,' he observed, his voice slumberous. 'No regrets.'

Clemmie raised her arms and wriggled luxuriously. 'Am I so terribly transparent, then?'

He shook his dark head, all mussed now, where she had run her frantic fingers through it. 'You just looked...' He shrugged his naked shoulders. 'Happy. That's all.'

All? 'Don't knock it, buster,' she chided, and kissed the tip of his nose. 'Happiness is a rare commodity.'

'And are you? Happy?'

'Mmm!' She closed her eyes dreamily. 'Totally.'

He shook his head. 'No. Not totally.'

Her eyes flew open again. Was this his way of telling her not to read too much into a very pleasant session of afternoon delight?

Aleck read the insecurity there and could have

cheerfully pulverised the man who had planted it so firmly in this woman's heart. And that man, of course, was one half of the problem... 'Total happiness would be me *not* sneaking down here like a thief on a winter's afternoon—'

She clapped her palm dramatically above her left breast. 'Why—you've stolen my virtue, sir!' she declared through a giggle.

He put his hand over hers and moved it down to cup the breast in tandem. 'Happiness,' he contradicted thickly as he saw her eyes dilate with pleasure, 'would be the freedom to make love wherever it took our fancy.'

'You want to do it in the car?' she questioned innocently.

He felt the blood rush exquisitely, to harden him. He slicked his finger down between her thighs to find her ripe and ready for him, and he watched her mouth suck in an *oh* of shocked pleasure as he slipped right into her without warning.

'I want to do it here. Right *now*. Like *this*...' He was helpless as he thrust deep inside her, as powerless as he'd ever felt in his life and yet filled with power, too. With this woman he became a mass of beautiful, puzzling contradictions.

It was as though her response was completely outside her control. In astonishment, Clemmie felt her climax building with rapid speed into explosive need, her body shattering into exquisite spasms around him. 'I'm coming,' she cried helplessly into his mouth, as he tipped her over the edge of some astonishing universe.

'Oh, *hell*!' he swore, and Clemmie's dazed eyes snapped open. She was startled by the look of fierce intensity on his face when he suddenly withdrew before climaxing.

It took a moment or two for them to gather breath to speak, and Clemmie wantonly trailed her fingers over him.

'You forgot the condom?' she guessed.

'I forgot my own name!'

She pretended to frown. 'Do I know your name?'

He started to laugh, and then remembered that life was never as simple as you wanted it to be. 'So what now? Is this a secret affair?'

Clemmie heard the troubled note in his voice. 'Do we have a choice?'

He thought about his young daughter, who looked so like his late wife. Would she be able to handle the idea of her father being this intimate with another woman? Was it going to be too much? Too soon? 'Isn't it living a lie not to tell them?'

Clemmie turned her head. Outside the window, the bare branches of the cherry tree rocked and shuddered in the grey lash of the rain. 'I don't know,' she said eventually. 'Maybe we should see how it goes for a while. Maybe it's too soon for any of the girls to accept a replacement in their lives.'

She didn't say what she was most afraid of—that 'replacement' was too permanent a word. What if the affair fizzled out after a few months—even weeks—once the novelty had worn off? Surely it would be better for everyone if their daughters were unaware of the depth of involvement between her and Aleck?

She turned back to face him and stroked her finger slowly down the sculpted curve of his cheekbone, wanting to tell him that she loved him. That she had always loved him. That she would never stop loving him. But she didn't want to scare him off! Heavens, the thought even terrified *her*!

The logical side of him—the paternal part—knew that her words made utter sense, while the emotional side of him—the lover part—wanted to tell the world and damn the consequences. But children altered you. Made you stop thinking about what you *wanted* to do. Instead made you think about what you *ought* to do. 'Maybe you're right,' he sighed reluctantly, and pulled her closer to him. 'But if you change your mind—or you think the time is right to tell them...'

'Then we'll discuss it.' She nodded, stupidly wishing he'd insisted. Thinking, too, that Aleck was the kind of man she could discuss *anything* with. Until she realised that there was one subject they had never discussed at all.

Alison.

Something unspoken hovered in the air around them. Their eyes met. Aleck read the question there, his heart softening as he acknowledged her tact. She hadn't asked him a damned thing. Not before bed. Not even *after* it! Clemmie Powers was some woman.

'Clemmie—'

'Mmm?'

'About Alison—'

She heard the tension in his voice, saw the strain which made ravines out of the laughter lines around his mouth, and shook her head. 'You don't have to tell me anything, Aleck,' she told him huskily.

'I know that. But I want to, sweetheart.'

And suddenly Clemmie was certain of only one thing. That this was their moment, hers and his, here and now. And nothing—*nothing* could take this away from them. Not guilt, nor recriminations. This was theirs, and theirs alone.

All along she had been getting mixed messages about Aleck's relationship with his wife. Alison the beautiful. Alison the cold. A woman no other could compete with. Yet Clemmie had noticed that Aleck was strangely reluctant to talk about his late wife.

So was all as it seemed? Or was it like most of life—neither black nor white but variations of grey? And did she really need to know the nature of Aleck and Alison's marriage at this ecstatic stage in *their* relationship? Couldn't the past taint the present that way?

No. She didn't.

Not today. Maybe not even tomorrow.

Clemmie shook her head. 'No, you don't want to tell me, Aleck,' she contradicted softly. 'Not really. In fact, there's only one thing you want right now.'

His mouth quirked into a smile as he saw the look in her eyes. 'And that is?'

She raised her open lips to his. 'This.'

CHAPTER SEVEN

NOVEMBER slid frostily into December, and the children began to get manic and excited. But for once in her life Clemmie was oblivious to the enticement of the Christmas countdown. She was too full of love for Aleck to think about anything else.

She tried very hard to concentrate on the normal yuletide routine of making puddings and cakes, but she was heavy-handed with the treacle, and for the first time ever her Christmas cake had the consistency of a rubber tyre.

Justine stared in wonder as she surveyed the blackened mess still smouldering in the tin. 'Mom, are you okay?'

Clemmie spun round, her eyes dreamy. 'Of course I'm okay, Justine. Why shouldn't I be?'

'You look *thinner*,' observed Justine critically. 'And you keep forgetting things lately.'

'And singin' all the time,' piped up Louella.

'Nothing wrong with singing,' said Clemmie robustly, wondering how on earth she would survive the Christmas holidays without her blissful afternoons in bed with Aleck, and then immediately feeling disloyal to her daughters.

The telephone started ringing and Clemmie absently licked at a wooden spoon before putting it back down on the counter.

'I'll get it!' said Justine and ran into the hall to answer it. She was back minutes later. 'That was Stella,' she announced, her face full of barely suppressed excitement. 'She says can we go up to her house to play?'

Clemmie's heart thumped like a drum. 'I'll walk you up there if you like,' she offered casually.

'Her dad wants to speak to you.'

'Well, why didn't you *tell* me?' exclaimed Clemmie, and then remonstrated with herself as she went out to pick up the phone. Oh, for heaven's sake! She was acting like a nineteen-year-old instead of a twenty-nine-year-old!

She picked up the phone, her stupid voice coming out more breathlessly than she had intended. 'Aleck?'

'Hello, gorgeous.'

Which, she assumed, meant that Stella was not within earshot. Clemmie tried to ignore the butterflies she felt far too old to be feeling. 'The girls said something about coming up to play?'

'That's right. Why don't you follow them up later and I'll cook us all supper?'

Clemmie sighed. 'That sounds perfect.'

His voice was wry. 'Not quite. Perfect would be if you didn't have to go home.'

'What, *never*?' she teased.

'Why not?' he growled.

Clemmie heard footsteps behind her. 'What time shall I come?'

There was a long, telling pause. 'Whatever time

you like, honey—I'll be happy to oblige!' he murmured, and rang off.

'Mummy, why have you gone all red?' demanded
Louella.

'Because it's hot,' lied Clemmie frantically.

She sent the girls off after lunch, and forced herself through her household chores. She found herself looking unenthusiastically around the sitting
room, knowing that she ought to paint it, and that
she really ought to try to get it completed before
Christmas.

What colour? Lemon, perhaps. Or turquoise.
Didn't they say that turquoise was a very restful
colour?

Clemmie sighed. The trouble was that she
couldn't seem to work up any great eagerness about
decorating. Come to think of it, she couldn't seem
to work up any great eagerness about *anything*. Her
mind seemed stuck in a groove, like a record on a
turntable, and the groove began and ended with
Aleck Cutler.

She washed the kitchen floor and went out into
the garden to clip at some foliage to put in a vase.
She needed to work on the garden, too. She had
hastily planted a few daffodil and tulip bulbs before
the frosts set in, and at least the lawn wouldn't need
cutting until the spring, but the bushes were all
straggly and in need of pruning, and the beds could
do with tidying up.

She glanced at her watch. It was only three
o'clock. She couldn't turn up *yet*. Aleck might be

working and it would look as if she couldn't keep away from him.

But did she care?

Not really. She suspected that Aleck knew just how much she wanted him. Her body language certainly wasn't subtle whenever he was within hugging distance!

She ran a bath, recklessly squirting her best bubbles into the running tap, and was rewarded with aquamarine water and the heady scent of tuberose. Then she lay submerged up to her neck, while the water cooled and the light faded from the afternoon sky.

It was quiet in the house without the girls. Too quiet. Leaving her too much time to wonder what lay ahead for them all in the New Year. Would this illicit romance continue indefinitely? she wondered. Or would they be brave enough to bring it out into the open?

She just couldn't imagine how they would tell the girls, somehow. Plus, if the truth were known, she had to admit that it was exciting to have Aleck come to the house most afternoons and make mad, passionate love to her. Aleck——her secret lover. It made her feel young and wild and free. And very, very desirable.

Clemmie wasted time until five o'clock, despising her inability to settle to a book or a newspaper, then she locked up the house and set off for Aleck's.

The sky was moonless, the December afternoon as black as pitch. All around her she heard the rustles and hoots of the countryside, but she felt no fear as she strode up the empty lane towards the Cutler house. When she reached the end of the drive, Clemmie paused for a moment and just stared.

From here, Aleck's house looked like an old-fashioned Christmas card—all lit up and bright and welcoming. She imagined a glossy holly wreath on the door, and a big, dressed Christmas tree in that cavernous hall, standing next to the knight-in-armour. Imagined baking batch after batch of mince pies to bring out to hordes of hungry carol singers.

And she had obviously been watching far too many corny old films!

Smiling, she rang the bell, but the door was opened by Aleck almost immediately, and it was as much as she could do not to throw herself into his arms and hug him tightly.

Aleck saw the eagerness on her face and resolved to take action. Hell, he wanted to kiss her. He didn't want her trailing back home to her lonely bed tonight, after he had cooked her supper. He wanted her *here*, in *his* bed. 'We're going to have to tell them,' he said softly.

'Who?'

'The children.'

'What—*tonight*?' Clemmie screwed her face up in alarm.

His expression was wry. 'Well, when would you suggest we do it? Christmas morning?'

'I suppose if you put it like *that*...' she said slowly. 'Where are the girls?'

'Here!' called Stella, and Clemmie and Aleck

turned around to see the three of them trooping out of the study.

'Hello, darlings!' beamed Clemmie. 'Been good?'

Her daughters quickly looked at Stella, as if seeking guidance.

For what? Clemmie wondered.

'We've made tea,' announced Stella. 'And biscuits. In the study. Would you like to come this way?'

'Of course,' smiled Aleck, and winked at Clemmie.

The girls had obviously been working hard to create an impression. A tray of tea stood on the hearth in front of the fire, next to two plates of home-made biscuits.

'Mmm!' said Clemmie automatically. 'Looks *wonderful*! Smells wonderful, too. So what's all this in aid of?'

'We want to ask—' began Louella.

Justine scowled. 'Shut up, will you, Lou!'

'Perhaps you'd like to sit down?' suggested Stella quickly.

Clemmie smiled into Aleck's eyes. Sweet of them!

There was a lull while the girls busied themselves pouring milk and tea, spooning sugar into cups and piling plates with lemon and spice biscuits; it wasn't until they were all settled, and the girls had demolished most of the cookies, that they put their cups down and looked with big eyes at the adults.

'I'm the spokesperson!' announced Stella solemnly. 'And the other two agree with everything I'm going to say. Don't you?'

Justine and Louella nodded their heads in accord.

Clemmie frowned, wondering what on earth was coming next, as Stella fixed her father with a fierce and determined stare.

'We'd just like to know when you and Clemmie are getting married, Dad. That's all.'

Clemmie slopped tea into her saucer while Aleck stared back at his daughter in bemusement.

'That's all, you say?' he commented drily. 'Then heaven help me the day you come to me with a serious problem! And is there a reason for this sudden question, Stella?'

There was a pause. 'Miss Cummings said that she sees you coming out of Clemmie's house every afternoon,' said Stella slowly.

Clemmie met the black expression in Aleck's eyes, and for a moment she almost felt sorry for Maggie Cummings.

'She said *what*?' he questioned, in a voice which was dangerously soft.

'She just started giggling and asked was there something going on that she didn't know about—'

'Only her eyes looked really *angry*,' put in Justine.

'And anyway, we'd kind of guessed that something was going between you two, hadn't we?'

'Definitely,' nodded Justine.

'Def-nitly,' echoed Louella.

'We just don't think you should have secrets from us children, that's all,' added Stella primly.

Aleck felt staggered. Dazed. Bemused. 'Er—do we have to discuss this right now?'

'Yes, we do!' answered Stella firmly. 'Why don't you just come out and admit it, Dad, and say you love Clemmie?'

Aleck's eyes narrowed with interest. This was a previously unrevealed side to his daughter he was seeing now! 'Maybe because I haven't actually got around to telling *her* that yet?' he murmured.

Clemmie stared fixedly at a spot on the carpet with all the intensity of a person who had spotted a stray diamond twinkling there.

'Well, why *not*?' demanded Stella.

Aleck looked at each of the four females clustered around the fire in turn. Stella and Justine were looking as if they had just taken a degree in determination, while Louella was trying very hard to mimic the expression on both their faces. Only Clemmie looked ruffled, staring down at the carpet, her shiny red-brown hair falling all over her face so that he couldn't see it. He wanted to go over and take her in his arms, love her and kiss all her doubts away. But there were more people involved than just the two of them. He had to take this step by step.

'I'm waiting for the right time,' he said slowly, and wondered if he was ever going to find it.

'Is it to do with Mummy?' Stella asked suddenly.

His eyes were suddenly watchful. 'What makes you say that?'

'Because you keep all Mummy's photos!' Stella accused. 'Loads and loads of them! And you've left the room how she did it—even though you hated it at the time! But you didn't love her, not really! And she didn't love you, either! You were always arguing—you know you were! So why are you always pretending to me, Daddy?'

'And you keep *saying* that Dad will come and see us!' babbled Justine, as if the words couldn't wait to come bubbling out. 'Only he never does, and we both know he never will! He never even writes to us, does he, Mummy?'

Clemmie lifted her head slowly to meet Aleck's eyes.

And suddenly Aleck knew that the only solution to this problem was complete and utter honesty. It might be painful. Probably would be. Some people might even say that it would be inappropriate to give these children an insight into what he and Clemmie were really thinking about their ex-partners. But anything less would be an insult to them all.

'I *did* love your mother, Stella,' he said, very carefully. 'How could I not love her when she gave birth to you?' He looked into his daughter's blue-green eyes, which were like a mirror reflection of his own, and saw the faith and love there which gave him the courage to continue. 'But what you say is true; we *did* argue. We argued a lot. We just weren't very good at living together. And when...' He swallowed down the lump in his throat at the sight of Stella's face turned so trustingly towards his. 'When your mummy died, sweetheart—I felt so bad about that. I wished we could have been happier together. For your sake, more than anything.'

'But you didn't get divorced, did you?' said Stella quickly. 'You stayed together.'

'Yes,' he agreed quietly.

'Because of me?'

'Yes.' Quieter still.

'Thank you, Daddy,' said Stella simply, and Aleck knew then that he had done the best he could. He felt overwhelmed with gratitude as she jumped up to hurl her arms around his neck and hug him.

Clemmie realised that Justine and Louella were now looking at *her* expectantly, and it certainly didn't seem the right thing to do to march them all off to another room to speak 'privately'. Not when Aleck had behaved so openly and so honestly in front of *them*. She cleared her throat as she struggled to choose the right words.

'I don't *know* whether Daddy will come over to see you both, and that's the truth. He has a new girlfriend and a new baby, and he might not have the time or the money to come all the way to England.' Or the inclination, she could have added, but didn't. 'If you like, you could each write him a letter—not the sort of "Hi, Daddy, how are you?" kind of letter that you usually write, more the sort of letter where you tell him exactly how you feel. Tell him you're worried, that if much more time passes by you're afraid he will forget you altogether. Because that's the truth, isn't it, darling?'

'Yes, Mom,' answered Justine softly, her eyes bright, because even at her tender age, she instinctively recognised how much it had cost her mother to say those words. Her mother's life would be easier by far, she realised, if Bill Maxwell just disappeared out of their lives for good. And yet Clemmie was doing everything she could for that not to happen because of *them*—her and Louella. 'Oh, thank you, Mom,' she said softly, and kissed her, and then Louella came over and put her arms around her, too, and it was as much as Clemmie could do not to start blubbing.

Aleck could feel all the heightened emotion in the room which was in danger of swamping them. Time to lighten up. And besides, he had things he needed to say to Clemmie. Alone.

'I think I'm going to get a drink for Clemmie and me. Anything for you girls?'

Silent messages flashed between Stella, Justine and Louella, and they shook their heads.

'No, thanks, Dad—not at the moment. We're going off to play!'

'Okay, then.' They skipped out of the room and Aleck forced himself to go out to the kitchen. He wanted to leave Clemmie on her own for a moment. To let her gather her thoughts and make up her mind what *she* wanted. Because he certainly knew what *he* wanted.

He found the very best bottle of claret he could—he was tempted to bring champagne, except that he couldn't bear to be that predictable. And besides, Clemmie's pale face had looked more in need of warmth than cold fizz.

Swinging the glasses between his fingers, he carried the bottle into the study to find Clemmie where he had left her, sitting by the fire with the flames picking out the red lights in her hair.

She glanced up as he walked in, then couldn't look away. She loved him. She loved him so *much*. But hadn't they both made mistakes in the past?

'Hi,' he murmured.

'Hi.'

He wanted to kiss her, because that would make everything right, and yet something told him that it was very important he *didn't* kiss her. Not yet.

Instead he eased the cork from the bottle and put it down on the mantelpiece to breathe. He looked at her. 'Don't you think it's time I told you about my relationship with Alison?'

'Yes,' she said quietly. 'I do.' She sat as silent as the night, her eyes never leaving his face while she waited.

His gaze was steady on her face, but his words seemed heavy. 'As you've probably picked up from what I just said to Stella, it wasn't a happy marriage…'

Quietly, Clemmie rose to her feet and moved close to him, tenderly putting her finger over his lips. 'And don't you think I hadn't started to work that out for myself, my darling?'

His eyes darkened. 'But I never said—'

She shook her head. 'No, you didn't. You never said a disloyal word about Alison, Aleck—and more power to you as a father for doing that. But all the signs were there if you looked for them, which maybe I did. The non-verbal clues, I suppose.'

'Like?'

'Like the fact that you looked tense whenever she was mentioned. Like your reluctance to remove some of her photos—which would be normal after all this time. But I guess your guilt stopped you doing it.'

He sighed. 'Shall I tell it like it really was?'

Clemmie's gaze didn't waver. 'Only if you think I need to know.'

'I do,' he said softly.

'Then tell me.'

There was a long pause before he spoke. 'All my life I'd had everything I ever wanted. I was good at everything I turned my hand to.' He threw her a look of mocking apology. 'If that sounds unbearably arrogant, it isn't meant to. Everything came so easily. *Too* easily. I'd never had to fight for anything or anyone before—'

'But you had to fight for Alison?' Clemmie guessed shrewdly.

He nodded, a faraway look entering his eyes as he tried to remember the boy he had been. Life had been so simple then. Or it had seemed that way. 'She was everything I thought I wanted. So exquisite, with that pale golden hair and those eyes like chips of turquoise...'

Clemmie had expected this to hurt. But not this much. 'Go on,' she said, in a low voice.

'She seemed so aloof and unobtainable...' His voice trailed off, and words spoken by other people about Alison came drifting back to Clemmie's memory.

'She was a cold fish'—Maggie's verdict, true, so it might not be the most reliable testament.

'Mummy never let me'—that had come from Stella.

'I *had* to have her,' he admitted reluctantly. 'And then, when I *did*—she was so...so...*remote*, I guess. So distant. Like a beautiful statue. You never knew what was going on in her head, and I suppose that her elusiveness was attractive to someone who wasn't used to it.'

Clemmie felt her cheeks colour with shame as she remembered the way she had virtually flung herself at him in the classroom. 'And elusiveness was the *last* thing you could have accused *me* of.'

He saw her crestfallen face. 'Sweetheart,' he said softly, 'believe me when I tell you that the way you behaved that night completely blew my mind.'

'So that's why you stared at me as though I was something the cat had brought in, was it?'

'Clemmie,' he murmured, 'I was feeling a) guilty and b) frustrated, and so I did the classic macho thing of blaming you. I told myself that you were outrageous, a temptress—and not the sort of girl I wanted to be involved with.'

'And what did Alison say when she found out?'

He sighed. 'That was part of the problem. There's nothing like jealousy to focus the mind. It's the dog-in-a-manger thing—you don't want a person until you think that someone else does. And when Alison discovered that I had been caught in a compromising situation with you, she started coming on to me *very, very* strong.'

Clemmie couldn't stop the sarcasm from showing. 'And you, of course, hated every minute of it?'

His gaze was steady. And rueful. 'Sweetheart—what do you want me to say? I was eighteen years old.'

'So what happened next?'

'We went to university. We carried on going out, but as time went on my feelings towards her began to change. And then, in our second year, Alison became pregnant.'

'And was it p-planned?' She saw the hurt and the anger in his eyes.

'What do you think?'

'I th-think I'd like to punch you and kick you and scratch you, except I know I have no right to be jealous,' she told him brokenly, but he pulled her into his arms and held her there, very tightly.

'Shh, sweetheart,' he said into her hair. 'Don't you think I don't feel the same way about Bill, even though *I* have no right to? And you can take it out on me as much as you like,' he promised, on a note of silky anticipation. 'Later.'

'Tell me the rest,' she urged.

He stroked her hair. 'I couldn't leave Alison then, and to be perfectly honest I didn't want to. Not when she was pregnant. I'd been brought up to honour my commitments, but it was more than that. I wanted this baby, Clemmie—she was *my* baby, too, after all. And I didn't lie to Stella when I told her that I loved Alison. She was the mother of my child, so how could I not love her?'

Clemmie heard the tenderness and respect with

which he spoke and realised that she admired him far more for honouring Alison's memory than she would have done if he had rubbished her.

His face darkened. 'I could *kill* Maggie Cummings for spreading gossip to a ten-year-old child.'

'Well, don't do that. I have no intention of spending the rest of my life visiting you in jail!'

He smiled. Maybe he *should* have brought that champagne, after all!

Clemmie raised her face to his. 'Aleck?' she whispered.

He thought of all the things she might say. All the things he prayed she would *not* say. 'What is it, sweetheart?'

It was all there in her eyes, and written in the huge smile on her face, but she said it anyway. Just so that there could be no misunderstanding. 'I love you, Aleck Cutler.'

He closed his eyes tightly and thanked God. 'I love you, too, Clemmie Powers,' he whispered huskily. 'And I'm damned if I'm going to wait until Monday afternoon to show you just how much!'

He lowered his mouth towards the sweet temptation of hers and kissed her very thoroughly indeed, and Clemmie was beginning to get that melty, gloopy feeling which meant that if they didn't stop what they were doing very soon...then things were going to get completely out of hand.

'Whoooh!' came a giggled shriek from the doorway. Their daughters stood there, giggling and blushing in equal measures, and when Clemmie

looked up into Aleck's face she saw that the two of
them were no better!

He cleared his throat. 'What can we do for you,
girls?'

'You said you'd cook us supper!'

'And I will,' he smiled.

'But Dad—it's raining really hard outside! And
Justine and Louella didn't bring their wellingtons!'

It took Aleck and Clemmie a moment or two to
get the message, and when they did Clemmie
blushed even more.

'Perhaps they could stay the night, then?' Aleck
suggested gravely, before turning to the woman at
his side. 'And we could hardly send you back on
your own, could we, Clemmie?'

Stella tugged impatiently at her father's sleeve.
'Isn't there anything you want to tell us?'

Aleck knew what they wanted. What he wanted.
And what he knew deep inside that Clemmie
wanted, too. 'I want to marry Clemmie,' he said.
'And for us all to be one big, happy family—'

'*When?*' demanded the three girls in unison.

Aleck looked at Clemmie. 'Whenever you like.
As soon as possible. Please.'

Clemmie wanted to pinch herself.

She thought of the way she and Aleck had looked
at this house from the classroom window all those
years ago. The way it had seemed so lit up and welcoming tonight. She thought of the corny films it
had reminded her of and she knew that their life
would be that good. No. Better!

'As soon as you like. How about later this

month?' She smiled into his eyes and nearly melted from the love she saw there.

'Can we be bridesmaids?' Louella's voice was breathless.

'You can.' Her mother smiled. 'And you can wear scarlet velvet and carry white muffs—if you want to, that is!'

'And you can move in here after the wedding— or before it, if you'd like that,' said Aleck as he looked tenderly at the circle of female faces smiling at him. 'Because I'm going to design Clemmie the most state-of-the-art professional kitchen she could wish for to make her cakes in.'

Her eyes shone as they looked at him, and she wondered whether now was the right time to tell him that she hadn't ruled out having more babies. Perhaps it could wait...! 'Everything has worked out perfectly,' she sighed happily, and leaned her head against his shoulder. '*Perfectly!* And just in time for Christmas!'

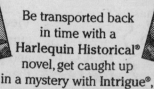

Coming in December 1999
Two award-winning authors invite
you home for the holidays!

'TIS THE *Season*
by
DEBBIE MACOMBER and
LISA JACKSON

CHRISTMAS MASQUERADE by Debbie Macomber

He'd stolen a kiss in the crowd—and taken her heart with it.
Then she met him again, engaged to another! Jo Marie
dreamed about uncovering the truth behind the engagement
and claiming Andrew for her own groom!

SNOWBOUND by Lisa Jackson

All Bethany Mills wanted for Christmas was peace and quiet.
But sexy investigator Brett Hanson stirred up the past and
then whisked her away to his mountain cabin for safety—but
from whom did she need protecting…?

Available December 1999 at your favorite retail outlet.

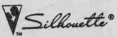

London's streets aren't just paved with gold—they're home to three of the world's most eligible bachelors!

You can meet these gorgeous men, and the women who steal their hearts, in:

NOTTING HILL GROOMS

Look out for these tantalizing romances set in London's exclusive Notting Hill, written by highly acclaimed authors who, between them, have sold more than 35 million books worldwide!

Irresistible Temptation by Sara Craven
Harlequin Presents® #2077
On sale December 1999

Reform of the Playboy by Mary Lyons
Harlequin Presents® #2083
On sale January 2000

The Millionaire Affair by Sophie Weston
Harlequin Presents® #2089
On sale February 2000

Available wherever Harlequin books are sold.

GREEK TYCOONS

Wealth, power, charm—what else could a handsome tycoon need? Over the next few months, each of these gorgeous billionaires will meet his match... and decide that he has to have her— whatever it takes!

Meet Constantine, Dio, Andreas and Nikolas in:

On sale January 2000: **Constantine's Revenge**
by KATE WALKER
Harlequin Presents, #2082

On sale March 2000: **Expectant Bride**
by LYNNE GRAHAM
Harlequin Presents, #2091

On sale May 2000: **The Tycoon's Bride**
by MICHELLE REID
Harlequin Presents, #2105

On sale June 2000: **The Millionaire's Virgin**
by ANNE MATHER
Harlequin Presents, #2109

Available at your favorite retail outlet.

HARLEQUIN®
Makes any time special ™

HEART OF THE WEST

Every Man Has His Price!

Lost Springs Ranch was
famous for turning young
mavericks into good men.
So word that the ranch was
in financial trouble sent
a herd of loyal bachelors
stampeding back to
Wyoming to put themselves
on the auction block!

July 1999	*Husband for Hire* Susan Wiggs	January 2000	*The Rancher and* *the Rich Girl* Heather MacAllister
August	*Courting Callie* Lynn Erickson	February	*Shane's Last Stand* Ruth Jean Dale
September	*Bachelor Father* Vicki Lewis Thompson	March	*A Baby by Chance* Cathy Gillen Thacker
October	*His Bodyguard* Muriel Jensen	April	*The Perfect Solution* Day Leclaire
November	*It Takes a Cowboy* Gina Wilkins	May	*Rent-a-Dad* Judy Christenberry
December	*Hitched by Christmas* Jule McBride	June	*Best Man in Wyoming* Margot Dalton

HARLEQUIN®
Makes any time special ™

us at www.romance.net

PHHOWGEN